EMIL'S LIST

Bruce Weiss

authorHOUSE®

AuthorHouse™
1663 Liberty Drive
Bloomington, IN 47403
www.authorhouse.com
Phone: 1 (800) 839-8640

© 2018 Bruce Weiss. All rights reserved.

No part of this book may be reproduced, stored in a retrieval system, or transmitted by any means without the written permission of the author.

Published by AuthorHouse 10/09/2018

ISBN: 978-1-5462-6264-0 (sc)
ISBN: 978-1-5462-6262-6 (hc)
ISBN: 978-1-5462-6263-3 (e)

Library of Congress Control Number: 2018911738

Print information available on the last page.

Any people depicted in stock imagery provided by Getty Images are models, and such images are being used for illustrative purposes only. Certain stock imagery © Getty Images.

This book is printed on acid-free paper.

Because of the dynamic nature of the Internet, any web addresses or links contained in this book may have changed since publication and may no longer be valid. The views expressed in this work are solely those of the author and do not necessarily reflect the views of the publisher, and the publisher hereby disclaims any responsibility for them.

Dedicated to my friend Bernice Barrasso

CONTENTS

Prologue ix
Chapter 1 1
Chapter 2 9
Chapter 3 24
Chapter 4 28
Chapter 5 45
Chapter 6 53
Chapter 7 59
Chapter 8 66
Chapter 9 69
Chapter 10 73
Chapter 11 79
Chapter 12 83
Chapter 13 94
Chapter 14 109
Chapter 15 117
Chapter 16 130
Chapter 17 134
Chapter 18 140
Chapter 19 144
Chapter 20 148
Chapter 21 152
Chapter 22 166
Chapter 23 172
Chapter 24 180
Chapter 25 187
Chapter 26 196

Chapter 27 199
Chapter 28 201
Chapter 29 204
Chapter 30 209
Chapter 31 212
Chapter 32 223
Chapter 33 227
Chapter 34 234
Chapter 35 239
Chapter 36 244
Chapter 37 252
Chapter 38 258
Chapter 39 265
Chapter 40 269
Chapter 41 272
Chapter 42 278
Chapter 43 286
Epilogue 289

PROLOGUE

Emil's List
October 1985

I received a surprising phone call from a very well respected and renowned journalist, asking if I'd like to work on a special writing project with him. The words electrified me, as if I'd just been struck by a bolt of lightning on a clear day.

Emil Breck, preeminent journalist and one time colleague as always got right to the point, stating he wanted help organizing his lifetime collection of personal papers in order to write a memoir.

I wondered if I were daydreaming, wondering why ask me? My first conscious thought was I'd have to think about it but the words wouldn't form. It was truly a once in a lifetime opportunity and most likely a one time offer.

Saying yes meant I'd have privileged access to a lifetime of incredible journalistic work, a half century of writings penned by someone most considered the most trusted journalist America ever produced. He was conspicuously quiet in recent years and at times I wondered if he'd retired, but there he was. I knew if I said I'd get back to him I'd most likely regret it the rest of my life. It was extremely difficult to say the one word I actually wanted to scream, which was yes. When the word finally came out I realized I'd been gripping the phone so tightly my fingers cramped.

The call came more than two years ago and it changed my life in ways impossible to imagine. I admired and truly respected Emil Breck, a man who'd ultimately faced more life and death situations than any journalist dead or alive I'd ever known. With fearlessness and daring he'd managed to expose inequalities and injustices, proving often the pen was much more powerful than the sword. I knew he'd nearly paid with his life many times in his long career, always searching for truths.

Emil was introduced at functions as the dean of investigative reporting, a writer blessed with remarkable insights and the ability to do exhausting research. He had a wonderful way with words that people admired, his op-ed pages fixtures in newspapers not only in America but in publications around the globe. His reputation was stellar, often referred to as the most discerning and decisive reporter America ever produced. I too was a journalist but I couldn't hold a candle to his work.

After I'd managed to say yes there was an indomitable silence, finally broken with the words he'd get back to me soon with a timeline. When he hung up, I couldn't honestly comprehend if the call lasted seconds or minutes. My mind was numb.

Emil Breck; I said the name over and over again, each time with more reverence. There were a hundred questions I should have asked, especially why he'd chosen me. I'd been in the writing and reporting business for as many years as him but my work never received the accolades Emil earned, the call so surreal I couldn't fully grasp the message. My prized book shelves ran the entire length of my living room wall holding a lifetime of books I'd collected and devoured. I though of one book I'd nearly forgotten. Somewhere among those hundreds of books was a scrapbook I'd fashioned many years ago

Locating the old scrapbook felt as if I'd just rediscovered a rare and ancient relic, and old friend. The fragile album contained hundreds of yellowed news articles and op-ed pieces painstakingly collected over the years, most touching me very deeply. Many were found in old microfiche files in the basement of the Boston Public Library, a place I'd spend days reading old news dispatches. I'd made copies of the best articles, hoping those defining pieces might make me a better investigative reporter. Many years ago I'd once thought about using those stories for a book tentatively titled, 'Journalists Who Used the Power of the Pen to Change the world,' and as a subtitle, 'For Better or Worse.'

I hadn't opened the scrapbook in many years but when I looked at the first news article from the 1950's, it was no surprise it was an explosive op-ed piece written by Emil Breck. I felt like I'd just located a long lost friend. Leafing through the hundreds pages in the album, I rediscovered most of the articles I'd fallen in love with were written by Emil. There were many other pieces written by other journalists I considered masterpieces, but there was something moving about Emil's work.

Page after page reminded me Emil put his life on the line quite often to get the perfect story. I remembered a speech he'd once given at a National Press Club annual meeting, telling the audience a good reporter never gave up on a story until all the truths as well as all the lies were exposed.

I was smitten by Emil's words as I was when I'd first read the pieces. Each one passed the test of time, crafted with forthrightness and outspokenness. Being in the right place at the right time was not luck he used to say when teaching journalism students, but achieved through hours of resolve and determination bordering on obsession. Only perseverance allowed a serious writer to find hidden truths and lies he emphasized.

I read a few of Emil's articles written in the 1940's and 1950's, Cold War years when Americans were constantly warned to be on guard for creeping Communism in America. Because his writings often cast positive views about socialism, Emil become public enemy number one in many people's eyes. He replied to his many critics saying Americans didn't really understand the righteousness in many Socialist doctrines, including free health care and education for all.

Some of the album's pages contained dispatches Emil wrote from Nuremburg Germany, one of the few American reporters to sit in during the trials of Nazi leaders.

Every turn of the page in the scrapbook was a reminder of how daring and insightful Emil was. Some of his pieces portended things that later brought great changes to America. One of his most poignant pieces written weeks before becoming common knowledge, was there existed a convoluted connection between President Nixon and Watergate. President Nixon once said someone ought to shoot the son of a bitch Commie Breck.

I read over a few very outspoken articles describing the actions of Freedom Riders in the 1950's, Emil's words drawing attention to oppressive segregation practices in the South. The articles praised the brave students willing to risk their lives so the world might understand the brutal southern segregation practices. I believed the articles Emil wrote about the Freedom Riders were his best.

Turning the page I found an old article written from Teheran, merely hours before hundreds of American citizens were taken captive from their embassy and imprisoned.

Near the end of the scrapbook I found one of my all time favorites, a reflection written by Emil on the first anniversary of John F. Kennedy's assassination. The story earned him a Pulitzer prize, a day he described as one of the darkest in American history,

I spent the next untold hours reading over the articles I'd collected; dispatches and opinion pieces, first hand accounts with eye opening snapshots into extraordinary times in the twentieth century. Write a memoriam? It would have to be several thousand pages long I mused.

I'd thought about Emil over the years from time to time but sadly, his writings appeared less frequently.

His written words literally jumped off the page, grabbing readers by their throats. Holding the album in my lap felt as if I was holding a dormant volcano ready to erupt, the writing juices flowing uncontrollably inside me.

Closing the scrapbook it was nearly impossible to comprehend that one of the greatest journalist the country ever produced actually called me. In truth, I knew very little about the man but I'd learned early on he wasn't in the business for wealth or fame. He called himself a most ordinary citizen driven to expose evils and wrongdoings anywhere in the world.

When the second call finally came four days later, Emil launched into what he called non negotiable ground rules. Apart from a number of confidentiality issues, one caveat was my solemn word I'd continue the work on his project if for any reason he could not. I remembered his exact words.

"I do this work now because I want ordinary citizens to understand we all have a moral obligation to speak out when terrible wrongs need to be righted."

He also made it clear that when the work was finished, it would not be published until after his death.

I was to come to his apartment on a Monday, five days after the second phone call. Those days felt like an eternity as I began to grasp the idea I'd be working with a man who'd seen the best and worst of twentieth century life up close and personal. I obsessed with the thought there were far better qualified writers he could have chosen, but curiously I never asked why he'd chosen me.

As a visiting part time lecturer at Northeastern University in Boston, my time was my own and I could fully commit myself to Emil. The thought I'd have complete access to letters, personal papers, diaries and news dispatches felt as if I'd won a lottery. Emil made a point of saying the work would rub a lot of raw nerves and certainly open old wounds. I'd have to have very thick skin to survive the work, said in ominous tones.

Waiting for the day I'd journey to his place, my thoughts were never far from Emil Breck. One evening over dinner, possibly twenty years earlier he spoke to me about his upbringing. I'd forgotten much but did remember he'd been born into a middle class family falling under the grip of Fascism in his native Romania. I recalled he'd been most fortunate to emigrate to America in 1933, the year Hitler rose to power in Germany.

It was slowly coming back to me and I realized I knew more about him then I'd thought. He'd once said he didn't just live the first thirteen years of his life in Romania, but rather survived. He talked a great deal about how Fascist repression influenced much of his future thinking and eventually his writing. I hoped he'd tell me more about his early life when we started working together. I couldn't remember the last time we'd seen each other, possibly when he was teaching at Harvard when I stopped by to sit in on one of lectures.

In days I would make my first journey to Beacon Hill after being away for years, a place well known as the home of writers, poets, politicians and artists. I lived in Copley Square, only a few blocks west but light years away in many aspects.

The hours preceding our first day dragged on, my mind solely focused on the opportunity I'd been given. When the day finally arrived it reminded me of how I felt the first day of school a lifetime ago; excited but cautious.

When the door opened at Emil's place I was unprepared for what I saw. Hundreds of cardboard boxes filled with papers were piled high to the ceiling. Couches sagged under the weight of plastic boxes busting at the seams. Untold numbers of dog eared file folders stretched to the ceiling and his bed look like a swayback horse under the weight of more cartons. The thought of actually finding one particular paper seemed impossible.

Our very first day working together was a blur, nine hours non-stop without a break or anything to eat. At the end of our first day my head was so numb I decided to walk back to my place, glad I did. Somewhere far from Beacon Hill I realized I'd learned more about certain events in history than I'd ever learned in a classroom.

During my first week I learned there was little to no time for idle chat, decidedly working with an indisputable task master. Carefully and painstakingly we began to organize papers, at times a task so tedious it felt painful, yet I had the most remarkable glimpse into lives and events that shaped the world.

Often it might take hours to search for one particular paper and I would use that time to ask Emil if he would tell me more about his work, but the response was always the same. "It's all in the papers."

There was one particular topic that would get him to talk however, with an edge to his voice. The greatest evil in the world he maintained was censorship of words, saying much of his life's work was devoted to fighting censorship, including the many times his own articles were reworded.

Morning coffee breaks became part of our second week, one of my favorite times because the work would be put aside for a few precious moments. On one of those occasions he told me he'd become a collector of rare books, each sharing one common theme. Each book had once been banned when first published and the author scorned. A day later during one of our short breaks he talked about life as a young boy in Romania.

"Even as a very young child, I not only saw but felt the dark shadow of Fascism smothering every aspect of our lives. I was a very curious child, my ears always open particularly when adults spoke in quiet whispers. It was from them I learned individual liberties that we once enjoyed and took for granted were being taken away, always to ensure national interests came first."

Another time he said as a young boy he knew one day he'd speak out without fear against Fascist regimes.

I hardly slept at night, my life totally absorbed in Emil's work. I'd became so involved I'd even forgotten to work on the lectures at Northeastern I'd promised to deliver.

I thought we were making excellent progress and getting along well, sensing he was trusting me with his extremely personal papers. One late Friday afternoon I had another one of those out of the out of blue experiences. As if he were talking about the weather, I heard the depressing words.

xiv

"I've decided do the rest of the work by myself," he said so quietly I had to strain to hear.

For a few moments I wasn't sure what was happening.

"Thank you for your time. You've been a great help but I've concluded this is what must be." When it finally sank in I was so beleaguered I didn't ask why.

I recalled he'd said something about the work becoming a one person job several times but I wasn't really listening. I used all my strength getting up to walk to the door without sniveling. When I got to the front door of the apartment building Jose the building super stopped me.

"I am so sorry because it's probably none of my business," he whispered so no one else might hear, "But is Mr. Breck alright?

I had no response.

"Last evening you see, Mr. Breck forgot to take his keys when he went out for his walk so he had to come to me to unlock his door. There was something about the look on his face that told me something was terribly bothering him. When I opened the door he asked me to wait a moment. When he switched the lights on he looked so frail. Mr. Breck looked about his place as if someone was hiding there but of course, there was no one.

"If you're not feeling well" I said, "I know a doctor who makes house calls but there was no response. That kind and gentle man always had a few minutes for me but at that moment, I felt we were strangers. I brought him soup later that evening but he wouldn't open the door for me. I didn't know who was more rattled, Mr. Breck or me.

"Walking back to my place I couldn't help wonder if perhaps Emil was ill. The more I thought about it, something told me there had to be more to my being let go than Emil just wanting to work alone. His words flashed through my mind..

"If I'm unable to continue the work, I must have your solemn word you will take full possession of all my papers and continue what we've begun. Everything is yours with the exception of my book collection. I have other plans for it."

I don't remember most of the walk home except a feeling of great sadness and confusion.

I could not have guessed in a million years his untimely death was only a matter of weeks away. I probably would not have known if I hadn't had such a morbid interest in the obituaries in Boston newspapers. One sad day I found Emil's.

I asked around about what happened with no answers until an old newspaper acquaintance told me something I hadn't known. He said he heard from a friend Emil suffered a massive heart attack and the building super found him slumped over the desk where he'd used to write his lifetime stories. Poor Jose I thought.

I couldn't accept the fact Emil was gone, grief stricken until a thought crept into my mind I could not let go.

Emil insisted I take possession of his papers but how would I get them? Had he put anything in writing saying so? Who might know he'd asked me to take his papers? Maybe not getting them was for the best I reasoned, believing I really wasn't up to the difficult task of finishing his memoir.

If the papers somehow did end up with me, would it be possible to change the format from memoir to a biography? I felt as if I were living in no-man's land, unable to move on and not able to go back. I could not have known during those dark days that one day, I'd need every ounce of energy in my body to fulfill Emil's wishes. In the middle of the work I would suffer terribly, something later identified as a nervous breakdown.

I would be remiss if I didn't mention someone who came into my life after Emil's death, eventually becoming my co-pilot and confidant. She was a young woman by the name Sucre Grande, born and raised in Peru and living in Boston. She was the person Emil wanted his book collection to go to.

Sucre was twenty-five years old, born with sight but sadly, now totally blind. She'd come to the United States at the age of seventeen to attend a U.S. college. After graduation while working at the Harvard University library she'd accidentally run into Emil Breck in the school cafeteria, a very fortuitous meeting. That single event lead her to become a valuable and endearing part of Emil's life.

Weeks after Emil's death I received a phone call from a man by the name of Steven Gould, introducing himself as the executor of Emil Breck's will. He said he did not want to speak about the will over the phone, but would I come in to discuss it. Nearly convinced I might inherit Emil's papers kept me from sleeping that night. One door closed behind me and possibly another door was about to open.

CHAPTER 1

My phone seldom rang but one morning it's annoying sound stirred me from a wonderfully deep sleep. Who could be calling at such an ungodly hour I wondered, causing me to miss the end a fantastic dream? I ignored it but on the fourth ring I had a strange intuition it was a call I shouldn't miss. There was no way at that moment I could have imagined my life was about to change in many ways, starting me on perhaps one of the most unusual journeys of my life.

"Mr. Darwin?" Is this Mr. Charles Darwin?"

Sales person possibly? I'd let him have a few moments of my time and hang up.

"Mr. Darwin, my name is Steven Gould and I'm an attorney with the Boston legal firm of Finley, Gould and Strong on Beacon Hill. If you have a moment I'd like to pass along some important information effecting you very much."

There were many people I knew who'd become very nervous at the sight of a police cruiser in the rearview mirror. My reaction to a lawyer calling had the same sickening effect. Several of my more critical newspaper articles in the past led to rather unpleasant experiences with lawyers. The sound of shuffling papers made me curious. Was I in some kind of trouble for something I'd written some time ago?

"Mr. Darwin, I'm the attorney for the late Emil Breck? I am assuming that you knew him."

Cautioning myself before I knew where it might lead, I managed to say a barely perceptible yes.

I wondered if the call related to Emil's personal papers. He'd said if

Bruce Weiss

something happened to him and he couldn't finish the work, he wanted me to have them. Was that what the call was about?

"I'm listening" I said, a bit guarded.

"May I ask your relationship to Mr. Breck?" I found the words rather personal.

Don't get tangled up with an attorney an inner voice screamed, sharks making a very good living off the misery of others. The attorney repeated the question when I didn't immediately answer, believing it had to be about Emil's papers. Hesitantly, I replied.

"Mr. Breck and I once worked together on a writing project, that was until about six weeks ago when our relationship ended. I'm curious though before this goes any further. How did you get my number because it's unlisted?"

There was no immediate answer troubling me.

"Mr. Darwin, may I call you Charles?"

"Actually I prefer Charlie.

"Charlie, I'm the attorney who prepared Mr. Breck's last will, actually the fourth revision done in the past six months. The final will was written one week before his fatal heart attack. As his life long friend as well as his attorney, I thought he didn't look well but as you might know, he was a very private man. Some people want to change their wills when they suspect or know for certain their lives are about to change.

"Mr. Breck dictated the words of his new will, actually just a few short paragraphs. As his friend and not his attorney I asked if there was a reason for writing a new will. I laughed at his answer, which was it was none of my damn business.

"Mr. Breck had very few assets but it would be nearly impossible to put a monetary amount on his personal papers. He was a rather quiet man of few words but he did insist his life trove of papers be given to the right person. Charlie, Mr. Breck spoke quite highly of you and asked that all his personal papers be given to you. That was how I got your phone number.

I realized I had not said more than five words.

"When Mr. Breck and I finished our business we talked a bit about the memoir he was planning. I believe our meeting lasted no more than fifteen or twenty minutes and then he left my office, the last time I ever saw him. His death hit me very hard.

Emil's List

"I'd like you to come by my office for the official reading of Mr. Breck's will because you are the heir to his papers. I should also tell you I've asked a young woman, someone who was quite close to Mr. Breck to also attend our meeting as she is to inherit his valuable book collection. You two are the only people mentioned in the will."

Who was the woman, I wondered. He'd never mentioned any woman in his life but obviously she must have been very important to him. I asked if there was anything else I needed to know.

"Only that the will is one page so our meeting shouldn't take more than a half hour. Massachusetts law requires the reading done in a legal office with witnesses but you need to be aware of something else. There's always the possibility a relative might come forward to contest the will's distribution and we'll discuss that in our meeting if it becomes an issue. Oh and one more thing. There could be tax implications on the value of the papers and the books and if there is, I can refer you to a tax lawyer in my firm."

Emil stated I was to take possession of his papers if for any reason he was unable to finish the project, but I was still stunned by the call. I'd almost convinced myself I'd probably seen the last of his papers. Who was the woman in his life?

"Charlie I want to get this settled before the end of the week so can you meet here in my office Wednesday? Do you know where we're located?"

Boston's most distinguished and oldest law firms were located on Beacon Hill, not very far from my own place in Copley Square. Emil lived most of his life on the Hill and I'd probably walked by Gould's office many times. I said Wednesday would be fine, even though I had a class to teach that day.

"Three O'clock then and please make sure you bring along some identification. Given the simplicity of the will it shouldn't take long and if you're wondering, Mr. Breck covered my fees so keep you checkbook home."

I truly had no affection for lawyers but Gould was not the usual adversary claiming I'd defamed someone in my editorials. Even thought Gould sounded sincere, I continued to believe all lawyers made a very lucrative living off other people's troubles.

When I hung up the thought I might actually finish the great man's work hit me as if I'd been punched in the gut. I thought of the question I wished I'd had the courage to ask Emil when he'd asked me to work with him. Why had he chosen me instead of any of the great newspaper people he must have known? I also wished I'd asked why he let me go. Did he know he had a bad heart and little time left?

There was a folder tucked into a nook on one of my book shelves and I hoped it was still there. It was a thick envelope containing a number of hand written notes from Emil to me over the years. Whenever he was touched by something I wrote he either sent praise or criticism. If he had questions about one of my articles he'd ask me to send along my thoughts.

I'd never seen his rare book collection, nor had he ever talked about it. Even though I spent countless hours at his place, the books must have been hidden behind the scores of cardboard boxes filled with his papers. Suddenly my mind was on fire.

The meeting was a day and a half away and I realized it would be impossible to not think about Emil's personal papers. If they were officially mine as Gould insisted, I'd have a lot of work to do just to get them all to my place. Looking around I wondered where I would find the room for all the cartons.

Across the street from my place in Copley Square was the ancient Boston Public Library. Curious about Gould and his law firm, I thought it wouldn't hurt to search for information that might tell me who I'd be dealing with.

I actually discovered more about Gould's law firm then I really needed to know. Steven Gould was the great-grandson of the firm's founder, Ezra Gould, originally from North Wales. He came to America penniless but according to an article, he managed to put himself through school, eventually studying law. The legal firm occupied it's current building for nearly one hundred and fifty years, designated an historic Boston landmark in 1930. Copley Square was a short trolley ride to Government Center, then a five minute walk to Beacon Hill. As much as I tried to put the papers out of my mind I could not, trying to force myself to concentrate on an upcoming lecture I'd be delivering to Northeastern University sophomores, the same day I'd be meeting with Gould.

At last the day arrived for the meeting. I found myself walking Boston's historical Freedom Trail to get to the law firm, a trip back in time in old revolutionary Boston. I hadn't been to Beacon Hill in a few years but as I walked about I realized nothing had changed and nothing probably would.

The neighborhood had a world class reputation where the rich and famous lived. The Gould building was a block from Louisburg Square, an enchanting collection of Greek Revival buildings, many still home to the upper class of Boston. I'd read several books about the neighborhood for one of my college courses, learning where architect Charles Bulfinch and painter John Singleton Copley once lived and where Louisa May Alcott spent her childhood. Jenny Lind once resided there.

Staring at the polished brass name plate on the front door, I wondered if the Strong in the legal firm was Milton Strong, one time governor of Massachusetts and abolitionist during the Civil War years. If I remembered the basement of the Gould building was one of the stops on the Underground Railroad.

A burnished sign with the Massachusetts coat of arms next to the building pointed tourists and locals across the street to an ancient burial ground. The overgrown cemetery was surrounded by a rusted iron fence and primeval looking trees. It was the final resting place for many early Boston patriots, including Ben Franklin's parents and John Hancock. The Gould building had a front row seat, looking down upon one of the most historic and often forgotten places in the city. What a gem I thought.

Mr. Gould walked into the waiting room, a man I thought my own age. Instead of an expensive suit he wore sweatpants and sweatshirt and seeing the look on my face he acknowledged he'd just come from the company gym after his daily workout.

He asked if I had any trouble finding the building so I told him I was somewhat familiar with Beacon Hill, working and living in the city for many years. Looking past his oversized desk my eyes were drawn to the picture window and the view below of one of Boston's premiere Revolutionary War burial grounds. I'd been inside the cemetery once a long time ago with my students and it impressed me greatly then, not recalling if I noticed the Gould Building at the time. Attorney Gould pointed to an area near a tall beech tree saying proudly one of his relatives was buried there. I wondered if it was Daniel Gould, one of the men accompanying Paul Revere on his famous ride. When he took a phone call

I looked over the photographs on the walls; Gould with politicians, most notably a young John F. Kennedy.

We chatted about our mutual acquaintance Emil Breck and I explained our recent work together. Looking at the great grandfather clock in the room, I wondered when the mystery woman might arrive.

"Why don't we begin" the attorney announced.

Attorney Gould removed a leather folder from his center desk drawer, the firm's name etched in large letters of gold. Inside was a thin folder which I assumed was Emil's will. It also contained a letter addressed to me.

The will was short and sweet as Mr. Gould explained on the phone, music to his ears he declared. Mr. Charles Darwin is to receive sole possession of all my personal papers the second paragraph stated. I almost shouted out with relief and happiness. I asked the attorney if he knew much about Emil's professional life as a journalist. At one time he was known by everyone who read the news I related.

"I was actually a devoted follower of his writings he said, "And like so many others, I learned his opinions were always forthright although at times quite irritating. I got to know him some twenty-five years ago when the firm did some legal work for him. I was so impressed by the man I actually attended a reading when he spoke about his reporting years in Europe. I can still remember him saying just because Germany, Japan and Italy were no longer evil powers, Fascism was still very much alive and well in the world, and had to be destroyed. We were in touch from time to time. I once convinced him to have dinner with me here in the law dining room."

When the attorney took another call I got up and walked to the large window, my eyes drawn once again to the ancient burial stones in the graveyard. Tourists snapped pictures, a few doing grave rubbings, oblivious to the sign warning against it.

When he hung up, Mr. Gould asked, "Did Mr. Breck ever show you his book collection?"

Shaking my head no, I replied I knew he was an avid collector but had no knowledge of what books he'd purchased or owned.

"Mr. Breck's books were kept somewhere in his apartment I believe and a few times I'd spy a book on an end table when we worked together. The titles knocked my socks off as well as the author's signatures"

Another phone call interrupted our conversation.

Emil's List

"That was my secretary telling me Miss Grande will not be joining us today. She called to say something came up at work at the last moment and she'd have to reschedule. Since she's not here I'd like to tell you a bit about her because it appears you were both very close to Mr. Breck.

"Miss Grande, Sucre was born in Peru, living here not as an American citizen, but with a green card allowing her to work. She is employed at the Harvard Library although I'm not exactly sure what she does. When you finally meet her I think you'll find her quite extraordinary. Miss Grande has been blind since the age of twelve yet she manages to enjoy a very full and active life, entirely on her own. I met her several times with Emil and was quite touched when she spoke about the traumatic events of her childhood in Peru. I think Emil was quite happy to leave his collection of fine books to her.

"From what I understood she was the only other person to visit him in the last few years besides you, as you know he was pretty much a recluse. He invited her to come visit everyday after he'd discovered the young lady had a very special interest in literary classics.

"On one of Emil's visits to this office he told me about Sucre and how he'd met her quite accidentally in one of the dining halls at Harvard. One of the things he learned was her love of classical literature and in time, he mentioned his rare book collection. To her great surprise he invited her to come by his place one day so he might read a few of his great books aloud to her. They became close friends and to repay Emil's kindness, Miss Grande began preparing lunch meals. I believe they spend hours together, usually during the middle of the day for nearly two years, reading and dining. About six months ago I called to check on him and he told me he'd read nearly fifty classics to Sucre, the highpoint of his day."

"Okay, enough chit chat" he announced. "I'll keep Emil's will under wraps for a while longer until Miss Grande can reschedule a meeting. I know the intent of the will and to allay any concerns, it states you are to inherit all his personal papers. As to Miss Sucre Grande, I have another handwritten note in his own words for her."

When Gould stood up I suspected our time was up. Walking me to the door he took a key from his pocket, explaining it would open the front door to Emil Breck's apartment. I was so overwhelmed I didn't remember my walk to Emil's place.

"The superintendent of Emil's building insisted with no exceptions everything had to be out of his apartment in three days or less because a new couple had put a deposit down. "Three days is all you've got to get the crap out" said with a tinge of anger in his voice. "Whatever is left behind will end up in a trash dump."

I disliked the man immediately.

"I'm counting on you to get all those cartons and furniture out," said with a snarl.

With Emil's key in my pocket I made my way to his apartment to take stock of what could be found, with the thought the landlord could and would make things difficult.

The moment I opened the door to Emil's apartment I was shockingly overcome with a great sorrow because Emil was not there. Feeling woozy I grabbed hold of the door steadying myself. I half expected to see Emil and the thought he was no longer alive hit me much harder than I'd expected. Looking about his place I sensed it would be near impossible to get everything packed and out in three days.

Regretfully, if I worked too quickly there would be no way to keep all the papers in the right order and I'd create a mess. When the super insisted three days I thought that was generous, but one long look around the place told me the task was going to be formidable. There was nothing I could do until morning so I locked the place up and walked back to my apartment in Copley Square. Looking about my place, a literal bachelor pad, I was slapped in the face with the reality the rooms looked smaller then I'd ever remembered. The image of overflowing boxes and cartons in my place seemed daunting.

CHAPTER 2

Emil's building was constructed with old Boston brick, part of an entire block of non-descript but well maintained buildings built in the late 1880's. I stood outside his place the next morning for a few minutes, recalling the very first time I'd come there, apartment 614.

I'd once worked with Emil five days a week for nearly a month, managing to avoid the rickety antique elevator on my visits after one frightening ride convinced me the stairs would be much safer. With a great sense of melancholy, it would be the first time working there without Emil. Looking about it felt as if the place was sacred.

It was so quiet inside the building the only sounds were my own footfalls. I'd met a few of the residents on my visits, usually sitting outside near the entrance with a nice hello and in particular, the kindly old man with the snarling little dog. The place felt so quiet it seemed as if no one lived there. The stair cases were so steep so I'd most likely have to use the old elevator to get all of Emil's papers out I guessed. As usual, the hallway to his apartment was unlit. On my previous visits I'd always felt a great sense of anticipation and excitement, awed seeing Emil already at work, nearly oblivious to my entrance. It was sadly very different because Emil was gone and I still had a hard time accepting it. What could I possibly do with the papers to make Emil proud of me?

Force of habit made me knock on the door, shaking my head at the absurdity until I heard someone walking around inside. To my great surprise the door opened and a very attractive young woman with dark oversized dark glasses greeted me. I immediately realized who she was. She had to be the blind Peruvian woman Attorney Gould mentioned, the inheritor of Emil's book collection. I hadn't expected to find anyone inside so I was a bit disconcerted, even uncertain how to address a blind person. I cleared my throat to let her know I was standing outside the door, a bit overwhelmed and flabbergasted.

"Would you like to come in Mr. Darwin," the words spoken with a slight hint of accent.

Could she possibly see I wondered, because how could she possibly know who I was? With a bit of trepidation in my voice I asked how she knew it was me.

"Mr. Breck's phone still works and when I called Attorney Gould to let him know I'd found the hidden key, he said you'd be coming by sometime today. I couldn't imagine it was anyone else. I apologize for missing the meeting with Mr. Gould but I had to finish a very important rush job before I could get here. I also wanted a few moments alone in Emil's place because in truth, since Emil's death I've been unsure what to do with myself."

I felt a nagging uneasiness having never encountered a blind person. She stepped aside to let me pass, thinking if I kept up a running conversation she'd know where I was.

"My reason for being here" I said meekly, "Was to begin packing Emil's papers. I also need to figure out how I'm going to transport all these cartons to my place. I'm not sure if you know, but we've only got three days to empty this place," said somewhat apologetically.

I realized I was shouting, reminding myself the woman was blind and not deaf.

"I need to box everything up and we'll have to do the same with the books Emil left you. I hope we can get everything out in time."

I was using my outdoor voice, wondering if I'd ever carry on a normal conversation with the lady. I also wondered if that was something she'd usually experienced when meeting someone for the first time. A long silence grew awkward until I found a few words. Had Emil ever mentioned my name I asked. She nodded, asking if he'd ever mentioned her name. I shook my head, realizing very quickly only words would do with a blind person.

"I want to look around the back room and figure out how many extra cartons we'll need in order to pack every notebook and folder. Keeping everything in the right order is going to be critical but truthfully, there's not enough time to be careful or truly thorough. I'm not sure if you knew,

Emil's List

but Emil saved sixty years of his work, possibly tens of thousands of papers stored so this is not going to be an easy task. I could certainly use your help."

When I reflected on those words a haunting thought came to mind. How could someone who was blind help me?

I peeked into Emil's bedroom turned storage facility, seeing wall to wall boxes piled high to the ceiling. I wondered if I should take Ms. Grande's arm leading her into the back room, but thought not.

I said I'd actually only looked into Emil's bedroom once because all our work was done in the front room. Obviously she could not know how overwhelmed I was seeing so many overflowing boxes, many bulging at the seams, having no idea where or how to start. Emil probably knew where every single paper was I guessed but without labels marking the cartons, I had no idea what we'd be packing. Something Emil once said though came to mind as I looked about. He said he'd never thrown a single set of notes away, even those written on matchbook covers and scraps of paper. I'm not sure how long I stood staring, shaking my head until I realized I needed to tell the young lady what I was looking at.

"Look at all these cartons," I said much too loudly. "There's no way we can keep all these years of reporters notes in their proper order."

When I thought about my choice of words I regretted saying them.

"What I really meant to say was Emil stockpiled a lifetime of notebooks, letters, news articles, diaries and who knows what else. Cartons fill every square inch of the room."

I knew I was shouting a bit too loudly again,

"Have you ever seen such disarray in your life?"

The moment those words escaped I'd just made the situation even more uncomfortable. A gnawing ache in my gut told me I'd made a terrible mess with my use of words in our brief introduction. The lady had not said a word and for a moment I wondered if she'd walked out. How could I be so thoughtless where she was most vulnerable? I spied her near the door in the front room, a red and white striped walking stick firmly grasped in her left hand. I wished she'd use the stick to knock some sense into me I muttered.

"It's Sucre Grande" said with buoyancy,"

I suspected I was about to get a needed lesson in manners. Using an indoor voice I said I was very sorry for being terribly insensitive.

11

She immediately responded saying I had nothing to apologize for. The words actually made me feel worse.

"I only use my walking stick when I'm in an unfamiliar place or if there are obstacles that might trip me. As you can probably see because I can't, there's quite a bit of disarray in Emil's place."

I was thankful she couldn't see the frustrated expression on my face or my hang dog look. Not sure what to do or say next, I thought it best to spend some time talking about our special relationships with Emil.

I explained Emil and I were in the same business of journalism and that he'd asked me to help write his memoir. I could have gone on and on about Emil's exploits but I suspected she knew much about his extraordinary life.

"His unexpected death was a great loss to me both personally and professionally" I added. "Anyone who grew up reading his incredibly insightful stories would certainly feel a great loss. I don't really know what your relationship was with Emil but I knew he chose his friends very carefully."

"He was truly the most incredible person I'd ever met or known," she said, a great sadness in her words. "Mr. Darwin, would you mind if we sat down and had a little talk because there are some important things you need to know about me. Please be patient because this is very hard for me.

"When I arrived on one of my daily visit's a month ago, Emil's super stopped me before I got into the elevator. He told me the dreadful news and how sorry he was. Mr. Darwin, for your information I've experience much loss in my life and a great deal of sadness but when I heard those words, the anguish was so intense I thought I might die."

I instinctively reached out to take her hand to say I understood and how sorry I was.

"In truth not a minute passes without thinking about Emil."

To my consternation she pushed my hand aside, throwing her hands up in the air which I took as a don't touch me gesture.

"Please Mr. Darwin, as I said only a moment ago there are a few things you need to know about me. First for your information, yes I'm totally blind and my world is darkness so please listen carefully. Despite my blindness, I still manage to get around quite well all by myself without anyone's help. I say this with all sincerity and I share that sentiment with

Emil's List

everyone. Thank you for trying to be helpful so don't take this the wrong way, but if I ever need your help I promise I'll ask."

As an old newspaper man I was seldom lost for words but staring at those dark glasses, I was speechless.

We'd both admitted we'd suffered a terribly painful loss, the grief almost impossible to bare. In our brief encounter I sensed she'd most likely lost her dearest friend leaving a great void in both our lives.

We shared Emil stories, knowing we'd never run out of things to say about the man. I said how surprised I was when he called and asked me to collaborate on his memoir. I said I felt as if I'd just won a lottery,

"Emil and I were colleagues from time to time in the news business, although I never thought of him as a close friend. Our paths crossed occasionally over the years however because we might be working on the same story. Journalists are funny people because we pretty much march to our own beat. Of all the writers and journalists I've met over my lifetime, there was no one as good as Emil."

"What's going to happen now since his work can no longer become a memoir?"

That question was very much on my mind, wondering even in her dark world if she could sense my uneasiness.

"I haven't made any decision yet but I'm leaning toward changing the format from memoir to biography. I know that wasn't Emil's wish or intent but that might be the only way to finish his work. As you can see......."

I didn't finish my thought, caught again by the use of those four words. Would I simply continue to be thoughtless?

"I'm really not totally insensitive," I said, offering another apology. "What I really meant to say is I think a biography would be the best way to use his personal papers, hoping my efforts would make Emil proud. There's one question I wished I'd asked however. With so many outstanding journalists to choose from, why did Emil pick me?".

"By the way my first name is Sucre."

"My name's Charles but people who know me call me Charlie. For whatever reason the name Charlie always seems to put a smile on people's faces. Just curious though, now that you know my connection to Emil what brought you two together?"

"I remember the day we met very well. It was in one of the Harvard dining rooms and in the course of our brief conversation, we both recognized we shared a common love affair with books. He told me about the extraordinary books he'd collected and I began to wonder if fate brought us together that day. From that moment on we built a friendship and in time, Emil was able to do something no one had ever done for me before, something quite simple and quite lovely. He offered to read his books aloud to me, knowing I would enjoy them very much. He read some forty books with the eventual goal of reading all one hundred and fifty in his magical collection.

"I learned so much and was so thankful for his kindness. You see, the stories he read made me forget about my blindness for a while. My mind came alive when he read but sadly, there won't be anymore stories. I will always look back on that time knowing in my heart they were the absolute best days of my life. I would get lost for hours during those enchanting readings and I don't think we ever missed a day. Emil had the ability to bring the stories and characters to life, a truly unexpected and special gift to a blind girl. It was possibly the greatest gift I'd ever received. I do miss him terribly"

I said I'd love to see the collection once everything was organized and packed up. That brought me to a question I wanted to ask. Would she like to help organize the papers, even though I wasn't sure how a blind person might help.

"I wish I could help you," she sighed, "But I'm afraid I'd just get in your way."

I said nonsense, emphasizing that much of the organizational work was going to be very time consuming and I could certainly use someone to help me. How would she do that? I'd figure that part out later, I hoped.

"Look around at all these.........The rest of the words stuck in my throat, difficult to believe I'd used that same damn trite expression once again. This time to my surprise she graciously smiled.

"Mr. Darwin, please don't concern yourself about the choice of words you use. I can't begin to tell you how many people shout things at me each and every day. 'Hey lady, watch where you're walking or hey lady, are you blind? I've developed a thick skin and have learned to live with it. I must have heard the word look at this or look at that or watch this a million times. Truthfully, it doesn't bother me as much as it did once a long time ago."

Emil's List

I was humbled, hoping not to make the same careless comments over and over again.

Sucre suggested we check out Emil's small kitchen because he'd kept a tin of coffee in one of the cabinets. The cabinets were empty but something nearby caught my eye. A book rested on top of the refrigerator and when I looked at the title, it was the Diary of Anne Frank.

"Did Emil read this book to you" I queried?

"I know this takes time but I really can't answer a question like that unless you tell me the name of the book."

"Of course" I said, apologizing one more time. "It's the Diary of Anne Frank."

"That was the book Emil wanted to read next but I'm afraid that's not possible now. I was so looking forward to that diary because what little I knew about her life, I thought Anne and I might share some things in common. I think all the other books are somewhere in that back room and if you're interested, you might move a few things around and find them."

I was certainly interested in the books Emil bragged about, even if it meant taking time from packing things up.

The books were indeed in the bedroom, buried behind stacks of cartons, resting on rickety metal shelving. They appeared to have no wear or tear, looking very much as if they'd just come off the press. I ran my fingers over the leather bindings, feeling the raised gilded letters of titles and authors.

As if handling pieces of fragile glass, I took several books from the shelf to take a closer look. The first book was one I actually owned and used once or twice in one of my classes at the university. The book looked as if it had never been opened.

"Sucre, I'm holding a very tragic and terribly sad story called All Quiet on the Western Front by Erich Remarque. This is unbelievable" I whispered. "It's a first edition boldly signed by the author so it's definitely worth a small fortune. Did Emil ever read this book to you?"

"Yes we finished it about six months ago. It was terribly difficult for me to concentrate at times because sadly, it reminded me of our terrible civil war in Peru."

The next book I took from the shelf was Andersonville, a book I'd read in college years ago. It too was a first edition, signed boldly by MacKinlay Kantor the author.

"And this book, Andersonville? Did Emil read this one to you?"

"He read it to me last year, a book I truly didn't care for very much. It was very distressing and the awful descriptions of men forced to live so terribly greatly upset me. It was hard listening to his words, again reminded of the wars in my native Peru."

I took Animal Farm from the shelf, a first edition written but not signed by George Orwell. Telling Sucre the title I said I'd read it in school in a combination history and English class many years ago.

"I don't think any of us understood the real meaning of the book at that the time I said. It's a rather simple story but underneath, it's quite frightening because the tragedy could happen anywhere."

"Mr. Darwin, did you know that Emil and George Orwell once crossed paths many years ago in Spain?"

I shook my head no, once again aware that every question or comment needed a verbal response and not a gesture.

"Doctor Zhivago by Boris Pasternak" I announced with great feeling, saying I'd seen the movie at least a dozen times but never actually read the book. I was just about to ask if she'd ever seen the film but mercifully I stopped myself.

"The Grapes of Wrath" I said excitedly. Before I could say the author's name Sucre shouted enthusiastically Steinbeck.

"He's one of my favorite authors" she said rather proudly.

Every book on the top shelf was in near perfect condition, most looking if they'd never been opened or read. I couldn't imagine how much the collection was worth,

Staring in awe at John Steinbeck's signature on the title page I asked, did Emil read the Grapes of Wrath to her.

"He did and you know what? From the very first sentence I knew it was going to be a very moving and emotional story."

"What about the Gulag Archipelago by Solzhenitsyn and the one next to it, the Manifest of the Communist Party by Karl Marx and Frederich Engels? Extremely difficult reading I acknowledged."

Neither one she answered. I said both books were highly toxic and at one time banned from America's libraries and schools.

"Mr. Darwin, I'm not sure if Emil ever mentioned this to you, but every book in his collection shared one common theme. Each book was once banned and some even burned. That's why he collected those specific books, traveling the world for first editions once damned and banned."

I hadn't put that together but thinking about the book I'd found on the refrigerator made me doubtful. Who would possibly want to ban or even censure Anne Frank's diary I wondered? Sucre reminded me there were many Holocaust deniers and perhaps they were responsible for censoring the book.

"Slaughterhouse-Five" I said?"

"One of my absolute favorites. Emil once asked if I could invite three authors living or dead to have dinner with, who would I choose? I said Kurt Vonnegut for sure but I'd have a tough time choosing two more. Emil promised we'd find the time to read all of Vonnegut's books."

"The Ugly American by Lederer" I said, awed by the author's bold signature. "I've never read this book but I know it sent shock waves though America when first published. Did you like the story?"

Yes she said, very much.

I took the Bible from the shelf, knowing throughout history it had been banned or censored in many places for many reasons. Interestingly, it was a book I'd never actually opened. Jokingly I said it wasn't signed by the authors, making Sucre laugh.

"An American Tragedy by Theodore Dreiser" I said with reverence. "It's a first edition in perfect condition. Here's another one titled The Bluest Eye by Toni Morrison, also signed by the author. Did Emil read you this one?"

She shook her head, no.

"Fanny Hill by John Cleland I said defiantly. "This book was once banned everywhere in America and in many places around the world. I recalled a group of us teenagers plotting to get our hands on a hot book like that but it wasn't to be."

"The Group by Mary MaCarthy," I announced.

I thought the book was out of place among the classics, believing it was never considered great literature. I asked Sucre if she knew why The Group was part of Emil's collection.

"I actually questioned Emil about that book because it did seem out of place. He told me there were very strong objections to the book because of references to homosexuality and promiscuity, therefore it was banned from libraries. I actually thought the book was beautifully written."

"Lady Chatterley's Lover by D.H. Lawrence and Lolita by Nabokov I said with a smirk. "These two book created a lot of problems for the authors and their publishers" I remarked.

I eyeballed The Adventures of Huckleberry Finn by Mark Twain, an extremely rare and valuable book. The book had once been banned from schools and continued to be removed from shelves in some schools because of issues about race.

"Another Country by James Baldwin" I said excitedly, adding it was a book I'd read many times because Baldwin was one of my favorite authors.

"I too fell in love with his writing because he had such a powerful way of expressing words. Emil told me he'd once met Baldwin in a coffee house in the Village in New York. How amazing is that?"

"Brave New World by Huxley, Catch-22 by Heller and the list goes on and on. Sucre, you have inherited a very fine collection."

I felt as if I were holding the Holy Grail in my hands. One of the first books I'd ever fallen in love with was The Catcher in the Rye by Salinger. "Did you like this one, The Catcher in the Rye" I asked?

"I was a little disappointed because I thought it was a bit dated," she surprisingly remarked.

"My parents found Salinger's book in my room when I was about thirteen and I never saw it again. Run Rabbit Run by Updike, The Tropic of Capricorn by Miller, Ulysses by James Joyce, Fahrenheit by Bradbury," I crowed. "You're absolutely right. There is a common them to each book. All were once thought controversial and either heavily censored or banned. Did Emil ever explain why he had such an interest in censored books?"

"He once told me while growing up in Romania he saw soldiers removing scores of books from libraries and private homes. He described watching books piled up in the middle of the streets and drenched in gasoline and burned. He promised himself he would spend the rest of his life fighting that type of ignorance and intolerance. You know his personal writings far better then me so I suspect you knew that was one of the reasons why he wanted to be a journalist."

I nodded, adding a yes a few moments late. I knew Emil felt strongly censorship ran against human nature, but I had no idea he'd created a collection of those books. Regretfully I'd have to put the books aside to begin packing Emil's papers. A few more minutes wouldn't make a difference I reasoned so I turned to the books again.

"Howl and other Poems by Allen Ginsberg" I said with a chuckle. "Still in the original dust jacket. I know exactly where I was when I first saw a copy of this book. I was a college sophomore and the book was required for an English class. From the very page, Ginsberg became one of my literary heroes.

"Naked Lunch by William Burroughs, Of Mice and Men by John Steinbeck and to Kill a Mockingbird by Harper Lee rested next to each other. I couldn't believe all those wondrous books were in one private collection.

I said with pride my granddaughter was named Harper because her mother had fallen in love with the story To Kill a Mockingbird when she was a child.

I was mesmerized by the books, losing track of time. Peeking one last time at the books I hadn't yet examined, it was obvious I was staring at one of the most eclectic collections I'd ever seen in one place. A few of the titles seemed relatively benign, wondering why a book such as The Arabian Nights was once censured. For each book I doubted, others certainly fit the bill including Hitler's Mein Kamph. Curiously, I felt bad there was no author's signature making it priceless.

I grew more conscious of the sounds Sucre's cane made when she walked about. Lost in the collection of books I'd actually forgotten she was blind, the tapping sounds bringing the reality back. Sucre said she could never have imagined the books would be hers one day, a bittersweet end to their relationship. I said I too had a love affair with books and was pleased his collections would go to someone who enjoyed great literature.

We'd finally run out of things to say about the books and I found myself staring at her, trying to guess her age. She was quite lovely although the large round oversized dark glasses hid her expressions.

I watched her move the walking stick from hand to hand, looking pensive as if she were deep in thought. To keep the conversation going I asked what she remembered about her life in Peru. I was relieved because she looked quite happy to respond.

"I was born in the mountain city of Arequipa, Peru's third largest city surrounded by the majestic Andes Mountains."

I replied I was a native Bostonian and in all my travels I'd never seen a mountain range. Sucre explained mountains were sacred sites in many places in the world, especially in the Andes and the Himalayas. There's much more but I'll save all that for another time.

I asked how she'd met Emil.

"I'll give you the short but very sweet version. When I started working at Harvard, Emil was a visiting lecturer and I was working in the school library translating books into Braille. In one of the Harvard dining rooms one fortuitous day I accidentally walked right into the professor. I wasn't concentrating and wasn't using my walking stick. The next thing I knew I'd walked right into a man who introduced himself as Emil Breck.

"I'd never heard his name until that most auspicious day. I simply wasn't paying attention, my mind on my work, thinking I knew the dining room well enough to not use my walking stick. Sadly, I was wrong. All of a sudden I crashed into someone carrying a full tray of food, the tray falling to the floor, the sound of plates breaking. My first embarrassing thought was everyone in the dining room had to be staring at poor me. Thanks to the man's good nature it wasn't as bad as I anticipated. He spoke loud enough for everyone to hear that he was sorry he wasn't watching where he was walking, and that it was his fault. I was too stunned to say it was I who'd created the problem.

"Instead of a scolding or berating me he said he really wasn't very hungry so no great loss. When the laughter in the room died he took my arm, telling me we'd find a table and have coffee.

"That basically describes our accidental meeting and over several of cups of coffee we talked about our work at Harvard, leading to a discussion about books. He asked If I'd ever translated some of his text books into Braille but I thought not. When we were about to go our own ways he asked what kinds of books I liked best. When I told him I preferred the classics he told me to sit tight and not get up and leave just yet,

"He said he had a very special book collection, telling me the name of a few titles saying he didn't think they'd been put into Braille. I don't know how long we sat, possibly two hours, maybe more. He said he'd just bought a new book for his collection, asking me to put my hands out, placing it in the palms of my hands. He whispered it was a first edition by Edmund Wilson titled Memoirs of Hecate County. I'd never heard of the book or the author but what he said next took my breath away.

"Would you be interested in coming by my place some afternoon, possibly later this week if you have the time because I've never read this book. I'm looking forward to doing just that and I'd be very happy to read it aloud so you too could enjoy the story.

"For one of the many times in my life I couldn't find the right words, surprised someone would want to do something for me other then trying to guide me along. We set a time and date and then one wonderful day I ventured to his place.

"The first afternoon reading eventually led to another and then many more afternoons until the meetings became a daily ritual. I'd arrive at his place usually late morning and after a little talk about our day and work, we'd sit down and Emil would pick up the book we'd left off the day before, reading for hours or until his voice tired. I truly never wanted our day together to end. When he'd finish reading for the day we'd spend priceless time talking about the meaning of the story. He told me he'd made special notes for himself about each book and author that he'd placed inside every book he'd read.

"All the books in my collection he stressed such as Memoirs of Hecate County were once ruefully banned and censored. When we'd finish one book Emil chose another to read aloud and you know what was most special? Those hours were one of the very few times in my life when I didn't think about my blindness. His words put lovely pictures into my head, as if I could actually see for a few hours everyday.

"I loved almost every book, some more then others and was getting quite an education. I'd often have to literally pinch myself, asking if this was really happening. I had such heartfelt appreciation because I could picture the stories and in my head. Emil was the only person I'd ever met who knew how to make a blind woman see."

"Did he ever talk about his professional career with you?"

"I heard little snippets about his life but not too much. Our friendship was based really on reading. If you're curious, once or twice I seem to recall he'd mentioned your name."

"Do you remember what he said about me?"

Bruce Weiss

I was instantly sorry I'd asked such a self gratifying question.

"I believe he once said that he was looking for just the right person to help organize his personal papers. A few weeks later he told me he had some very good news. He'd found just the right person so I guess that was you."

We hadn't started packing yet my thoughts eventually turned to the seemingly impossible task of collecting all the papers and trying to keep them in some type of order. I suggested we get right to work re-boxing some of the torn cartons and get things ready for the move that would take place the next day. We'd have two full days to move things out including the books. Before I could say more I saw a perplexing look on her face suggesting I wasn't making a whole lot of sense.

"I'm not sure what you know about blindness Mr. Darwin, so I'm going to give you a short education. Most blind people including myself adapt to a dark world and many of us lead a reasonably good life. There are many sightless people though who sadly feel their lives are over. I consider myself one of the very fortunate ones although in truth, I felt like giving up many times. If I hadn't bumped into Emil I'd hate to think that I'd just be going through the motions of life with little feeling. Regretfully there are limitations to what I can do so I'm not sure how I could ever help you."

I truly wanted to learn know more about how she managed her dark life. How and when did she lose her sight I asked, adding if she said it was none of my business I'd understand. Her response was we'd better sit down because her life was truly very complicated.

"Here's the shorter version for now. As I said I was born in Peru in the country's third largest city of Arequipa. The first twelve years of my life were sighted and I was quite happy all the time I seem to recall. My life regretfully turned upside down when I was twelve years old when I lost my sight, a story I'll relate later. I will say however I lived though years of sorrow and misery because of a tragic event one innocent Sunday morning. I'll save the rest for another time but I'd like to tell you more about my life here in this country."

"After high school I came to America to attend college and when I graduated with a degree in literature, Harvard University recruited me to work with students with impaired vision. I began a program at the university turning college text books into Braille, something I'd learned

22

in Peru. The work was rewarding but I thought about moving on until the fortunate and accidental day I bumped into Emil Breck.

"Two strangers came together because I thought I knew how to negotiate the dining room without my walking stick. Of course I couldn't have known at the time that both our lives would change after that fateful moment. It didn't take long to realize Emil was the most perceptive and kindest person I'd ever met. When we left the dining room late that afternoon I felt he was probably the first person to truly understand the darkness in my life. It was always seemingly difficult finding the right words when people asked about my blindness, but the words with Emil flowed easily as if a magic spell had been cast. When he began to read aloud the very first book at his place, I knew it was not just a story he was reciting, but the beginning of great changes in my life. We spent several years together and looking back now it seemed to have passed in a heartbeat. I wished a thousand times I could have found a way to repay him for his extraordinary kindness.

"I can't really explain how Emil was able to get a blind person to see words and pictures but he did. Maybe it wasn't that difficult though because unlike others with my affliction, I did have twelve good years of eyesight. Emil was generous with his time and truly understanding when I told him things about my blindness. One day I'll tell you how I lost my sight, a long sad story difficult to talk about even many years later. I would love to hear about your relationship with Emil but for now, I want to ask you about a phrase he used often. Did he every say the words there was more to his work than met the eye. I'm sorry I never asked what that meant."

In truth, I had no clue. As she spoke I realized I was cradling the Scarlet Letter by Nathanial Hawthorne in my hands. I could have listened to her all day but time was an issue. I wanted to ask one more question though. What did the name Sucre mean?

"It's the word for sweet in Peru, the name the nuns gave me because I had such a sour personality when they took me in."

I said my full name was Charles Darwin although I did not write the Origin of the Species. Sucre replied she'd studied Darwin in school.

"I was named after the scientist because he was a distant relative and my parents hoped I'd become a scientist like him.

CHAPTER 3

I asked if Sucre if she would like to stop for a bite to eat and have me walk her home.

"You mean like a blind date" she replied, laughing loudly at the sentiment. I merely shook my head, glad she'd said yes.

Waiting for our dinner Sucre recalled memories of her life in Peru and what eventually happened ending her childhood.

"When I was a very young girl my family lived in a rather spacious apartment above the main post office in the city of Arequipa. I was born with full sight and my earliest recollections of the city buildings were nearly every building was constructed with a white quarried rock found in the nearby mountains. That's why Arequipa today is called the White City.

"When I was very young our country experienced a very bitter and dangerous civil war. There are no official numbers but many believed the number of dead were in the hundreds of thousands. Sadly, many others simply disappeared never to be seen again. Rebels calling themselves the Shining Path waged war against what truly was a very repressive and authoritarian Peruvian government. It didn't really matter which side you were on because the war eventually touched everyone. The guerilla attacks and brutal responses from the government were not unlike many conflicts taking place in other Latin American nations.

"We were very fortunate in the early years of the war because Arequipa never experienced a direct attack by the rebels. Life was not easy though because there were many days we couldn't go out into the streets because of rumors of an impending attacks. Often the power lines were blown up by the rebels and we'd be in the dark, having only enough food for one meal a day which wasn't much.

Emil's List

"On one of the stormiest days of the year my father decided it was safe to go out to find food. Sadly, the rebels infiltrated the city during the night and the Shining Path soldiers captured him. The rebels erroneously believed my father ran the postal service in Arequipa, which he absolutely did not. We only rented an upstairs floor in the same building. The rebels tortured him to make him confess what government documents were received at the post office.

"The rebels kept him blindfolded for five days far from the city but on the sixth day he managed to escape. He was badly hurt but slowly made his way back to us. While his wounds healed soldiers from the government came to our apartment to question him about what he'd learned about the terrorists. When he said he'd been blindfolded and didn't know where he'd been taken, the government soldiers took him away. Like the rebels, he was tortured for days because they felt he was not being truthful about the Shining Path. One day they simply let him go but he was never the same.

"On a very quiet ordinary Sunday morning we were dressing for church when someone, either a government soldier or a rebel broke into the post office building planting high explosives. When the bomb went off the only thing I remember was the blinding flash and the sound of thunder seemingly never ending. I must have been knocked unconscious because when I awoke, I found myself lying in the street, bloody and hurt but alive. Days later I learned my parents and two brothers lost their lives that morning."

I was horror-struck by her tale, sorry I'd encouraged her to talk about her Peruvian life.

"My body eventually healed but my eyes were far too damaged to repair. A cloister of nuns searched the streets for orphans, finding me wandering in search of something to eat. They took me to their convent in a valley far from the city and the war, a village called Lares.

"The village was very poor with almost no contact with the world outside the valley. There was only one road in and that dead ended near a very steep mountain. We were safe there however, far from the terrors plaguing the rest of Peru.

"I hated the sisters at first but they never gave up on me, teaching me how to take care myself. School lessons took place in a one room school and I knew from the very first day I had a love affair with learning. Once

Bruce Weiss

a week a priest would come to the village and after mass he would teach me Braille.

"When I was eighteen Sister Juanita arranged for me to travel to America to attend a small religious university. I knew very little English and nothing of the world outside the village of Lares so I was quite frightened. I majored in American literature, devouring books purchased in Braille.

"When I graduated I moved to Boston because Harvard offered me a wonderful position in their library and bookstore. My first job was translating books from Spanish and English into Braille. Then of course I had that unexpected meeting with Emil."

I said she'd done very well for herself.

"Do recall any conversations you might have had with Emil about his life as a journalist? He had quite an excellent reputation."

"I'd probably have to say yes and no. He seldom talked about his private life, seemingly always interested in my life. It turned out he knew much more about Peru's war with the Shining Path than I did, telling me things I had not known.

"Good memories or bad ones he emphasized; they all needed to be kept alive because memories of one's childhood fade in time and are eventually lost. As to his work, at times he would read aloud what he'd prepared for his next lecture at the University, one of the few times I learned about his life experiences. All his lectures were based on personal experiences so part of the answer is I did knew a little about his work.

"Sometimes in the morning preceding a lecture he'd practice the delivery and it felt as if I were getting a free Harvard education. Emil as you probably discovered had the uncanny ability to paint pictures of people and places and events he'd investigated. One day I woke up realizing I was probably more fortunate then most other blind people because I didn't lose my sight until I was nearly twelve years old. Many things Emil read or discussed I was able to picture."

"Did you know he was planning to organize his nearly fifty years of personal papers into a memoir" I asked? She answered with an emphatic yes.

When I looked at my watch she somehow knew what I was doing surprising me with her words. The time is a few minutes after ten she declared.

Awed, I asked how she knew, saying that was the exact time according

Emil's List

to my watch. Her mischievous smile touched me deeply as if I'd asked a wondrous question.

"I've had to overcompensate for my blindness and learn to use my other senses. One of the things I've learned is to listen to the extraneous sounds sighted people might not hear or ignore. I knew the time because I heard the church bell in the distance chime ten times a few minutes ago."

I hadn't heard the chimes, nor had I ever been aware of the bells tolling on the hour I replied.

"I really should go back to my place now and then to work," she declared. "I'm finishing up the translation of a text for a professor of letters."

"I'm going to give you my phone number" I said, "just in case you need get in touch with me. Don't worry about the books because we'll move them to your place tomorrow."

When I said those words I realized she wouldn't be able to read the books, nor my phone number. I later learned she could memorize an entire phone book of numbers if said aloud just once.

"Why don't you give me your number" I said, "and I'll call you the morning."

I watched from the window as she made her way down the street with her trusty walking stick. I hoped she'd say yes to helping with the work on Emil's papers because in truth, I liked her very much and could use the company. I turned my attention back to the task of packing up Emil's papers.

CHAPTER 4

I hardly slept that night thinking about the horrors Sucre experienced in her young life. I replayed her words in my mind but even if I'd not heard her poignant story, I doubted there would have been much sleep. My overactive mind was never far from Emil's trove of papers and the enormous task of organizing. I couldn't stop fretting the what ifs. What if I'd hadn't been let go by Emil? What if I'd been able to discover Emil only had weeks to live? What if I'd known he was working too hard, his heart unable to keep up with him? His book collection was also in my thoughts

One of the local literary critics once advertised a first edition of To Kill of a Mocking Bird for sale, signed and offered for five thousand dollars. Sucre would have no way of knowing the collection could easily be worth hundreds of thousands of dollars.

Each time I looked at my bedside clock I became more frustrated, my mind unable to slow or shut down, doubting I'd ever sleep. When I was finally able to drift off for a few minutes, I'd invariably wake up perplexed by a series of disturbing dreams. When I looked at my clock again I realized I had a stack of books resting on my night table. I'd forgotten Sucre asked me to take three or four home to read in my spare time. I switched on the light and brought the books to my bed.

The first was The Last Temptation of Christ and curiously, tucked between the pages was a handwritten note in Emil's handwriting. 'The book and author were savagely attacked by censors when the book was first published.' There was more but I'd save it until I actually started to read the book. The second book was Charles Dickens' Oliver Twist. For the life of me I couldn't fathom how or why a book by Dickens would be censored.

Thanks to another note found inside I had the answer. It was suppressed and banned in England because of it's criticisms of religion per Emil.

I was well also aware of the evils of censorship, not only in literature but in my own reporter's articles and in my profession in general. I knew many books were censored on political grounds, others because of sexual content. Dr, Zhivago, one of the books Sucre left with me also contained a personal note stating something I'd already known. The book was banned because of it's open and not so hidden political undertones.

Lady Chatterley's Lover was the fourth book, a novel once fodder for critics who'd objected to literature with sexual overtones,

It was true. All the books Emil collected were once banned, not only by censors but by tyrants ruling over totalitarian states. Many were banned by the Church, especially when religious fanatics objected to language and descriptions.

I thought about a lecture I'd once heard Emil deliver about The First Amendment in our Constitution and the right to free speech. He'd used the term self-righteous describing censors, claiming they had no right to decide what was or was not in the public's best interest. Uncle Tom's Cabin was debated nearly every year I recalled, as were several of Judy Blume's books. In my scrapbook there was an op-ed piece where Emil demanded all citizens needed to stand up to their local authorities who'd taken it upon themselves to remove books from school libraries.

Certain censored books gained great international notoriety because of their politics I'd learned. Solzhenitsyn's books including the one Emil owned were removed from libraries, book stores and even private homes in the old Soviet Union, often burned in massive bonfires in public areas, just as the Germans did in the 1930's. Banned books were available to those who defied the authorities at great risk. The Nazi's burned thousands of books deemed anti-Aryan and anti-German, old black and white newsreels still popping up in movies from time to time showing the smiling faces while the books burned.

Copies were burned in public displays in many small towns. Catch-22 was removed from my high school library when I was a student I remembered because adults feared the theme would harm young readers. Many journalists including myself had stories censored but certainly none more then Emil. A very dirty business in truth. I wanted to call Sucre but it was an un-Godly hour mostly to say hello. That was my last thought, falling shortly into a very deep sleep.

In the morning the sound of my ringing phone startled me, wondering immediately if it might be Sucre. The moment I heard her voice I sensed something was not right.

"I couldn't sleep last night so late in the evening I walked to Emil's place. The front door of the building slammed quite loudly and unfortunately woke Emil's landlord. He was very angry, scolding me about trespassing, saying I didn't belong in his building. He shouted get out or he'd call the police. When I left he continued yelling full volume including we didn't have three days to pack everything from Emil's place, only two."

Damn I muttered. Even with three days I doubted we could get everything packed but two? I sensed we would not have enough time to empty the place.

"Charlie, there's something else I need to tell you before I meet you there. When I began retracing the route back to my place the landlord caught up with me, saying he was privy to some very juicy information gotten from one of his police friends. Charlie, are you sitting down?"

Grudgingly I said I was.

"According to the landlord, an extremely arrogant man by the way, the police might be looking into Emil's death not as a heart attack as reported, but possibly as a homicide. I didn't believe him but if it's true, maybe we should talk to the police or Emil's attorney before we go back into the building this morning."

A score of thoughts inundated my head, none good. Most likely a rumor I suspected but having been in the reporting business for years, many rumors later turned out to be true.

"Murder," I whispered?

It wasn't possible because the medical examiner ruled a heart attack killed Emil. Rumors could easily ruin lives and I knew that too well. Emil certainly had his share of spiteful enemies but someone murdering him was preposterous.

I told Sucre to meet me at Emil's place in exactly two hours because I needed to rent a van and buy cartons. I also said somewhat assuredly not to believe what the super said. My head ached terribly and it was still very early in the day.

It took longer then planned to rent the van making me extremely edgy by the minute. Once on the road I realized I wasn't used to driving Boston's ancient roadways. The streets were originally created as cattle paths and the traffic patterns hadn't changed in nearly three hundred years. I mistakenly drove down a one way street to the consternation of Boston cabbies.

I'd tried to call Attorney Gould from the rental agency but was told he wasn't in yet. Tepidly I asked his secretary if she knew of any new issues surrounding Emil's death. She sounded surprised and said no, she hadn't heard anything.

When I finally arrived at Emil's place I found Sucre sitting on the front stoop. She'd once told me she could not form tears because of the damage to her eyes, but she looked damned close to losing it. We took the rickety elevator to Emil's floor, managing to avoid the super.

During the slow rode I tried to imagine what the place might look like if there were yellow crime tape baring the door. Fortunately there was none and the moment I opened the door I realized the place looked just as we'd left it the day before. So much for rumors.

Sucre brewed the last of Emil's tea and we toasted the beginning of our work relationship, vowing to work non stop packing until the apartment was completely empty. Time was the enemy so I anticipated working all day and night after losing the third day.

We first packed Emil's books because of their value. Carefully removing the rare books from the shelves, Sucre packed each with great care into the cartons I'd purchased. After filling two cartons Sucre's voice broke, saying how much Emil loved those books. I wished she could have a good cry but strangely, it was me who felt tears forming.

There were long periods of silence as I handed each book to Sucre who'd placed them ever so gently into the cartons. I was mesmerized by her gentle movements. When one of the books fell to the floor we both gasped and then laughed.

When the quiet grew too painful to bear I thought of something to lighten the heaviness, asking if she would allow me to take over Emil's role and read the unread books to her. The thought put a wry smile on her face, saying she'd think about it.

Progress was slow but we finally got all the books packed into cartons ready to be moved downstairs and into the van. We'd filled the elevator sending it on it's way down without us, fearful too much weight might cause it to crash down to the basement. We were both sweaty and dirty, complaining in jest who had the most aching muscles.

Just as I was about to lock the door Emil's phone rang, a truly haunting sound. Mercifully it was Attorney Gould's secretary calling to ask how the packing was going. I told her we were working our butts off and about to close up for an hour or so. There was no response, hearing someone whispering to her.

"I'm very sorry Mr. Darwin but there is a new development regarding Mr. Breck's cause of death."

It felt as if my world was about to collapse.

"The Boston police issued a statement a few moments ago saying they'd gathered certain evidence suggesting foul play was the cause of Emil Breck's death. I'm sorry to have to be the one to tell you but Mr. Gould is not here right and I thought you needed to know."

I sensed I was in a freefall to a place that felt very frightening. On the drive to drop books off at Sucre's I tuned into the hourly news on the radio. The lead local story stunned us.

'Boston police authorities received a court order to exhume the body of esteemed Boston journalist Emil Breck, a second autopsy requested because new evidence pointed to foul play.' The newswoman added Mr. Breck was found slumped over his desk in his Boston apartment several weeks ago.

I took a deep breath, a death grip on the steering wheel cursing the word exhume. The idea of Emil's remains being disturbed was repulsive. My heart was breaking and poor Sucre looked horrified. I assumed there had to be very strong evidence to get an order of exhumation, doubting the process was ever taken lightly.

Sucre asked why Emil had to have to have an autopsy when it appeared to be a heart attack. Sadly, I had an answer.

"When someone dies an unattended death Massachusetts law requires an autopsy. The earlier tests performed were probably fairly routine given his age and everything pointed to a fatal heart attack. From what we've just heard it's possibly someone has disputed that finding. For what reason, I have no idea.

The moment we walked into Emil's place the phone began ringing.

Emil's List

Once again it was Attorney Gould's secretary giving me the reason for the second autopsy.

"After a thorough review of the medical examiner's notes, the notation that an unknown substance was found in his blood stream sounded an alarm bell. The Boston medical examiner initially thought that not important, declaring it was an open and shut case of massive heart failure."

I couldn't believe what I'd just heard.

What happens now Sucre asked.

I shrugged my shoulders, remembering to reply verbally. I said I had no idea although if someone suspected foul play, I guessed there needed to be a full investigation.

We began the urgent task of packing with a great heaviness in our hearts. My nerves were on edge.

The plan was to fill the van and drop the cartons off at Sucre's and making a quick u-turn to head back to Emil's to pack papers. Every minute counted but I needed to call Attorney Gould to possibly find out what was happening. Put on hold for nearly twenty minutes sitting in stone silence, I rued the lost time. Each passing minute meant we might not get all Emil's papers out in time.

When at last the attorney answered what followed was one of the most painful phone conversations I'd ever had.

"Going over the first autopsy results more carefully it's possible that a poison known as strychnine could be the unknown substance. We'll know more when the results of the second autopsy are available. Let's hope that's not the case."

Who would want to poison Emil? What could I possibly say to Sucre who'd taken Emil's death harder than anyone else?

"Don't draw any conclusions" Attorney Gould warned. "We wait until all the lab work is done. Charlie, I too came to the conclusion it was a tired or a weak heart that finally gave out."

We should have been in the van on our way back to Emil's place but after the call I couldn't get myself moving. I projected terrible scenarios if it were true, including the police thinking me a suspect. When all was said and done I suspected, the police would realize Sucre and I had been the only ones benefiting from Emil's death. Would the police consider that

Bruce Weiss

motive if poison was truly found in Emil's system? I hated the thought of Emil's body being exhumed because it felt so ghoulish.

It was actually a good thing we had not driven off because the phone sprang into action once again, my heart racing. It was attorney Gould calling to offer some solace.

"I'll be the first to know what the police are up to but if they should contact you for any reason, my advice is don't say anything to them. If they insist, tell them you want your attorney present. By the way, that's not an admission of guilt. While the situation is still fluid, please, not a word to anyone."

I relayed the conversation to Sucre, trying my best to make it sound as non-threatening as possible. Despite my best attempt the words did nothing to calm her. Her senses were never wrong and she knew from the sound of my voice that we might be in trouble.

"We've got nothing to fear or fret about right now but I'm going to guess sooner or later we'll be questioned" I said cautiously. "Remember, we've done nothing wrong and we've got one of Boston's most powerful lawyers handling this possible situation."

My attempt at reassurance was met with a look of skepticism. We had fewer hours to pack the papers but getting the valuable books to Sucre's place offered a little peace of mind. It would be nearly impossible to put a price on the papers but the books were definitely priceless.

Sadly there had been little time to mourn Emil and when we returned to his place the reality he wasn't there hit me very hard. We pushed and pulled packed cartons down the hallways to the elevator, then through the lobby to the van. On one trip I spied something on the windshield of the van. To my astonishment it was a rather costly ticket. A perfect storm was brewing I sensed. When the van was emptied at me place we rushed back and when I opened the door I sensed we'd hardly made a dent in the work.

Driving the narrow streets of Beacon Hill in a large van was difficult enough but with the new stress it felt as if each pothole stirred a new terrible thought in my head. Had the press gotten wind of a police investigation into a murder? If the super at Emil's apartment heard about Emil's situation, I feared it was a good bet the press would soon be on the case.

We loaded more cartons into the van speeding to my place, dropping the cartons off before making the round trip once again. Traffic crawled at times along with an orchestra of horns driving me out of my mind.

We filled the cartons haphazardly, packing a lifetime of personal papers without a glance, knowing they'd all be mixed making the task of organizing them like putting a thousand word puzzled together. We worked all afternoon until it grew darker and when I switched the overhead light on, nothing happened. Trying the lamps did nothing, making me realize the electric company or the super pulled the plug. So much for putting in an all-nighter.

We worked as best we could in the darkness piling paper on top of paper until a carton was full, the darkness actually making me more sensitive to Sucre's sightless life. I stumbled into cartons feeling totally lost. Sucre knew where all the cartons were located and while I tiptoed nervously around, the darkness did not slow her down. I was getting a taste of what it was like to live in a dark world but it was only temporary for me.

Banging into boxes and tripping over chairs made me greatly admire Sucre's ability to negotiate a dark world safely. To my amusement she let out a little laugh each time I cursed after whacking my shin. When the work in the dark became impossible I suggested we grab the boxes we'd packed and take them down to the van, calling it a day. One last glance about Emil's place told me we still had much work to do and only one more day to do it. I asked Sucre if she'd like to stop at a diner for a bite but she said she really wasn't very hungry. Curiously, neither was I.

We drove the streets of Boston in silence, doing my best to keep my mind on the driving. Dwelling on the awful exhuming process nearly causing me to hit a parked car. My scattered mind eventually got us lost somewhere in East Boston.

I lugged all the packed cartons with Emil's papers into my apartment, exhausted as mentally and physically as I'd ever felt. The empty van pretty much summed up how I felt. Driving Sucre back to her place, I barely had the strength to say I'd see her in the morning.

Aching muscles did little to calm my overactive mind that night. A half hour after I'd gone to bed I was still wide awake so I decided to open up one of the cartons and peek inside.

Grabbing a handful of loose papers, I turned the overhead light on, needing a few moments to get used to the brightness. In the quiet of my

Bruce Weiss

place I immediately new I was holding history in my hands. Reaching deeper into the bottom I discovered a weathered leather bound book, wondering if it was a diary or perhaps a date book. I settled back in bed turning to page one. Curiously, I found myself reading aloud as if Sucre was nearby.

'I was seventeen years old in 1936, lying about my age saying I was twenty-two and a recent college graduate. Without any appointments I headed out into the big city hoping to get a few job interviews, beginning with the city's largest newspapers.

'I thought I'd put together a pretty good plan. I'd work for a few months as hard as I could proving to my bosses I was a gem in the rough. In time after proving myself I'd get up the nerve and ask my bosses to pay my way to the Soviet Union where I would report for the paper. There were many mysteries waiting to be uncovered behind the Iron Curtain and I knew I could do the job. The plan was to sail to Barcelona, Spain finding the cheapest fare possible and then find overland transportation to Moscow. That was my hope but to my disappointment, the plan turned out to be an exercise in futility. It was a depressing day of knocking on doors and being told to go away.'

I put the diary down leafing through the loose papers in the carton. The earliest dated articles I pulled out were obituaries written for living movie stars and politicians. I knew from personal experience the work was hardly rewarding but early in one's career it paid the bills. I'd once asked Emil what personal papers and articles he'd saved. His answer was he'd saved every one of them and looking at the piles of cartons, that was an understatement.

I pulled a file folder out of the same carton of articles written from Spain in the late 1930's. He actually got there I said aloud, part of his dream

I had no idea how long he'd remained in Spain because from the diary, his final destination was the Soviet Union. It appeared the earliest article were written from Spain in 1937 with attached long hand notes. In his diary he rued the fact getting to the Soviet Union was nearly impossible. Shuffling through the papers in the folder I realized Emil unknowingly had a front row seat to what would become known as the Spanish Civil War.

As absorbed as I was reading the news dispatches, Emil's poisoning was

Emil's List

never far from my thoughts. Although nothing was official yet, I couldn't help sense I'd certainly be a suspect, so why hadn't the police come to talk to me?

I wasn't going to get much sleep so I gave some thought to returning to Emil's place with a flashlight to do more packing. We had only one more full day to pack Emil's papers and I had many doubts we'd finish the task. Even if we somehow managed to pack up his place there were other issues. If I couldn't give rightful credit to Emil's life I'd fail him. I'd had my share of life's disappointments in my work but I'd never tackled anything as challenging as writing a great man's biography.

It was a little after three with still no sleep, stirred by Emil's Spanish articles I couldn't put down. I said over and over again just one more page. Just as I was ready to surrender the phone rang. For several moments I felt paralyzed, my heart beating so slowly I thought I'd pass out. It was near four in the morning.

"I'm at Emil's" Sucre whispered" and I needed to call you because I simply couldn't sleep. There's really nothing I can do here but I wanted that warm feeling I'd always felt when I visited to hopefully take away some of my sadness, Charlie, you need to know that when I arrived this time there was tape across the door and I'm assuming it's the yellow police tape your police use at crime scenes."

I told her I'd be there in thirty minutes and leave the apartment immediately, sitting tight on the staircase waiting for me. I hated to bother Attorney Gould at four in the morning but he'd insisted I could call anytime in an emergency. When he answered I knew he wasn't thrilled with my call, saying give him five minutes and he'd call me back. When he called there was a definite angry edge to his voice.

"I had a long sober conversation with the police chief yesterday afternoon so yes, I knew about the tape but assumed this could wait until morning."

I replied there were still thousands of papers needing to be packed and removed from the apartment. He said he was very sorry but no one could enter the apartment anymore because it was considered an active crime scene. Before I could bemoan the bad news, Attorney Gould said all was not lost however.

"Charlie, as a personal favor the chief said he'd make a one day exception in your case, emphasizing quite strongly not only was the apartment a crime scene, but the papers potential evidence. I assured him if the police needed those paper they could come by your place and take them anytime. By the way, the super in Breck's building isn't thrilled with the police presence so I'd stay very clear of him. Remember, everything has to be out by the end of the day because the super is going to change the locks at midnight.

"Oh, and there's one more thing. A police officer will be sitting in an unmarked patrol car near the front of Emil's building but he won't interfere with your packing. I'm sorry but what you can't get out will most likely be hauled away by the super and taken to a landfill. He's on the warpath, complaining to anyone who'll listen that the bad publicity will drive present and future renters away."

I grabbed a taxi to Emil's apartment building, worrying about Sucre knowing an angry super was lurking. Looking up and down the street when I arrived, I saw no police car but many cars that could have been unmarked.

Sucre was sitting on the sixth floor landing when I approached in the dark with my flashlight. Sitting down next to her I whispered my conversation with Gould. A few minutes later I stopped talking because we'd both heard footfalls on the stairs below. I hoped it was the cop with a flashlight but when the light hit us it was the building super.

With a threatening tone he snarled we had one day to get everything out of the apartment, adding he'd better not see either of us or the police at his place after that. The light was then directed toward the door with the torn tape. The super said nothing more, walking away. One floor below we heard his footfalls stop.

"This used to be a quiet respectful place but thanks to your kind it's now got a bad reputation and it's driving my tenants away. I want everything gone and as a precautionary note, you'd better not do anything in that apartment you'll later regret."

Before I got the key in the door we heard his footsteps coming back up the stairs. Fortunately this time though it was a cop, a visible badge on his vest.

"I want to see some IDs right now," definitely not the voice of the super.

Eying the shield I didn't know if I should be thankful or terribly worried. Staring at my ID the officer nodded his head, removing the tape thus allowing Sucre and I to enter.

With the first rays of light it was with much relied nothing seemed to have been disturbed. Sucre said wait before we walked inside. I soon knew why. Looking about I saw a paper cup with cigarette butts floating in a brown liquid. Hopefully it was left by the police because someone else would certainly have been there for sordid reasons I reasoned. Sucre's sense of smell was right on target.

In all the morning confusion and uncertainty, one overwhelming thought plagued me; there wasn't going to be enough time to gather everything up. Time was the enemy and sadly, the job would be so helter-skelter it would be impossible to keep Emil's papers in order.

We worked nonstop filling cartons, frustrating me to no end. When we had four of five filled we pushed and dragged them down the hall toward the elevator. To my dismay the super anticipated our using the elevator, finding a sign on the door saying, '**for use by residents only**.' Things were coming to a boil inside me, fearful about having to use the rickety narrow old stairways to bring the heavy cartons down.

Each trip to the building front door was greeted by the super's irritated glare and snide comments. Every time I walked by my anger ratcheted up another notch but on the positive side, it did speed up our work.

On the fifth precarious trip down the stairs I nearly knocked an old woman down, swerving to avoid her. The carton fell and broke open, careening down the stairs scattering papers everywhere. Apologizing and picking up papers, the woman said she'd known Emil Breck for more then twenty years, adding no one really knew the man though. I managed to collect the papers listening to her annoying voice, talking non-stop about her daughter who never visited.

Sucre and I worked all day without taking a break, constantly eyeballing the wall clock and looking out the window to see how much daylight was left. With another three hours of sunlight, I was somewhat pleased at our progress and knew if need be, we'd work right up to the deadline at midnight when we had to be gone.

As the sky grew darker the work grew more chaotic. We tossed loose papers into cartons and what felt like the hundredth time that day, we took

Bruce Weiss

the perilous trek down the daunting staircase to the van. The cartons were getting heavier and forever fearful of a header down the stairs. Near eleven I looked around Emil's empty place and should have been elated. Sadly, I was overcome with great sadness. Sucre sobbing quietly. It took us nearly an hour to get to my place getting lost once again.

With my apartment building in sight I was pulled over by the police. For several long agonizing minutes the officer sat in his patrol car talking on the radio. I wondered if an APB had been put out for me, a person of interest in the Emil Breck case. When the officer finally approached my car he informed me I was driving without my headlights on. The incident took twenty minutes and cost me a two hundred and fifty dollar ticket.

The long day despite mishaps and worrying turned out alright. We were able to get every last paper and book out but I knew it would take weeks just to put every paper in the correct order.

The steep narrow stairway killed my back and an anger was building because at no time had any resident used the building elevator. My legs were so tired I debated leaving the cartons in the van until morning, a comforting thought until I remembered the number of car thefts in my neighborhood. The bottom line though was we'd beat the clock and the papers were safe so the work could begin.

I'd purposely left behind Emil's old mattress and a few broken chairs behind just to piss the super off. In my rear view mirror when we pulled away there was a sight that wiped away much of my anger, the super running after the van. The small taste of revenge made me smile.

We were tired and dirty but the van still needed to be unloaded. Fortunately my elevator was not off limits making the move fairly easy. When we'd hauled the last carton into my place I remarked we both looked as if we'd run an obstacle course. I was too tired to change but not having a bite to eat all day I was starving. We walked to a small twenty-four hour dinner and sat down for the first time all day.

Walking back to my place after dinner to drive Sucre home to my unsettled dismay, the van was gone. Damn good thing we'd removed all the cartons was all I could say after the initial shock wore off. We took a taxi to Sucre 's place and called the police to report a stolen rental van.

Home at last near two in the morning I called Sucre to say a quick goodnight but the call turned into a thirty minute discussion about Emil.

Emil's List

Before we hung up Sucre said something making all my aches and pains and even my stress go away.

"I know working with Emil's papers will probably be very frustrating but you need to remember this Charlie. Emil spoke quite highly about you, saying he'd always admired your work. Charlie Darwin was the only person he could trust with his very personal papers he emphasized. I know you're concerned about doing a good job but remember this. Emil had a great deal of faith in you and he knew you'd never let him down."

The words were touching and for the moment they'd chased much of the doubts about doing an honorable job away.

"Charlie, Emil also said it would take several years to write his memoir because the papers encompassed a full lifetime of work. I'm certain there will be bad days but I know they'll pass."

At the end of a very trying and arduous day, Sucre's words gave me a feeling not so much of hope, but of determination to shine a light on Emil. I told Sucre to come by anytime the next day if she'd like, or take a few days off because it had been a long grind.

"I'll probably go over to Harvard some time tomorrow to finish work that I've avoided these past few weeks. If there's time late in the afternoon I'll try to stop by."

I told her there was something I'd like her to think about.

"If you finish your work early, why don't you and I take the rest of what's left of the afternoon and go to the Franklin Park Zoo. I haven't been there in years and I know you'd love the place."

The answer was a hardy yes.

"I have never been to a zoo in my entire life but the thought of wild animals always reminds me of the time my father brought home an orphaned baby spotted mountain bear in Peru. I think I was about ten years old and the bear might have been a birthday present. My dad built a cage behind the post office but in a matter of weeks, the bear managed to pry the bars apart, wandering into the post office and frightening the patrons while looking for food. We brought him up to our apartment but the very first day he managed to rip the door off our refrigerator to feast. The bear regretfully went back to the mountains the next day".

The zoo turned out to be a wonderful adventure on a picture perfect late fall afternoon, the moment we arrived feeling as if all was right in the world. Stopping by each cage I described the animal, listening to Sucre laugh hysterically when the animals made sounds.

"Charlie I know this a vacation day away from all that's happened but there's something's on my mind. Is it okay to bring it up?

Sure I replied.

"Possibly four or five days before Emil died I had this strange sense something was greatly bothering him and my senses are rarely off base. He just didn't sound well as if his mind was far away, distracted and seemingly sad. He'd easily recalled every event in his life but suddenly he'd become very forgetful. I said nothing but knowing he was so good at recalling names and dates, I was a bit dismayed. I'm not sure why I didn't say anything because when I have certain feelings or intuitions, I'm usually right. As you know, Emil was a very private man."

The thickening dark clouds felt like a bad omen, suspecting we were in for a good storm, Minutes before there had not been a cloud in the sky so I was quite shaken. Sucre actually felt the change in weather even before I said we'd better go. We took a cab back to her place arriving just as the skies opened.

The rain came down with such force we decided to sit in the taxi to wait for it to slow. Sucre said she'd changed her mind and wanted to put her work at Harvard on hold for a while so she could help me start working with Emil's papers.

I hope my condition doesn't hinder the work, she said. I replied there was no one else I'd want to work with on the papers because no one knew Emil as well as she did. She gave my hand a good squeeze.

The weather and the cab ride made me very sleepy, the rhythm driving over the cobblestones most comforting. When we got into my place the phone was ringing, a daunting sound because the police were never far from my thoughts. The caller identified himself as Lieutenant Philips of the Boston Police, asking to talk with Charles Darwin. It's over was my first thought, girding my loins in anticipation of some bad news.

I said I was Darwin, the nervousness in my response very obvious.

"Sorry to bother you Mr. Darwin but I'm calling to tell you we've recovered the stolen van. Normally I wouldn't call someone who'd rented a vehicle but a book was left behind and I thought it might be yours."

I nearly collapsed, asking the lieutenant for the title. He replied it written by someone named Kant and the volume looked very old and possibly valuable.

I said I'd be down for it in the morning and when I hung up, I realized my shirt was soaked and it wasn't from the rain. The phone rang again a few moments later, making me suspect there was more to the stolen van than just a book. Someone spoke with an accent explaining the merits of fine solar panels. I thought of scores of terrible things to say but hung up instead.

"Since we're going to work together," I noted to Sucre, "There are some things I need to tell you about Emil that might give you a different perspective. Emil always maintained his professional life was extremely complicated and many of his writing were very litigious and contentious, creating avowed enemies over the course of his lifetime. He also noted his life had been threatened too many times to remember. Fortunately most of the threats were bluster and although the threats were very real he said. There was little retaliation and nothing bad ever happened. The truth hurts he often said, the reason why so many people took offense to the things he wrote. There's a reason I'm telling you this Sucre.

"Emil once said in words that were meant to be a caution. Whoever had access to his papers was potentially in harms way, although he wasn't certain how. From that sentiment I want you to know there are possible dangers lurking out there. If Emil was murdered as the police now believe, it might have been because of something in his myriad of papers. We now own them and I don't say this to frighten you, but it's possible someone else is interested and might do anything to get them. What I'm suggesting is, if you feel the need to retreat, I'd perfectly understand.

"No way Charlie. The only thing I ask is that you be patient with me" Sucre replied. "Charlie all the things I do in my life have great risks so don't worry about me. I'm tougher then I appear."

At that moment a magnificent rainbow appeared in the sky. Sucre said it was a good omen and looked forward to her walk home.

In the morning the phone rang, waking me from my first decent night's sleep, certainly not a good way to start a day. Thankfully it was Sucre saying she'd come by shortly because she'd made a special tea using traditional Peruvian cocoa leaves. The tea was indeed intoxicating, a relief after several hectic days.

"Reporters and journalists by are by nature very private individuals," I said. "We tend to keep things very close to the vest because our livelihoods depended on getting the scoop. Any number of us might be working on the same story so we never dared sharing any information. Journalists by nature work alone, generally keeping what we were working on very private. Emil and I often traveled in the same circles, usually at press dinners or news conferences but like most reporters, we were tight lipped about what we were working on.

"Possibly eight or ten years ago we did collaborate on a story although I can't quite remember the specifics now. In 1979 we both did a story on Iran and since he'd been in country when the hostages were taken, he held all the cards but here's something. I was fairly new to the work yet he came by my office one day with information he'd uncovered, offering it to me.

"I never considered Emil a friend but I respected him more than any other journalist I'd ever known, taking our work extremely seriously which meant little time to socialize. From my personal experience, a reporter always creates enemies, most who don't follow through with their threats but there have been incidents. Again, I'm not saying this to frighten you off. I just want to be totally upfront.

"Emil's papers represent the best journalism you'll ever find anywhere in the world. I do think it'll be a great experience for you and I know that you'll learn much about twentieth century American history. Emil kept everything he ever worked on, some rather toxic and others mostly benign. The work is not going to be the memoir Emil wanted so I can truly use all the help you might offer. Two passionate minds working together can produce great results and besides, I've never written a biography."

To my surprise Sucre said there were certain conditions before we began, saying she'd fill me in later.

We rummaged through a few cartons, soon discovering we were really too tired to begin the work. It would have to wait one more day.

Chapter 5

Sucre arrived at my place just before eight the next morning and the first words were the conditions she'd referred to a day earlier.

"First and foremost, you'll have to be very patient with me because I'm not a reporter and in truth, I'm not familiar with much American history. I'll help in any way I can but you'll have to be candid and honest, especially if I become a liability. You must agree to be patient and you must agree to let me go if things don't work out."

I agreed and said I totally understood her wishes. "We're going to be working at a very slow pace because this is also very new territory for me also. I think we'll make a good team though and I look forward to working with someone who knew a different side of Emil."

Sucre nodded although not as enthusiastically as I'd hoped and to make matters a bit more convoluted, I put my big foot in my mouth again,

"We haven't started organizing any of Emil's work so why don't we first gather up all the loose papers and see if we can't put everything in some kind of order."

I regretted the words as soon as they came out, turning a shade of red hoping she wouldn't sense. Her response was immediate.

"Condition number two. You can't beat yourself up every time you say something about looking or seeing. I've worked quite hard becoming immune to those statements and expressions. Believe it or not it happens all the time, even among my co-workers at Harvard who know me well. I can't tell you how many times someone shouted hey lady, watch where you're walking or are you blind?' I can't let those words ruin my day so my response is usually a smile and a wave. Please don't worry about what you might say because I've developed a very thick skin over these past years."

I assumed there were other conditions but Sucre suggested we get down to the work saving the others for later. The carton I'd randomly selected for our first endeavor held many notebooks, all written in long hand. Buried beneath were scores of news articles most likely written from those notes. I promised to read every paper aloud.

We'd organized stories by date, the only effective way to start. Sorting through countless papers eventually felt like an endless task. To take an edge off the repetitiveness I asked which books of Emil's were her favorite.

"Actually I enjoyed almost every book Emil read aloud with the possible exception of Rabbit Run by John Updike, not one of my favorites. The others Emil read held my interest and I truly fell in love with each and every book. Emil had a wonderful speaking voice, especially when he'd assume the role of one of the characters right down to the accents. I learned much more than just plots or subplots because he had a way of really understanding the characters. This might sound a little crazy but I swear Emil had the ability to make a blind girl see again."

Several old leather bound diaries were buried among the loose papers, some dated in the late 1930's apparently written in Spain. Each entry contained personal insights into what he was seeing or thinking at the time. The diaries enabled us to place many undated papers about Spain in one large folder we'd created.

When we'd emptied all the contents in the first carton which took us nearly three hours, I wasn't quite ready to open another just yet, saying at least a dozen times we'd work slowly and deliberately. Over cups of Peruvian coffee Sucre brewed I asked again to tell me more about life growing up in Peru, admitting I knew very little about the country with the exception of the famed lost city of Machu Picchu. Talking about Peru usually uplifted her.

"I think I told you that I'd once traveled by train from Cusco to Machu Picchu with my school class. The entire experience was magical and fortunately permanently etched into my mind. When I lost my sight I vowed I'd return one day and happily, one of the nuns took me there. Machu Picchu is a very spiritual place and when you touch the stones they seem to come to life. A few were warm to the touch, even those not exposed to the sun for centuries so it was a very different experience for me without

Emil's List

sight. Regretfully, many parts of my childhood were lost forever but there are places like Machu Picchu still living in my soul.

"Charlie, I still see the world from a child's point of view but sadly, my childhood ended when I was twelve. Some memories are very vivid and alive and I'm extremely thankful I can still recall them. Other images have faded over time and unfortunately, there's really no way to get them back.

"You remember I told you my family lived in Arequipa, Peru's second largest city? It's surrounded by the incredible snow capped Andes Mountains year round. Did you know the Andes are the longest mountain chain in the world."

I shook my head, reminding myself to say no.

"I miss the mountains very much because Peruvians consider them sacred places. The ancient Inca worshipped the mountains and certain ones became religious ceremonial sites still visited these days. The sun was also very important to the early Inca and it's still worshiped in many daily rituals. In many homes the only source of light and warmth is the sun. If you walked on the sunny side of the street in Arequipa you'd easily become overheated but if you walked on the shaded side, you'd need to bundle up because it was quite cold. The air was cool and dry most of the year in Arequipa although we did have a rainy season. If you looked up into the winter sky during the day, you could actually see stars.

"The main square was a child's wonderland because thousands of pigeons lived there. Somewhere in my apartment I have a picture of me with my arms held out, pigeons standing on them and one on my head. Sadly, most of our photos were destroyed in the explosion. Am I boring you yet?"

Hardly I replied,

"I think about my family and often wonder how my life would have been different if the bomb hadn't detonated. On that fateful day I think I told you we were preparing to go to church, and if we'd only left ten minutes earlier......well, we didn't. If I dwell too much on that terrible day I can get very down on myself and end up hurting for days. I used to feel so sorry for myself all the time but after I was taken in by the nuns that stopped. They wouldn't allow me to sulk and because of that I hated them for the longest time.

"There's one thing about my childhood still permanently etched into my mind and I'm extremely grateful. Outside the city a new airport was built and near it stands a magical mountain towering high over Arequipa. It's not part of the Andes chain but a large free standing mountain in black, an inactive volcano last erupting thousands of years ago. It's shaped like a perfect Egyptian pyramid reaching nearly 19,000 feet into the sky. For many Peruvians it was a favorite although especially difficult weekend climb.

"After church my father used to take us to the base of the mountain for a picnic dinner. We'd pack a traditional Sunday lunch including guinea pig and we'd sit in the shadow of Misti Mountain. When I was five or six I fell in love with the flights into and out of the airport, making me dream about all the places I'd like to see one day.

"The airport took up much land but the surrounding fields remained unchanged, used mostly for grazing alpaca. At times the mountain could look most foreboding, especially when wisps of smoke escaped from the cone at the top. To many it was a symbol of peace and strength. When smoke poured from the top on dark days you could often see the deep red of fire. Every birthday I asked my father if we could climb Misti Mountain because Peruvians loved to summit the mountain on their birthday. You could make a special wish at the top and it was certain to come true. Just before each birthday my father would say wait another year because it's a very strenuous hike. Regretfully, I lost my family when I was twelve and I've not been back to the city since. Still, I've promised myself one day I'd return to Misti Mountain and climb it, not only for myself but to honor my parents and brothers."

I was deeply touched by her words. Keep the good memories alive I offered, adding I truly hoped she'd return one day, maybe even on her birthday.

"What else do you remember about your childhood," I asked?

"My brothers and my parents of course. They're frozen in my mind especially our last morning together. Our apartment was totally destroyed and the few pictures we had burned up, but I'll save the part about growing up with the nuns for another time. What about your childhood. Are there good memories? Did you like school?"

The question caught me off guard because I rarely thought about it.

"I think I enjoyed my childhood but it really was a long time ago.

Emil's List

Maybe it's due to age but I really can't remember an awful lot, although I have warm memories of a very caring family. I loved school the most and the moment I walked into my first classroom like you I was hooked on learning. Years later I finished my education with two degrees in journalism at college. In my senior year I was the editor of the university newspaper, a very prestigious position getting my foot in the door after graduation with several newspapers. My first job was actually reporting local Boston stories, occasionally writing editorials including a few that actually circulated nationally.

"So if I think back on my life, it's the news business that's etched in my mind. I loved the work until regretfully, it came to an end five years ago. On my sixtieth birthday I was abruptly fired because I'd crucified one very powerful Boston politician my publisher adored. I'll spare you the sordid details right now because it's rather complicated but I'll tell you about it one day. When I left my paper I freelanced for a while until it became terribly obvious nobody wanted my stories anymore. I was considered a person non-grata. After all the doors were shut in my face so I became a part time lecturer at Northeastern University in Boston to pay the bills and still do that work."

"What kind of reporting did you do? That's how you met Emil, right?"

"It was how I first met him and I'll give you the highlights as well as the lowlights. After college I spent many rewarding years working for a newspaper sadly no longer in business. The paper was the old Boston Evening Times and like many afternoon papers in the late sixties, declining circulation due to television news eventually led to it's demise.

"I worked for the paper for nearly twenty years, the last ten as chief editorial director. We were a very liberal newspaper supported by important people such as the Kennedy's, with occasional nods of approval from the more conservative Lodges. I wrote op-ed pieces mostly designed to shake things up and like Emil, I made many enemies along the way. I thought I'd work until my pen ran dry but sadly that was not to be. About seven months before the paper folded we were bought out by the Boston Sun, becoming the Boston Sun Times. The new owners were politically far to the right and many of us had a very difficult time with the paper's right wing philosophy. Shall I continue?"

"Are you getting to the highlights now or the lowlights?"

Bruce Weiss

Sucre couldn't see my Cheshire Cat grin.

"I'm not sure if you've ever heard the name Raymond Baldwin, once governor of Massachusetts serving nearly fourteen years."

Sucre replied she knew very little about American politics.

"I spent the better part of a year investigating the governor's office because I'd gathered evidence the man was dishonest and worse, a thief. My new bosses were tucked into the governor's back pocket so I was ordered to stop the criticisms but of course I continued. I was told to write flattering articles about the governor which I refused to do.

"I listened to my conscience when it was time to stand my ground or give in to keep my job. It took about two minutes to figure out what I was going to do. I went after Governor Baldwin with the proverbial sledge hammer and in the end, even though I was right and my evidence of terrible corruption portrayed him as a crooked politician, I paid dearly. I was demoted from the op-ed desk and no longer able to write editorials. I even lost my corner office and was considered a bad influence because I caused problems.

"I'd exposed Governor Baldwin's shadiness and the many underhanded and illegal deals he'd made while in office. During his last two months he refused my interviews and our paper was not included on the list of correspondents invited to hear him speak. Obviously my bosses were not happy with me and I was called into the owners office several times, lectured about being a good team player. I was warned one more nasty word from me though and I'd be out on the street. I left the office that day as angry as I'd ever been in my life.

"I went back to my office the next day and wrote a long articulated article about the Governor's corrupt practices I'd uncovered. Every word was true, describing the taking of a lot of money on the side while fronting for some very shady people. The governor denied the allegations of course, threatening to sue me and our paper if the words were not retracted.

"That unfortunately was the last straw for the bosses. The following week the snot-nosed young son of the owner who'd taken charge of the paper called me to his office. I clearly saw the handwriting on the wall and knew my days were numbered. By the way, three months later his father who'd turned the reins over to his son was sent off to prison for tax evasion. The kid refused to print any of my articles and one day I was ordered to

Emil's List

clean out my desk, ending my tenure with the paper. To add insult to injury I was told I'd never write for any newspaper anywhere ever again."

"What did you uncover that was so bad?"

"I'd gotten information from very reliable and trusted sources who'd put their careers and lives on the line, telling me absolute truths. I found several internal State House memos in my mailbox proving Governor Baldwin was in bed with some very formidable financial people, essentially lining his own pockets. It turns out he was a silent partner in a company manufacturing devices used to send signals to the police when a car was stolen, something you'd call a tracking device.

"I forget the name of the company now because they're no longer in business but unbeknownst to state regulators, the governor ordered the device put into every vehicle the state owned. That included motor scooters to semi-trailers and everything in between, some twenty thousand vehicles in total. The governor's secret take amounted to almost a million dollars.

"That was my final story and even though I knew I'd be tossing myself under the bus, the truth had to be told. You know what got the boss the angriest? I didn't send my article to the top brass for their approval which they would not have given anyhow. I'd taken it right down to the press room and ordered it front page news.

"I was fired but was actually quite proud of myself, knowing I'd done the right thing but unfortunately, that's when bigger troubles set in. All the evidence I'd collected mysteriously disappeared and word got out I was vindictive and dishonest. Someone made sure the word about me being a trouble maker got out and it was soon very obvious nobody would hire me. Fortunately Northeastern University hired me to lecture graduate journalism students."

"Oh please go on."

"Okay, this is the part of my story when I first got to know Emil well. Years before he'd became the Governor of Massachusetts, Raymond Baldwin was the youngest representative ever elected to the U.S. House of Representatives. In short time he earned his first chairmanship on a rather new and at first, powerless committee called the House Un-American Activities Committee. In his new leadership position he lorded over what eventually became one of the most shameful eras in US history, setting

Bruce Weiss

the committee on a course eventually ruining the lives of many good Americans, including Emil.

"I didn't know Emil at the time and it wasn't until much later I learned he was one of the sacrificial lambs crucified by Baldwin, claiming Emil was un-American. When Emil and I began to work together weeks ago we discovered we both had Raymond Baldwin in our past and not in a good way."

The phone rang before I could get to the good part.

"Attorney Gould calling" were the first words. "I'm just calling to make sure you got everything out of Mr. Breck's apartment."

I told him it took much longer then we'd thought but we got everything out. When there was no immediate response my old reporter's instinct told me something else was on his mind.

"Charlie, all the results of the lab tests done on the tissues taken from Emil's body are in and I'm sorry to pass along some thorny news. The chief medical examiner tipped me off so this can't go any further so you also might want to keep this from Miss Grande. We knew traces of strychnine were found in the body tissues but the new lab tests revealed it was a massive amount, meaning someone definitely wanted him dead. The coroner confirmed poisoning was the legal cause of Mr. Breck's death and the evidence has been turned over to the Boston police. The big question being asked now by the detectives is, who would want Emil dead and why.

"Stay with me because this doesn't get any easier. I was given very privileged information the police have no choice but to investigate a murder, and you're going to be high on the list of suspects. The other will be Ms. Sucre Grande."

CHAPTER 6

Someone driving by the cemetery during the exhumation process became curious, spreading word a murder investigation might be underway. When the press got news that an extremely high dose of poison had been discovered in Emil Breck's system, all hell broke lose. Calls swamped the switchboard at the central police station looking for answers. Television crews arrived at the cemetery en masse and the story was soon the talk of the city. A reporter friend called giving me a heads up that his paper was going to print an article about the exhumation and investigation. He also said the word on the street was several persons of interest were linked to the death of Emil Breck."

I wondered if the day could get any worse and if the press came after me, how would I react?

I called Attorney Gould's office once again asking what might happen now the press was involved. He replied there were a number of other suspects on the detective's list including Emil's landlord, a neighbor who'd complained often and several unnamed individuals who'd once made direct threats against Emil.

My back was still killing me from lifting the heavy cartons of books up and down too many narrow flights of stairs. Wishing it were possible to put my mind to rest and concentrate on Emil's papers, sadly it was not to be. Staring about my apartment the sight of box upon box beleaguered me, carton upon carton piled one on top of another nearly reaching the ceiling. Climbing over and around the cartons to get to my bathroom told me I'd made a mistake. Two of the cartons contained Emil's books belonging to Sucre had been moved to my place.

I called Sucre just after noon, intuitively hearing great tiredness in her

Bruce Weiss

voice. It was difficult to know exactly how she felt because emotions were hidden well behind her big dark glasses. I asked if there was anything I could do for her but she replied no, saying exhuming a person properly buried would never happen in Peru. I understood her horror. Before we hung up she said she'd very much like to be alone for a while.

The thought of where and how to begin the work on Emil's papers had no definitive answer yet. A burdensome weight rested on my shoulders, knowing it wasn't because I'd lifted cartons. Worse, the thought the police could enter my life any moment was never far from my thoughts.

Trying to concentrate on the task before me I admitted it would take weeks just to put all the papers in some kind of order. Did I have the fortitude or even the talent to produce something distinctive or exceptional with Emil's papers? My usual pit bull approach and the fire in the belly was dying, feelings of gloom and doom settling in. I spent the rest of the day as far from the cartons as I could, trying to put my mind at ease.

Sucre took the day off arriving early the next morning. It was obvious even with her dark glasses there were new worry lines on her face. As daunting and challenging as the work was going to be, I knew the sooner we started going through the papers the better we'd feel.

I often reminded myself that I had to keep up a verbal explanation about what I was reading and doing. I said we'd start categorizing all the loose papers and she could put them into the different folders we'd put together. She had only one request. Would it be possible to take an hour off each day, possibly the lunch hour.

"I've decided to take you up on your offer and read one of Emil's books to me if you still want to."

I hated the idea of losing an hour but it would give Sucre something to look forward to each day. I make it clear I was no Emil but would do my best to make the books come alive.

We worked all morning making slow progress, wondering if there might be a way to speed up the process of sorting papers. Every paper needed scrutiny and a verbal explanation to ensure Sucre remained part of the work. I warned myself to avoid references such as take a look at this or that.

Near one in the afternoon we put the work aside as it was time to reach into one of the cartons of books I'd accidentally moved into my place. The book on top was The Bell Jar by Sylvia Plath. I asked Sucre if Emil had read it to her. She replied no, acknowledging she'd never heard the title or the name of the author.

I knew a little about the Bell Jar because shortly after it was published my mother's book club met in my home to discuss it.

"Whenever the ladies gathered in our living room once a month, I'd usually sit at the top of the stairs where no one could see me, listening to the questions and comments about the books. For the Bell Jar, the group discussed the great backlash the book received because critics called the book trash, having no place in America. I remember listening to sections of the book so I think you'll be as rapt as I was. It's actually a very interesting story.

"If I recall after the group finished the discussions and left, I came downstairs to read the back jacket. In Emil's edition there's an interview with the author where Plath admits the book was a thinly veiled account of her own inner conflict and eventual mental breakdown and recovery."

Staring at the cover I wondered if the book was a poor choice for Sucre, given the turmoil in the main character's life. I told her I seemed to recall Plath said the book was written through the eyes of a character at an all female college in the 1950's, based on her own experiences.

Opening the book I had a pleasant surprise. An envelope fell to the floor and I immediately recognized Emil's handwriting. He'd left a note inside as he'd done with the others and after a quick glance, I realized it was Emil's insight into the book and the author. I began to read the note to myself until once again I realized I was not including Sucre. I proceeded to read the observations word for word.

'The novel The Bell Jar was quickly taken to task by literary critics because of it's descriptions and discussion of sexuality, as well as the use of objectionable terms describing a lifestyle not talked about at the time. The novel rejected traditional marriage and motherhood and the result was the swift removal of all copies from high school libraries and college bookshelves.'

Reading Emil's notes it became obvious his thoughts were very perceptive. In bold pen strokes he decried the book's censorship, writing down his own thoughts about the rejections and censorship he'd experienced in his own life. I told Sucre I'd hold off on the reading for a

Bruce Weiss

few minutes because I wamted look through the other books to see if any others contained Emil's personal thoughts.

In no time I discovered each book contained notes written by Emil, information about the story, the author and why it was banned and censored. It became obvious every book was once considered too controversial for public consumption, either banned and some even burned in huge public bonfires.

I asked Sucre if Emil talked about why he added his personal thoughts to each volume.

"We spent out time together talking about the books and learned each book was once repudiated by critics and censors. Emil once told me he'd became interested in those books because so much of his own work was treated with the same disdain. I got the same introduction and discourse every time we started a new book, ending the day's reading with his favorite expression. There was much more to the book than met the eye. Why he added his own notes I never asked."

Neither of us truly understood what those words meant although Sucre guessed it probably had something to do with her blindness.

Returning to the Bell Jar and reading chapter one, from the very first paragraph I rediscovered the book was considered far too racy for the times. When our hour was up, I told Sucre I was going to look through the second carton of books to see if they also held thoughts by Emil.

"Sucre, I'm now holding a first edition of a book which means it's quite valuable. The title is The Satanic Verses by Salmon Rushdie. Do you know the curious story about what happened when it was first published?"

Sucre said she knew about the problems the book created "Wasn't a price put on the author's head?"

I nodded, reminding myself to answer verbally.

"Most of the Moslem world including Iran condemned the book. When the Ayatollah Khomeini, Iran's religious and moral leader called the book blasphemous, sales exploded. When the Ayatollah called for the author's execution it became number one on the best seller list. If you want we can put the Jar aside and read Emil's notes in the other books."

Sucre wasn't keen on the idea of putting the Bell Jar aside but she relented.

"Emil wrote eleven pages of personal thoughts about The Satanic

Emil's List

Verses and the controversy that ensued. I'll quote him. 'It is sheer lunacy when books are banned or censored. I once wrote a scathing article about a senator and he actually contacted a hit man to shoot me."

I pulled out another book once banned, announcing I was holding Jude the Obscurer by Thomas Hardy. I said I couldn't recall if I'd ever read it but obviously Emil wanted it to be a part of his collection. Choosing another, I discovered Moll Flanders by Daniel Defoe, a book I'd never read.

Each volume contained an envelope with Emil's thoughts, each cursing the evils of censorship. I asked Sucre if Emil ever mentioned the notes he'd put inside each book. She replied no. His common phrase there was something more to each book than met the eye intrigued us.

"He used those same words every time we'd start and end a new book. Emil read Moll Flanders to me, a book I was so looking forward to but after hearing the first chapter, I realized it was terribly uninteresting."

Looking inside the rest of the books in the carton I was aware I was taking valuable time away from Emil's papers. Curiously, I found myself unable to put the books down.

A very thoughtful six page note was tucked inside Jude the Obscurer. I read the note aloud and when I was done, Sucre went into the kitchen to make us breakfast. I continued to keep up a running account of the books Emil commented on.

'The author has written a book that was regretfully crucified by the critics, referring to the story as grimy and steeped in sex. The reviews stoked the fires of censorship around the country causing many religious groups to demand the book be banned. Thomas Hardy lost heart and the desire for writing when an English bishop burned all the copies of his work in the main square near a church in London. I too felt that way when my own work was censored.'

I realized we'd probably find personal notes in every book stored at Sucre's place and we'd get to them when we had more time. When Sucre ran out to get more eggs, I browsed through the remaining books in the second carton, curious about what Emil thought about each book. Force of habit made me read aloud even though Sucre was not there.

'Moll Flanders was banned and taken out of circulation when critics claimed it was filled with nothing but debauchery and wickedness. One self appointed book critic insisted it should not be allowed in the homes of good Christian people. Several cartons of Moll Flanders were seized by United States Customs inspectors at several American ports, claiming the books were too obscene to be read. They were summarily dumped into the Hudson River'.

I was impressed with Emil's perceptions, thinking about the times my own words were changed and how it riled me. I was certain his interest in those particular books was born from the sad reality many of his own early writings were heavily censored, some never going into print.

I suspected he felt a special kinship with the suffering many prominent authors experienced. When Sucre returned I thought we should save Emil's papers for another day. After a late breakfast we decided to go for a long walk, promising ourselves the real work would begin another day.

CHAPTER 7

Sucre arrived unusually early the next morning holding a large brown bag. She'd once said she used to cook Peruvian foods at night, bringing her pots and pans to Emil's place the next day to show her appreciation for the readings. The wonderful aroma drove thoughts of several dreadful dreams I'd had the previous night out of my head.

I'd dreamed my life was in total disarray, chaos everywhere beginning to believe that was the new norm for me. I'd hoped once we started with the papers those upsetting dreams would go away but they lingered, even after I was well awake.

With no more procrastination it was time to organize Emil's papers again, Dutifully cataloging Emil's work by date and subject matter. The first folder we filled was dedicated to the letters and articles written when Emil lived and worked in Spain in the late 30s. Sadly, the Spanish articles were scattered about in several different cartons, the result of packing up Emil's place in such a hurry.

By noon we'd filled fourteen folders with notes, letters, and newspaper articles written in Spain. The Spanish papers as we called them dealt with Emil's experiences covering nearly fifteen months of turmoil in that country. The earliest writing found was dated September 18, 1938, a hand written letter addressed to a woman by the name of Clarissa announcing he'd arrived in Spain safely. I began to read each letter aloud.

'Dear Clarissa, September 18, 1938

'I've finally arrived in Spain, hoping it's only a temporary stop before traveling on to the Soviet Union. Planning a trip to the dark side of the moon would have been much easier. There were a number of things I couldn't tell you before I left so allow me to fill you in.

'You once asked if I'd joined the Communist International in my youth and I can truthfully answer that question now. The answer is yes.'

Damn" I shouted. making Secure scream what happened.

"I think we found the answer to a very contentious issue I'm certain few others knew. I'm not sure if Emil ever mentioned this but he was once called before a congressional committee in Washington called HUAC. Under oath he was asked if he was then or ever a card carrying member of the Communist Party. Someone probably learned about his membership and gave his name to the committee in the business of finding Communists in America. Being called before the committee was nearly a death sentence but let me get back to this letter from Spain before I explain the committee's work."

'In truth Clarissa, there was never a good time to divulge my membership to anyone. I was very proud being a member but given the highly inflammatory times, it was best to keep the secret to myself so the authorities would not find out. If I'd been a bank robber things would actually have gone easier for me. Did I lie to the committee, something that could have gotten me a long prison sentence? More about that later.

'Was I an active member? Oh heavens yes. I considered my membership a badge of honor, knowing deep in my heart we could change the world for the better. One of the reasons I didn't share that information with you was because of your father. You and I both know how he would have reacted and I was also concerned about you.

'My earliest infatuation with Communism actually began when I was in my mid-teens. I was always very idealistic as you probably know, reading any and all materials I could get my hands on about Communism. I hid the literature from my parents and never told them about my membership. Communism was an engaging system but a way of life most Americans feared greatly, very toxic to many people but not for me. It was quite alluring and truly practical to an impressionable teenager. I was always interested in American politics but the tenets of Communism touched me quite deeply. Why might you ask?

'Because I felt the Communist doctrine was remarkably humane,

Emil's List

recognizing all people were truly created equal, unlike our capitalist system favoring the wealthy.

'Years later when I earned my reporter's credentials one thought dominated my thinking. One day I vowed I'd find a way to get to the Soviet Union so I could see the country and it's people's way of life. Since the revolution, very few reporters have been allowed into the country to report Soviet news and I desperately wanted to be one of the first.

'Looking back I knew I was a bit naïve but I never gave up my dream. I was far too raw and inexperienced and a bit naïve in my late teens but didn't understand that until I was much older and wiser. Every fiber in my body told me there were remarkable stories to be uncovered in that most secret land. The dream of going to the Soviet Union regretfully hit every roadblock possible, but it only made me want to travel there more.

'I read as much as I could about life in the Soviet Union to prepare for my journey but sadly, much of what I was able to get hold of was pure propaganda written by the American State Department. The readings however managed to stoke my yearning because I wanted to know the real unadulterated truth. I wanted to be able to make an honest personal assessment about Soviet life.

'I kept my thoughts and more importantly my papers from prying eyes and ears because most people were obsessed with the Red Scare. If my readings were somehow compromised or discovered, I knew I'd be in big trouble and could possibly lose my press credentials and ultimately, my freedom.

'I spoke in confidence with several well trusted editors about my plans to travel to the Soviet Union even though at great risk. I was hoping one of them would take a chance on a hungry young reporter but it was not to be.

'The editors decided it would be a waste of my time and more importantly, their money and their paper's reputation. Disappointed and terribly hurt, I left the paper, a very good paying job by the way to find a newspaper that might believe in me.

'After much searching I discovered a small Greenwich Village newspaper with access to secreted leftist and Communist news. After much vetting by the owner Sam Solomon, he decided to take a chance hiring me, making it clear nothing about my work could be traced back to him. There would be little salary and no expense money and I could

Bruce Weiss

leave no paper trail behind. I didn't care about the money because getting to the Soviet Union was worth a million dollars to me. Sam said he'd help me obtain the necessary documents allowing me to enter the Soviet Union legally. I walked on air all the way home.

'I took all the money I'd saved and made some preliminary travel plans. 1937 was going to be my year and I was convinced nothing or anyone could stop me.

'Unfortunately the best of plans hit unexpected obstacles but even during those darkest days, I never gave up hope. When I'd reach a dead end I looked for other options, believing my travels would eventually work out and in time they actually did.

'My journey began on a steam ship out of New York City, bound for the port city of Barcelona Spain. The crossing was uneventful, spending most of my time in my cabin writing my diary. Once I arrived in Barcelona I wasted no time and began to look at options for overland transportation to Moscow. Everything looked and sounded promising until one day I came up against a wall I could not to get over. Getting documented travel papers for Moscow proved more difficult then I ever imagined, spending day after day inside the Soviet Embassy talking with bureaucrats telling me to come back the next day for a final decision.

'I grew more and more depressed, disappointed by the reality I might not get travel papers. Equally depressing, I found myself running out of my savings and nearly broke. I found a room I could not afford, promising to pay the homeowner rent when I published my first article. I didn't know at the time but delaying my journey to the Soviet Union and remaining in Spain turned out to be one of the greatest accidental turning points in my life.

'I was in constant limbo, stuck in Spain without money, eating in food kitchens and often sleeping in shelters, spending days knocking on newspaper doors that would not open. One particularly depressing afternoon I found myself alone by the sea, finally accepting the reality it was the end of my dream. It was there however I accidentally discovered something quite extraordinary was happening literally right under my nose, and I hadn't noticed.

'I'd never envisioned any future in Spain but that all changed when an elderly man came by and sat next to me. I got up to leave but he grabbed

Emil's List

my hand asking where I was from. Telling him I was an American his eyes lit up, saying he had a story he wanted to tell.

'Why I didn't get up and run is a mystery, perhaps reporters intuition so I stayed. He spoke excellent English, telling me about a terrible Civil War happening in Spain, something few people outside the country knew about. He said one day, possibly very soon the war would tear his country apart and create much death and misery. The more he spoke, the more I was inexplicably drawn in his story.

'I learned early on that a good reporter must remain neutral but I learned that afternoon it was nearly impossible. Hearing frightening stories about life and death in his country, particularly in the south moved me greatly, creating great compassion for the Spanish Republicans. The Republicans had taken up arms to stop a Fascist uprising determined to take the reins of government. The goal of the Fascist Party in Spain was to first partner with Germany and Italy and help create a new Europe.

'I realized my life in America was becoming a distant memory as the stranger related tales of the violence destroying his country. Hours later my journey to the Soviet Union for the time being was put on hold. The old man who's name I never knew explained things I knew nothing about, a dirty civil war tearing Spain apart day by day, wincing when he told me about the many indescribable acts of killing and destruction. The Republicans supported Spain's legally elected democratic government doing their best to ward off attacks by Spain's renegade military but to no avail. The head of the rebels was the avowed Fascist and murderer Francisco Franco. If you could have looked into Franco's office as I did one day, you would have see a large portrait of Adolf Hitler on the wall behind his massive desk.

'From the old man's words I began to believe that the Spanish Civil War could very well turn into the greatest tragedy to hit Europe since the closing days of World War One. I was fully absorbed by the man's words, wishing I could have written them all down. He did not know I was a reporter but as an American he said I needed to let the world know what was happening. At that moment I began to suspect I'd be in Spain for a very long time, almost prepared to put the Soviet Union out of my head.

'For the next fifteen months I wrote articles about the war, every one from personal experiences and observations. Unfortunately, the world

Bruce Weiss

did not seem terribly interested in what was happening in Spain at the time. World War One was still on everyone's mind and most people and governments were tired of war.

'In America the only newspapers picking up my reports were the leftist press, their circulations rather small because they were looked down upon. In the meantime of course, America was having it's own problems in the late 1930's.

'When I'd sailed away from home the country was facing it's own crisis and even though I was a great distance away in Europe, I kept my eyes and ears open to what was happening. It was terribly disturbing to read of worker's strikes, often met with violence from the police or the military. Across an ocean looking back I began to believe the best days of America were behind her. The country was still mired in the great American Depression and the economic crisis was impacting millions, driving American families into deep despair. I saw many of those people during my travels from San Francisco to New York before I left for Spain, families sleeping beneath underpasses or lined up for blocks to get hot soup at free kitchens.

'As Karl Marx prophesized and I came to believe, capitalism was failing to meet the needs of the people. Bank accounts were wiped out, the government was running out of money and many companies declared bankruptcy. Failed banks swallowed life savings. My thoughts turned even more toward Communism as a cure because the government of America could not take care of it's citizens.

'I'd first thought often about joining the American Communist Party when I was a freshman in college, especially after the stock market collapse and economic woes deepened. I grew wary of the American capitalist system operating without safeguards, unable to help people. In the 1930's twenty million Americans were still living in households with no wage earner. Traveling cross country I saw children ravaging through garbage dumps looking for scraps of food and a government unable to deal with the crisis. I and many others began to think about other forms of government.

'Communists were transforming Russia into a true worker's paradise while FDR's New Deal was doing little to lift the nation from the Great Depression, the outlook remaining bleak. The Soviets created full employment and I wondered why we could not.

64

Emil's List

'What was so attractive about Communism? I came to believe it was a more just and equitable system designed creating full employment, universal health care, free education and so much more. There were no bread lines in Russia, no worker's strikes and nobody lacked the basic necessities of life. Healthcare and education were free from cradle to grave, something we couldn't manage in America. Some politicians tried, paying dearly for those sentiments. Sadly, they were the ones labeled Communists.

'One day I might discover Communism doesn't live up to my expectations and if that happens, I hope America finds other means to insure equality.

'Clarissa, I need to ask one favor. Burn this letter when you've finished reading it because it can only bring trouble to you and your dad, certainly to me. I officially joined the International Communist Party in 1937 in Spain and right now that is just between you and me. If my membership in the Party became known in America, my family and close friends including you would be in someone's crosshairs. I will try to write again if and when I reach Moscow, but that might be a while. Emil.'

We were truly mesmerized by Emil's sentiments, knowing it was just the tip of the iceberg of a very full life.

"Let's read another letter to Clarissa," Sucre urged.

CHAPTER 8

Dear Clarissa, 1938

'I'm traveling through the Spanish countryside with a very distinguished group of European journalists as the only American. I'm amazed at how far I've come since I first arrived, penniless without a job, unable to understand the language and having no place to live. I've been accepted as a fellow journalist and many of the reporters have complimented me on my work.

'The Soviet Union continues to pull at my heart in many ways, often writing letters to Josef Stalin (don't tell anyone) asking if I might come to the Soviet Union to interview him. I have not gotten a response and am beginning to believe it was just another pipe dream.

'Why do I think it necessary to stay here in this volatile country of Spain? Because America has isolated itself from the rest of the world, ignoring European affairs which become more and more complicated everyday. I do this because I've seen brutality and tragedy in a very dirty war with many innocent civilians caught in the middle. America needs to know what's happening here. From a distance I observed Franco's firing squads executing men, women, and children in small forest villages. I saw the entire population of another town marched into an old bull ring where machine guns shot them down, including infants.

'Because of neutrality laws in the United States, the Spanish Republicans have no one to help them. They're using old World War One weapons, some rifles dating back to our own Civil War. They're up against modern weapons of war supplied mostly by the black market. The only real aid the Republicans receive comes from the Soviet Union supplying arms and materials and even technical advisors to fight the Fascist threat.

Emil's List

Without our help I suspect Madrid will soon fall and the Fascists will stamp out the last wisps of democracy here. Thank God for the Soviets. If someone wants to see how Fascism stifles life, let them come to Germany or sadly, to Spain.

'I'm not a risk taker and bravery is not one of my strong suits. I try to stay some distance from the intense bombardments from the air but every now and then I find myself in no man's land and wonder how I'll survive. I'll give you a history lesson.

'A cadre of generals met secretly in the mid 1930's plotting a revolt against the legally elected Spanish government. They justified their cabal because they feared the government was encouraging growing Communism. Personally and professionally however, I would prefer to call it socialism. The renegade group called themselves the Nationalists, their leader a Spanish general by the name of Francisco Franco. Rising through the ranks of the military he gained followers with the message he would cleanse Spain of all Bolsheviks. He's probably got many supporters in America because of that sentiment.

'A good number of European journalists have been in the right place at the wrong time, sadly paying with their lives. I've lost some good friends covering the war but the work must go on.

'I continue to be fully committed to writing and exposing what is happening here in Spain. Germany and Italy were the first to have Fascist regimes and the world still has not come to grips with the dangers presented to world peace. There is no question Fascism is spreading rapidly throughout Europe. Portugal, Greece and, Romania as well as several other nations including Spain are in trouble. For the time being Spain still has a democratically elected Spanish Republic but nobody knows how much longer the Republicans can stop the Nationalists. I want to write more but things are heating up where I'm staying. More later, Emil'

Sucre asked me to read more letters from Spain, saying sadly the situation reminder her what happened in her native Peru. Another letter found was written in January from a tiny village in western Spain.

Dear Clarissa, it's a new year and I wish you a healthy and happy 1939. Let peace reign here and all over the world. I want to write about my work these days.

'I'm traveling with a small group of Republicans who's task is to set

Bruce Weiss

up machine gun nests. This morning we were overlooking a small ravine and this is what took place.

'After an hour of waiting in silence with only the sound of the men's breathing, I heard several shots coming from the woods some two hundred yards away. The machine gunner did not respond immediately and when I stood up to get a better look with my field glasses, I'd made a terrible mistake I shall regret the rest of my life. In seconds I felt a sharp pain as if something exploded inside me, my immediate reaction shock and surprise like stepping on a live wire. When I fully realized I'd been shot in the leg a feeling of helplessness overcame me, my knees crumbled as I collapsed onto the ground. I felt no pain but did sense I was slowly falling unconscious from which I would never wake up.

'I was angry with myself for placing myself carelessly in harms way, a moment regretfully that could have killed me. What if the bullet struck twelve inches higher I thought? Would I have survived? I felt no resentment toward the person who fired the shot, it being war of course. I heard our soldiers yelling pick him up and move him to the rear.

'In and out of consciousness I heard soldiers saying get him to a medic. I had no idea how bad I was hurt or where in my leg I'd been hit. When I tried to ask questions I realized I had no voice although finally able to mumble the words so many men must have uttered. Am I going to die? Someone leaned close and said I would be alright, the bullet passing through a fleshy area of my thigh and I'd be up and around in no time.

'The next thing I remembered was being put on a stretcher and a voice telling me I'd be alright. Those words were very welcomed and in days I was back to work with a great story to tell.

'Every day there is less and less hope the Republican government can survive. I believe my heart is firmly entrenched in Spain and it's breaking. If you can find any of the news articles I've written for the American press, you might find a few stories about the war written by your friend, Emil Breck'

Sucre and I read twenty more letters before noon, all addressed to the woman called Clarissa, each describing life as a reporter and condemning America's lack of involvement.

The words were heartrending and distressing. The morning flew by so quickly I asked Sucre if she'd like to take a break to start reading James Baldwin's Another Country.

CHAPTER 9

Later in the afternoon we discovered not all the newspaper articles in Emil's Spanish papers were written by him, but by other reporters traveling with him so we moved on.

I grabbed a a handful of old newspaper articles from a different carton, written in the early 1950s by a Baltimore reporter by the name of Max Roth. We started a new file for Roth as we would do for every phase of Emil's reporting career. I'd never heard the name Roth before but it was soon obvious Emil thought enough about his writings to save many of his articles.

We filled three oversized folders with newspaper clippings from the defunct Baltimore World, written by it's Washington DC chief reporter Max Roth. I racked my brain but for the life of me I couldn't recall ever hearing the name.

We gathered as many of Roth's articles we could locate and organized them by date, the oldest June 18, 1952. Once again I forgot I needed to read out loud until looking up and seeing the now too familiar quizzical look on Sucre's face. I apologized, telling her I was looking at what appeared to be a an op-ed piece written about a Washington DC committee known as HUAC, the House Un-American Activities Committee. How it related to Emil I said we'd soon find out.

'Before World War Two, fear and contempt for Germany and Italy got all the headlines in the daily news. After the war however it was the Soviet Union and the Communists making the world an uneasy and dangerous place.'

"Ain't that the truth" I declared. Before I read the full article I want to give you a brief history lesson about HUAC, a congressional committee

69

Bruce Weiss

growing extremely powerful at a very contentious and disturbing time in this country. In the early fifty's the Cold War, a war of frightening verbal threats between the US and the Soviets became everyday news, words drawing us closer to a full scale nuclear war. The prevailing thought was not if another world war could happen but when.

"I want to tell you a little what it was like growing up during the Cold War years because it had a great effect on me." I quickly realized I might have been talking in a foreign language.

There were two op-ed pieces stapled to Roth's article, both addressed to Emil Breck. I read them aloud next.

'Dear Mr. Breck. I've recently learned the Committee known as the House Un-American Activities Committee has summoned you to appear before them. Make no mistake and do not take this lightly, but this is a very dangerous group with seemingly unlimited powers.

'I want to give you a little background history about the committee since I've been following it's work very closely for many months. The panel of senators and representatives rarely met during the war years but at the start of the new decade, it became a daily part of Washington's business. You'll soon have a front row seat when you stand before what has quietly become one of the most powerful and feared committees in Washington. I'm enclosing an article I've written which will appear in the Baltimore World this Sunday, two days before your appearance.

'Committee subpoenas are handed out like candy, often preceded by a threatening knock at one's door by federal authorities. Anyone, absolutely anyone suspected of having Communist sympathies or ties even if the evidence is entirely suspect or manufactured can become a target for the committee. As a young reporter but not new to the business, I found myself in the right place at the right time in Washington. The early days of the committee's work were hardly newsworthy and I alone was the sole reporter documenting what eventually became a committee with an insatiable thirst for power. It didn't take long for the committee to blatantly abuse it's given power.

'High on the committee's hit list were reporters and I came to believe it was only a matter of time before the committee came for all of us. The committee subpoenaed magazine and newspaper editors, playwrights, authors, and a number of producers and directors. I've heard rumors actors will be called on the carpet soon. What was their crime? The committee claimed to have evidence many were closet Communists.

'I was one of very few reporters observing the committee observing it make it's own rules, unchecked by any government authority. I had a front row seat hearing their shenanigans, watching it slowly evolve into a monster with seemingly unlimited powers.'

I paused explaining that when I first heard of HUAC I was too young to understand. "I'll continue the letter."

'Most Americans at the time felt any endeavor by our government to weed out Communists was good and just. It took time but eventually the hearings became nothing more than a witch hunt, a very dark stain on America. Hundreds of innocent lives were ruined by HUAC.

'Unlimited power allowed the committee to dig for as much dirt as it could find or in many cases manufactured. The panel grew more menacing and more powerful every day, assuming blanket subpoena powers and the authority to threaten witnesses with contempt of Congress if questions were not answered. If those called before the committee failed to turn over names of their acquaintances, there was hell to pay. Those who tried to fight back against the Committee's attacks were labeled Reds and Communists, the labels ruining their lives.

'The rules of the Committee changed daily as it relentlessly pursued the lives of anyone in their eyes who was deemed un-American. The president of an advertising agency was summoned before the committee because the color red used in the company's ads looked very much like the color of the Soviet flag.

'The Chairman of the committee, a young second term representative by the name of Raymond Baldwin claimed the committee's goal was to return the country to the honest, freedom-loving, God-fearing Americans it belonged.'

When I saw the name Raymond Baldwin in the article I was shocked, taking me back to another time and place I though I'd put far behind. I told Sucre the sordid tale of how Raymond Baldwin single handedly ended my writing career years later.

"Sucre, Raymond Baldwin was the person blacklisting me from the news industry, discrediting me so ruthlessly I was never able to work for another newspaper again, an act of revenge I could not overcome."

Bruce Weiss

I realized I had a special kinship with Emil because we both had Raymond Baldwin as a nemesis in our lives. I read on.

'As an objective reporter I saw and heard what others did not or simply chose to ignore. Criticize the committee's work and you might find yourself the next victim sitting under the bright lights in the hot seat. Most reporters sadly turned a blind eye to the evil work for fear they might be the next one having the axe fall on their necks. The committee was clearly on a rampage without checks or balances, free to accuse anyone of being un-American and the power to punish without due process of law.

'I applaud my own newspaper because it was the very first in the nation to openly expose the workings of the committee. My editor in chief Charles Anderson wrote a piece claiming HUAC was having an impact on every reporter's creativity.

'I'm quoting from the Congressional record the exact words of Chairman Raymond Baldwin.

'We must do our work so we can dutifully alert the good American people to those who bring this nation harm.'

'I was given a private ten minute audience with Chairman Baldwin, my first question asking why people in my profession were being singled out unfairly. He said and I quote again, 'writers are part of an underground network of subversives bent on using devious words to tear America down,

'Today's reporters do nothing more then tear the fabric out of our free-enterprise system' proclaimed the Chairman. 'You people cause good Americans to lose faith in our country, sadly causing them to look elsewhere for reassurance. You might not be aware of this but the Communists are just sitting back idly, waiting for the masses to turn to them. If you don't know yet, you and your colleague's writings are weakening this country and your work is clearly designed to destroy the American nation.'

CHAPTER 10

We drank endless cups of coffee to stay awake and alert, reading disheartening and at times, frightening articles about HUAC, particularly reports filed by Mr. Max Roth. Another Max Roth article described one of Emil's several appearances before the committee.

'Today the HUAC (House Un-American Activities Committee) called a foreign born American journalist to answer the committee's questions. The writer called to the hot seat was Mr. Emil Breck.' Damn I yelled, making Sucre laugh so hard she choked on her coffee. "This is where things get interesting I'm certain."

'Concerned citizens across the nation are finally understanding what's happening in Washington with the HUAC committee. I knew very little about Mr. Breck but I'd read some of his writings and in my opinion, he was nothing but a true blue American. Like others called before the committee, I assumed there were hints of a Communist connection the committee wanted to investigate.

'I was most fortunate to speak with Mr. Breck before he began his slow walk to the table just below the committee dais. We had just a few moments but he told me it was a pleasure and a civic duty to talk to the press, and that perhaps we could sit down and talk further at another time.

'I wished him luck, saying the committee liked to make it's own rules. What he said next surprised me.

"I've always anticipated being called before this committee and now it's my time, suspecting the chickens might have finally come home to roost. I will be forthright. The committee has been feasting on writers and now it's my turn, an easy target because of my words."

'Unlike others who'd been summoned I saw neither fear nor anger in

Bruce Weiss

his demeanor but instead, a determined look suggesting he was ready to do battle. I thought he'd be an aggressive defender and certainly not cowed by the anticipated bullying.

'We learned right away Mr. Breck's writings were the exact bone of contention for the committee, the type of person the committee members referred to as leftist. He turned around to look for me and at that moment I saw something in his eyes, suggesting I needed to be careful because I might be next.

'Mr. Breck was allowed only two minutes to make an opening statement including a brief synopsis of his work. He sounded strong and determined and I detected no apprehension or fear in his voice This man was different because he seemed not to be intimidated.

"I want to make it crystal clear to the committee and those in attendance here today" Mr. Breck began, "that I speak for all writers who believe in freedom of speech, the people you so unfairly threaten. The opinions you will hear today however are strictly mine. If the committee deems me un-American because of my writings, I would remind you I'm just a drop in the ocean because ultimately, you'll need to subpoena every good newsman and newswoman working in this country."

'The committee members wore blank stares on their faces, as if they were terribly bored or perhaps they'd already made up their minds about Breck. For the record Breck stated he was a journalist, a writer, a columnist and a proud naturalized American citizen. He swore to tell the truth saying somewhat tongue in cheek, he hoped the committee would do the same.'

'Chairman Baldwin's reaction to Breck's initial statement was a scowl and the words holding back information or lying would lead to a contempt of Congress citation. When Breck's two minutes were up the assault came immediately and quite ruthlessly.

"There is clear evidence before this committee Mr. Breck indicating you are an active member of the Communist Party. Would you like to deny that?"

'There was a bullying manner in the Chairman's words. I'd been covering the committee for a few months but I'd never heard accusations come so quickly or with so much vile.

"Sitting before the committee today is a member of the Communist

Emil's List

party I maintain but in fairness, I will give you Mr. Breck a chance to rebut my accusation."

'It took several minutes to quiet the spectators before Breck was able to respond. The spectators reminded me of the citizens of Rome sitting in the Coliseum waiting for a thumbs up or thumbs down.

"Mr. Breck, or should I say Comrade Breck, this committee has proof you are now and have been for some time a card carrying member of the Communist party."

'Mr. Breck did not look the least bit threatened or troubled by the accusation, detecting a slight smile on is face. He leaned into the microphone refuting the charge, his voice remarkably calm.

"A Simple yes or no will suffice very nicely because Mr. Breck, we already know the truth."

'The few spectators in the gallery collectively whispered loud enough for the committee to hear the words, where's the proof? The members sat in stony silence, like ancient museum statues.

"May I please see the proof you claim to have against me Mr. Chairman" Breck declared.

"This committee does not answer questions Mr. Breck. We ask them."

'The words were condescending, as if a young child was being chastised. "You sir are here today to answer our questions and even though you are foreign born, this is an American institution and you must play by our rules."

'Mr. Breck pushed his chair away from the table, his arms crossed.'

"Mr. Breck, I take your silence and the smug look on your face as an admission of guilt. For all practical purposes we can adjourn now because even in your silence, we have all the proof needed. There is no reason to waste any more of our time but I'll give you one more chance to admit your guilt. Mr. Breck, lets put an end to this nonsense now."

'Breck leaned forward, his voice even stronger and more pronounced.'

"Yes Mr. Chairman, you have aptly described this charade referring to it as nonsense. I have a right to face my accusers who've falsely labeled me a Communist. It's true I was not born in America but I know all my rights and I'd like to remind the committee even if I speak with an accent, I do not have to answer any question that might incriminate me. I'm referring of course to the rights guaranteed all Americans both naturalized and

Bruce Weiss

those born here. The Fifth Amendment to our Constitution protects us and there are good reasons. I will gladly stop responding so you and the committee members can take the time to read the amendment."

'Laughter erupted in the room, an angry snarl on the Chairman's face, ushering in an awkward silence.'

"Mr. Breck, the Fifth Amendment only applies to loyal Americans, definitely not Communists. You have two minutes left before I use my authority to silence you and your subversive writings."

"Mr. Chairman, I put my professional and personal life on the line every working day defending the freedom of the press. On the airwaves, in news print, in books and in the cinema, I believe writers have consistently demonstrated to the world our commitment to the freedoms you outlandishly question. Again, I ask you to show me what proof you have."

"I have all the proof I need right here in front of me Mr. Breck."

'The Chair waved a pile of papers in the air, a smug grin on his face.

"These sworn statements prove beyond a shadow of a doubt you are indeed a member of the Communist party. If I look carefully I'll bet I could even find your membership number."

'Breck remained remarkably calm, proclaiming once again his right not to answer questions that might incriminate him. His response turned the Chair a deeper shade of red.'

"You've perverted the real intent of the Fifth Amendment," Baldwin shouted. "You use the same argument all Communists use and I'm sick and tired of hearing it. You say you have the right not to answer the questions asked by this committee and if that is your prerogative, I pity you. The proof is overwhelming so I suggest you stop hiding behind the Iron Curtain you obviously embrace and respond to this charge. This is your last warning and if you continue this silliness I'll order your arrest by the Capitol Police."

"Mr. Baldwin" Breck responded respectfully. "I tell you again I do not have to answer your questions. Every citizen in this nation is protected by the Constitution and you more then anyone else ought to know that."

I stopped reading Roth's story, telling Sucre all the time I'd known Emil he'd never once mentioned an appearance before the dreaded House Un-American Activities Committee.

"I'm completely stunned and totally awed by Emil's appearance and

76

Emil's List

the bizarre coincidence Baldwin is the same man who torpedoed my newspaper career years later. He seemed to have made a habit of ruining careers. Let me read more of Roth's article.

"If you change your mind Mr. Breck about coming clean," Baldwin hissed, "I would probably welcome your return to this room, but only when you've learned how to tell the truth. We have much work to do here and you've certainly wasted enough of our time. I hereby use the authority invested in me to charge you with contempt of Congress. If you change your mind and agree to cooperate with this committee, I believe we can get beyond our poor start."

'The spectators collectively gasped when the Chairman ordered the Capitol police to take Mr. Breck into custody.'

"Sucre, Emil never mentioned this terrible event in his life to me. What about you?"

Shaking her head she replied no.

"Did he ever mention the name Roth in any conversations with you?"

Again she shook her head no.

"There's still more to the story so lets find out that happens next."

'I left the chamber and caught up with Mr. Breck in the bowels of the Capitol Building. There was no van available to transport the prisoner so we had a little time to talk and wanting to be fair, I wrote down every word. He immediately impressed me.

"I know who you are Mr. Roth and I know your writings so this is what I'd ask of you. Describe what has taken place here not for me or you, but for the American people so they understand the freedom of the press is not always free. I want you to document everything that's been said here because the American people need to know our Constitution is being mismanaged. My writings and my voice will never be silenced and I will not answer a single question until I'm informed who my accusers are. I would also demand the opportunity to question my accuser."

'An officer with the Capitol police announced it would be a few more minutes before the van arrived, eyeing me with some suspicion. I couldn't completely take in what had actually taken place inside one of the most important and revered buildings in America.'

"I'd always expected to be called before the committee," Breck contended, "so I was not terribly surprised by this. Mr. Roth, I hope you can

Bruce Weiss

truly relate what has taken place here. If this committee succeeds in their witch hunts they'll be able to put you and I and every other newsperson out of business. I have no idea what proof Mr. Baldwin alleges but of this I'm certain, it's none of his damn business. All reporters including yourself Mr. Roth are in danger of being censored or worse. If this committee can take away the guaranteed rights of one citizen, no one would be protected by our Constitution and none of us would have unalienable rights. Mr. Roth, be very careful."

'I wrote down his exact words, watching Mr. Breck marched down a ramp to the prison van accompanied by Capitol police. Alone in the deepest recess of the Capitol building, I felt an overwhelming sense of powerlessness and then anger, and then great sadness.'

Chapter 11

We were both a bit hungry so Sucre began preparing what she referred to as a typical Peruvian dish of fish and rice. Lunch she explained was the main meal in Peru so it was quite filling. The food was excellent followed by a nice long break before we got back to work, my thoughts never far from Roth's tale.

"Sucre, I'm going to begin the afternoon with another article written by Mr. Roth and from the first sentence, I can tell you he laments the fact Emil spent nine days in a jail cell not a half mile from the Capitol building. This seems so unbelievable it could actually be fiction. I think you'd have to have lived through the Red Scare in the 1950's to fully understand the country's mentality at the time, but I'm sure Matt Roth will make you understand."

'I received a note from Emil Breck saying he'd been summoned back to the committee room at their request. I rushed to the jail hoping to catch up with him while he waited for the Capitol van transport. My timing was perfect because I was fortunate to have ten minutes alone with him. My first question was did he know why he was being recalled. His response was simply a shrug of the shoulders. I asked if he had any sense what might happen next.

"All I can tell you is that early this morning I received word I'd been summoned to the Committee room again, assuming I'd be asked the same questions. Why? Hopefully we'll find out soon."

'I asked if he would answer their questions this time and as I'd expected his answer was a resounding NO. He maintained HUAC was violating his civil rights, reiterating his politics was truly none of their business or anyone else's.

Bruce Weiss

"Joining a political party including the Republican Party or the Democratic party is not against the law," he said with a Cheshire Cat grin brightening his face. "This committee has put this country on a treacherous and dangerous path."

'When the van arrived I drove to the Capitol taking my usual front row seat. At the time Jake Blum, a reporter for a Philadelphia newspaper was being grilled. I dutifully wrote down a few notes while mentally preparing my next article. Looking about the chamber I was dismayed, seeing only one other reporter at such a critical time. Word must have gotten out however because the moment Breck appeared, spectators and reporters streamed into the room. It was standing room only.

'When Blum was dismissed, Representative Baldwin rose from his seat whispering something to each of the members. When he finished he returned to his seat, calling Emil Breck to stand before the committee. The atmosphere in the room was tense, as if a battle was about to take place. I switched my pocket recorder on because I wanted every word to be accurate.

'Chairman Baldwin had the same demeaning tone and grimace, not giving Mr. Breck a chance to say anything before accusing him of being a Communist and a liar. Mr. Breck was then given five minutes to deliver a second opening statement.'

"Congressman Baldwin and honorable committee members, I've always kept my political views to myself. Truthfully, it's no one else's business. I've not broken any laws and more importantly, I've never advocated harm to any individual or institution, yet I've never been ordered to defend my beliefs to anyone. Mr. Chairman, you claim to have evidence suggesting someone pointed an accusing finger at me. I would very much like the opportunity to meet that person or persons.

"I don't believe I've ever said, written or done anything illegal. I'm an American citizen, albeit a naturalized one born in Romania where Fascists ruled with no opposition. There were no individual rights in my native country and those who opposed the Fascists were tortured, imprisoned or killed. Everyone in my country was required to state their political views and that is what you are espousing here. Those who opposed the regime paid dearly.

"If you deny just one American his or her rights guaranteed in the

Constitution, no one would be safe. I grew up under a government quashing all personal freedoms and in Romania you either followed the party line or you disappeared. You have stated for the record I wrote subversive articles, yet those writings have often lead to noble ideas. I remind you of our own Declaration of Independence.

"You do not have the authority to force me or any American citizen to answer questions about their political beliefs. The first and fifth Amendments to the Constitution protect me and every citizen in America, and this committee has no right to take those away.

"You are suggesting Americans must have a system of loyalty checks, the first step I might add in the short walk toward Fascism. If you insist on loyalty tests, I assure you it would eventually lead the nation down the path to a form of government you claim you want to destroy.

"This committee is operating a witch hunt, plain and simple. The Salem witch trials started this way and years later we have still not learned their sad lessons. I will not appear before this committee after today so I respectfully refuse to answer your questions. You can silence me but you cannot silence free ideas. If you send me back to jail I shall go gladly."

'Are you through," Represented Baldwin asked?'

"You've given me five minutes so no sir, I'm not. The Bill of Rights protects the citizens of this nation from witch hunts like this. To my dying day I will always insist the people of America should not be persecuted because of their political views. Now I will say my time is up."

"In more ways then one, Mr. Breck. Things will go easy for you if you give this committee the names of the Communists you associate with."

"I will never give up names to this group or to anyone else. Whether I'm a member of the Communist Party or the Republican party or even the Bull Moose Party, it's none of your business."

"Mr. Breck, I resent your tone and ill manner of speaking. You disrespect this committee and all good Americans with your flag waving and grand-standing. I am this close to holding you in contempt again. Is that what you want?"

"Representative Baldwin, this committee is vilifying me and many other good Americans and thanks to your efforts, our names and pictures grace many newspapers and magazines across America. The word guilty and subversion are used liberally in those publications because of your work.

My family has suffered because I was ordered to appear, the assumption anyone who appears is guilty. I and others who've appeared before this committee have been deprived of our due process so I will never condone your work and will fight to my last breath your kind of tyranny. I'm certain my time is up so thank you for allowing me the opportunity to speak my mind."

'Several minutes of eerie silence shrouded the room until Mr. Baldwin announced he was prepared to deal with a new contempt of Congress charge.

"Your speech has fallen on deaf ears in this room and I'm certain all across this great land. The United States will never tolerate subversives or anti-American sentiment. You and the others called before this honorable committee are simply fabricators, saboteurs and troublemakers.

"Lewisburg Prison in Pennsylvania will by your new home for a while Mr. Breck because you've refused to truthfully answer questions asked by this committee. We cannot and will not allow Communist subversives to destroy this nation and as an aside Mr. Breck, I've read your articles and it's obvious your views give power to those who would harm this great nation. You are not a good or loyal American sir as you describe yourself and I believe if you asked the general public, they would agree.

"Given the powers entrusted in this committee, I hereby sentence you to an indefinite term in Lewisburg Prison. While you are there let me assure you this committee will continue to expose internal Communist plots against America and it will continue to do so until the very last Communist in America is ferreted out.

"I see a smile on your face Mr. Breck but I assure you this is no laughing matter. We'll see how prison life changes your attitude. Perhaps one day you'll come to your senses and leave your foolish and traitorous beliefs behind. Bailiffs, you may take this man away."

CHAPTER 12

I read several more Max Roth's articles, many expressing personal feelings about what took place during Emil's hearings. We had a few more hours before dark but I had to admit we were very tired and thought it best to knock off a bit early.

Sucre claimed that she was getting an extraordinary education about Emil and his life and times, things she'd never imagined.

"It's all truly bittersweet she said, making me feel hurt, angry and nervous deep down inside. I don't like those feelings. Yet I also feel a great deal admiration for his courage."

I shared the same emotions, my mind constantly afire, still unsure how I might put Emil's extraordinary life stories into a deserving biography. We'd barely scratched the surface but thankfully, I already had some inventive ideas.

Sucre began humming a Peruvian tune making me realize I hadn't thought about her blindness all day. It wasn't until I saw her waking stick leaning against the wall by the door I'd remembered. She was truly a remarkable and exceptional woman who'd never once complained about the life she'd been dealt. Sadly the stick also reminded me she'd never see any of Emil's writings or the biography I hoped to write. I told myself it was terribly important to read everything aloud, letting her know she was an equal partner in our project.

Over a late dinner I related more stories about what I knew about HUAC, recalling a few names of soldiers, actors, writers and even businessmen called before the committee. Sadly, they were all subjected to the arbitrary whims of the members on the committee I rued.

I explained what I remembered about Senator Joe 'Tail-Gun'

Bruce Weiss

McCarthy, the man replacing Baldwin as chairman of the committee. I said his blistering character assassinations made Baldwin look like a rookie.

"When Baldwin left the committee and eventually his congressional seat, he explored the idea of running for governor of Massachusetts. As to McCarthy, he viciously attacked all who came before the committee and it wasn't silenced for a very long time. He ruined the livelihoods of many respected and good people. Never apologizing for his work, he remained a bitter man until he finally drank himself to death and for all practical purposes, that was the end of HUAC."

I wished Max Roth was still alive because I would have loved to have had the opportunity to talk with him about Emil. I wondered if he'd continued his work at the Capitol after Baldwin, hearing the nonsensical ramblings of Joe McCarthy.

After dinner Sucre said she needed to return home but would return as usual early the next morning. I wanted to call a cab but she said no, walking and being independent was more important than a ride.

When Sucre left I glanced around at the unopened cartons, most overflowing with thousands of news articles Emil collected. Many were letters still in their original envelopes, Spanish stamps and Spanish postmarks clearly evident. I felt terribly tired and regretfully came to the conclusion anything to do with Emil would have to wait until morning.

Sucre arrived early the next day but it was immediately obvious she had a look of concern on her face. When I asked if she was alright she said it was nothing more than not getting enough sleep. We left it at that.

"The more I hear and learn about Emil and the injustices he faced, the sadder I feel" Sucre said sorrowfully. "That's not the America I dreamed about when I was growing up and it's all so disappointing. I probably spent the entire night thinking about Emil."

When I read the letters to Clarissa I began wondering if talking about the terrible civil war in Spain made her recall her own tragic days in Peru. I decided to put the letters aside and explain what I knew about the Spanish Civil war, mostly from textbooks and my college studies I said.

"In hindsight Sucre, if America paid more attention to what was happening in Spain perhaps as Emil suggested, World War Two might not have happened. Today's history books tell us the Spanish Civil war was a prelude to World War Two, a practice run for the Axis powers of

Emil's List

Germany and Italy. Many of the tactical decisions how to wage a more aggressive war in Spain came from the Germans secretly preparing the next great world war.

"A new generations of weapons, most extremely lethal were developed in the late 1930's, particularly in Germany and tested in Spain. Most of the new weapons were experimental, designed with one terrible thought in mind; would they became the ultimate weapons the Germans might use one day? Their military studied what weapons were most effective and which ones could produce the most damage and destruction. The Germans tried new explosive compounds, storing useful information for future military campaigns. Battle strategies were perfected in Spain, including how to terrorize civilians who were fair game, something avoided during World War One. If the world paid attention to what was happening in Spain from Emil's reporting, it's possible the Fascists might have been stopped cold. In the end the new arms and weapons designed to kill as many people as possible became the horror of World War Two."

The melancholy look on Sucre's face concerned me, fearful the deeper we delved into Emil's personal papers might actually harm her. She hadn't had the time to mourn her great loss and I wondered if the work was too much to bear.

"Did Emil ever talk about his reporting days in Spain," I asked?

"No, I really don't recall any conversations about his time there. Most of our conversations were about literature and good books. Emil rarely discussed his working life so everything you've read in his papers is very new to me. I knew he was a great man but I had no idea what he'd faced in his life. He seldom talked about his personal life but he seemed awfully interested in mine. I don't think we ever discussed politics other then how it might relate to censorship."

I opened another file folder from one of the cartons and by chance, it turned out to be a collection of newspaper and magazine articles written by the mysterious Max Roth. There was also a thick packet of letters written between Roth and Emil.

"Sucre, the more Roth's name pops up, the more I wish I knew more about him. This first article was published in the Sunday Times and it's all about Emil."

'It took me nearly four months of knocking on doors, writing letters

85

and making phone calls but I'd finally received permission to travel to Leavenworth Federal prison in Pennsylvania. My purpose; to interview prisoner number 386-082, Mr. Emil Breck, a colleague I'd written about bravely faced down the HUAC committee. I must admit I found much to admire in this man.

'To the readers who did not catch my earlier articles in the Baltimore Sun, Mr. Breck distinguished himself with his stirring first hand accounts of the Spanish Civil War in the late 1930's. In this reporter's opinion, those pieces were the finest war time reports every written, most from the front line. I had never laid my eyes upon him until his appearance before the HUAC in 1952 but I knew his stellar reputation.

'In my early days as a Capitol Hill reporter I'd accidentally stumbled upon the work of a rather unknown committee called HUAC, or the House Un-American Activities Committee. The committee had been around for some years but it's early work was not considered newsworthy. I knew little about why the committee was formed but as their work became more eccentric, I grew very surprised more people weren't aware of it. In the early days there were very few newsworthy days resulting in little or no press coverage. One individual ordered to appear to explain his politics was a distinguished journalist by the name of Emil Breck.

'I was somewhat familiar with his prolific writings but in truth knew very little about him, other then he'd put his life on the line reporting the deadly Spanish Civil War. HUAC went after him because they believed he was un-American. The first question out of Chairman Baldwin's mouth was, was he or was he not a member of the Communist Party.

'Anyone suspected or rumored to have Communist ties became fair game for Representative Baldwin, taking it upon his committee to weed Communists and Communism out of American society. All the rules of civility were radically altered when Chairman Baldwin sensed he'd uncovered a real Communist. Decorum was not part of the committee and in it's place, a malicious aggressiveness grew to be the norm.

'The questioning and personal attacks went on for nearly two hours the first day and not getting answers the committee expected or wanted, Mr. Breck was eventually jailed on a contempt of Congress charge. Like others who'd been called before the committee, he'd refused to answer questions or to incriminate himself.

Emil's List

'The committee chaired by Mr. Baldwin demanded Mr. Breck either admit or deny he was a card carrying member of the Communist Party. Given many chances to reply to the accusation, Mr. Breck refused each time, citing the Fifth Amendment and his right not to incriminate himself. The Chair sentenced Mr. Breck to an undeterminable term in prison until he agreed to testify truthfully, answering all the committee's questions.

'I'd covered enough HUAC hearings to see first hand the unlimited powers the committee generated. The hearings grew more contentious with personal attacks stopping just short of slander. Most of the nation supported the committee's work because Americans had been brainwashed, told there were Communists all over Washington, possibly even hiding in closets and under beds. The committee defined Communists as un-Americans who by words or actions showed nothing but disdain for the American way of life. Many of the accused were charged with fomenting terror or writing un-American sentiments to incite violence.

'When I'd finally received permission to visit the prisoner I was told I'd have fifteen minutes with Mr. Breck so I knew had to prepare carefully.

'I'd never seen either the inside or the outside of a prison so I wasn't prepared to be traumatized. When the prison first came into view from my car I thought a large black cloud hovered above it, something that actually turned out to be coal burning providing heat and electricity.

'I'd written several letters to Mr. Breck indicating my desire to interview him, saying I wanted to let the world know his story. I said I was a very good listener but most of my letters were returned unopened, some with the notation it could not be delivered.

'As my car approached the outer gate it felt as if something alien had dropped from the sky, the dark imposing gray walls stretching to the horizon. I was unprepared for the desolation because as far as I could see, there were no trees or signs of life.

'On the medieval looking ramparts guards with rifles carefully watched my car approach.

'Signs directed me to the visitor's parking area where only two other cars were parked, doubting many people made the trip to see friends or relatives inside. The permission form enabling me to visit was a gift from a Congressman who'd asked to remain anonymous, saying he'd once

Bruce Weiss

condemned the work of the committee and in return was threatened with a subpoena.

'At the main gate I was asked a score of questions; Why was I there? Who did I want to visit? How did I know this person and did I realize if an incident occurred inside the prison, I would be on my own? I thought I'd eventually be asked to write down the name of my next of kin.

'A uniformed guard led me through several dark tunnels through locked doors to an office where I waited and waited. I sat for nearly an hour until a man in tie and jacket entered the room. Without an introduction he proceeded to preach prison protocol, all the do's and don'ts within the prison and with the prisoner. He spoke rapid fire as if he'd given the speech hundreds of times.

'Another guard entered and patted me down and went through my bag. I had a small recorder I'd planned to use and expected it to be taken, but surprisingly it wasn't. When everything was deemed in order I was led down empty hallways to a small glassed-in room, seeing no cells or prisoners along the way. Inside the room there was one metal table and three chairs chained to it. The guard explained in the strictest terms I would be alone with the prisoner but someone would be nearby watching and listening very carefully.

'Waiting I tried to remember what Emil Breck looked like, thinking back to the day he was called to testify before the House Un-American Committee. I was certain prison changed him and I wondered if I would recognize him.

'As I'd written in a series of articles several months ago, Mr. Breck like others was subpoenaed because the Committee claimed to possess clear evidence that he was a Communist. The verbal assault came early with an angry edge from Chairman Baldwin, asserting defiantly he would only accept a yes or no to the charge. When Mr. Breck did not answer quickly enough, Representative Baldwin pounded his fists in rather dramatic fashion, demanding Mr. Breck acknowledge whether he was a Communist or not. Again there was no response.

'The Chairman seemed to seethe with anger because of Mr. Breck's silence. He repeated the question again, a bit quieter but more pointed yet there was still no response from Mr. Breck. With a nod from the Chairman Mr. Breck was led away by the Capitol Police. I got up to follow him,

Emil's List

hoping to have a brief moment of his time. Thinking about the hearing, I'd almost forgot I was in America.

'The slamming of a metal door somewhere in the prison made me jump, the place a true house of horrors. I very much doubted Mr. Breck was a violent man but I sensed he was in a very violent place.

'Another loud door slam made me jump again. With his head slightly bowed and legs shackled and hands cuffed, I watched Mr. Breck shuffle to one of the chairs, sitting when ordered by the guard. Time was valuable but I did not want to start a discussion with the guard hovering. Precious moments passed while the guard stood stone faced and motionless. I finally asked if I could talk to the prisoner alone, saying I was a reporter and needed a few uninterrupted minutes to interview Mr. Breck.

'The guard glared at Emil, a warning I suspected before he grudgingly walked from the room, the door left open behind him. When we were alone all the questions I wanted to ask became a jumble in my mind. I must have looked terribly dazed because a moment later I heard a gentle voice as Mr. Breck asked if I was the reporter he'd seen in the back of the hearing room a month ago. I nodded and seeing his reassuring smile I settled down.

"I'm curious about you," he said, the words barely audible. "I would like to know why a reporter would want to come out here to interview me."

'I told him I'd been covering HUAC hearings since they'd begun and was very familiar with the Committee's work. I asked what it felt like to be called before a hostile Congressional committee. He didn't answer immediately so I pointed at my watch. He nodded slowly, understanding our time was limited. I whispered the committee was a danger to American democracy.

'My next question I hesitated asking. Leaning close I asked if there was any truth to the committee's charge he was a card carrying member of the Communist Party.

'Mr. Breck seemed to think about the question until a sly smile appeared. There was no admission or denial, just the words he preferred not to answer that question, at least not until he knew me better. I then asked if he thought HUAC actually had hard factual evidence he was in fact a party member.

'His smile grew even wider, stating emphatically he would not allow anyone to make him provide details about his private political opinions. I asked if he thought he was in for a long prison stay. He responded with a shrug of his shoulders.

"Whether I'm a Communist or not is none of the Committee's business, or anyone else's."

'Those words are a direct quote.'

"There are things I've done in my life that would greatly disturb the Committee and there are things I've said and written they might take issue with. However, I've never advocated violence in this country, nor have I ever campaigned or expressed an opinion calling for the overthrow of the government. I covered the Spanish Civil War for nearly three years giving me great insights into what happens when the laws of the land are manipulated by those who should protect those rights. I pray to God this country never goes through the type of tragedy I saw in Spain. I pay taxes, I vote and I have the freedom to express my political thoughts without fear of retribution, just like any other American. I like many others certainly have issues with some of America's policies but in a free country, we all have the right to speak out. I love the first amendment but I doubt the Committee considers it when making accusations.

"I can tell you this Mr. Roth. If the committee does have damaging information about me, I have an absolute right to see the evidence. I made it quite clear in a note I sent Mr. Baldwin that I will continue to refuse to answer any question until I was able to confront my accusers. The Chairman refused and that response violated my rights as an American citizen. Mr. Baldwin has hijacked our Constitution and is ignoring the rights it guarantees.

"Mr. Roth, if you manage to get this interview published which I doubt, I want you to emphasize that if I can be called before Congress to discuss my private life, anyone could."

'The longer we sat with each other, the more admiration and respect I had for Emil Breck. How long do you think they'll keep you here I asked?

'His reply was probably forever or until one of two things happened.

"If I answer all their questions, which would mean allowing them to take my rights away, I'm certain they'd be lenient but at what price? I haven't broken any laws and I'm hardly a candidate for sedition. I know writers who eventually bowed to pressure, turning over names of colleagues and fueling the feeding frenzy. I won't do that."

Emil's List

'When the guard returned I thanked Mr. Breck for his time, wishing him peace. There was one last question I wanted to ask but I knew our time was up.

'He bowed at the guard's command to be returned to his cell. Whether Mr. Breck was or wasn't a member of the Communist Party, I could not guess. I strongly believed however he had every right to keep that answer to himself. We looked at each other one final moment, a wink at me and the words, keep the faith. I asked if he needed anything but there was no response.

'I sat in that icy room for five minutes until someone came to walk me to my car. While I'd waited I realized I'd totally forgotten my recorder and hadn't taken any notes. How I might process all we spoke would not be easy, believing Breck's liberty might depend upon my writing.

'The managing director of the magazine Liberal Times Review heard about my visit and contacted me about publishing my interview. I preferred more mainstream organizations but no one else would touch my story. When it was about to go to press the story was unexpectedly pulled without explanation. I knew someone censored it because the subject was too hot to handle.

'I doubted many people subscribed to the Liberal Times Review so I tried to convince myself it was no great loss. A week later New Nation Magazine approached me and published my article in its entirety. To their brave editor I have much respect.

'I received much negative feedback but I knew I would always stand by the thought, even if you are a minority of one, the truth is still the truth.'

I told Sucre I'd never heard of New Nation Magazine but the story piqued more interest in learning about it's writer, Max Roth. Reluctantly, I put the folder down.

There was still much organizing to be done and scores of cartons had not yet been opened. Sucre said she was tired it was time to return to her place. At my doorway she paused and gave me a funny look. Then I remembered. It was the night I was to come by her place for a traditional Peruvian meal at the usual Peruvian dining hour, ten in the evening.

I knew very little about Peru so I'd purchased a copy of the Lonely Planet Peru mesmerized by one long section devoted to Peruvian food, including recipes for alpaca and sheep and grains. The writer described the national dish as something everyone should try at least once on a visit; an oven roasted spit fired guinea pig usually served on Sundays. I truly hoped that wouldn't be our main course because when I was growing up, I had two pet guinea pigs.

The evening walk along Boston's streets alone to Sucre's place seemed different and I knew why. When we'd walk together she'd make me hear things I'd never noticed before. I'd become awed by her ability to negotiate Boston's perilous streets as drivers sped by, usually one eye on the road and a hand on the horn.

Thankfully the dinner was not guinea pig although Sucre amused herself by making guinea pig noises during dinner preparation. She explained that guinea pig had been prepared the same way for a thousand years, spit roasted in a community oven. She said the cooking process began with the breaking of the animal's neck, demonstrating how one quick twist did the trick. I flinched.

"The carcass is then dropped into hot water to make it easier to remove the fur."

I asked where one purchased the furry critters.

"Most people have ten or twelve living in their homes on straw mats, usually the living room. When it's time to begin the cooking, the wife always did the honors. The organs were removed and cooked separately on spits in a wood fired oven and then placed back inside the animal. Most homes in Peru do not have ovens so communal ones are used. On any Sunday you might see dozens or more roasting at any time inside wood fired clay ovens in special buildings."

I couldn't help think about the large Boston rat I'd seen walking to her place. Fortunately the chicken dish was a great meal and much appreciated.

Back at my place late, I decided to call a friend in California who wrote for the San Francisco Examiner. Reaching Phil Mathews at his desk we shared a little small talk about our lives. Then the reason for my call. I asked if he'd ever heard of an old time reporter by the name of Max Roth.

"I haven't heard that name in a very long time but yes. I believe he passed on possibly eight years ago in the Bay Area where he'd retired. I recall reading his obituary and felt sorry we'd not kept in touch. I believe I wrote a note to his children, two sons expressing my condolences. I haven't heard his name mentioned in all those years until your call. Can I ask what's the interest?"

I said I'd come across old articles he'd written and wanted to use them in a project I was working on. We spoke for another ten minutes, mostly about mutual friends until there was nothing more to say.

In the morning I called a Boston newspaper friend, asking if he might look up Max Roth's obituary, saying it might be difficult because he'd never lived in the Boston area. Two hours later he returned my call, saying he'd found a rather short obituary in the files of the old Baltimore Sun. It mentioned Roth's writing career and the names of two living children, Jamie and Jed Roth.

I knew in a flash I needed to find the sons to learn more about their father.

Sucre arrived later then usual, saying she'd made a stop along her travels to pick up a fresh bouquet of cut flowers, something she bought once a week. Even though she couldn't see the colors she said, she was always overcome by the wonderful scent infused into her life.

CHAPTER 13

Another work day began with the opening of another cardboard carton, anticipating we were really opening a treasure chest filled with stories for the ages. We certainly hadn't been disappointed yet. Resting on the very top was a memo written from Raymond Baldwin to members of his HUAC Committee; the subject, Emil Breck. I wondered how Emil managed to get his hands on it but in truth, nothing he ever did surprised me.

I read the first few words until Sucre cleared her throat quite loudly, another lapse on my part for not reading aloud. Before I could apologize she asked if it would be alright to bring up a subject that had nothing to do with Emil. I nodded, then saying yes of course.

"I've been wondering about something Charlie and I hope you don't mind if I ask you a very personal question. You don't have to answer but it's something I've been awfully curious about for some time now. You know a little about my family but I know nothing about yours. Charlie, have you've ever been married?"

I was bemused by the question because in our working days together we'd rarely talked about anything but our work, Emil or Sucre's Peruvian life. I was surprisingly taken aback but my words came out rather easily although it was a subject I'd rarely thought about or discussed.

"I was married for a little more then ten years and sadly toward the end, my wife's health problems grew worse. We both knew before we married that our time together was probably going to be limited because she was born with a very weak heart. Even though I thought I was prepared for the inevitable, the day she didn't wake up nearly destroyed me. She's been gone a long time now but I think about her quite often, especially around the holidays. It's been six years since I lost her and time has gone by in the blink of an eye.

"My wife, who chose to be called Francesca which was not her real name, was quite a remarkable woman. Her doctors did everything possible until we realized that the end was near. Looking back we were most fortunate to have those wonderful years together, many more than the doctors first thought. I've lived alone since then but I have two grown daughters probably around your age. Robin is married and living in London and Sasha is married to her work in New York City. I have one granddaughter."

I thought about the picture of my wife in my bedroom Sucre could not see.

"What about you?" I asked finding myself a bit shaken.

"Anybody special in your life now or ever?"

Sucre laughed, turning a slight shade of red.

"No marriages although when I was eleven years old living in Peru, a young boy by the name of Martin proposed to me. Sadly, I'd heard he'd died years later during the war with the Shining Path, one of so many young men to lose their lives. After I lost my sight I knew it wouldn't be fair having someone just to take care of me or watch over me, so no prospects. Can I ask you another personal question?"

I truly wanted to get back to work but I let Sucre go on.

"Would you please tell me what you look like?"

I laughed out loud because I'd never been asked and was completely unsure how to answer. For several moments I thought about the image in the mirror I'd seen every morning, but I could not quite put the right words together.

"Okay, I'm a little over six feet tall, fairly thin, black hair, a stubble of a beard rarely trimmed, brown eyes and rippling muscles," adding I was only kidding about the muscles.

"And me," she asked shyly? "What do you see when you look at me?"

Without hesitating I told her she was quite beautiful and the proof was the number of men we passed on the street who took long stares at her, saying she'd turned many heads.

"I think the first thing people notice is your long straight beautiful black hair."

Bruce Weiss

We both began laughing like children, both a little embarrassed realizing it was far easier dealing with Emil's work than talking about ourselves. I added I was very fond of her because of her great courage and for not allowing her blindness to interfere with her good life. Beauty is only skin deep I said, immediately wishing I'd not said that. The ensuing silence suggested we get back to the work.

"I'm going to read the memo from Chairman Baldwin that appears to be addressed to his fellow Committee members on the HUAC. How he got this confidential note I couldn't guess."

'I have absolutely no doubt in my mind Emil Breck is a leftist and earnestly believe this man and his writings are legitimate threats to this nation. The newspaper articles written from Spain in the late 1930's clearly illustrate a very strong affection and fondness for Communism and the Soviet Union. The articles blatantly praise the Soviets while offering strong criticisms of America. I believe he's taken calculated steps to disguise his past and I wonder if his interest in coming to America from Romania was suspicious. I don't want to waste any more of the Committee's time with Mr. Breck so I think it's time we squash him like a cockroach. I've highlighted several statements demonstrating beyond any shadow of a doubt, Emil Breck was then and probably still is an active card carrying member of the Communist Party. If we can't get him to admit this, I suggest we set a good example and throw the book at him." RB

"What's the date on the memo" Sucre asked?
"March 30ᵗʰ 1953 which tells us he was probably in prison when the memo circulated. There's something stapled to the memo appears to be more transcript of Emil's final appearance before HUAC. Here it goes."

Representative Baldwin (R-Massachusetts) delivers his opening remarks, repeating earlier key questions for the record.

Badwin - Are you now prepared to admit you were once or still are an active member of the Communist Party? That is the only issue here Mr. Breck and we can put this all behind us if you will enlighten the committee about your status.

Emil's List

Breck - I ask again, may I please see the evidence you claim to have indicating I am now or was once a member?

Audience reacts with loud talking. The Chair pounds his gavel saying he will not tolerate interruptions.

Breck - I respectfully refuse to answer your question until I see the actual evidence against me.

Rep Baldwin - That's not going to happen until you answer all the committee's questions. How many times do I have to tell you that? Were you raised in Hungary to be a troublemaker?

Breck - I beg to differ but I came from Romania."

Shuffling of papers and whispering among the Committee members

Rep Baldwin - The Committee has gone over a number of your published articles which I'm certain you're well acquainted with. I'm also looking at statements gathered by intelligence officials who investigated your active political years in Romania. I strongly maintain it's in your best interest to answer all our questions and keep this in mind. We did not request your presence before the committee today. It was you sending word you wanted to return to testify. Is that a fair statement?

Breck nods, asked to say yes or no for the record.

Rep Baldwin - I will ask this one last time because my patience is wearing very thin. Are you now or have you ever been a member of the Communist Party either in American or the International?

Booing from a spectator. Chairman demands the police escort the violator out.

Breck - Representative Baldwin, That particular question is asked of every person you've called before this committee. It is true I'm a naturalized America citizen and yes, I was born in Romania which is not a crime.

Bruce Weiss

I was not a member of the Communist Party in Romania despite what people like you assume or what your so called intelligence people allegedly reported. I have always held deep resentments toward the Soviets because of what they did to my country after the war.

Rep Baldwin - Is you answer you've never been a member of any Communist Party at any time?

Breck - "I think we should move on Mr. Chairman.

Laughter

Rep Baldwin - Okay for the sake of argument let's assume you weren't a member of the Communist Party growing up in Romania. It is my understanding however Romania became a Communist nation. How is it possible you were therefore not a Communist?

Breck - You are correct about Romania but you are wrong about me and millions of others. Even though Romanians lived under a Communist regime, very few people were actually members of the Party. An as an aside, I was living in America as an American citizen when the Soviets installed a Communist government in my homeland.

Rep Baldwin - As you said let's move on for a moment but make no mistake, I'll get back to some of your earlier statements. Did you write news articles between 1936 and 1939 supporting Communism and Communist causes in Spain? Be careful how you answer because lying to this Committee is a punishable offense. I've shared your writings with intelligence experts who agree wholeheartedly you supported the actions of the Soviet Union in Spain. Would you care to comment?

Breck - As a journalist I've always tried to be impartial but at times that's impossible. It was no secret the Fascists in Spain, led by General Francisco Franco were in collusion with the Fascists in power in Germany and Italy. Franco's followers were ruthless torturers, murderers and plunderers, employing very sophisticated new weapons of war provided mostly by the Nazis. If my writings appear slanted in favor of the Republican war effort

Emil's List

fighting Franco, then I will admit I was partial. You must understand something. The Soviet Union stood by the Republican efforts to stop a Fascist takeover in Spain. When other nations ignored the catastrophic crisis in Spain and the senseless slaughter of civilians, the Soviets were the only ones to stand up against Fascism. Any praise directed or even perceived toward the Soviets by me was strictly in response to their humanitarian efforts to help the Republic survive.

Rep Baldwin - Mr. Breck, this Committee isn't interested in a history lesson but we'd like to know if you were acting as a Soviet agent living and writing in Spain. The record will show we've read many of your articles and the Committee agrees there is an obvious bias not only for the Soviets, but for Communism in general. This committee also located reports proving many of your articles were reprinted in Soviet newspapers. My next question sir is, did you ever write articles for the Soviet press? Did you collaborate with Communists in any way? Did the Communist party pay for your news reports? Mr. Breck, you need to explain why the Soviets were so flattered by you and your articles.

Breck - The answer to all those questions is no. I did not work for any Communist organizations, nor was I ever asked and no, I did not receive any money from the Soviets. Any newspaper in the world was free to pick up my stories.

Rep Baldwin - Your reporting makes the Communist fighters in Spain seem heroic. Can you look the Committee members in their eyes and insist you were fair and impartial in your writings?

Chairman Baldwin rapped the gavel several times to quiet the spectators.

Rep Baldwin - Please tell this Committee how or why your articles were also picked up by leftist newspapers in America. I have several reprints here.

Breck - Mr. Baldwin, I have no idea because I did not work for them. My articles were picked up by many papers and I had no control over their use or distribution. My only concern was they spell my name right.

Bruce Weiss

Laughter

Rep Baldwin - Have you ever knowingly written articles for the Soviet Press or were you ever asked to submit articles to them? Has any Communist organization including those that possibly exist in this country tried to influence you in any way? Did you take money from known Communist organizations?

Breck - I have written hundreds, possibly thousands of articles over the years, some as recently as this past year from prison. I don't know which articles of those thousands you're referring to so perhaps you might share your notes with me so I can better understand exactly what it is you want.

Rep Baldwin - That will not happen Mr. Breck. As stated earlier, I have several hundred of your news stories in front of me and most speak for themselves. Do you think we're naive? Why would you need to look through these articles when you yourself wrote them? Before you answer my next question however you might want to comment on an article I have here you apparently wrote for Le Monde, a French newspaper. In the article you extol and glorify the efforts of Soviet Communist forces fighting in Spain. Did you write that article?

Breck - I don't remember specific articles however if you read what I wrote about the Soviets, you'll see I was decrying the fact America didn't aid or support the free Spanish. I would also encourage you to read about 1930's American neutrality laws under FDR. The absence of our involvement allowed the Fascists to gain control of Spain and they ran the country with an iron fist for the next thirty years.

Rep Baldwin - Were you aware the managing editor of Le Monde was a member of the French Communist Party?

Breck - I was not and if he was, it was none of my business.

Rep Baldwin - Did you visit the Le Monde office in France either during the Spanish Civil War or any other time?

Emil's List

Breck - Yes.

Rep Baldwin - And did you meet with the managing editors either socially or for business reasons while in France?

Breck - I believe we did get together socially but we did not discuss politics.

Rep Baldwin - I'm going to introduce evidence for the record Mr. Breck, that you spent much time in France. Now, there is no crime in visiting but if you went there to write stories for a newspaper with leftist leanings, one can only assume you understood and approved of their political philosophy. Did you realize there were strong connections between many of the editorial people at Le Monde and the French Communist Party?

Breck - As I said, I don't recall talking politics with anyone at the newspaper.

Rep Baldwin - Have you ever traveled to the Soviet Union? Be careful how you answer this question because perjury is a very serious crime.

Breck - Yes I was invited three times by various cultural organizations and when I traveled there, I spoke about my Spanish civil war experiences.

Rep Baldwin - I have a copy of an interview with a Soviet magazine written about your visit there in 1950. 'Emil Breck, the noted American newspaper reporter will appear at the Moscow State University this evening with a broad and varied range of topics for discussion. Mr. Breck has written hundreds of news articles highlighting Soviet efforts fighting Fascism. He has also written a number of articles on Stalin.' Do you remember that article about Stalin?

Breck - I do remember the article and I was actually asked to write it for the New York Times, hardly a Communist newspaper.

Laughter

Rep Baldwin - I'd be happy to debate the New York Times with you. I'll show you the magazine Mr. Breck to refresh your memory.

Bruce Weiss

An aide brought the magazine to Mr. Breck

Rep Baldwin- Well?

Breck - Representative Baldwin, I've never read this magazine or given anyone permission to use my work in it. From the very first paragraph I can tell you someone changed my words. I would not have said those words so I can only guess a Soviet journalist exaggerated the situations I wrote about.

Rep Baldwin - Let's talk about the section in this article where you talk about Lenin. Have any of your articles or political opinions extolled the philosophy of Lenin.

Breck - "No, I don't believe any of my writings were anything more then biographical. I've studied Russian history like thousands of others and that by the way is not a crime. Many people have written about Lenin and Stalin including several Pulitzer Prize winners. I've spent hours reading about Karl Marx but that too is not a crime, even though his manifest was banned in America. These are important people who changed the world whether we like it or not. Reading about them or having knowledge of them is not against the law.

Rep Baldwin - Mr. Breck, since you've been an American citizen, have you ever attended a meeting of Communist sympathizers?

Breck - I have attended hundreds of meetings Mr. Baldwin. If there were Communist sympathizers there that was never my purpose for going. However, allow me to add a bit more to my previous answer. I believe a person can be changed and influenced by historical figures living or deceased.

Rep Baldwin - Have you ever visited the Soviet embassy to the United States or any Soviet consulate?

Breck - I might have for articles I was researching but I can't remember specifics.

Rep Baldwin - Perhaps you had better think more about that answer Mr. Breck.

Rep Baldwin - Have any members of any Soviet organization ever come to visit you here in this country?

Breck - I do not recollect if any did or did not. I've lectured on the freedom of the press quite often and it's very possible some in the audience night have had Soviet connections.

Rep Baldwin - Tell me about your address to the Young Republicans at Yale College on April 4, 1952. Do you recall your visit there?

Breck - I do. Wonderful hamburger place nearby called Louie's Lunch.

Rep Baldwin - That response is not necessary. Were you aware after your address you spent time talking with a man by the name of Gregory Povich?

Breck - I don't recall that name, so no.

Rep Baldwin - Think again, Mr. Breck.

Breck - I don't remember that name but it's possible we chatted as I spoke with several students and faculty members interested in my work. I cannot say for certain if one of them was the Povich you mention.

Rep Baldwin - Are you telling this Committee that you've never heard the name Gregory Povich, even though I have a picture in front of me taken by the Yale Student Newspaper, and you're shaking Mr. Povich's hand?

"Stop there" Sucre interrupted. "The more you read the angrier I'm getting. Many Peruvians have always looked up to America including my family so this is very hard on me. Emil was an honorable man and the undignified manner he was treated by your government riles me terribly. The more I understand the work of HUAC, the more I wonder how and why your nation tolerated it. Why didn't people speak up to support Emil? Before you read anymore I want you to know Emil Breck was the most

Bruce Weiss

honorable person I'd ever known. I'm terribly mystified and confused because the more I learn about his life and the way he was treated, the more I wonder why good people didn't speak out. You might as well continue reading."

Rep Baldwin - When did you discover your reports were being published without your permission as you say in a number of Soviet publications?

Breck - One time I actually discovered one of my articles was published in a Soviet paper, appearing without my permission but there was nothing I could really do about it.

Rep Baldwin - Do you remember the titles of any of your articles turning up that way?

Breck - No.

Rep Baldwin - Did you ever write articles describing the Soviet Union in healthy or glowing terms?

Breck - Probably, along with thousands of other reporters who were free to express themselves without worry of censorship.

Rep Baldwin - Would you please answer my questions with a simple yes or no. In your naturalized citizen life in America, have you ever contributed articles to any Communist publications either here or abroad?

Breck - I have submitted many articles because that's how I support myself. That's my profession. I very rarely concern myself with the politics of newspapers and magazines if they express interest in my work.

Mr. Breck was reminded to give verbal answers for the record.

Rep Baldwin - Are you familiar with a newspaper called The New Worker?

Breck - Yes, I've heard of the paper.

Emil's List

Rep Baldwin - Did you ever submit an article to this paper?

Breck - No, not to my knowledge but I can't be one hundred percent certain.

Rep Baldwin - Did this paper ever publish any of your stories without your knowledge?

Breck - I couldn't answer that but it's possible.

Rep Baldwin - Couldn't or wouldn't?

Breck - To my knowledge the New Worker published nothing of mine. Most times I had little or no control over how or why or where certain articles were published.

Rep Baldwin - That sounds like an excuse a Communist would use Mr. Breck. You once wrote an editorial for the Memphis Oracle in 1947. I'd have to look up the exact date but that's beside the point. You advocated sharing technical information with the Soviet Union to help their scientists and engineers develop an atom bomb. Do you remember that story?

Breck - I do, but you wouldn't understand the reasoning because you've taken many of my words out of context, painting an erroneous picture of me. I would humbly suggest you read the entire piece and perhaps you could share it with this Committee.

Rep Baldwin - As I've said before and hope I don't have to say it again, you're not here to suggest anything. You're here to answer questions and the committee would appreciate precise answers. I have several more articles in front of me with your name on the byline, this one published in something called The Worker's Paradise, an underground newspaper allegedly tied to Communist groups. Are you aware of the Worker's Paradise?

Breck - As a reporter I knew the names of many different publications. I cannot recall if I'd ever heard that particular name.

Bruce Weiss

Rep Baldwin - I have just a few more questions for you. Did anyone ever approach you about joining the American Communist Party or any organization with Communist ties? If so, I want their names.

Breck - Once, yes.

Rep Baldwin - Who was that individual and what did you discuss?

Breck - You asked me if I'd ever been approached and I said yes. When I told the gentleman I was not interested in what he was peddling, that ended the conversation. I don't believe we exchanged names.

Rep Baldwin - Why did this mystery man approach you?

Breck - Maybe it was his job to approach anyone and everyone to seek support. I've also been approached by Republicans you know.

When the laughter died Chairman Baldwin said the committee did not want to hear catty remarks.

Breck - Mr. Chairman, I apologize.

Rep Baldwin - Are you familiar with a man by the name of Archie Sampson?

Breck - Sure, he wrote for the Chicago Tribune and I believe he won several Pulitzers for his reporting.

Rep Baldwin - Mr. Breck, many of the members of this Committee have other commitments requiring their attention. We have more questions for you so I am ordering you to re-appear tomorrow morning at 10am. Is there anything you'd like to say to this Committee before we adjourn?

Breck - I would Mr. Baldwin. The world is always changing and if we don't adapt to those changes we'll be left far behind. This Committee believes the world is threatened by a mysterious, shadowy Communist conspiracy and I believe you've taken a wrong approach. You insist anyone who sees merit in a socialist state is America's mortal enemy. The United States Constitution has guided us for two hundred years, yet you would change it's meaning to fit your goals.

Without a true understanding of how our Constitution changed the world for the good, you have chosen to turn it into a weapon that needlessly destroys good and decent lives. I would ask who gives this Committee the authority to pry into people's private lives? If you can demand a person's political views, what would be next? A religious test?

I've never yelled fire in a crowded movie theater even though I have freedom of speech. If writing opinions and op-eds you don't agree with makes me a Communist, then I am. Mr. Baldwin, your Committee can only succeed in strengthening the public's belief in the systems and organizations you attack.

Character assassination is all that you've managed to produce here and there's not a shred of evidence proving I or others were out to destroy America. Your accusations have made criminals out of good Americans so I would ask this of you Mr. Baldwin. Have you no shame?

Rep Baldwin - Mr. Breck, the only person in this room who harms good Americans is you. We are adjourned until this afternoon.

Sucre and I sat in silence at the insanity Emil had once been subject to, supposedly in the land of the free.

"The early 1950's were not kind to people like Emil Breck," I said dejectedly. "Many lives were forever ruined and careers lost. I think Emil came out of those hearings strong and determined to fight those type of injustices the rest of his life, and he did."

Later that afternoon we discovered a trove of papers near the bottom of another carton, mostly editorials written by reporters and editors offering their take on Emil's Congressional performance. Many of the letters praised Emil for his stance but others damned and condemned him as a Communist.

I asked Sucre if Peruvian leaders made their own laws, flaunting the country's Constitution. She replied that was the norm in Peru no matter who was in power.

Bruce Weiss

"Good people get elected because they offer help but in the end, most ruled as they pleased, something not uncommon in other Latin American nations also.

"Peru dealt differently with enemies of the state and instead of government hearings like HUAC, people simply disappeared, many killed by midnight firing squads. During our darkest days we turned to America for help, knowing it was a towering beacon of freedom and liberty. Reading Emil's transcripts makes me think America had more in common with Peru than people thought.

"I honestly couldn't imagine what happened to Emil could ever happen in America so I'm numb, confused and very saddened by the terrible affront. Emil was such a gentle and caring person who truly loved his country, warts and all. The accusations must have hurt him appallingly but the Emil I got to know was never resentful or bitter. I could never have dreamed this country would ever turn against its own citizens. As I said, Emil and I rarely talked politics so this is all very new and truly upsetting for me.

"Charlie, Emil always painted a beautiful picture of America and we rarely talked about it's dark side. As I've said, we spent most of our time talking about great literature. The only time I ever heard disappointment in his voice was when he'd rage about censorship not only effecting the authors of the books he'd collected, but also his own writings. The books brought us together for nearly two years and I'm eternally grateful for that time. In truth, if you'd read all those letters and articles without mentioning Emil's name, I would never have connected that terrible committee to him.

Chapter 14

'Rep Baldwin - Mr. Breck, I hope you've enjoyed a good lunch and I hope we can get through everything in short order, depending of course upon your willingness to come forth with the truth. This session has dragged on far too long and I think we all need to move on. There is something however I'd like more clarification on. I'd like to discuss the articles written 1936 to 1939 from Spain again. I realize it was twelve or thirteen years ago but perhaps you might answer a few questions so we can get past it and move on. First, I would like to ask once again your reasons for painting such a convivial picture of the Soviet Union. Did you have a special arrangement with them?

Mr. Breck shook his head, again admonished to give verbal responses for the record.

Rep Baldwin - What I'm getting at is did you deliberately travel to Spain to join up and fight with the Communists and not actually work as a reporter you pretended to be? Were you turned by the Soviets knowingly or unknowingly becoming a propaganda arm for the Communist Party?

Breck - It's a bit complicated so please allow me to answer without interruption Mr. Baldwin. My studies in college focused on the First World War and early twentieth century Europe. The more I read and understood, the more interest I had in European affairs. It was folly to believe nothing like the First World war, once known as the great war could ever happen again, which of course it did just a mere twenty years later.

Bruce Weiss

I wasn't alive during World War One but for my senior thesis I interviewed nearly two hundred World War One veterans and many others involved in the war effort. Everything I wrote was based upon first hand accounts and experiences using original documents. That work gave me the opportunity to understand how wars not only begin, but how they could have been avoided. I learned like many others World War One's conclusion created events and situations leading directly to the Second World War. In the 1930's Fascism devoured much of the European continent, something particularly alarming to the Soviets. Because of America's neutrality laws, we kept our noses out of European affairs and as you know, we didn't confront Fascism until Pearl Harbor was attacked in 1941. By that time, Fascism was spreading like a wild fire.

Europe was still feeling the awful effects of the First World War and many governments including our own didn't have the desire or the money to take up arms again. Even the most enlightened people declined to stand up against nations planning a more devastating war. I believe we most likely could have stopped Italy and Germany from building their powerful war machines long before they were ever used. Germany was first to prepare for the next war, followed by other nations falling under Fascist regimes. I'm sure you're familiar with the word appeasement.

In 1936 the democratically elected government of the Spanish Republic was forced to take up arms to defend itself against a Fascist military uprising led by Francisco Franco. Fascist Italy and Fascist Germany eagerly supported Franco with arms and soldiers and the end results were destroyed cities and towns and untold civilian deaths. In the chaos only the Soviet Union made a concerted effort to help the Republic of Spain. Why? Because the Soviets feared Fascism even more than democracies like ours. The civil war in Spain lasted three years and during that time Fascism spread throughout Europe and Asia and sadly no country had the will or the desire to stop it. In 1939 Poland the fuse was finally lit, the sad beginning of another tragic world war. Spain was the time and place where Fascism could have been stopped so why did I stay there during those turbulent years? Because few people understood the consequences and I wanted them to know.

Emil's List

Rep Baldwin - Mr. Breck this committee doesn't need a complete history of the Spanish Civil War so I'm going to cut you off. Can we wrap this thing up?

Breck - I can but I want to finish my thought. As soon as Franco took up arms against his Spanish Republican government he received the blessing of the Germans. A non-intervention treaty was drawn up and signed by most western European nations, isolating Spain and promising not to interfere in a civil war. The pact literally handed the Fascists permission to solidify and expand their aggression.

General Franco was the voice and the leader behind the anti-government war, proudly calling himself a Nationalist. He openly sought and accepted aid and weapons from the Fascist nations of Italy and Germany who were more than eager to accommodate him. Mr. Baldwin, in the first months of the Spanish Civil War, Germany sent hundreds of aircraft, tons of bombs, mortars and more then ten thousand machine guns and tanks to wipe out Spain's democracy. I stayed there because I believed the conflict would eventually cross borders and the entire continent would go up in flames again. It was a time when few other reporters were willing to risk their lives. Someone had to document the wrongs of appeasement and non-intervention, someone who would enlighten the world how Fascism would eventually destroy Europe.

Joseph Stalin, the Russian leader was alarmed by an armed Germany to its west, believing a Fascist victory in Spain would be a direct threat to the security of the Soviet Union. The United States response was to do nothing; call it appeasement or non-intervention. Stalin's fears came to fruition when Hitler and his Fascist forces attacked Russia.

Rep Baldwin - Mr. Breck, I'll tell you again I don't need a course in history or a review of the entire war. Try to answer my questions in a couple of sentences please. Only prophets could have predicted World War Two so I don't believe you went there for any other reason then to join up with the Soviets. Do you think your writing helped the Soviets?

Bruce Weiss

Breck - As I've said for the record, I was in Spain to cover a war few people in America understood or cared about. Its entirely possible if we'd put an end to Fascist expansion in 1936 Spain, World War Two might not have happened. That was the theme of most of my articles.

Baldwin -I'd debate that point but let's move on.

Breck - Stalin ordered his military to send an International Brigade to Spain to help the Republicans defeat Franco. America's neutrality position would not allow us to help what a few wise men called a terrible mistake, empowering the Fascists. It did not stop good Americans from going to Spain to support the Republicans however.

'Brigades of young men sailed from America to Spain putting themselves immediately into harms way to fight for the Republic. Keep in mind the only one's giving support to the Republic were the Soviets, so why should I have portrayed them as merciless? Many of my articles indeed approved of Soviet actions because the Soviet effort was the only thing keeping the entire nation from falling into the hands of Franco. My stories were personal observations and I took orders from no one. If they elicited positive feelings for the Soviets then that was clearly fact and not opinion. The Soviet Union took in many Republican refugees including many women and children while a poorly armed Republic fought a desperate battle for survival.

Rep Baldwin - I would strongly argue with everything you've just said.

Breck - Do you know how many Americans went over to fight with the Republicans for a free Spain? Did you know those brave men and women were branded criminals by our government? I met many of these honorable men while I was there, many who were members of the American Communist Party. Many gave their lives trying to keep Fascism from swallowing Spain.

Rep Baldwin - So let me get this straight? Did you join the Communist Party when you were there?

Emil's List

Breck - I refuse to answer that question. I praised the Soviets for their efforts in Spain but I willingly acknowledge I have never advocated Communism. If you read my writings carefully, you will never find any avocation for Communism.

In 1937 twenty thousand Americans of German decent joined the German Bund and staged mass rallies in New York supporting Hitler's Fascists. Thousands of Italian Americans rallied in support of Mussolini. Millions of Americans listened to Father Charles Coughlin on the airwaves condemning Jews and supporting lynching's in the south. Why are those people not here before this committee? Did they get a pass so you could devote all your efforts toward finding Communists in America?

Rep Baldwin - Mr. Breck, you're beginning to try my patience. Are you aware of the chaos your Soviet friends are up to in today's world.

Mr Breck -My purpose in Spain was to report the news fairly with no one and no government telling me what I could or could not write. If I criticized America's inaction and praised the Soviet Union's efforts well sir, that doesn't make me a Communist. I met many Russians and many Communist Party members in my three years there and for your information, I did attend some of their meetings, purely as a responsible journalist. You claim to have all my articles written during those three years but I believe you haven't read any of them. Until you do, I refuse to answer any

Rep Baldwin - How about just one question. Were you then or are you now a member of the Communist Party?

Breck - I refuse to answer that question.

Rep Baldwin - I then ask the Capitol police to return you to Leavenworth post haste so you might think a bit longer about changing your tune.

I didn't know if we'd find any more transcripts detailing Emil's experience before HUAC, ruing again the fact Max Roth was long gone and could not help.

113

Bruce Weiss

"There are countless thousands more articles and letters and when we go through each one we'll better understand Emil's view of the world. He was certainly full of many surprises and I'll bet if he'd been able to write his memoir, it would be required reading in all journalism classes."

"I wish I'd knew more about Emil to help you Charlie. I can only say I could never have guessed he'd led such a remarkable or challenging life. Sadly, the world truly doesn't seem to learn about great deeds and great people until that person is gone."

If I could truly document his extraordinary life for a biography I thought, Emil would certainly get the much warranted attention he deserved. At that moment though Sucre looked scared and lost.

"You know when Emil read aloud I actually heard the voices of the characters in his books. My blindness never stopped me from being able to picture the many wondrous things he described. I wish you could have heard his uncanny way with words, especially when he read the courtroom scene in To Kill a Mocking Bird. His inflections made me feel a full range of emotions I didn't know I could feel, including salvation and resilience. All Quiet on the Western Front also touched me deeply, mostly because it reminded me of the war I'd experienced in Peru. I too thought Emil and I would be a team for many years to come but it wasn't meant to be I guess. No matter how busy he was with his work, he'd always found the time to read the marvelous books in his collection to me."

I said I'd also believed we'd have many good years working together but still wondered why he'd let me go. Could he have let me go because he'd been threatened again and was concerned for my well being?

"Emil talked about his various travels searching for books" Sucre whispered, "describing places I used to dream about when I watched airplanes taking off from the new Arequipa airport. I would still love to visit many of the places he spoke about so lovingly, even if I could not see them. Despite my blindness Emil encouraged me to travel and experience all the different languages, the smells in the markets and to listen to the sounds of the different languages.

"Charlie, I wanted to tell you early on I really didn't want to work with you but you managed to stir feelings in me the same way Emil did. Very few people ever effected me that way. You too have managed to make a blind girl see again."

I was always touched when she spoke about Emil but I hadn't known she'd felt that way about me. I asked if Emil ever talked about his native Romania.

"Romania was talked about on several occasions, mostly because we were both foreign born ands our experiences moving to America and beginning a new life were similar. Emil hadn't returned to his homeland but I believe he'd hoped to revisit after finishing his memoir. He encouraged me to consider returning to Peru, saying it was always possible to go home again.

We dove into another carton overflowing with papers, many editorials written by Emil over the years. We placed those in our folders, each one dedicated to a specific time or place. The work at times was terribly tedious and after reading the last transcript which greatly touched us, I asked Sucre if she'd like to knock off early so I might read to her. I knew it was impossible to replace Emil but it would take our minds off the scores of cartons we had not yet touched. Sucre seemed relieved at my suggestion.

I chose a book one of my absolute favorites, Another Country by James Baldwin. Sucre asked if Baldwin was related to the Baldwin in charge of HUAC. I had to stifle a laugh, replying absolutely not.

After reading a few pages Sucre's face lit up, pleased to see the worry lines melt away. All was right with the world for a few precious moments.

I read for nearly two hours knowing she'd fallen under the spell of James Baldwin's words. When I closed the book I told her FBI director J. Edgar Hoover demanded the book be banned in America because of its interracial descriptions and homosexual sex scenes.

"What did Emil write about Another Country in his notes," she asked?

I'd entirely forgotten Emil wrote personal notes about the books and their authors. Sure enough there was another envelope in the back of the book. It was like finding the prize in a Cracker Jack box.

'I'd once met a bookseller in New Orleans when I was visiting who'd been arrested and charged with obscenity when the book Another Country was discovered in his shop. The old gentleman spoke about his troubles fighting the charge and the enormous fine he was ordered to pay. To my delight we shared our common admiration for James Baldwin and was greatly surprised when he opened his safe, removing the one copy of

Bruce Weiss

Another Country the police had not found. His hands trembled slightly when he handed me the book, saying there would be no charge.'

There were several more pages written about Baldwin including the negative reactions espoused by the critics decrying references to homosexuality.

At end of the day we ate our light evening meal and then it was time for Sucre to return home. I felt the need to stop her to give her a big hug letting her know how much I appreciated her in my life. I didn't however, sensing the physical contact might startle her. She turned at the door saying please don't read anymore Another Country until she returned the next day.

CHAPTER 15

A half hour after Sucre left the phone rang and to my surprise it was Attorney Steven Gould. I thought it odd he was calling so late, portending bad news. His voice sounded strained, the words very terse. If it couldn't wait until morning I felt I was in for very unfortunate news. Getting right to the point he said he needed to see me first thing in the morning at his office, no later than seven. I asked what it was about but he insisted it was not phone talk. My heart ached. His last words were please bring an account about where I was with Emil's papers.

I'd been feeling slightly optimistic lately, dwelling less on the murder investigation and beginning to think it could not lead to my door. Poor Sucre I rued, poor me.

Sucre and were a team and our work kept Emil alive and in our thoughts. The late night call dampened the good feelings and as hard as I tried to remain upbeat, negative thoughts swirled about my head. The entire day with Sucre had been wonderful and productive but the call rekindled the nagging nervousness I was trying very hard to hide from her. Our early morning meeting could be for only one reason I suspected. I would likely be charged with Emil's murder.

In the morning after a night of very little sleep filled with disturbing dreams, I arrived at the Gould Building just as the sun began to illuminate the downtown glass towers. I was a loose bundle of nerves and as hard as I tried, I couldn't seem to stop the panic I felt.

When Gould walked off the elevator into the waiting room I thought I saw a troubling look on his face. My only clear thought was the proverbial shit was about to hit the fan.

Walking into his office I felt like a prisoner being lead to an execution

Bruce Weiss

chamber. His first words were to his secretary, telling her he would take no calls and no interruptions, not even if Jesus Christ himself was calling. It was crunch time.

"Mr. Darwin, Charlie, as you know a lethal dose of strychnine killed your friend Emil Breck. The police ruled out suicide and all the investigating authorities agree this was definitely murder. The chief of detectives informed me yesterday this particular poison would cause a very painful and agonizing death so someone definitely wanted your friend to suffer before he died There are many less painful ways to end a human life and this poison was not one of them. An accident? Hardly given the amount of poison ingested and that brings us to where we are right now.

"Mr. Darwin, Charlie, as murder investigations go, things generally get very nasty the longer the investigation goes on so I need to be completely up front. There is a very good chance you will be charged with murder sooner rather then later, so we need to prepare our case."

"Why me" I shouted? "Why would I want to kill Emil?" Were the police in the outer office waiting to arrest me I wondered?

"Charley after the police got the full lab report they investigated how and where the strychnine was purchased. No one in the department ever worked a case involving strychnine poisoning which is way this investigation is taking so long. The detectives have done their diligent homework however, discovering even without a prescription strychnine in large amounts can be purchased at certain veterinarian's offices. I know that sounds odd but there's a good reason why it's still around.

"Rats and other rodents live in and around barns and farms and the rodents do a number on the food supplies. Agricultural people say the vermin can eat a fifth of what is meant for the farm animals and vets claim strychnine in the right hands and in the right amounts can eradicate pests in the areas where farm animals don't stray. You with me so far?"

Reluctantly I nodded.

"The reason the police talked to me about this case is because for many years I was Emil Breck's attorney. I also know a few good men and women who work in police services so occasionally I'm privy to certain inside business.

"Griffin Family Vet is located just over the border in a small village in New Hampshire and that's where the police struck gold. They'd contacted veterinarian offices within a hundred mile radius of Boston before they found the right one. One individual purchased a good amount of strychnine apparently with your credit card and signature just three days before Mr. Breck's death. That my friend is called pretty damning evidence."

It felt as if all the air in the office had been sucked out, struggling to catch my breath, my head felt it might explode. I wanted to scream that it wasn't me and I'd been set up. What's the use I thought so I remained silent.

"As your lawyer I want to ask you if there's anything you need to say right now that might tell me what we're really up against. Remember, anything you say to me cannot be used in a court of law and I'm damned serious about that. It's personal privileged information and anything said here stays here. By the way, my only concern is to provide a good solid defense and a client's innocence or guilt has no effect on my effort."

Gould thinks I did it I thought. My chest tightened but there was nothing I could do or say to relieve it. I wanted to shout my innocence to impress the attorney but I was certain the effort would be futile. Think calmly and rationally I cautioned myself, sensing I could not hold myself together much longer. I gathered my wits and finally spoke.

"Mr. Gould, are the police absolutely certain it's my signature and my card because I swear, I've never bought strychnine nor have I been to New Hampshire in probably more than twenty years. Furthermore, I have no farm animals and I've never been in any vet's office. I didn't poison my friend so I know I've been set up to take the fall for a murder I did not commit. Why? I have no clue but I feel it might have something to do with Emil's latest work.

"Charlie the police are only doing their job and in all reality they're not making this stuff up. I promise if and when the police decide they need to talk with you I'll be there. When you leave my office shortly keep in mind you're probably going to be watched so just go about your normal routines. The situation is fluid and I'll keep you informed of any changes."

I began to protest my innocence again but attorney Gould threw his hands up in the air, stopping me, saying it didn't matter.

I was so distraught I didn't remember getting up and walking to the window, staring forlornly at the Revolutionary cemetery below. What's happening to me I whispered to my reflection in the window? Attorney

Gould asked me to sit down a few more minutes to pull myself together before I left.

My head was spinning, facing something impossible to comprehend. What will become of me I moaned a little too loudly? I didn't purchase the strychnine but the evidence was pretty clear. I began sweating profusely, suddenly thinking there just might be something in Emil's work I now owned, putting me in danger as well. When I looked up Attorney was tending to some paper work.

"Charlie there's something else. There was a surveillance camera in the vet's office and the police have the tape made the day of the purchase."

Oh God I whispered. I'll be cleared.

"The request to purchase strychnine according to the vet was the first in nearly a year so he remembered it quite clearly. The police watched the tape many times but due to the poor recording, no exact identification was possible at least yet. The out of focus frames do show the buyer wearing a Red Sox hat pulled down producing a shadow on his face, making identification impossible. The veterinarian, Doctor Pittman was interviewed by the detectives and he gave them all he knew about the customer, which sadly for the police wasn't much.

"The tape shows a conversation but the audio unfortunately was not working. The man paid with a credit card, seemingly yours and then simply drove away."

Did the doctor see the car I asked?

He did not Gould responded.

"Am I the only suspect"?

"No, but unfortunately you're at the top of the list. If you're curious about Miss Grande, she too is a suspect but the police don't think she was involved so she's merely a person of interest at this time. The detectives believe her physical disability clears her."

What happens now I asked meekly, not sure if I really wanted to hear the answer.

"The police are keeping me in the loop and I'll just end this meeting saying the investigation is ongoing. Don't investigate any of this yourself because I can assure you you'll regret it later. I just wanted you to be prepared and I was afraid if we'd met later, it might have been too late."

"That's it" I shouted?

Emil's List

"As I stated earlier our conversations are protected by the attorney client privilege and I would strongly urge you not to discuss this with anyone, even your Peruvian friend. Second, if and when the police make contact with you, you need to let them know you're more than willing to cooperate but only with your attorney present. By the way, those words will have no bearing on your guilt of innocence. Say nothing to the police, not even have a nice day. No arrest warrant has been issued yet but if one eventually is, I'll be the first to know. Don't discuss this conversation with Ms. Grande because its possible she might be called to testify at some point so the less she knows the better."

"How long do you think I might have before the police want to see me?"

"First, they won't do anything without informing me so if that hour or day comes we'll meet here in my office and I'll prepare you. I'll drive you to the station; no handcuffs, no news people, clean and simple. It could be hours or days or even weeks from now, or it might not happen for six months. One thing I've learned in this business is justice moves very slowly. Keep yourself busy and one more bit of advice. Stick around Boston and no trips to New Hampshire to investigate on your own. Assume someone's keeping an eye on you so try not do something that would jeopardize your position."

I left the Gould Building so disconcerted I was nearly hit by a taxi. The driver slammed on the brakes screaming was I blind? At that moment the man's words actually brought me a bit closer to understanding what Sucre felt and heard on the streets. The familiar friendly streets of Beacon Hill could often be dangerous.

The idea that a real killer was out there was something I truly hadn't dwelled on a lot, that was until the meeting with my attorney. I wondered if my life was in danger or worse, what about Sucre? Emil made hundreds of enemies in his lifetime so the big question was, which of them wanted him dead? What if Emil was killed because of something he was working on? I now owned those papers and if there was something potentially explosive in them, were I and Sucre now in someone's crosshairs?

Without direction I strolled around Beacon Hill, stopping at a few old Boston bookstores, places I'd always considered a refuge when life became difficult or too overwhelming. The sign on my favorite shop proudly proclaimed it had been in business since 1849 and entering, the first thing I became aware of was the smell of the old worn wood flooring and book shelving, weathered by more then a century and a half of wood fired stoves. I'd whacked my head on low beams more times then I could ever remember and did it again before my eyes got used to the darkness. As always, I felt insulated from all the troubles in the world among the great books, a healthy dose of tranquility. I tried not to think about Gould's words as I examined various titles but simply couldn't put his words out of my mind. I wasn't looking for a special book, just seeking a sense of peace to give me the strength to walk home. A few minutes later I became light headed and ran out.

Wandering past the Gould Building I paused to peek into the Revolutionary War cemetery. Staring up toward the sixth floor of the Gould Building I saw Attorney Gould staring down at me.

Questions swirled through my head, none with answers, each adding a feeling of hopelessness and despair. Nothing made any sense. Who would want to kill Emil and for what reason? Had he discovered something toxic or had he uncovered some great injustice, causing someone to silence him? Had he stirred something up and if he had, what was it? If there was something in Emil's papers directly tied to his death could the owner of those papers now become the next victim? Was there something hidden deep inside those papers possibly known only to Emil and his assassin? I knew I'd have to go through every article and paper extremely carefully hoping to find clues.

Would I have enough time to find answers before the police came calling? Could I possibly find something in those papers before someone came after me or Sucre?

I walked into the Puritan Book Shop on Boylston Street, a fairy-tale place I'd spend many rainy afternoons reading. It had a musty smell of ancient books, treasures locked behind glass doors due to their age. The prices were quite steep although I was still tempted enough to purchase one or two over the years. Several volumes dated back to Revolutionary War times, a few containing bold signatures by Adams, Revere, Paine, Franklin, Washington and others. The owner recognized me, asking if I was looking for something in particular. Actually I was but it was a long shot.

Had she ever heard the name Emil Breck I asked? She shook her head

Emil's List

no, asking who he was. I replied he was a very prominent journalist who'd recently passed away.

"If you're interested in journalists I do have a first edition in the back room signed by Ernie Pyle of World War Two fame. I've also got one or two news dispatches signed by Ernest Hemingway reporting from Europe. They're quite valuable you know because of the signatures so I keep them locked away. If you're interested in reporters I also own several original documents signed by John Peter Zenger, Joseph Pulitzer and a very rare first edition signed by Benjamin Franklin. If you'd like I can show you those books."

I thanked her saying I wasn't interested right now nor could I really afford them, but asked if I could see the Franklin book out of curiosity.

It took several minutes to open a rustic safe but it was worth the wait, told the book could be mine for a mere $125,000. The look on my face told her my answer.

I didn't want to go back to my place just yet, especially since Sucre was working at the Harvard library. I hated the thought of wasting the day though and wasn't sure I wanted to be alone. I took the metro to Cambridge to walk around a place I'd not seen in a very long time.

Walking away from the underground subway I realized the village of Cambridge and the Harvard University campus had not changed over the years. It felt as if I were a million miles from the hustle and bustle of Boston and my problems there, although the city was just a few miles away across the murky Charles River. Cambridge still oozed quaintness and stately elegance, a community where politicians, businessmen, doctors, writers and poets studied and lived. Emil taught at the University some years ago and that gave me an idea. Did anyone at the university still remember him?

I asked at the admissions office if it were possible to talk to someone who might have known professor Emil Breck. The woman suggested I follow the walkway across the campus to the office of Silas L. Evans, dean of the school of arts and sciences.

"Dr. Evans has been at Harvard for more then fifty years and he probably knew everyone."

Dean Evans was in his office, motioning me to come in after watching me standing outside his door for several minutes. His full head of white unruly hair reminded me of photos I'd seen of the poets who'd once called

Bruce Weiss

Cambridge home. He seemed genuinely pleased someone came by, asking what he could do for me. I told him I had a friend and colleague who'd once taught at the University by the name of Emil Breck.

"I'm a writer beginning work on a biography of Emil Breck and I was hoping you might have known him. If you did I'd very much like to ask you a few questions if you have the time. He'd written many thousands of news articles over the course of his journalistic career and not long ago I began working with him organizing his memoir. Sadly, he passed away recently, regretfully before we got very far into the work. These days I now spend my time putting his notes and letters in order to write his biography."

The professor nodded but said nothing.

"Emil Breck gained fame as an exceptional war reporter in the late 1930's, posting news articles and letters during the Spanish Civil War. His career blossomed from there. Later in life he lectured at this university about the dramatic events he experienced during in his lifetime."

Dean Evans nodded but still said nothing.

"I have all his original documents as well as hundreds maybe thousands of news articles he'd written during his fifty year reporting career. I have a roomful of cartons filled with his notes, most first hand accounts of some of the most important events taking place over the last fifty years. My partner and I are now going through his papers and at this point we've discovered some very worthy of note articles especially the ones describing his appearance before the House Un-American Activity Committee in the early 50's. I'm not sure if you knew but Emil Breck was once called before that committee. Would you have known him? I'm not certain when he retired from the university."

"You say he retired but that's not why he left. Did you know he was forced to resign?"

The professor leaned back in his oversized chair, closing his eyes, letting out s slow pronounced chuckle. Jumping from his seat like a surprised cat he dashed to his window, motioning me to stand next to him.

"Lovely view of the old campus, don't you think?"

I said yes it was.

Emil Breck, he said several times, waving to a few students walking on the campus paths.

"I haven't heard his name in quite a while but yes, I do remember him and quite clearly. You never forget someone like him. You see that large Elm tree over there? That's where you would always find him holding classes even in the dead of winter. He hated teaching indoors.

"Not only did I know him but I admired him and his work very much" he added. "I did know about his Spanish Civil war reporting days and his appearance before the HUAC and was familiar with many of his writing. I don't think I've heard his name mentioned in years. You say he passed on?"

I nodded.

"I'm very sorry to hear that but before we continue our conversation I have a question for you. You're not with any government agency are you?"

I definitely was not I replied.

"Let me see what might interest someone writing about Professor Breck. Correct me if I'm wrong but I believe he was a naturalized American, born in Romania or Hungary."

Romania I interjected.

"I think I actually might have been the person who hired him but I'm not certain. When he first began teaching here I mentored him and attended some of his first lectures. It doesn't happen often but I was immediately impressed by his knowledge and his manner of speaking. I believe during that first visit to his classroom he was recounting his days in Spain to his foreign affairs class. Apart from being a damn good professor, he was particularly devoted to social issues and causes. Find a worthwhile cause and fight for it as if your life depended upon it he told his students. Maybe you'd better sit down because if you've got the time, I've got a few stories I can relate, that is if you're interested."

The dean had my full attention.

"What I remember most about him wasn't what he said, but what the Harvard University students said about him. He was constantly challenging students to go out and make their own history, saying with much conviction it was the right thing to do to; being at odds with those in power when you found something wrong or immoral.

"I believe he referred to himself unabashedly as a socialist but I always thought more of an anarchist actually. He was heavily involved in civil rights issues and often taught tactics to certain chosen students to prepare them for the first Freedom Rides into the segregated south.

"He supported labor movements and of course his anti-Viet Nam War

Bruce Weiss

efforts were well known. Emil was a full professor of history here for many years, seemingly always finding the time for the underdog. He might have a class of fifteen or so students but another twenty or thirty would always show up just to hear his lecture.

"I had the pleasure of sitting in one of many of his classes over the years which I enjoyed immensely. By the way you are correct. He did appear before HUAC as you said but I'll bet you didn't know he was once considered public enemy number one by J. Edgar Hoover and the FBI."

I did not know that but wasn't surprised.

"He didn't talk very much about his personal life but he'd chew your ear off about current issues. Ask him what was on his mind and you'd better be prepared to spend a few hours listening. Professor Breck and I met over dinner a few time and when he had more then one glass of wine, we'd commiserate on the current state of affairs until the place closed. Did you know in the early 1950's he was once sent off to prison?"

I nodded.

"You know he never had his day in court and his career like so many others was nearly ruined by those damn committee hearings; Judge, jury, and executioner during a very frightening time in America. Many of Professor Breck's op-ed pieces written for the Harvard paper showed great disdain for the committee but sadly, many people thought it was nothing more then sour grapes.

"I called him my friend but in truth, I believed he didn't have many friends here at the University, preferring to keep to himself. If you can listen to an old windbag a little longer there is one incident that touched me deeply. Would you like to hear it?"

I told him I certainly would.

"You've probably heard of the SDS, the Students for a Democratic Society."

I replied I knew the organization and its role in the turbulent sixties.

"You're correct. The group was very active in the sixties and early seventies on this campus, avowed enemies of the establishment and in particular the terrible mess in Vietnam.

"SDS began on the west coast as a student activist movement, gradually reaching the eastern schools and eventually Harvard. I think the press referred to the awakening here as the emergence of a new ultra left.

Emil's List

"The Harvard newspaper in those days wasn't a fan of SDS or their philosophy, vilifying the group in editorials and calling them thugs and degenerates. The group on campus made a lot of noise, advocating direct action against what they saw as injustices in this country, including Harvard's neutral stance on the war. The group wanted all Harvard students to re-examine their feelings about Viet Nam and to speak out, and they weren't afraid to turn to violence to get their points made.

"I believe it was the fall of 1967 when a number of university students attempted to shut the campus down. The SDS demanded all military on campus including ROTC be tossed out unconditionally.

"The leaders of the campus SDS approached Professor Breck, knowing he was sympathetic to many of their causes. The group sought his support, guidance and advice, many students aware of his earlier battles with HUAC. In late 1967 he was somehow able to get hold of a secret memo sent from the board of trustees to the University president. The gist of the note was to find ways to dismantle SDS and expel their leaders. The president of the University became outraged, not to mention greatly embarrassed when Breck published the memo in the University newspaper. His writing demonstrated among other things the secret links between Harvard and government institutions supporting the United States involvement in Viet Nam.

"The group held candlelit protests just outside where that elm tree still stands, and Emil Breck was with them every night for the silent protests and some not so silent. Looking out this very window, I had a front row seat as you can imagine.

"The protests turned a bit more violent each day until one evening, students began to break into and occupy many of the university's administration buildings, essentially shutting down key parts of the University. Emil wouldn't stand for that, believing in non violence so he turned his back on the group until they came to their senses. The shutdown went on for days, each new day attracting more sympathizers and unfortunately, more outsiders. Governor Baldwin finally called in the National Guard when the situation began to unravel."

I'd nearly forgotten Baldwin was governor at the time.

"Professor Breck was harshly criticized for publishing stolen secret documents showing evidence of collusion between Harvard and military

Bruce Weiss

think tanks in Washington. The University's response was to shut down the paper. The demonstrations continued getting a little more violent each day.

"The police were finally called and after ugly street battles with hoses, tear gas and dogs and horses, the buildings were retaken and the protestors arrested. An armed presence on campus stopped the nightly marches so in response, a few SDS members broke into the president's office, barricading themselves inside.

"Professor Breck was very active in the student causes but shied away from the use of violence to achieve aims. He met with SDS leaders discussing ways to force the university to use it's influence with the government to pull troops out of Viet Nam. He even met with the university trustees. hoping they could resolve the crisis. One major sticking point however was the Professor's demand for amnesty for those arrested. You might recall seeing the cover of Look Magazine back then, showing one of the protest leaders sitting behind the University president's desk, smoking one of his cigars.

"Professor Breck and the students put together a non-negotiable list of demands that once met, would make them give up their protest. Unbeknownst to Breck, some of the protestors kidnapped an acting dean and held him hostage. The University and the police said the line in the sand had been crossed and there was to be no more appeasement, no more negotiations. The school president stated he had no intention of meeting any demands as long as the assistant dean was detained, He also added he would not meet any demand until all the protestors left the buildings and the marches stopped.

"Everything was moving very quickly as the university fell into total anarchism. Some faculty members spoke out against the chaos, pushing for a relaxation of tensions and hoping to find a civil way to deal with the crisis. More then half the university students had sympathy for the SDS actions, half were very against. The protestors remained adamant about their positions but after nine days an agreement was hammered out. Anyone occupying the buildings who wanted to leave could do so without punishment. Only a few left though so in response the University and the police blockaded the buildings so no more food could be brought to the protestors, also shutting off the electricity.

"Three days after the blockade went into affect the protestors

Emil's List

surrendered. Hearings were held the following weeks with expulsion orders given to the leaders. After days of hearings Professor Breck was cleared by the university of any wrongdoing but in return, he would be forced to retire from the University.

"I believe he moved to Washington after that to work with an organization planning a march on Washington demanding an end to the war. That was the last time I saw Professor Breck until the day he was re-hired as a part time lecturer some years after his forced retirement. He lectured about the turbulent years of the late sixties and early seventies, mostly personal stories. You did say you were writing his biography?

I said I'd just begun the preliminary work and hoped it would highlight the career of a most remarkable man.

We spoke for another half hour, mostly stories about my own writings and the confusing and confounding 1960's. I thanked him for his time and when I got up to leave he asked if I knew Emil was also an avid collector of rare books.

I told him there were one hundred and sixty books in his collection, all first editions, many signed by their authors. I then said they shared a common theme; all the books he'd purchased over his lifetime were once considered extremely controversial when first published."

The Professor laughed saying of course, knowing Emil, everything in his life was controversial.

"He left them to a young woman he'd befriended," I said.

CHAPTER 16

When Sucre arrived the next morning I was very thankful she couldn't see my face. I hadn't slept more then an hour, my head pounding all night obsessing over Attorney Steven Gould's fear-provoking news. To my surprise the minute Sucre walked in she knew I was having a difficult morning. Her extraordinary senses beyond sight never ceased to amaze me but I did my best to assure her I was fine.

Part of me wanted to relate the conversation I'd had with Attorney Gould but I needed to protect her innocence, knowing Gould I could possibly put Sucre in an awkward position, especially if the police decided to interrogate her. She could be forced to say things that could eventually pound nails into my coffin I suspected.

I hated the feeling of being fragile and worse, vulnerable as I tried to hold my feelings inside. On a certain level though I knew her keen insights could read the thoughts in my head.

I talked about the meeting with Professor Evans and his remarkable tale of what took place some years ago at Harvard just outside his window.

"Charlie, months before we met I walked into Emil's classroom because I wanted to hear one of his lectures. Everyone at the university talked about how incredible he was, wishing they'd gotten into his class. Listening to his students from the back of the room I realized they truly loved him, whispering much praise. Much later I also happened to attended Emil's very last college lecture and because of my blindness, I heard things others most likely did not.

"His final lecture was about Martin Luther King and the highlight of the class was his recitation of the I have a Dream speech from memory, admitting later he'd been one of the half million in Washington that day.

When Emil walked into the cafeteria after class the students and teachers gave him a standing ovation. He noticed me and stopped at my table, saying with mixed emotions he'd just put his resignation letter on the dean's desk. Emil then said something I've never forgotten. If you always speak the truth, you will make the world a better place.

"A week later at work I'd heard he was in the library so I went to find him. I was a bit nervous but I wanted to know what he was going to do next. I can still remember his exact words.

He said it was the right time to use the remaining years of his life to organize a life time of personal papers, no easy task in order to write his memoir. Emil said it would take most of his remaining years and when it was done, he hoped it would bring new light to the turbulence and uncertainty of the 30's, 40's, 50's and 60's. He insisted there were many good stories to tell and many lessons to be learned so history didn't repeat itself. I was somewhat taken aback when he said it would not to be published until after his death."

That should have been many years from now I added ruefully.

"Emil told me the job was too big for one person and one day he'd find someone completely objective, someone he could work with. On the days you were working with him I was spending long hours at the Harvard library so our paths never crossed while you worked there. One day he stopped by the library to tell me he'd found the right person and the only reason I remembered who it was because the name was Charles Darwin. Of course I thought of the famous Charles Darwin."

Reluctantly it was time to get back to work.

"I know you'd really enjoyed the letters Emil wrote to Clarissa" I said. And with some extraordinary luck I actually found a few more stashed under a pile of loose articles. Why don't we start there. You know, I still wish we knew Clarissa's last name because if she were still alive, she'd have an amazing tale to tell about Emil. This first letter I'm going to read discusses some of his political views, hardly a love letter."

I started to read aloud but curiously found it difficult to concentrate, losing my place several times. Weighing heavily on my mind was the discussion with Attorney Gould, my mind flooded with frightening extraneous thoughts. Putting the letter down in mid-sentence I decided

Bruce Weiss

to go against Gould's advice to tell Sucre what the police suspected and what I supposed I was up against. I purposely did not use the word we.

I repeated the conversation I'd had with Attorney Gould practically word for word, trying my best to make it sound non-threatening. When I saw the worry look on her face I said don't feel bad because Mr. Gould was on top of things and he wasn't going to let me down. Once those words were out I felt a bit less scattered.

"I wanted to tell you about this the moment you walked in this morning but I couldn't get the words out. Seriously, Mr. Gould didn't want me to tell you anything about the police work because if you spoke with them, you might be forced to divulge incriminating information."

Sucre took the news rather stoically, reminding me we were a team and teammates never kept things from each other.

"Charlie, I have a lot of faith in the police in your country and your American legal system. We truly feared the police and the judges in Peru for very good reasons. From what you've told me about Attorney Gould, I think we can trust him and we're very lucky to have him. Try not to let it impede the good work we're doing here because it's really all about Emil."

I didn't want to beat myself up any longer but was well aware I could be arrested at anytime. The best cure for my worries I suspected was to pick up Clarissa's letter again and make it my sole focus.

"From the opening paragraph Emil writes about joining a secret organization but sadly he doesn't explain what it was. Here we go Sucre so as usual, fasten your seatbelt."

'Dear Clarissa, 1939 is almost over and I fear dire things will happen not only in Spain but all across Europe in the new year. I'm not a seer but if you could see what I've been observing in Spain, you'd have that same sense. The world must absolutely crush Fascism before another day passes and the free world needs to deal with this. America has done nothing to date to fight this growing menace, sitting on the sidelines while Fascism spreads like wild fire without resistance across Europe. Regretfully, the politicians in Washington feel it's not an American problem and Europe will have to come to grips with it. I believe America must respond before all of Europe and eventually Asia fall under Fascist regimes. The present foreign policy in America is wrong and everyone needs to stand up and

Emil's List

say it must be changed. Democratic Socialism is the only answer for a peaceful Europe but that might be a moot point now, depending on what Mr. Hitler does in the coming months. Sorry this letter is short and heavy but I wanted you to know what I've been thinking."

CHAPTER 17

Sucre brought a backpack full of Emil's books to my place the next morning adding to the ones already in my place. It would take time to read each book but I looked forward to the noon hour, especially the books I'd never had the time to read.

Extending lunch hour to two hours enabled us to finish James Baldwin, a captivating story taking our minds off the work. Next up was 1984 by George Orwell, discovering he was one of Emil's favorite authors. Like the other books we'd gone through he'd left his personal notes behind, referring to 1984 as one of the most extraordinary books ever written at the perfect time. From the very first page it was obvious his notes were going to be insightful.

'I had an unexpected meeting with George Orwell, recognizing him immediately sitting alone in a small dark restaurant. I introduced himself and said I'd traveled to Spain to report on the war. He said he had also traveled there but not as a writer or a reporter like me, but as a fighter.'

'He claimed to have read all my reports from Spain, adding serving with the Republican army fighting Franco was one his finest moments.

'Mr. Orwell told me he was shot by a sniper as I had, suffering a terrible wound to his throat. Like me he'd also feared he'd die or if he survived, be unable to ever talk again. He eventually recovered his voice and was fortunately able to live a normal life. The wound eventually healed and he was able to talk, although in a quieter and more compelling lilt.

'During Orwell's recovery he and his wife moved to Morocco for a half year. It was there away from Spain he wrote the book Coming up for Air, his last novel before World War Two.'

I told Sucre what I knew about the novel, stressing it was a pessimistic

Emil's List

view of Europe's future not because of war, but because of creeping Fascism. I then proceeded to read more of Emil's notes about 1984.

'George Orwell argued industrialism and capitalism were failed systems, sadly believing old England was dead. When 1984 was written it became the most censored novel ever penned and it will probably hold that distinction forever. Days after it's publication in the mid fifties it was unceremoniously banned from school libraries, considered far too controversial and convoluted to be read. With the pervading fear of a nuclear war with the Soviets on everyone's mind, it was considered fodder for the Communists.

'There was much criticisms of Orwell's work including his seemingly obsession with sex. Orwell always maintained he was not a Communist and that his books and other writings were nothing more then a study of Communism, showing it in an unfavorable light. The critics and the censors disagreed. I could relate fully to him.'

I started to read chapter one and an hour later reluctantly putting Orwell's 1984 aside to return to Emil's papers.

I'd found another fourteen letters written from Spain with other references to Orwell, making me ask Sucre if any of Orwell's books were put into Braille at the Harvard library. Her reply was she didn't think so. I told her she should bring the book to the library one day and find out if it might be translated into Braille because it was an important work. Our productive day of work sadly came to a rather abrupt end with a rather loud knock at my door. No one ever comes to my door I whispered uneasily to Sucre.

When I asked who it was the response was another menacing knock. Cautiously opening the door I saw a man and a woman, ID tags on their jackets identifying them as Detective Dreselly and Detective First Class Lee of the Boston Police Department. In a very polite manner Detective Dreselly said they'd like to come in to ask a few questions. Attorney Gould's words flashed through my head like a bright neon light, the admonishment to say absolutely nothing. I knew that was the right thing to do, saying somewhat hesitatingly I would feel better if my attorney were present. Would that possibly tell them I'm guilty I wondered. What would happen if I said no?

Neither officer spoke, boring a hole in me with their eyes. Detective

Dreselly spoke up with a kindly voice, saying I could be a great help to the police in their ongoing investigation into Emil Breck's death. Detective Lee added I really didn't need a lawyer because it would just be a friendly chat.

"Besides" Detective Dreselly interjected, "You might actually help us find his killer."

Those words made me consider the possibility they somehow believed I wasn't the murderer. I finally relented when Detective Lee used the word please.

Cautioning myself to be very careful about what I might say and knowing too well it was probably the wrong thing to do, I managed to say the word okay.

"How did I know Emil Breck" was the very first question, a soft ball lowering my anxiety level a notch.

Several more questions also felt rather benign and answered freely without hesitation. The situation became a little dicey though when Detective Lee asked if Emil had any enemies. The obvious answer was Emil made many enemies during his lifetime because of his writings, but I really didn't want to go there. I replied I simply had no way of knowing.

"When did you see him last?"

Before I could answer Officer Dreselly said I should think very carefully about my answer. After the benign questions new ones came in rapid fire giving me less time to think of an appropriate response. It was obvious I didn't answer fast because they crossed their arms showing impatience.

"Did Mr. Breck ever talk about suicide? Who was he in contact with regularly? Was Emil Breck of sound mind? Had I ever overhear a phone conversation upsetting him?"

To each question I said I had no way of knowing.

"In the days leading up to his death, did Mr. Breck seem more nervous or more upset then usual? Did he mention he was having any physical problems? Did he own any pets?"

"Pets." I shouted, caught off guard. "No, Emil had no time for pets"

"Was he strapped for cash? Did he mention any medications he might have been taking? Had he ever talked about dying? Had he mentioned the name of someone who might be threatening him and were you aware of any threats against him."

Emil's List

Even if I knew the answers I had no time to respond before another question was fired, the questions running on endlessly, each time a bit more personal and seemingly more threatening.

"Did you harbor any ill feelings toward Mr. Breck? Were you jealous of his fame and success?"

The last two questions raised my ire and if the detectives were trying to get a reaction from me, they'd sadly succeeded while I clenched my teeth.

"Did you," followed by a long silence, "have anything to do with Emil Breck's death?"

The question felt like a punch in my gut. Detective Lee hardly blinked, staring at me, making me very nervous. I wondered if the detective was more interested in my reaction or my answer.

"No I did not," said barely above a whisper, praying the detectives would finally stop and go away. Surprisingly, Detective Dreselly closed his notebook thanking me for my time. It was then I realized there were dark sweat stains on my shirt. Detective Lee said she had one more little question. Are you familiar with a substance known as strychnine?

My nerves were nearing the breaking point and it took all my strength to shake my head, saying no.

Detective Lee turned toward Sucre sitting on my sofa.

"Sucre Grande I believe?"

When Sucre began to respond I interrupted, my exasperation getting the best of me. Trying to sound unruffled I explained we were working together on Emil Breck's papers, adding Miss Grande could add nothing to their investigation. The look on Detective Lee's face told me the kid gloves were off.

Ignoring my attempts to save Sucre from being questioned, Detective Lee moved so close to Sucre I thought she might actually fall on top of her.

"Miss Grande, how did you come to know Mr. Breck?" When I started to protest Detective Lee raised her voice startling me.

"We're not talking to you right now so keep your mouth shut." If she'd pulled out her gun I would not have been surprised.

Why hadn't I simply said we'd only talk about Emil's death with our attorney present and end the inquisition? Sucre's first words were noticeably shaky when she spoke. I tried one last time to intervene, arguing it was alright to ask me questions but to leave Sucre alone.

Bruce Weiss

"Mr. Darwin, if you're the talkative one, why don't you describe Miss Grande's relationship with the deceased? We know the woman is blind but I don't believe she's deaf."

When I didn't answer Detective Dreselly moved in front of Sucre so I could not see her.

"Miss Grande are you totally blind or can you see shapes," Detective Lee shouted?

I begged this time, saying in exasperation, please leave her alone.

"Alright then Mr. Darwin, I've got one last question for you, the tone suggesting it was going to be accompanied with a warning. Mr. Darwin have you visited any veterinarian offices lately?"

I said I would answer no more questions and anything else that needed to be said would have to wait for my lawyer to be present.

"We're not here to incriminate you or Ms. Grande," Detective Lee said in a conciliatory tone. "This is just part of a standard investigation so there's really no reason to get a lawyer involved. You do know Mr. Darwin that lawyers are only interested in one thing, and that's making big money off your misery. You do want us to find the person who killed your friend, don't you?"

I was through talking, hoping I'd simply shut up.

"Let me ask you this" Detective Lee said, moving closer to me. "In the past three months have you ever visited a veterinary office purchasing any medications?"

I finally kept my big mouth shut, overcome with such anger I was afraid I would do or say something regrettable. Why had I not taken Attorney Gould's simple precious advice?

"With all due respect detectives, I have nothing more to say. We have to get back to our work so would you kindly leave?"

Both detectives smiled.

"Of course" said Detective Dreslly "We'll talk again but let me leave one thought with you."

Detective Lee removed a clear plastic envelope from her inside pocket, holding it inches from my face. There was no mistaking what it was. It was a receipt of a credit card transaction with my account number and signature. I knew it was not mine but it seemed pointless to say anything

Emil's List

more without Attorney Gould present. My mouth was so dry I couldn't have uttered a word even if I'd tried.

"We'll continue this conversation at a later date," Detective Lee announced. We'll definitely be in touch."

When the detectives finally left my body ached so badly I needed to lean against the door frame for support. In the hallway outside my door I heard the detectives laughing. I didn't know whether to cry or open the door and scream fuck you.

My name was definitely on the credit card receipt so I could hardly blame the detectives for wanting to question me, but why hadn't they arrested me I wondered? When I heard the front door of the apartment slam shut I told Sucre we ought to go out the back door and get some needed fresh air.

We walked the Boston streets in silence, thoughts about what had just taken place cruelly running through my mind. There was not a doubt in my mind the police suspected no one but me, ruing it was just a matter of time before I was charged. As to Sucre, I promised myself I'd do whatever was necessary to keep her out of the mess.

There was really only one question I'd truly wanted to ask the detectives but the thought of asking scared the hell out of me. Had the detectives uncovered a motive?

Strolling the Boston streets did nothing to calm my nerves, night noises making me extremely jumpy. Why hadn't the detectives arrested me? Was someone else out there in the dark shadows watching us besides the police?

CHAPTER 18

I heard a loud crash in the middle of the night causing my heart to pound uncontrollably. A car crash possibly? Half awake I heard the loud noise again eventually realizing it was the sound of someone banging quite loudly on my door. Not quite fully awake I thought it most likely the detectives with an arrest warrant. Without bothering to ask I opened the door and surprisingly there stood Sucre. I'd somehow slept until ten, far past our normal working hours and the door had been securely latched so Sucre's key would not open it.

I wasn't sure who was more crazed at that moment until she threw her arms around me saying she'd become terribly disturbed when she couldn't get into my place. It took many more moments to clear the fog and the confusion from my head. What time was it I asked? Her response took away much of my craziness, telling me the church bells tolled ten times a moment ago.

"What's in the bag you're carrying," I asked?

"I stopped at a liquor store on the way over here to buy a few ingredients to mix later, something we can drink after the work day is over. I'm going to make something called a Pisco Sour, the world famous Peruvian national drink. The mixed drink has wonderful medicinal powers curing almost everything from a broken heart to bad dreams."

Over coffee I realized Sucre was acting unusually quiet and when she was like that, I knew something bothered her.

After a very long awkward silence I asked if there was something troubling her. Without hesitating Sucre described something that happened after I dropped her off at the front of her building the previous evening. From the sounds of her wavering voice I knew it was not going to be good.

Emil's List

"First, forgive me for not calling you last night but to be honest, I wasn't sure you could handle much more after the police incident at your place. About twenty minutes after I walked in I heard a knock at my door. I wouldn't open it of course but I did ask who it was, suspecting the answer would be the detectives and I was right.

"It's the police was the reply. It's detective Lee. You know I never forget a voice after I've heard it once so it only took me a few seconds to know it was not Detective Lee.

"I ran to the phone and dialed 911 but just before the call was answered, I heard footsteps running down the hall and then down the staircase. I have no idea who it was or ever if it was a police officer but the woman on the phone cautioned me. Don't open the door and just sit tight. Ten minutes later a police woman arrived asking permission to check about my place. I told her what occurred trying to remain calm as she announced no officer from the Boston police department had been to my place. The next moment I was getting the blind test."

"What's the blind test?"

"When you tell someone you're blind they'll often wave their hand before your eyes to see if you react. Don't ask me why people to that because it's terribly offensive. When I walked her to the front door to leave we bumped into Estaban, my apartment super. He's an extremely caring man and I dearly trust him. I heard tiny sounds realizing it was the officer was removing her weapon from the holster. It dawned on me she might have thought this was the man who'd had pretended to be a police officer. I shouted Estaban was not the one who'd knocked because I knew his Spanish accent. The officer asked for identification and after handing it back, she said goodbye and walked away.

"I told Estaban what happened and he told me to wait in his apartment while he gave the building a good search for any strangers. The man who'd come to my door was long gone. That's the end of my story. Poor Estaban seemed more upset than I was especially because he had a gun pointed toward him. He insisted he'd sit outside his apartment near the entrance to make sure I was safe. Despite my objection he walked me to your place this morning. I don't believer either of us slept a wink."

The last thing either of us needed was another twist to what was happening in our lives. Finishing our morning coffees I said I needed to call Attorney Gould right away, adding I should see him immediately.

It was near eleven but regretfully I was told Attorney Gould had not come to the office yet. I left a message saying it was somewhat urgent and please have him call me when he got in.

Too agitated to start the day's work I decided to hold off until Gould called. While waiting I thought about what I could do to keep Sucre safe in case things spiraled totally out of control. My head told me she needed to move into my place for a while so I could keep an eye on her. Surprisingly, she listened patiently to my idea without interruption. She cherished her independence above anything else so I knew all too well the answer would most likely be no.

Sucre put her ear buds in to listen to her Peruvian music, ignoring me while I tried to put everything out of my mind so we could return to Emil's papers. An hour later Sucre still had not responded to the suggestion she move into my place so I thought it best not to push the issue.

By noon with no call back, I suggested instead of doing any work why not read a few more chapters of 1984. The story was difficult to follow and reading a difficult book was probably not the best read at the moment. My thoughts were not far from the police showing up at my place and Sucre's mystery man. I was drowning myself in worries and doubts while the walls of my place closed in.

The daily grind of going through the seemingly endless cartons became too methodical and with hundreds of files yet untouched, the work was all consuming. Still, I tried to convince myself we'd accomplished more than I thought we would.

Surprisingly I'd forgotten about Attorney Gould who still hadn't returned my call. I was near certain we were not going to hear from him so I announced the work day was done, time for Sucre to prepare the special drinks she'd planned.

Sucre closed the door to my kitchen and began to mix the ingredients. Ten minutes later I tasted my first Pisco Sour, one of those tender moments reminding myself we needed to take more time out for ourselves. After the first one all seemed right in the world.

At ease and with the day's lack of work behind us, I thought it might be a good time to push the request for Sucre to stay at my place, emphasizing

Emil's List

of course it was just temporary. Not to my surprise I was met with what I'd expected; stubborn resistance. I truly believed she could be as stubborn as mule at times so I backed off a bit, sweetening the deal saying she could have my bedroom as I'd gladly take the comfortable living room couch. From the look on her face I knew too well she was going to resist, her usual refrain she was a big girl and could take care of herself.

There was nothing more I could say because I didn't want to frighten or upset her, but a moment later she said something that relieved some of my fears. She agreed to a temporary move and although she could not see the relief on my face, I know she sensed it. One less thing to worry about I thought.

Sucre gathered things at her place and returned. I pulled the living room sofa closer to the apartment front door so I could hear any sounds while she unpacked. Moving furniture around was a problem for Sucre so I had to describe the location of new obstacles. It had been a stressful late morning and afternoon and evening but grudgingly, I realized that feeling would be the norm for a while. Get used to it Charlie.

CHAPTER 19

I called Attorney Gould the next morning because I'd never received a call back, only to be disappointed again with the words he was not in his office. I said it wasn't an emergency but needed to talk with the attorney about my case. The secretary said call back later and hung up. I smashed the phone down, something I quickly regretted because it frightened Sucre.

The mysterious visitor to Sucre's place reinforced the feeling we were most likely in someone's cross hairs, most likely because I was in possession of Emil's papers. As unruffled as I tried to sound, Sucre's perceptive senses felt my trepidation. Gould was on my mind and I could not turn the angst off. Gould was no longer the life raft but suddenly a painful thorn in my side. I told Sucre I was going to taxi to his office and sit in his waiting room until he showed up.

Mr. Gould's secretary scowled when I said I didn't have an appointment, waving me away, saying it would do no good to wait. I refused to leave the office so she simply acted as if I weren't there. The phone rang several times and after one of the calls, she motioned me to come to her desk. Attorney Gould was taking a couple of weeks off on a well deserved fishing expedition in Nova Scotia I was informed

When I turned to leave she said she had an envelope for me, left by Attorney Gould. The hastily looking scrawled note said he'd turned my case over to a trusted member of the firm by the name of Sanford Roberts. I hated the though of starting all over again but there was little choice because any minute the situation could literally explode. I supposed if I didn't see Roberts, I might find myself going it alone.

I felt appallingly disappointed, disillusioned with lawyers once again.

Emil's List

I'd been disappointed many times but this time it felt even worse. The hopeless look on my face was not lost on the secretary

"Why don't you see Mr. Roberts because from what I understand he's a very fine counselor, so why don't you let me call his office and see if you two can't meet right now. I'm sure he's familiar with your case and I know he can help."

I honestly didn't know if I had the energy or even the desire to rehash a case seemingly spinning more and more out of control, but I couldn't live with the craziness any longer. I called Sucre saying I'd be back in an hour.

Sanford Roberts was a giant of a man, towering over me but it wasn't his height striking me as much as the fact that he looked like a young school boy not old enough to shave. He actually looked as if he'd just graduated from high school, let alone law school. My immediate thought was he looked far too young to be experienced with the law yet despite my doubts, I reluctantly sat down on a hard chair in his small windowless office on the third floor. I held little hope our meeting would be productive.

While he shuffled papers I asked if he was familiar with my case but the blank look on Robert's face revealed nothing.

With obvious urgency in my voice I raced through the tale of Emil's untimely death and my eventual meeting with Attorney Gould as well as the contents of the will. I also said I was most likely considered the number one suspect in a murder I didn't commit. The more I rambled on, the more I had the sinking feeling there was nothing he could do to help me. I kept many things to myself including Sucre's unknown visitor but did make reference to the reality there was a murderer lurking somewhere out there. When I was through talking I forlornly believed Robert's understood nothing I'd said so his first words surprised me. He talked about my case and I realized he was familiar with it. He seemed genuinely supportive and empathetic, assuring me Attorney Gould would not have passed the case along he if had any doubts about his ability.

"I've read your case file and I've seen a copy of the will. Since you spoke last with Mr. Gould there are a few new developments to report. A little over an hour ago I was actually on the phone with Assistant DA DelVechio and happy to report you're not going to be indicted now or in the foreseeable future. Mr. Breck's death is still an ongoing murder investigation which tells me the police believe there are other suspects.

Bruce Weiss

The detectives who came to your place will certainly need to speak with you again but as Mr. Gould made it clear, say nothing unless he or are there. I don't know if you said anything damaging but if you did, I think we can fix it."

The words put me a bit more at ease and the anger began to ebb. I impressed upon him there was a very good possibility someone connected to the murder was capable of doing Sucre and I the same harm that befell Emil. It was not a feeling I maintained, but the actuality Emil might have been killed because of something he'd been working on. I said I'd come to believe there is something buried in his extensive notes that could have led to his death but I hadn't found it yet.

The words I didn't have to worry about the police for a while was really no great consolation. Who should I be more worried about I wondered; the police who had clear evidence I'd purchased the poison or the unknown individual or individuals who murdered Emil?

"Mr. Darwin, I read the autopsy report on Emil Breck and there's no mistaking the cause of his death. The strychnine was absorbed into his body but how it got there is still the great mystery. The chemical numbers were off the chart and there was enough poison in his body to kill a hundred men. We're talking first degree murder but I want you to understand I don't have Attorney Gould's experience but I'm all you've got right now.

I asked if my partner Sucre was considered a suspect and did she need a lawyer.

"Someone ingesting that much poison most likely got it through his food, something Mr. Breck would not have smelled or tasted. The police know your partner Sucre Grande prepared most of his meals but they're giving her a free pass for now because of her blindness. As to whether she wants to speak with a lawyer, I would be happy to represent her if she does."

I asked if he'd seen the video tape from the vet's office purportedly showing someone buying the poison.

"I saw the tape and it's no help because no matter how hard the lab people worked, there was no definitive picture any court would accept as evidence."

When I arrived home Sucre was sitting in the dark, listening to the ever present news station on her old portable radio. I told her about the

Emil's List

new temporary lawyer, doing my best to paint a rosy picture saying he seemed genuinely interested in helping. I didn't tell her my gut feeling that even the best lawyer in the world might not be able to help me. There was something about Roberts but I couldn't quite put my finger on it in our short meeting.

"My only problem Sucre is his young age and probable lack of experience in murder cases."

"Did you tell him you suspected there might be something in Emil's papers worth killing over?" I nodded, forgetting I needed to be verbal.

"Are you or I going to be arrested?"

I was suddenly very sorry I'd ever asked Sucre to work with me on Emil's papers. She was a sweet innocent young woman with a horrid past and did not deserve to be involved in the chaotic situation.

"No, neither you nor I are going to be arrested."

CHAPTER 20

There were still untold numbers of Emil's papers we hadn't examined and more mind-numbing organizational work was required. At times the work wasn't foremost in my thoughts but thankfully, I was able to get lost in the remarkable tales of Emil's extraordinary life, still holding out hope that we'd find something in Emil's papers explaining the reason for his murder. It felt if we were looking for the proverbial needle in the haystack.

Sucre, usually upbeat started complaining she missed her place and wanted to go home. I sincerely believed she'd wouldn't be safe there even though I realized she probably felt like a fish out of water at my place.

"Ever since I came to this country to go to college, I've managed to take great pleasure in my time alone. Even though you've been wonderful Charlie, my blindness taught me some very important life lessons that regretfully, I've never been able to explain to a sighted person. I'd probably would have dropped out of life and become miserable until the day I died if I couldn't manage alone. I miss that unique feeling of independence and when I'm around most people I feel very self conscious. You might not understand but even when I'm around people I deeply care about, I still get that feeling. Too many colleagues where I work still go far out of their way thinking they have to watch over me. When I'm alone I depend upon myself quite well."

We passed more hours doing organizational work discovering the most extraordinary papers. When things were a bit slow, somehow we'd always manage to find a hidden nugget infusing us with fascination.

To my chagrin, I found myself becoming more unreasonable, more argumentative especially when I couldn't find something I was looking for, or forgot where I'd put something. When we finally broke for lunch I looked closely at Sucre, seeing how incredibly tired she looked, her trusty dark glasses unable to hide worry lines. I suggested we take the afternoon off, possibly going back to her place for a few hours to do our reading there. That sentiment seemed to relax us.

It was a most pleasurable walk to her place and the moment she put her key into the door, she paused to tell me how wonderful she felt being home again.

"This place is my refuge and sanctuary Charlie, a safe place for me and to be truthful, I honestly believe I'd be alright staying here alone. This is my comfort place because the outside world can be a terrible place for a blind woman at times."

When she opened the door she suddenlu jumped back, falling into my arms.

"What's wrong I shouted?"

"Can't you smell it Charlie?"

My first thought was the gas stove must have been left on but I smelled nothing.

"Charlie, someone's been inside my place because I smell stale cigarette smoke. Can't you smell it?"

In truth I could not.

"Oh God Charlie, someone's broken into my place."

The words crushed me, praying it could not be true. I said not to enter until I'd turned on her seldom used lights to look around.

The blinds and curtains were permanently drawn so it took precious moments to find the lamps. The moment I turned the first one on I nearly cried out. There was bedlam everywhere as if someone had torn the place apart. Even more distressing was the sight of Emil's books taken from the shelving and tossed haphazardly about the room. Many of the volumes were open suggesting someone had gone through the books expecting to find something.

I was so distraught what I was seeing I'd forgotten Sucre was waiting at the door. When I turned thinking of right words to say, she was standing right behind me. She couldn't see the jumble but it didn't take long for her senses to tell her something was terribly wrong.

"What's happened" she asked, her hand a death grip on my arm?"

Bruce Weiss

I was nearly too broken hearted to describe the mess but there was no sugar coating what I was seeing.

"Sucre, honey, someone broke into your place and I believe they were looking for something inside your books. They were all pulled off the shelves and now they're scattered about the floor. Don't move an inch from this spot until I can clear away some of these books. They're everywhere."

A strange thought came to mind. Was it possible there were hidden clues in the books describing what Emil might have been working on? If that were true, how and why would someone know or even suspected that? We'd gone through almost every book but the only thing we'd found were insightful personal notes; nothing suspicious or unusual. Why would someone deliberately look through every single volume while ignoring the potential value of the books? Why not steal them? Counting the volumes scattered about I doubted any had been taken. Sadly, many of the bindings and spines were torn.

"Take my hand" I whispered. "Your place resembles a mine field and I don't want you falling and getting hurt so stay with me. First, I'm going to lead you into your bedroom so you can tell me if anything was taken."

"There's a jewelry box on the chest near my bed. Can you see if its still there?"

It was and when I opened it, the mystery grew deeper. Describing the valuables inside the chest Sucre declared nothing was missing.

"Charlie, walk me around my bedroom because I need to feel everything so I might know if something was taken or moved."

The watches and jewelry in the top drawer were there, as was the Peruvian music box holding Sucre's money and credit cards.

"Whoever did this was apparently not interested in stealing valuables so tell me Charlie, why go after Emil's books?"

"I don't know" I said apologetically. "Whoever broke in obviously knew you'd inherited Emil's book collection and as Emil always said, there was more to the books than met the eye and I still have no clue what those words meant if anything. We've gone through those books and found nothing unusual so this is all a great mystery. I'm afraid nothing makes sense right now."

"Charlie I wished I'd asked Emil why he repeated that phrase so often.

Emil's List

I guess I always assumed it was just a trite expression but now I'm not so sure."

Sucre's spare set of keys were still on her dresser as well as several change jars packed with old silver dollars.

"Sucre, whoever did this was only interested in finding something inside those books. I have no idea what that could be but we have to go through them again because its possible we've missed something. You own a collection of books worth hundreds of thousands of dollars and you have cash and jewelry here in your place. Wouldn't someone want to steal those things?"

"Should we call the police Charlie?"

That thought unfortunately was on my mind.

"Let's hold off for the moment because I'd like to call Sanford Roberts get his take before dealing with the police again. Sadly, I'd like to keep a comfortable distance between the detectives and us."

The ongoing craziness that once seemed somewhat manageable like a small brush fire quickly turned into a forest fire.

"I'm going to pick up all the books and place them back on your shelves for now. I doubt whoever did this will come back."

My mind was smoldering, wondering who I should fear more; the detectives with evidence against me, the unknown person or persons who'd killed Emil, or the person who broke into Sucre's place to search inside the books.

CHAPTER 21

It took most of the morning to go through every page of every book before I shelved them, discovering nothing out of place. We found nothing more then Emil's notes and to boot, none of the pages had been torn out. I assumed nothing of any interest had been found. When all the books were back on the shelves Sucre called a locksmith to have the locks changed.

I felt awful because many of the bindings were broken and although I knew it didn't matter to Sucre, the value of the collection was adversely affected. I knew it could have been a lot worse but that thought did not make me feel better. Sucre would never sell any of the books saying she knew a world renown book binder at Harvard who might made repairs.

Sucre was more positive than I was but I knew the intrusion hurt terribly. She'd always tried her best to hide the pains she felt. The place was put back together but it would never be the safe haven for her. When the locksmith left I told Sucre to grab some things and we'd head back to my place.

"I'm not a very happy person, mostly because I've had to give up my private space, although I understand the reason. I hate feeling sorry for myself and it's a life and death struggle for me to fight those feelings. I couldn't begin to explain Charlie how very difficult it is for a blind person to uproot and learn to navigate new places."

I did my best to reassure Sucre it wasn't a permanent move but by the somber look on her face, I knew there was nothing I could say to make things better.

Walking out her apartment house front door I thought only about the books. Even though the new locks were supposedly impregnable, we weren't dealing with a simple thief. I remembered Emil's old storage facility thinking we should find the time to move the books there for safe keeping. There was no response from Sucre when I made the suggestion, knowing the intrusion and forced relocation was sucking the life out of her.

I called Attorney Sanford Roberts to ask if the firm owned a van needed to move a number of cartons to a storage facility a few miles away. Sanford replied he'd be happy to help.

An hour later Sanford arrived with a company van and after loading cartons we dashed to the old warehouse, feeling a sense of great relief the books were safe.

Sanford was a tremendous help and all the while he was with us, he'd never once mentioned Emil's case or the law. I offered him a few bucks for his troubles but he shook his head, saying he'd been fully rewarded because he got to see a few very valuable author's signatures.

I gave Sucre another ten dollar tour of her bedroom at my place as well as a tour of the full bath and kitchen. I promised not to move a thing which finally put a small smile on her face to my delight.

"Charlie in my place I knew where everything was kept. Everything I owned had a special place and if I needed it, I always knew where it was. Anything I needed to move went right back to where it always was. Sadly, one of the cruelest jokes I'd ever heard when I first came to America was how did Helen Keller's parents punish her? The terrible answer was they moved the furniture. When I first heard those words I wanted to die so please be careful. I know you'll be thoughtful and if you don't mind listening to my chatter there's one more thing.

"You can make life easier by putting everything back in the exact place every time, even it it's only your easy chair moved a few inches. Give me a day or two and I'll figure out my new surroundings and Charlie, I don't tell many people this but one of my biggest nightmares is walking into something and hurting myself. Be patient with me Charlie. I've learned to get through most days of my new life without mishaps although there have always been frustrations,"

I vowed to be extra careful and by her tone, believed Sucre had learned to accept she'd have to have a roommate, at least for a little while.

I said I'd make us a couple of cups of coffee but she insisted she wanted to do it. I watched her touch and sniff everything in the food cabinet, turning her nose up at a few things obviously spoiled. When she finished

Bruce Weiss

going over all my kitchen supplies she said it was very obvious I was a bachelor.

I felt a bit more at ease and about to say things couldn't get any worse when there was a rather abrupt knock at my door. So much for feeling calm because once again Sucre put another death grip on my arm. To my enormous relief it was Jose my apartment super coming by to make sure everything was alright, saying he'd seen the police walking around his building earlier.

Jose was a good guy and I'd always made time to say hello and ask how his family was. I didn't want to go into why the police were around because in truth, I didn't truly know the reason myself. I explained my friend Sucre's place had been broken into and perhaps they needed some information from her.

"You've always been very kind to me Mr. Charlie so if there's anything I can do, you just ask. If you ever have a problem you remember, I will always have your back as long as you live here."

I wanted to hug him for those kind and generous words. Before he left I told him the young woman with me would be staying for a while, asking if he might keep his ears and eyes open for any strangers inside or around the building. When he left I knew he could never have guessed Sucre was blind.

Thanks to the kindness that day from Jose and Sanford I was less consumed by the feeling I'd just been in a car wreck. I would admit however I felt bruised and scraped, but still standing.

With the day behind us I said I was going to close my eyes for a few minutes on the couch. What felt like a very long relaxing snooze was actually only ten minutes to my surprise. Moments later I realized I had not been as calm as I'd thought when my terrifying dream came to mind. My clothing was soaked and my teeth tightly clenched. This was the new life I rued.

Later in the evening Sanford Roberts called saying he was just checking in asking if there was anything else he could do for us. When I hung up I still very much doubted his legal skills because of his youth. but I'd come to believe he was a good and decent man. Where did Steven Gould fit into my case now? I had no idea.

Looking about the new bathroom arrangement I saw all Sucre's toiletries arranged by size. She must have heard me stirring because she called my name, thanking me for looking out for her. I told her we were doing important work and said I'd always look out for her.

We both slept reasonably well although Sucre did a lot of tossing and turning during the night. Our new arrangement was working so far and in the morning it would be time to dive back into Emil's papers.

I kept thinking about the books being searched, nearly certain the intruder probably had not found what he or she was looking for. One thought flashed in my head like a neon sign at night however. Was it possible something was hidden in one or more of the books neither the intruder or we had discovered? When the first rays of the sun lit up my place and hearing Sucre up and about, it was time to start a new day.

"We're going to hold off on Emil's papers this morning because I'd like to go though the thirty or so books we have here."

Painstakingly perusing each book and Emil's personal notes, adding to my frustration we found nothing out of place; no hidden messages and nothing suggesting there was more to the books then met the eye. Near three in the afternoon when we'd finished I halfheartedly said I just didn't have the desire to start working with Emil's papers just yet, suggesting I do some reading.

I picked up the copy of a Clockwork Orange by Anthony Burgess, announcing the title and the author's name. Sucre replied she knew nothing about the writer or the story but it had an interesting title. I said we'd start with Emil's notes and if they sounded interesting, we'd begin reading the book. Here's Emil take I announced.

'The book a Clockwork Orange was banned by government authorities first in England and then in the United States. Censors called the book nothing more then an expose on sexual violence and unadulterated brutality. An Aurora Colorado school superintendent was so outraged discovering the book in the high school library he took the time to look into the more then five thousand volumes on the school library shelves. In the end only one book was removed; A Clockwork Orange. The same scenario took place all over the country in schools and libraries.'

There were several more pages of notes but it was getting late and I wanted to get through chapter one. Sucre reminded me again how Emil

Bruce Weiss

strongly believed censorship was one of mankind's worst evils. I read for an hour and suggested we do one or two more hours of work.

We were still in the organizational stage placing articles and letters into folders based on date or subject matter and at times, it felt as if we were constantly shuffling decks of cards. When I was ready to call it quits out of the blue Sucre asked if I knew that I talked in my sleep. I said I wasn't aware of that.

"Last night you yelled several times, loud enough to stir me but what you were saying really didn't make any sense. Do you remember what you might have been dreaming?"

Because of her prompting my dream came back to me. Replaying it in my mind I knew I could not share it with Sucre because something terrible had happened to her. I said I seldom remembered dreams.

Thinking about dreams, I realized since Emil's death I was dreaming about peril and danger all night long. Getting ready for bed began to make me uncomfortable because I knew what awaited. Seeing my reflection in Sucre's dark glasses for the first time I saw telltale signs of weariness, proving I probably wasn't sleeping as well as I thought.

"Sucre let me bring this up again because I think it's critical. Do you have any idea now what Emil meant when he used the expression there was more to the books then met the eye? I'm a bit obsessed with that sentiment and just can't put it out of my thoughts."

"Charlie, I really don't think I'm the one to ask about what meets the eye," said with a mischievous smile. "I'm not sure what those words meant because we've looked through all the books and there doesn't appear to be anything more then stories and wonderful and insightful personal notes.

"I too have the sense there's got to be something more to Emil's expression but if I were to guess, the words probably had something to do with my blindness. However, I believe like you that whoever went through the books during the break in at my place had to have been looking for something Emil might have been working on. You probably know better than most people Emil truly knew how to ruffle nerves. Nothing was found in the books so why don't we spend a little more time reading over Emil's news articles once again. Maybe we're just missing something because I seriously doubt our friend wrote messages in invisible ink. We should consider every possibility because maybe it's just something we just haven't figured out yet."

Sucre was right, There were so many times Emil's life was threatened but he'd never shied from exposing things that might cause someone to harm or quiet him.

"Sucre, "I'm nearly convinced we won't find any magical answers in his books or papers but if there's really something there, we haven't found yet so maybe we just need a little luck."

"Wherever this eventually takes us Charlie I want you to know that I'm extremely grateful you asked me to help. I'm not sure if you knew but when you asked, I really wanted to say no for a lot of very good reasons. Now I'm so very thankful I said yes because if you hadn't asked me, I'd probably be incredibly lost and very lonely.

"When I feel down I wished so hard I had the ability to cry, something very soothing when I was a child. Sadly, there was too much damage to my eyes and the tear ducts from the explosion. I've experienced an awful lot of sadness in my life in the months and years after I lost my family but you know something? Losing Emil somehow feels much worse than losing my parents. I've never had a friend like him or knew anyone who could be so thoughtful and kind. I truly believe he was the very first sighted person who could truly understand what it was like to be blind.

"My doctors in Arequipa, the best in the country told me I'd never see again and sadly it took me a long time to accept the reality. I can't tell you how badly I wanted to die each day, afraid of everything. If it weren't for the hard-headed nuns who took me in I truly don't know what would have become of me. The nuns insisted I learn Braille but like everything else I fought them tooth and nail until I was finally too tired to fight anymore. I owe them much and now I'm finding joy working on Emil's papers because he reminds me of the good nuns.

"Before I met Emil, Charlie, I was just going through the motions of life, feeling sorry for my plight in life and feeling blue all the time. The nuns told me something very special would happen in my life and I didn't believe them at first but I think fate brought me to Emil allowing me to rekindle the joy in my life, something I'd thought I'd lost forever. Charlie, it's difficult to tell anyone I'm hurting but I can honestly say I'm hurting without Emil."

I said we'd keep Emil alive through his work and one day the entire world would get a glimpse of the life of a remarkable man.

"Charlie did you ever wake up feeling life wasn't worth the daily struggle anymore? Did you ever think about giving up and saying I can't go on much longer?"

I didn't have to think about that.

"There were times in my professional life when I'd hit rock bottom, especially the day word got out don't hire Charlie Darwin because he's poison. I felt that pain for a very long time, maybe even the same pain you felt when your life wasn't worth living anymore. I wondered, why wait for the inevitable because my work was done. In my journalism career when the best of projects didn't work out there was little joy and much heartbreak. Everyone goes through difficult times when all seems lost but somehow the strongest survive."

"Charlie, there were times when I'd stumble over things and constantly hurt myself. I didn't dare ask for help because I didn't want to become someone else's burden or be dependent upon others the rest of my life. I'm extremely grateful I can manage now although at times my shins are permanently black and blue. When I fall down these days though I pull myself up and get on with life, which by the way is more meaningful now thanks to you and Emil. It's not the big things in my life jumping up and hurting me today, it's actually the little things like putting my coffee cup down and forgetting where I left it. I was terrible at the convent until I accepted what the nuns were offering because they were able to teach me how to live. Later, Emil taught me how to live joyously with literature.

"Years after the explosion destroyed my family nearly killing me, I'd still obsess with the thought why hadn't the explosion killed me too? There were many times I knew it would have been better if I hadn't survived. I was always resentful and extremely jealous of other people because they took their sight for granted. Thanks to those very stubborn nuns grabbing me by the ears and getting my attention, I learned how to survive in a dark world. The nuns were relentless and I laugh now although it was no fun at the time. It got to the point in my life when I just didn't have the strength to fight them anymore. They unselfishly taught me how to live and how to accept who I am and gradually, I found myself more comfortable in my world of darkness.

Emil's List

"I still have to remind myself everyday I was very fortunate to have twelve good years of sight because I have wonderful memories etched into my mind. The nuns taught me many simple lessons, such as you can always start your day over again. They taught me it was okay to take a step back every once in a while, just as long as I didn't stay on that step very long. After Emil died I was really just drifting through life, going through the motions but then you came into my life and in a way, Emil still lives. Charlie this is one of those moments in my life when I wish I could cry tears. I'm sorry because I'm dumping my issues on you."

I was overwhelmingly but incredibly moved by Sucre's words, making many of the problems I'd faced in my life pale. She'd certainly traveled a very difficult road and her sentiments made me understand she was not as fragile as I'd once imagined a blind person to be. I admired her tenacity and courage. She'd overcame so much, refusing to let her blindness define her life. When the spell in the room lifted I didn't have to ask because Sucre announced it was time to go back to work.

"Make yourself comfortable Sucre because there's more urgency to go though everything now since the break in."

I grabbed a handful of papers appearing to be more transcript from the Congressional Records taken at the HUAC hearings,. I had not realized there were more.

"I know Charlie. I need to fasten my seatbelt.

Breck - You've asked me nearly a dozen times if I was a Communist and I'll tell you once again my response has not changed. I refuse to answer that question because you have no legal right to ask about my personal beliefs. I'm an American citizen protected by our time tested Bill of Rights and as I've said before, no one should be forced to reveal their political leanings. Saying that however, I've decided to give you an answer this time because I believe one of us has to take the highroad. Yes Mr. Baldwin, I was once a member of the American Communist Party, but no longer.

The spectators in the upper gallery booed loudly, the Chair responding with a loud pounding of his gavel, threatening to empty the room of spectators.

Bruce Weiss

Chairman Baldwin - This is not the Roman Coliseum so keep your thoughts to yourselves he crowed.

Breck - If you would allow me a few more minutes Mr. Baldwin, I'd like to expand on that remark. Americans have always been taught any form of Communism is un-American but I beg to differ. I believe the sole purpose of the American Communist Party was and still is to help the working class citizens in this country, and if that is Communism, who would argue that's bad? Caring for others is when we humans are our best. Is it not? The Communist party in America has never, and I repeat never called for the overthrow of America's democratic systems. Mr. Baldwin and members of this committee, I say in all honesty I do not know a single American Communist who is loyal to the Soviet Union. American Communists have always felt true power resided not in an oppressive government, but with the American people. American Communists have put their lives on the line defending America against foreign enemies, many fighting bravely during World War One. During World War Two some four thousand American Communists gave their lives fighting Fascism.

American Communists are not disloyal citizens sir, but people dedicating their lives to enrich America's welfare. Too many industrialists, bankers, and super-rich put their loyalties in profits and cartel interests first. Given their unstoppable power, is it wrong to stand for the American worker who makes a non-livable wage? American Communists are not betraying their country, they only seek to make it fairer. During World War Two many American companies made huge fortunes selling to whoever would buy their chemicals, arms and fuels, regardless of their political views.

Do American Communists serve the interest of the Soviet Union? The answer is absolutely no. If the tenets of the American Communist party were expressed without mentioning the word Communism, most Americans would agree with what they say and do. I've never heard any spokesman for the Party advocate an overthrow of our democracy. Our greedy capitalist ways? Yes.

Does the American Communist Party receive instructions or money from the Soviet Union? Absolutely not. They would however argue against the outrageous financial support and weaponry the American government sends to dictators around the world, making sure American interests are not tarnished. I maintain Communists in American have not plotted, nor ever intended to plot an overthrow or insurrection. That idea is pure myth, perpetrated by those who fear giving rightful power to those who are oppressed in this nation.

And finally I will close by saying being a member of any political party is not a crime. We have freedom to choose our politics in America and if you create laws to outlaw one party, what would prevent you from outlawing any party you disapprove. Thank you for giving me the time to say what is in my heart. I have nothing more to say about Communism but may I please have a few more moments of your time?

The Chair nodded.

I am one of many who believe the American system is broken. I would love to have our Constitution changed legally and certainly not by violence. Economic troubles created by our government have cause many Americans to live beyond their means. Even the very principles of liberty are in question for the poor and downtrodden.

I believe during this co called Cold War we are facing desperate times because there are serious problems in America. Your attacks against the free press are accelerating the crisis.

Many, many people in this country are sick and tired of being unable to support their families and your time and efforts here are making people sick. There is a general hysteria out there Mr. Chairman and good people of every political party are being neglected while you hold these hearings. Thank you, that is all I have to say for now.'

"What an impassioned speech I gushed," sensing the words were not well received by Baldwin and his committee.

"Okay Sucre. In his own words we now know Emil was an active member of the Communist Party but I'd always believed he was actually more of a socialist when I first met him. It took an awful lot of guts to say that to the committee, especially in Washington with the cold war heating up. I haven't looked over the next transcript but I'll bet the committee sent him off to jail again. You know, if it weren't for Matt Roth's reporting and

Bruce Weiss

Emil's testimony, people would have no clue what this country was going through and I very much doubt this isn't taught in American civics classes today. I'll read this next section and then we'll find out what happens.

"From the first sentence according to a Roth op-ed, Emil was in fact sent back to jail but released forty-eight hours later due to a surprising public outcry."

Late into the evening I read fourteen more letters addressed to Clarissa, all written during his Spanish years, each an eye opening look into the past. Finally putting the papers aside I told Sucre I was starved and could probably even eat a guinea pig.

"Charlie, I'd like you to continue reading if you're not too tired, maybe just a few more letters while I go into the kitchen and prepare a special Peruvian meal for us. It'll take a little time but I promise it'll be worth it. Oh and Charlie, if you can work and listen to music at the same time, I like to play Peruvian music when I cook."

It was nearly impossible to concentrate on Emil's letters because of the wonderful aroma coming from the kitchen and the music I'd come to love. My curiosity eventually got the best of me and I got up and peeked in the kitchen.

Sucre heard my footsteps because before I got to the door, she'd covered the large pot on the stove so I couldn't see what was cooking.

"What smells so good" I asked?

"Well if you must know, I stopped at a pet store not far from here yesterday and saw two very fat guinea pigs for sale."

I couldn't tell by her words or look if she was kidding but suddenly I wasn't very hungry. I returned to Emil's letters, wondering if I could stomach the meal.

"I'll read another letter to Clarissa" I mumbled, even more roiled because there were no clues to her last name. The envelopes were all addressed to CLARISSA in large block letters with a post office box number in Baltimore.

"Do you think she was his girlfriend I yelled into the kitchen?"

Her response made me laugh.

"I'm blind but I'm not deaf."

The rest of Sucre's answer was lost in the whirring of the blender but that did not stop me from reading

Emil's List

'Dear Clarissa. I've added a crown jewel to my book collection. After many months searching in Barcelona's book stores I located an excellent first edition of the Communist Manifesto. Karl Marx didn't sign it but get this, Friedrich Engels his co-author did. I'd once tried reading it when I was a teenager but it was much too complex to truly understand. I did learn some interesting things though and it only whetted my appetite to learn more about Marx. With this copy I plan on getting reacquainted with the writer.

'I've read the first one hundred pages so far, devoted to the history of working class movements around the world. I'll quote from the book so you can get an idea how he used words.

"I don't advocate violence but when the working man becomes convinced there must be social change, revolution would become necessary."

The book was then and is still considered extremely dangerous and controversial I added. I said I agreed with much of what Marx wrote, but never believed revolution was necessarily a good thing because it only makes the world a more dangerous place.'

"Sucre I'm going to read the notes Emil wrote about the Communist Manifesto before I continue with the letter to Clarissa.

'Class struggles between the bourgeoisie and the proletariat have always favored the rich because they are the ones who make and carry out the laws. That is still very prevalent in this country today and until it changes, the rich will get richer and the poor will simply die.'

There were scores of papers we hadn't gotten to yet but it was time to put the work aside for dinner. I was curious about what was being prepared in the kitchen, my stomach growling. Sucre said she needed another a half hour and although I was beat, I pulled out another letter addressed to the mysterious Clarissa and again read aloud..

'When I was called before HUAC in early 1953, many organizations including the church were calling for laws granting our government the right to seize and destroy any writings sympathetic to Communism. Clarissa, you know my position on any type of censorship because if someone is able to pass laws censuring certain writings and banning free thought, any writer could have his or her words changed or even destroyed. Writers have gone to prison and worse for their words. Who gets to appoint censors giving them unlimited powers?

Bruce Weiss

'I've always said when religious groups, government officials and civic authorities order libraries to rid their shelves of books mentioning the word Communism, we must speak out no matter the cost. Censorship is a crime committed against every human being and no one should be told what they can or cannot read.

'School committees are having field days removing books and magazines from high school shelves deemed Communist propaganda and sadly, that censorship also includes many excellent American novels. Senator Carlson of Minnesota claimed there were more then thirty thousand dangerous volumes in circulation in high schools in his state serving only one purpose; to subvert the minds of young Americans.'

"Sucre, Emil's notes highlight the number of authors accused of writing subversive literature. You'd laugh or even cry at some of the works censured, including Mark Twain's books. In fact, Twain once confessed he was once a member of the Communist Party.

"Emil also added his thoughts about authors who'd been silenced, especially those ending up in prison. During his long journalistic career, many people found Emil's articles extremely controversial. It's entirely possible some of his recent writings caused someone to take great exception to his work. It's also within the realm of possibility he was about to publish a story that might incriminate some very important people. There's still a lot of material to go through and we can only hope we'll find some answers, if there are any."

"Dinner will be ready in five minutes so you should put the papers down for a while,"

I made a quick call to Attorney Sanford Roberts, asking if there was anymore information about the case, a bit surprised because he'd answered my call on his home phone.

"I'm glad you called and hoping you're remaining positive because for all appearances, the investigation is still on the back burner."

I was beginning to like Roberts more and more. At least he took my calls I mused.

"So this is where the case stands right now my friend. The police know about your work with Mr. Breck and that remains an issue to the detectives but it's still an open case. Much more investigative work needs to be done. You've heard the saying justice moves very slowly.

Emil's List

"The police definitely have a credit card receipt with your signature for the purchase of strychnine which is pretty damning evidence. However, if the police can determine that's not your signature, then the case takes on a new direction. I know the DA and he's a good man so when he said he wasn't prepared to issue an indictment at this time I believed him. The detectives still have too many unanswered questions about who administered the poison so keep this in mind. If the detectives ever want to talk to you again, you must stay tight lipped until I'm there. You do not talk to the police on your own and do not discuss this with anyone other then Ms. Grande. I'd be very careful about what you tell her."

When I hung up and peeked into the kitchen I realized Sucre listened to our conversation on the extension phone. I smiled to myself.

CHAPTER 22

Mercifully it was a chicken dinner along with a very special Peruvian dessert. I couldn't remember the last time I'd eaten such rich food, the wait worth it.

"I'm very comforted by the fact you're staying here Sucre, even though I know it's incredibly difficult for you to settle into new surroundings. I'm sorry for being overly cautious but we really don't know who we're dealing with. If you're up to it and not too tired, we could burn the midnight oil and maybe find some answers leading us to a killer."

From the sound if my strained voice and Sucre's yawning there would be no midnight oil. Sucre rather effortlessly learned her way around my apartment, well enough to put her walking stick aside. She'd become so adept so quickly I believed if someone came by and didn't know Sucre, they would not realize she was blind.

Over cups of rich Peruvian coffee for dessert we sat back and talked about the work we'd accomplished.

"We should probably reread Emil's notes several more times, hoping we'll find something we missed telling us what might have led to his murder. Whoever broke into your place had to somehow know something of great importance was inside those books. I'm actually confused by the fact after looking through all the volumes during the break-in, the intruder had not removed a single page or note."

With Sucre at my place I grew more sensitive to sounds, hearing city noises differently. A car stopping in front of the building or the front door to the apartment house opening or closing immediately got my attention. My wall clock suddenly sounded like Big Ben chiming on the hour.

Despite saying the work day was over we went back to Emil's papers

Emil's List

and worked until nearly three in the morning. To my relief, the number of unread papers was shrinking fast. It was hard to believe that one person could gather and save so many valuable pieces of information about their life and times.

Sucre dutifully stopped the work on the hour listening to the news on her radio, the five minute break all the time we afforded ourselves. We laughed hearing the woeful tale of a man who's car had been stolen some months ago and abandoned in the huge underground parking lot beneath the Boston Commons. Nine months after it was reported stolen the car was tagged by a police officer with a ticket. To the owners dismay, the ticket amounted to seventeen thousand dollars in parking fees. Normally I didn't listen to the news but something told me to listen this time.

The story leading off the three O'clock morning news grabbed me by my throat. WBOS newscaster Thom Griffin, an old newspaper friend said rumors were circulating that former governor Raymond Baldwin would be declaring for the presidency as an independent candidate, possibly in the next twenty-four hours. The words Raymond Baldwin shocked me. Sucre said something but rather rudely I asked her to be quiet.

"Several unnamed sources said the former congressman and one time governor of Massachusetts would be tossing his hat into the ring, possibly as early as the next afternoon on the steps of the Massachusetts State capitol building. How about that sports fans?"

Impossible I thought, certainly a joke. He wouldn't have a chance in Hell running for dog catcher so I wondered if old Thom was doing a little more sipping than usual.

It took a few deep breaths to get over my initial shock, apologizing to Sucre telling her what the report boded.

"Raymond Baldwin vanished from public life after resigning the governorship in disgrace and I don't believe anyone knew what he'd been up to the last number of years. Some said he was just biding his time hoping people would forget or forgive his past bad deeds. A political comeback" I muttered under my breath. "I hope to God it was a joke, maybe announced by Thom to see if anyone in his radio audience was listening at three in the morning."

It can't be possible I said over and over, picking up the phone dialing Thom Griffin at the radio station. When he answered he sounded sober.

"Yep, it's a done deal" he said chuckling, "and you my friend can take that to the bank. I'm on the air until six this morning and if I hear anything I'll dial you up but between you and me and from reliable sources, it sounds like it's really going to happen."

I could only shake my head at the absurdity. Was this really the same man who resigned the governor's office in disgrace, rising from the dead like Richard Nixon? When I hung up I told Sucre why I was so upset and confused.

"It's a very long story and its very late but do you remember my telling you once about my run in with Baldwin when he was governor and I was on his enemies list? Not only was this man once my sworn enemy, but if you remember from Roth's reporting, Emil went through a hellacious time with him during the HUAC hearings."

It was getting late but I was suddenly wide awake.

"Sucre, about five years ago I exposed Baldwin's shady business deals and corruptive practices while governor, maybe the most difficult investigative reporting I'd ever done. I spelled out his misdeeds leading to his resignation. People all over the country couldn't have forgotten what he'd done but maybe they might have. When my stories were published he knew he'd be facing some very serious charges but unbeknownst to the public, he struck a secret deal with the juridical people and got to walk.

"I hadn't known that Emil and I were both a bone of contention to Raymond Baldwin until I read Roth's reports. I know it's late and I'm awfully flustered but there's something buzzing inside my head and I don't like that feeling. Emil was murdered and I was set up to take the rap. It's pure speculation at this point but I'm starting to wonder if Emil chose me to work with him because of something he'd discovered about Baldwin, and of course he and I were directly affected by him."

I felt like I was alone out in left field, unable to stop thinking it plausible that Emil might have been working on a critical piece about Raymond Baldwin. The thought sent ice water through my veins.

"Sucre I'd documented even the tiniest details about Baldwin's crooked dealings, double and triple checking all my sources very carefully. My reporting eventually made front page news in nearly every newspaper in New England and later nationally. I was lauded for my work exposing Baldwin but regretfully there were many stern warnings to watch my back.

I'd created some very powerful enemies as Emil had, but after five years of silence the truth was I hadn't thought about Baldwin until we read the transcript of the HUAC hearings,"

"Two weeks after the series of my articles were printed I was fired from my editor's job and given ten minutes to clear out my desk and leave the building. Three days later I received a subpoenas issued by the Massachusetts Attorney General ordering me to turn over all my notes about Baldwin. I did and to no one's surprise, a small fire in the courthouse storage area destroyed my notes.

"It seems as if days not years have passed since Baldwin denied his wrong doings and disappeared. He'd lambasted me in the press and then simply vanished. I never thought I'd ever hear his name mentioned as a candidate for any elective office and I would have bet the house on that.

"I still clearly recall his very first press conference less than twenty-four hours after he'd left office, defiantly saying when all was said and done he'd come out smelling like the proverbial rose. Days later he filed a multi-million dollar law suit against my newspaper and me. The man was bent on revenge but fortunately for me, nothing came from the law suits and he simply crawled under a rock someplace,

"Baldwin had also fallen off the radar screen when he left Congress and the HUAC committee for nearly five years. Why? It's anyone's guess. I'm not sure if you've ever heard the name but Joseph McCarthy took over the chairmanship of HUAC after Baldwin. It was impossible to imagine things would go from bad to worse but it did.

"Five years after leaving his congressional seat Baldwin ran successfully for the governorship of Massachusetts, a rather popular choice. I knew much about his behaviors as governor but I never knew he and Emil had once come face to face in the dark ages of the Cold War until we read Roth's reporting. I know a leopard can't change its spots but if anyone could, I wouldn't put it past Baldwin. When he resigned I honestly thought I'd never hear his name again."

"Could he really become a presidential candidate," Sucre asked? "I didn't think independents could run in America because you only have two parties."

"Anyone can run for any office and anyone can come back to life, including Richard Nixon who famously said after a political loss, you won't have Richard Nixon to kick around any longer. Anything's possible in American politics."

I suggested we try to get some much needed sleep as it was nearing five in the morning, catching up on the news later. I quickly discovered I was too wired to sleep staring out my window waiting for the night sky to lighten I was as worked up and energized as I'd once been when working on a great news story. This time it was because thoughts about Baldwin were running around inside my head. Sucre was awake too. Rather than rehash Baldwin, wanted to change the subject so I asked her to tell me about Braille. Sucre said she was more than happy to talk about that and her work.

"In the process of translating books you have to be very careful not to change the author's intentions meaning the work can be very time consuming and frustrating. When I'm working with a novel I feel as if I'm walking a tightrope because I can't veer from the author's purpose. When you get it right and the Braille truly sounds like the voice of the author, it's one of the most rewarding feelings."

Neither of us could fall back to sleep so I suggested we brew a pot of coffee and talk a little about where we saw ourselves when our work was done. Sucre said she didn't have to think about that, saying with certainty one day she hoped to go back to school and get a degree in education.

"I'd like to be able to work with the blind as a teacher and mentor."

I told her I couldn't think of a more rewarding job than teaching. For me I said, most of my time would be devoted to writing Emil Breck's biography.

Sucre asked about my reporting years, including what areas I concentrated on and how I'd gotten into the field. I said the idea of being a writer hit me hard very early in my life, and that I'd fallen in love with the written word as a young child.

"I was allowed to stay up late when I was very young as long as I was reading and that pleasure never waned, not for one minute. When I first heard the expression the pen was much mightier then the sword I was completely convinced what I wanted to do with my life. Looking back, I wouldn't have changed anything."

"Charlie, when I was finally able to accept my blindness I promised myself it would never stop me from living a full life."

Emil's List

"Do blind people who once had sight still dream" I asked?

She laughed, adding often in color.

"I still dream about El Misti, our mountain in Arequipa because to climb it took perseverance and determination, two things necessary to have a good life. Sometimes I dream about my parents and wake up truly thankful for that wondrous dream. Did I ever tell you how difficult it is to climb Misti?"

Not being a climber or knowing much about mountain I said I had no idea.

"The trail leading to the summit is very steep and icy and of course the weather is very unpredictable. Even though Arequipa is nearly two miles above sea level, the mountain stretches nearly four miles into the sky so you can imagine how very thin the air is, not to mention the incredible cold."

When I asked why people climbed it there was no response. Those were my last words before drifting off to sleep. Hours later when I awoke I remembered I'd curiously dreamed about mountains.

CHAPTER 23

We got a very late start the following day, beginning where we'd left off with the last section of the HUAC transcripts. Fifties music played on Sucre's radio while she awaited the morning hourly news.

At ten we heard the unbelievable words it was official. Raymond Baldwin would be declaring for the presidency of the United States as an independent candidate at noon on the steps of the Boston State House. The last time he'd made an appearance on those steps was to announced his resignation.

I still could not come to grips with the absurdity. The steps of the State House? The place where he'd shamefully resigned the office of governor five years earlier, saying the public had seen the last of him? There was no mention about his great fall from power in the newscast, only his emergence from hibernation. When the broadcast ended I was nearly too bewildered to return to our work, sensing we'd get little done. Suggesting going out for breakfast and a slow stroll over to the Commons and the State House to hear Baldwin's declaration seemed like the plan of the day. Sucre asked what Baldwin looked like, saying she pictured a giant of a man in her mind.

"I haven't actually seen him or pictures of him in some time, but the image at his last press conference reciting his resignation speech is still very clear in my mind. He's rather short and stocky, bushy gray curly hair, mustache trimmed to perfection and quite the dresser. His most distinguished facial feature from what I remember was his overgrown bushy eyebrows nearly hiding his eyes behind tiny wire rimmed glasses. I still find it impossible to fathom that he's actually going to declare he's a candidate for the office of president. I don't see him getting very far and not only because of his corrupt background, but because no third party candidate has ever won many electoral votes. Third party candidates also don't get front page news like the Republican and Democratic candidates so it would definitely be an uphill battle.

"When he finishes whatever he's got to say, I'm going to ask you not so much about what he said, but I want your take on his tone, the delivery and what people in the audience were saying about him. Forget what I told you about his past and keep an open mind. He's always had the reputation of being an excellent speaker and as governor, he held more press conferences than any other public official in America."

Walking across the Commons I caught my first view of the staging area in front of the State House, describing the layout to Sucre. Banners and balloons gave a festive look to one of the oldest state houses in America. There were only a handful of people milling around with only a half hour until the scheduled speech. If the audience remained small I remarked he'd easily pick me out of the crowd, certain he'd still recognize me.

"He once knew every local reporter by name and knew things about their families."

I asked Sucre to eavesdrop because I was interested in what people though about Baldwin, certain most would not speak highly of him. With ten minutes to go before the scheduled speech sounds of microphone tests boomed out over the Common while media crews went through their final checks. When the event should have started there was no one on the stage and more press people than curious onlookers.

Sucre surprised me with a question I wasn't expecting. What did I know about strychnine?

There were times I'd forgotten Sucre was unable to read print unless translated into Braille. When I read Emil's novels aloud she'd often ask me to explain what a certain word meant, realizing it would be extremely difficult for a blind person to know about something as obscure as strychnine. I replied I new a little.

"From what I've read and heard about Strychnine it's a white power, highly toxic, colorless and odorless and mostly used as a pesticide these days. It kills rodents on farms and has a very long life so it's usually applied only once a year. The poison is fatal to humans if inhaled, swallowed or even absorbed through the eyes or skin. If you purchased it you'd really

Bruce Weiss

need to know what you're dealing with so you didn't accidentally poisoned yourself. In Emil's case, someone knew what they were doing."

I didn't explain what I'd learned from Attorney Gould about strychnine, which was the poison would cause a rather slow and painful death. Gould said Emil most likely died as a result of convulsions and asphyxiation, a terrible death. Someone infected would live in agony for one or two hours before death, the attorney's words running through my mind.

Sucre replied a friend had given her a Braille copy of one of Agatha Christie's novels but she'd forgotten the title. She recalled poison was used as the murder weapon."

Minutes past the announced starting time a handful of onlookers arrived to see what the festivities were all about. We moved a bit closer to the stage.

Hands appeared in an upper window of the State House unfurling a large banner with the words, Raymond Baldwin will make our nation strong again. The cameras aimed at the banner and that was when I saw my friend Thom from the radio station, standing just to the right of the stage with his tape recorder.

I grabbed Sucre's hand and moved another few feet closer until we were standing directly in front of the platform, a place so quiet I had to remind myself we were in the middle of the city of Boston. We heard people speculating what Baldwin might say. Several said he probably wouldn't show. I whispered a running account of what was happening which unfortunately wasn't much. Ten minutes later a school bus pulled up and a band exited, the young musicians carrying instruments marching smartly toward the staging area. One trumpeter played a few notes of God Bless America.

Several people turned and walked away shaking their heads. People out for a midday stroll through the Commons didn't seem interested in what was happening.

Another ten minutes passed before a large group filed out the front door of the State House taking up the empty seats on the stage. The school band commenced playing God Bless America as people surged forward. Cameras were turned toward the driveway in front of the State House because two black limos with darkened windows drove up. I continued my jabbering, giving Sucre a full account. When Baldwin got out of the first

Emil's List

car I couldn't have been more stunned if I'd seen a ghost. The five years had obviously been very good to him because he looked fit and jaunty. He'd lost considerable weight and was not sporting his trademark wire rimmed glasses. His eyebrows no longer covered his eyes. Behind us the Commons came to life looking like an army on the move, stopping traffic and carrying signs supporting Baldwin. The crowd reminded me of many of the political rallies I'd once covered. Keeping Sucre informed was not easy because the band was playing quite loudly.

The former governor's hair was obviously dyed because the gray was gone. To my surprise he looked much younger than the man who's last public appearance on the same stage portrayed a tired and angry man.

Baldwin waved and glad handed people as he approached the stage, eliciting loud cheers from the growing crowd. A raucous chant 'make the Nation great again' began the moment he stepped onto the stage. Someone whispered something in his ear and moments later Baldwin's eyes were fixed clearly on me. We were so close to him Sucre commented that someone was wearing a very cheap cologne.

The ex-governor stepped back, flashing victory signs to his audience. My eyes were glued on Baldwin but when I surveyed those standing behind him, someone on the stage curiously caught my attention. I actually had to convince myself I wasn't seeing things but standing and waving to the audience was my attorney, Steven Gould.

He whispered in Baldwin's ear while the band played For He's a Jolly Good Fellow. Someone leaned into the microphone saying we were going to hear a speech for the ages.

"You who are gathered here today are about to become part of a great historical event, the start of a renewal to put American on the right road again.

The crowd roared loudly chanting Baldwin, Baldwin, Baldwin. I squeezed Sucre's hand so tightly she yelled.

What's happening now she asked.

"I don't know the man who's speaking but there's someone on Baldwin's stage that has all my attention right now. I'm afraid it's my attorney Steven Gould. Sucre, I was told Roberts was filling in because Gould was supposedly on a fishing trip in Canada. Oh dear me."

I released the death grip on Sucre's hand wondering why a distinguished

Bruce Weiss

Boston attorney would want to lend his support to a scoundrel like Baldwin. I couldn't take my eyes off Gould, missing the rest of the introduction but fortunately Sucre had her recorder going. For a few moments I'd entirely forgotten about Raymond Baldwin, stunned by Gould's surprise appearance.

"Friends, you are here today to support my good friend Raymond Baldwin in his fight to bring our country back to the greatness it has lost."

Looking around the crowd had grown considerably. The evening Boston paper would later peg the crowd at five thousand but at the time I thought easily many more. When the long winded introduction finally ended, the school band performed the National Anthem and then it was time for Raymond Baldwin to begin his speech.

"A very good morning to you all and my heartfelt thanks for coming out to this truly great historical event. It is with a great deal of humility and American pride that today I am announcing my candidacy for the presidency of the United States of America, running as an independent. I run as an independent because backroom politics should be a thing of the past. I have no political bosses telling me what to think or say, only you good people and I promise to listen to you."

The crowd cheered, the sounds echoing off the buildings surrounding the Commons. I suspected anyone within a mile of the Commons could hear his words.

"Our country has some very serious problems and it should be no surprise that our current leaders are no longer able to fix them. The do nothing occupant in the White House is all talk and of course, no action. I'm tired as I'm sure all of you are of the same old rhetoric spouted by Republicans and Democrats, meaningless words because nothing ever changes.

The audience was certainly tuned into each work Sucre remarked.

"My friends, I solemnly swear on this day that I will become the leader who offers solutions to cure the ills that have afflicted this great nation. If America was a business, it would look rusted and a large going out of business sale sign would sit on the front lawn of the White House. Over the past four years the windbags in charge have done nothing to stop America's disheartening fall from its once great heights.

"I have spent the last five years of my life working on a solid and

Emil's List

workable plan to right this wayward ship before dry rot completely sets in. We desperately need new leadership, someone who has no ties to any political party and who owes no favors. Both parties have let you down and all they've succeeded in doing is dividing us. Our beloved America is a failing state and no longer the land of dreams or opportunities. If you elect me I will make America's great promise become a reality again.

"Years ago as governor of the great state of Massachusetts I said the difference between our state and others was our strong determination to make the next generation of citizens better off. Sadly, we have lost touch with the things that once made us great, because the current leaders know nothing and do nothing. I'm terribly saddened when I hear people say that America's best days are behind her. I truly never want to hear those words ever spoken again. This country will not get better unless someone stands up and sends this message; THIS....SIMPLY....WON'T.... DO..... ANYMORE.

"We can do much better because we have untold resources our current administration chooses not to tap into. We have enough coal to fuel the entire world for five hundred years but this administration ignores that.

"We've been told we'll have to live with less and that is the solution to all your problems. I find that thinking one hundred percent unacceptable and truly offensive to all good Americans. I will not allow people with that frame of mind to ever be a part of my administration. Some say we are incapable of solving our problems and to those people, I say watch me."

It sounded as if a hundred thousand voices were cheering.

"I won't pay attention to naysayer's because they are the problem. I'm running as an independent and my allegiance will not follow standard party line, but the needs of the people of this great nation. Our leaders talk about our ills but do nothing to change things for the better. That my friends is the least effective way to govern.

"There are too many failed children in our education systems, possibly your own so we must start holding teachers responsible. Everyone needs to be held accountable.

"The sad state of our economy and the outrageous number of unemployed in the richest country in the world is shameful. There is no reason for economic ruin in a land of plenty, a land blessed in every sense.

"The workers of American have not created our present economic problems. It is the fault of the political leaders who sadly suffer from brain paralysis. I'll cut your taxes because our current administration has shown it does not know how to spend your hard earned money wisely. I will help create good jobs and guarantee the next generation of Americans will be better off then us.

"The current leader in the White House has perfected the blame game. He says America cannot keep up with other nations because other nations have different laws. We have the world's most capable labor force yet the current administration has done all that is possible to handicap businesses with overly excessive and punishing rules.

"I believe all things are possible in America and I know you want our next president to think about that every working day. Achieving greatness again will not be easy, but if we don't start today, when do we start?

"Since the end of World War Two we've gotten into wars on nearly every continent with few success and certainly no exit plans. Our allies no longer look up to us and the real fear is those old friends might easily turn to others, others not in our best interest to take our place.

"The American people worked hard to make this nation great and we've forgotten that the American worker is our greatest asset. We've lost the sense we can do anything if we put our hearts and minds into it. The people of America deserve better leadership and I make this solemn promise to you today. I will lead this nation to greatness again. We have to do more to protect our individual liberties and to preserve the sacred things that got us here."

The ground beneath our feet was actually shaking as people jumped and shouted the name Baldwin over and over.

"Massachusetts is the cradle of liberty and names like Bunker Hill, Lexington and Concord, the Boston Tea Party and the USS Constitution still mean something to the people of this state. I don't want America like ancient Greece or Rome becoming a footnote in future history books. The spirit of patriotism has waned but I promise I'll rekindle that spirit not only in Washington, but wherever Americans work, live, play, or pray.

"I ask for your support but it comes with a warning. Our journey will not be easy and it will take each of us to move forward and we'll only succeed if we work together. I'll stand by the helm twenty-four hours a day and get us out of reverse and neutral and move forward. There is

Emil's List

tremendous potential in this country and for too long like the American worker, it has been ignored.

"In the coming days I will speak to you about specific issues that will make American great again. God Bless all of you who came out today and God Bless America."

It would be difficult to argue with the man's words but I knew from personal experience the man was extremely treacherous and untrustworthy. Putting my arm around Sucre's shoulder I said it was time for us to go. One more glance back at the group surrounding Baldwin on the stage and in particular Steven Gould made me feel like screaming why. Gould seemed to be gushing with pride, as a father might look showing off a new baby.

"I've never been terribly interested in American politics," Sucre alleged while we walked away from the Statehouse. "If I knew nothing about what you've told me about Raymond Baldwin I'd have to admit he'd just delivered a very moving speech. He sounded sincere and respectable and I think people will generally respond to him well."

"Sure he sounded sincere" I responded snippily, "but he has inherent flaws that makes him a very dangerous person. He's always had the facility to fool people and I deeply fear what he would do if he indeed became a viable candidate."

We walked toward a hole in the wall lunch place I liked very much. A few patrons who'd followed us talked quite passionately about the speech. I felt double crossed by an attorney who should have known better and had a hard time convincing myself Attorney Gould was actually there. A brilliant legal mind and an intelligent man like Gould standing with Baldwin made absolutely no sense. How could a man with a stellar reputation ally himself with one of the slickest political operators of all time? He had to have known Baldwin's past behaviors so what could his interest possibly be?

Sitting at an outdoor table we listened to Sucre's tape of Baldwin's speech. Listening again I had to admit he did sound sincere and commanding and it would be very difficult to find fault with anything said. I suspected poor Emil was rolling over in his grave.

CHAPTER 24

There was a phone message from my new attorney Sanford Roberts asking for a meeting to touch base. I called his office but was told he was gone for the day, giving me the uneasy feeling that maybe Gould and Roberts were part of Baldwin's cadre.

I didn't really trust Sanford yet but I knew for certain there was no way I could ever work with Gould again. A young and inexperience lawyer like Roberts could easily be my ruin but regretfully, he was all I had at the moment. If the police wanted to talk to me again, could the rookie actually negotiate the complicated legal system or even manage a potential murder trial?

Sucre and I worked late on Emil's papers with a new urgency, hoping to discover answers to the question; why was Emil killed.

Sleep did not come easy or quickly once again, inundated with bad dreams I remembered all to well after each wakeup. My anxiety level knowing no bounds. I couldn't stomach breakfast so decided to walk to the Gould Building to wait for Attorney Roberts. Fortunately, he was in his tiny office.

"Mr. Darwin, Charlie, just as a precaution I think we should spend a little time this morning preparing for any number of legal scenarios and eventualities."

The introductory words made me feel I was a condemned man.

"First I want to share some good news with you. I got a call from the Assistant DA last night saying any arraignment or possible charges were still on hold in the Emil Breck's case. He reiterated that although the receipt and the charge card were pretty damning evidence, for now it's not enough to charge you. Even if you did purchase the poison, there is

Emil's List

still now way to connect you to Emil Breck's death. He took me into his confidence saying the evidence so far gathered would probably not hold up under good cross examination. The bottom line right now is we're looking okay but you've still got to be very patient because this case is far from closed."

I didn't know whether to collapse in relief or scream, asking if there were other known suspects. Shaking his head he replied if there were, that was something the police were keeping to themselves.

"Have the police figured what the motive might have been," I asked?

Maybe Roberts knew more but I suspected that he was not letting me in on everything. A motive seemed too obvious. Someone didn't want Emil Breck uncovering something possibly very explosive.

Attorney Roberts smiled.

"They're being very tight lipped about that too so I can't give you an answer right now. However I do believe the detectives are looking at other individuals, people who've held grudges against Mr. Breck and some who'd sent threatening letters. I didn't learn any names however.

"There is something you once floated by me and I'd like to bring that up. Remember you once said it was possible Mr. Breck was killed because of something he was working on? I'm curious. Have you found any hard evidence to back that up?"

My heart began racing, recalling the names of certain individuals who'd threatened me during my career, people I'd rightfully brought down. I assumed Emil was often in the same position. I answered it was possible something important could be found in Emil's papers but so far, no luck finding it.

"Charlie the detectives are extremely thorough but they know it's not an easy case because the killer used strychnine. Nobody in the department ever worked a case involving this particular poison so it's taking some time. To sum up where we stand, for the time being you're okay and I'll keep you informed if anything new comes up."

I wondered if the police thought I was a frustrated writer, insanely jealous of Mr, Breck's work and success. Was that a motive? The nagging though Sanford knew more than he was letting on made me uncomfortable.

"Charlie, the value of Mr. Breck's book collection is around a quarter

Bruce Weiss

million dollars" Roberts injected. "If someone wanted those books, that could be considered motive so there are other theories out there.

Should I ask if he thought I'd been chosen to take the fall because I was now working with Emil's papers? I kept quiet.

Sanford asked if I was aware of any vindictive people threatening Emil lately. I answered there were many people including Raymond Baldwin who'd once used his position to harm both Emil and I, and who still could be holding a grudge.

"Let's suppose Emil was murdered because of something he was working on" I said deliberately. "If that's the case, his killer might now be watching Sucre and I right now to see if we can find what that is."

I regretted the words as soon as they came out.

The image of Gould sitting on the stage with Baldwin was eating at me, making me wonder if Roberts knew Gould would be on the podium with Baldwin. I debated whether to lay all my cards on the table but if that involved criticism of his boss, would he toss me out on the street? I knew no other lawyers I could turn to so I wasn't quite ready to give up on or rile Roberts. My head was spinning. Should I ask about his boss's politics? I knew I should throw a little caution into the wind to find out which way it was blowing.

"Attorney. Roberts, when Raymond Baldwin was governor of Massachusetts he assembled a team of very shady individuals who were at his disposal day and night, settling problems quickly, efficiently and quietly. I uncovered this secret cabal. They weren't government officials nor were they on the state payroll. My investigation discovered evidence that Baldwin was supporting them monetarily. Please bear with me for a few more minutes because this isn't easy to talk about.

"Five years ago I also uncovered evidence of a secret slush fund the governor created to pay unknown individuals for work that often broke the law. I also discovered through some secret pirated memos that Baldwin met often with his team, usually the first thing in the morning. Nothing however was ever put in writing. As far as I know, nobody was killed but there were many curious and perplexing incidents happening to people who spoke out against Baldwin. Several of his outspoken opponents were mugged, several others were run down by speeding cars and a few found themselves falsely involved in made up scandals, names and reputations smeared. I had proof many of those dealings were connected to the Statehouse but most of that ended up burned up in a mysterious fire. The notes I'd used had been court ordered over to the DA who could have used them to bring charges against Baldwin. It's possible Baldwin has put his old gang together again so I'm going to go out on a limb here. Your boss might be a part of that assemblage."

I couldn't tell what Robert's was thinking because his expression never changed. Had he heard my inference that Baldwin and Gould might be up to no good? Roberts's silence unnerved me and all I could do was keep my mouth running.

"Mr. Roberts, I did have an axe to grind with Mr. Baldwin because he was dirty but it was strictly business when I went after him. After these long years I'm still hurt by the great pleasure he took in trashing my reputation. He also did his best to trash Emil's reputation years earlier. I wrote a series of scathing articles exposing his administration's shady dealings and that should have ended his political life forever, but now he's back and somehow Attorney Gould is connected to Baldwin.

"Baldwin was solely responsible for my firing and the ensuing blackballing, orchestrated so effectively it ended my professional career. I'm guessing you don't know much about Raymond Baldwin but if it would be alright, I'd like to ask you about your boss Steven Gould."

The expression on Sanford's face changed as did it's color, giving me the impression I was skating on thin ice.

"Are you talking about my boss, the well respected honorable Steven Gould? Are you questioning his character and if you are, what do you want from me?"

I couldn't take back what I'd said and there was no retreat. Curiously the edginess I'd felt since I sat down evaporated.

"Please listen to me a bit longer. How can such a fine man as Attorney Steve Gould support a man who'd disgraced himself in office, resigning in shame? It would take hours to tell you all the injustices and illegal acts his administration committed but believe me, the list is long."

I wondered if Sanford Roberts actually knew anything about Raymond Baldwin's past but then again, why would he? After all I thought, Roberts was probably a schoolboy during Baldwin's tenure as governor.

"I'm still not sure where you're going with this Mr. Darwin, Charlie.

Do you think its okay to judge someone by the candidate they support, one you obviously have a bone to pick with?"

I couldn't shut myself up, describing the corruption I'd uncovered and publicized as well as the consequences leading to my firing and blackballing.

"Was ex-Governor Baldwin ever charged with any crimes" Roberts asked?

My frustration got the best of me, making me want to get up and walk out. Either Roberts was extremely naïve or he'd come to the conclusion I was sour grapes. I wanted to say why don't we just forget we've had this conversation but the words would not come out.

"I think Mr. Gould's political views like yours and mine are based on our values. You do realize Attorney Steven Gould is one of the finest legal scholars in the nation. Did you know that fifteen years ago he was considered a candidate for the US Supreme Court? As to Baldwin, I really only know what I read in the paper these days and there's no mention of his past. I read his speech in the paper and truthfully, it impressed me greatly as it would Mr. Gould I assume. Let me get something straight. Are you sure you want to question Attorney Gould's integrity?"

I managed a slow shake of my head no. I was terribly sorry I'd brought up the subject but nothing could change that. Without any further discussion I announced I'd been away from my place for more than an hour and my friend Ms. Grande was alone.

Walking out of the Gould building I grew more and more perplexed by Sanford Roberts. I hoped the subject of his boss would not come up again and that I might limit our discussions to any legal troubles I might find myself in.

My apartment door was triple locked and my worries about Sucre disappeared when she unlatched them letting me in. I told her she was certainly a sight for sore eyes.

Over Pisco Sours I talked about my meeting with Sanford Roberts, emphasizing the positives, especially the fact the police were not pursuing me or us for the time being. I deliberately left out the convoluted discussion about Gould and Baldwin, asking if she'd heard anything more on her radio about Baldwin.

Emil's List

"Just that he's the number one news story every hour but interestingly, nobody has mentioned a thing about his problems when he was governor."

Damn I muttered, wondering why the sordid information was being held back. Had Baldwin put his team together quashing any discussion of his bad deeds? Despite my overactive mind it was paramount I put those two out of my head and get back to our work. The second Pisco Sour took the edge off, at least for a while.

"Sucre, I'm curiously focused on Emil's words there was more than met the eye. I've come to believe it wasn't a reference to your blindness so it's got to be the key to this. I know we've gone through the books a number of times and nothing seemed out of place and nothing suggested any hidden meanings. No matter how many times we might go through the books looking for something, I suspect we'll still end up finding nothing but the words written about very exceptional writers."

Opening another cardboard carton containing scores of handwritten notes, some apparently written when Emil was the Moscow correspondent for an independent news agency based in Washington in the late 50's. I read all the notes aloud telling Sucre that reporter's notes were the heart of the work that followed.

"Charlie, I hear a new frustration in your voice loud and clear, maybe even a bit of anger too so please hear me out before you read anything else. First, I agree with your assessment there's probably nothing in those books that might reveal what Emil was working on. I'm also convinced there are no hidden meanings. I've listened to Baldwin's speech several more times and I hate to say this but he sounds very formidable and even with his past misdeeds. He's going to become very popular. I'm no expert on American politics but I think his message is going to resonate with a large national audience, especially when he starts campaigning so can you can explain something to me? Are you upset and angry Baldwin has suddenly reappeared and are you thinking about using your old information to derail him?"

I wished she could have seen the devilish look on my face.

"No, although the thought has certainly crossed my mind a few too many times. No, I'm not going to dig up old history because I'm certain it would make no difference. The past is the past.

"Charlie there's something else I meant to tell you but regretfully

I kept it to myself. Remember you told me to keep my ears open to hopefully pick up private conversations at the Baldwin rally? Well, as soon as Baldwin finished his speech I heard him whispering to someone close to the microphone. I wanted to tell you about this a few times but didn't want to see you hurt anymore. Charlie, he whispered that's the son of a bitch Darwin who screwed me. Keep your eyes on him."

CHAPTER 25

Sucre strolled to Bunker Hill in the late morning to hear candidate Baldwin deliver his first official campaign speech. Bunker Hill was hallowed ground I explained so before she left I gave her a brief American history lesson.

"Baldwin should attract a rather large audience but first things first. Do I have to worry about you?"

"You never have to worry about me Charlie, honestly. I've negotiated these streets for many years well before I met you." That was the end of an attempt to keep Sucre home and safe with me.

After she'd left I continued working on Emil's papers, surprising myself reading aloud for several minutes. Force of habit I realized.

I accomplished much but a feeling came over me I hadn't anticipated. I missed Sucre not being around while I read about Emil's storied life. I also missed listening to Sucre's on the hour news reports.

When she returned mid afternoon I was so absorbed reading Emil's dispatches about Freedom Rides in the early 60's that I didn't hear her enter.

"What's got you so mesmerized? Didn't you hear me fumbling with the locks?"

"I was reading news articles about a very intense life and death situations Emil found himself in during the first bus rides into the segregated American south. Do you know about segregation and the Civil Rights struggles in America in the 1960's?"

"Charlie, the whole world was watching what was happening in your country and although I was far too young to understand everything, we knew it was wrong. In school the nuns told us about American segregation practices, stressing it truly offended the human soul."

Bruce Weiss

"Sucre while you were at the rally I read a number of extraordinary first hand accounts describing Emil's bus travels and the inhuman attack on the riders, courtesy of enraged white mobs. I'll tell you more about the freedom rides later, especially the part about the brave young men and women who knowingly put their lives on the line to bring about racial equality. First however, I'd like to hear your thoughts on Baldwin's speech at Bunker Hill."

"I'll play the tape for you so you can hear for yourself."

Sucre apologized she could not get as close as she would have preferred so the sound quality wasn't particularly good. I sat back closing my eyes and listened while Sucre described how she felt.

Baldwin's opening remarks were testy and terse right at the get go, not like the man who spoke rather eloquently the day before at the Statehouse. There was an angrier tone to his words, introductory remarks most likely meant to inflame the crowd. punctuated with diatribes and nasty attacks on both Republicans and Democrats. If the words were meant to stir up the crowd he'd certainly succeeded. The cheering and chanting was so loud Sucre turned the recorder volume down when she hit play.

"America is in big trouble and if we don't act immediately, our problems will soon become insurmountable so sadly acknowledge this to you. America will become a second rate nation on the world stage, sooner rather than later."

Baldwin had obviously taken a page out of his old demagogue playbook I thought, decrying the lack of backbone and courage in our current leaders and their do nothing approach to everything. The malaise he stressed, was like a dangerous flu.

"As a third party candidate I have no allegiances or alliances to party bosses. Therefore, I am the only candidate you can count on to stop the downward spiral we've become trapped in. Friends, I say this not to frighten you but it's the reality of America today. The current cast of characters in Washington are effectively moving America toward a failed nation status."

Baldwin slammed liberal judges soft on criminals and a military too inept to defend our nation. His voice reminded me of an old time pastor railing at his audience, the tone more powerful than the words.

"The police have their hands tied by such outrageous restrictions you have to wonder, who is actually handcuffed; the scum on our streets or the brave men and women in blue?"

Ranting about the military, he referred to the Department of Defense and today's generals as traitors to America.

"Our current military is second rate to our enemies, stymied at every junction by a do nothing Congress and a naïve president. The liberals consistently take money away from our nations defense, rendering our military practically useless. It's déjà vu ladies and gentlemen only the culprits this time aren't the 1950's communists; it's the lackeys in Washington who continue to make no investments in America's future.

"Have any of you seen the morning newspaper polling results?"

The crowd roared to life.

"Then you know that the majority of registered voters in Massachusetts support me. According to this morning's poll seventy percent of eligible Republicans and Democrats in the state have a favorable impression of me. I can promise you this, you ain't seen nothing yet."

The crowd was on fire. Sucre paused the tape.

"Charlie, the crowd was so loud at times you couldn't hear the candidate's words."

An old Baldwin trick people fell for before. Sound imposing but don't let too many cats out of the bag just yet. I realized he'd also learned a few new tricks during the five years out of pubic life including how to grab headlines. He once spoke with the same belligerence and bravado when he ran for governor but this time it felt a hundred fold more. When the speech ended there were endless minutes of clapping and shouting until Sucre mercifully turned the recorder off.

"Where's he going to speak next" I asked?

"No one is really certain but I heard someone near me say he was taking a day off before going on the road for three days of campaigning around Massachusetts. There's also a rumor next weekend he's taking his show on the road to Madison Square Garden in New York."

I shook my head in disbelief, finding it nearly impossible to accept the fact the clown was making a comeback. Did he actually believe the general population would simply ignore his past transgressions? They would I rued, unless someone pointed them out and it wasn't going to be me this time.

Baldwin's voice always grated on me because it was so phony but five

Bruce Weiss

years later, the thick Boston accent he was so proud of was gone. I knew I should stop upsetting myself to get back to our work but sadly, it took nearly an hour to put myself in a better frame of mind. Time to go back to work I announced, more for myself than Sucre.

"I discovered a few handwritten notes buried under a pile of notebooks and attached to one in particular was a letter Emil received just months before Baldwin resigned. It's possible Emil might have been working on the same story I was writing but I beat him to the punch.

I have no proof but my instincts tell me he was starting a new investigation into Baldwin, probably in the very preliminary stage. The date on the note was the real kicker. We've read papers dating back decades but this one note was written only weeks before he died. It could be our key to discovering what he was working on and possibly why he was killed. His penmanship is like chicken scrawl so it took some time to decipher the wording but here it goes."

'I've worked with the most dedicated and competent people my entire life, enabling me to expose greed, corruption and abuses of power. These individuals who asked never to reveal their identities were a treasure trove of sources and without their assistance, I probably would have been a footnote in some old reporter's journal. One of my oldest and most reliable sources wrote me an eye opening letter six years ago when she was a secretary in Raymond Baldwin's office.'

"This appears to be the letter the woman wrote to Emil" I said.

'Governor Baldwin meets secretly with a group of individuals every morning behind closed locked doors. The group is extremely loyal and carry's out the Governor's private wishes. One day the notes were not disposed as usual because I found them jammed into an overloaded shredder. The notes were dated March 17 describing the meeting in which the Governor asked his posse to identify any individuals and groups opposing him. The secretive group was ordered to create a list of names for the governor to be classified as enemies. Governor Baldwin issued orders that morning to do whatever was necessary to stop those who spoke or wrote unfavorably about him.'

"Sucre I had wind of this when I was investigating him five years ago but the group covered their tracks too well, not knowing Emil actually had hard evidence the shadowy group truly existed. It's a fact of life reporters don't share what they're working on or their notes with other reporters. Stapled to the note is the list of names brought up in the morning meeting that day. Sucre, I say fasten your seatbelt often but this time I mean it. It's ancient history but guess who was at the top of that list those many years ago?

"You're going to say it was you, right?"

I nodded, remembering to verbalize a moment later.

"There's more to the note." I added.

'A source I trust implicitly believes that former Governor Baldwin has put together another formidable team in anticipation of a run for an elected office. There are unsubstantiated rumors Baldwin is planning to return to public life."

Maybe we've just uncovered the tip of an iceberg I thought because in truth, I hadn't known Emil was working on a new investigation into our old nemesis Raymond Baldwin.

"Sucre it's possible, just possible Emil had the goods on Baldwin and someone on his team silenced Emil realizing he might be ready to blow the whistle. I realize that sounds like something out of a third rate crime novel but there might be more to the eye as Emil often insisted.

"Let me explain a bit more about Baldwin. The ex-Governor once carved out his own personal empire in Massachusetts, built entirely upon illegal and dishonest business dealings. The empire stretched from the Berkshire Mountains in the west to Cape Cod in the east. I'm now starting to believe its entirely possible Emil discovered Raymond Baldwin was secretly planning to build a new empire on a much grander scale. Now, if Emil knew Baldwin would eventually emerge from his cocoon to become a political force again, was he working on something to stop him? I don't know who his sources were or how he even discovered Baldwin was going most likely ready to re-enter politics.

"Where to you think Emil was going with this Charlie?"

"I can't be certain but it's entirely possible Emil always kept an eye on Baldwin going all the way back the HUAC days. He knew more than most the inherent evil in that man. It's possible Emil knew what Baldwin was up to during those very quiet five years. I don't know if there's more notes related to this but we still have a few unopened cartons. If we're on the wrong road, sadly this will all be a waste of our time."

"Charlie, do you really think Raymond Baldwin, a presidential could possibly be behind Emil's murder?"

"I begin to actually consider that possibility this morning but without definite proof I'd say its far out of our reach, at least for now. The election is four weeks away which gives us a little time to play detective but clues are going to be very difficult to find. Right now it's all speculation but with a tinge of real possibility. Baldwin never accepted responsibility for his shady dealings I'd exposed, blaming me and others for creating lies about him. If he's somehow involved in Emil's murder, I'm certain he's covered a very convoluted trail because he's always been very good at that.

"Sucre, in his farewell address on the steps of the State House Baldwin held reporters completely responsible for smearing his good name, declaring their slanderous fabrications made it impossible to govern the state. He saved most of his venom for me however, still powerful enough to destroy my credibility and making certain no one would ever hire me. When he left the governor's office I was sure I'd never hear his name again but now, I can't get him out of my mind."

"Why wasn't he brought up on charges when his wrongdoings were exposed?"

"Because even before the ink dried on the formal charges against him, one of my inside informers at the State House told me he'd struck a deal. He agreed to disappear for a number of years, make no political statements during that time and in return, there would be no indictments. His very last words were directed at the reporters who'd gathered on the front steps. Even though I wasn't there he labeled me a blatant liar, a fake news creator and someone in bed with leftists and yellow journalists. I never heard a peep from him after that until now."

There was a little more to Baldwin's Bunker Hill speech on Sucre's tape recorder and reluctantly I said we might as well listen.

'I thank you all for being here and I feel your heartfelt support. I'm greatly encouraged by the size of this audience and if the press would only tell the truth about the size of my crowds, I'd have no problems with them. I don't believe the press has been very honorable these past years and they've certainly had it out for me.

'It's an honor to stand before patriotic Americans at this historic site and like the patriots who defended this hill against overwhelming forces,

Emil's List

I will never retreat and never give up without a fight. I'm an independent candidate running for the presidency of the United States so I owe no allegiance to anyone but you. You are my political party and I'm counting on you to spread the word that we're going to change the status quo. I'm running for this office because like most of you, I don't like the direction this nation is moving. America is on a respirator and the patient is dying.

'Who's to blame for the unacceptable high unemployment rate, the sky high taxes, our shoddy military performances around the world and the failures of our educational systems? There's plenty of blame to spread around but personally, I fault the liberals who've bankrupted our nation both morally and economically. We desperately need someone in Washington to bring this country back to it's good old glory. Sadly, we've become a laughing stock to much of the world and the reason? Our political correctness is smothering the life out of us. Political correctness has taken on more importance then the real issues we're facing.

'I believe in strong leadership that emphasizes making political and economic change, rather then waiting for the winds of change to come along. If you examine my record of leadership in Massachusetts you'll see that our students were better educated, our cities were wealthier and less dependent on charity, and law and order was established throughout the state. If we don't move from the welfare state the liberals have painstakingly created, we will lose everything we've ever worked for. Now let me be specific.

'I've always supported the rights guaranteed by the Second Amendment of our Constitution and you know what it stands for. I'll never give up my guns because as wiser men have explained, when guns are taken away only the bad guys will have them. If you think registration of firearms is a good thing, I would remind you first comes registration and then confiscation.

'Look at our failed systems of education in America. Are you really happy with your child's schooling? I'll bet you're not. I'll put an end to Common Core in our schools and get the federal government out of education where it has no business. I say common sense, not common core. Let individual communities determine their own educational requirements without Washington telling them what to do. I declare, let's put the power back into the hands of local community school boards where it belongs. I would also insist on litmus tests for teachers to make certain they are not brainwashing our children, or worse.

'The liberal establishment has turned our country into the status of a third world nation. Friends, the liberal philosophy is obsolete and only a complete reversal of years of poor decisions can save us.

'We must put the word UNITED back into America again and the only way to do that is to elect strong leaders capable of maintaining a stable and orderly society. I've always been a law and order man because it guarantees a safe society. We can no longer allow ourselves to condone strikes and protests and certainly not liberal lies.

'New and very powerful protectionist laws would be a priority in my administration, protecting American industries and workers against unfair foreign competition. We can be number one in the world again, but only if we put America first.

'We must have the ability and capability to flex our military power anywhere and any time. If it is in our best interest, let the military do their job. The word will go out to friend and foe alike these colors don't run.

'I believe capitalism and capitalists like all humans have defects, but it is the best system for us. We need to make it easier for America to be more competitive in today's world. Excessive rules and regulations harm our businesses and I promise to repeal any regulations strangling our ability to compete on the world stage. I want America to be strong again and to do that I need your support. If you're like me you're sick and tired of our current leaders lamenting we are a failed state. I'd fire the first person in my administration who even thought that.

'I promise you I'll stop Washington from telling you what's best for you. Think about this. Do the actions of the federal government serve your best interests? The so-called leaders in Washington are weak and incompetent and that appears to be the only job qualification to work in Washington. Neither party has the will or the means to fix what ails us so we need a leader who's not afraid to shake things up. The current politicians in Washington are suffocating the liberty that many Americans have lived and died for, including those who died here at Bunker Hill.

'Look around this great hilltop monument and think for a moment about the brave patriots who defended the land then called Breed's Hill. Those brave men didn't run and neither will I if I'm in charge in

Emil's List

Washington. Are you tired of having the federal government tell you how to run your schools, your hospitals or your health care facilities? We've relinquished the power individuals once held, turning our lives over to the incompetents in Washington. It's time we make this country great again. Thank you for coming by today and God Bless you all, and God Bless America."

Chapter 26

Due to Sucre's blindness she'd developed other perceptions and insights most sighted people weren't aware of. It took me some time to learn her uncanny ability to overcompensate for her lack of sight. As a blind woman she'd learned how to listen to voices and sounds others could not hear. If she heard someone's voice once, she had the ability to recognize it in the future. Sucre also knew the sounds of danger, such as the sound of a speeding car or someone riding a bicycle on a sidewalk. She'd learned how to use sounds such as the chimes on the church steeples announcing the time. The world makes wonderful music she'd once said, all you had to do was listen well.

Listening to Baldwin's tape I sensed his words would easily attract the masses who shared his sentiments. In many Boston coffee houses customers were talking about the changes Baldwin could deliver.

Five years ago I'd been extremely outspoken about the graft and corruption so I wondered, how did this man reinvent himself and why weren't citizens holding him accountable? Had they forgotten what the city and state went through? I was obsessing with Baldwin, spending time fretting only succeeding in taking the edge off some of my own problems.

I continued to learn things about Sucre, particularly her resolve and determination to be as independent as possible. She often remarked Emil's papers read aloud filled her with joy, a free education in twentieth century American history. To have the grit to overcome the pain after her life was tragically torn from her was nothing short of remarkable. I believed she was one of the most courageous people I'd ever befriended, every minute of every day dealing with something as seemingly impossible as remaining positive in a darkened world.

Emil's List

Another phone call from Sanford near dinner time presented a new problem, and it was a big one.

"I'm sorry to tell you this but someone in the DA's office leaked information about Emil Breck's case to the press."

Sanford warned me to gird my loins because I could soon very well be at the center of a media frenzy storm. As if on cue the reality came to full fruition when the first news trucks, reporters and camera people arrived at the front of my building. Eye balling the scene from my 6th floor window, I knew my privacy was gone. Scores of reporters milled around waiting for an appearance and hopefully a statement. I knew the routines because I was one of them early in my career.

My attempt to ignore the commotion didn't fool Sucre because she instinctively knew I was standing on shaky ground, hearing me walk to the window at least a dozen times.

With much ado on the street the police finally arrived, their vehicles with flashing red lights reminded me of a disaster scene. I told Sucre the press people were setting up camp in front of the building and there was nothing we could do about it. Very few residents of my building however knew there was an unmarked back alley which would become our safe exit and entrance. I was somewhat certain I could deal with the press if I had to but what would happen if Sucre got caught in their grasp?

After dark I got a bit careless, standing by the window looking up and down the street. We both heard the loud collective shout 'there he is.' I flashed back to what it felt like a life time ago when I was one of them, probably using those same words.

I felt Sucre gently pulling me away from the window.

"We can't allow ourselves to become prisoners here" I whispered, worrying powerful microphones pointing at my window might catch our words. "I have to make sure there are no reporters in the back alley so wait here. To my relief the alley was clear.

I managed to stay clear of the window but was ever mindful of the noise and flashing lights on the street below. It was just the two of us dining but in my mind, Baldwin had pulled a seat up to the table, my overactive mind loosening old resentments I thought I'd gotten over. Would the press ever tire and go home I muttered? Sadly I knew the answer. At nine that night only one reporter and film crew remained and I suspected they were camped there for the night.

After dinner we listened to the radio and organized more of Emil's papers. Sucre put her earphone on listening to her Peruvian music, interrupted only by her new found fascination for the hourly news reports.

An hour later a loud knock on my door brought our quiet evening to an end, convinced it was the nosy reporter who'd grown tired of waiting below in the street. I was prepared to do whatever was necessary to protect our privacy but to what extent, I had no clue.

To my great delight I heard the voice of my building super calling my name. When I opened the door I did not miss the unhappy look on his face. I checked the hall and told him to come inside.

He said it was probably none of his business, but did I know why there was so much turmoil around the building, saying he'd talked to the police but got no answers. I didn't want to go into a long narrative mostly because the situation had become so convoluted. I said the issue was a large group of reporters wanting information for their news outlets from me. Thankfully, he did not ask why but offered his wife prepared too much food and since I hadn't gone out all day, he wondered if we would like some of his wife's home cooking. The sentiment floored me.

With things quieting down, Sucre drifted off with her earphones still in her ears. Looking over at her, I hoped she was at peace and dreaming about Misti Mountain. The Peruvian music always soothed her, bringing back warm thoughts about Peru she said often. I turned my attention back to Emil's papers because I knew I would not be able to fall asleep. The upside was the work kept my mind off Baldwin's campaign and the press and even my troubles for a while. There was another reason why I wanted to return to Emil's papers. There was a spark burning inside and I hoped tonight might be the moment a mystery unraveled that might conceivably solve a murder.

CHAPTER 27

In the morning the news trucks were back in full force, still not recognizing any of the reporters. I was awed by the fact they all looked like school children and I wondered if I'd ever looked that young and hungry.

After breakfast it was back to work, starting with the personal notes Emil deliberately tucked into each book in his collection. Sanford Roberts came to the rescue again, moving the books in storage back to my place so we could go through each of them again.

"We need to go through each one of his notes again, page by page to see if there's anything more then meets the eye we might have missed."

It had been days since I'd read aloud, feeling refreshed having Sucre by my side.

"Let's see if any of Emil's words sound out of place or if we suspect something written had other possible meanings." I soon realized it was a bad start to our work day because I'd promised myself not to use the words let's see.

We labored over each page, word for word. The work used up our morning discovering absolutely nothing suggesting any type of hidden meaning. By the afternoon we were both convinced there was nothing in the notes other then Emil's thoughtful and insightful comments about the books and their authors. I put the papers aside disappointed.

Nothing we'd gone through suggested a riddle or a hidden secret code. The expression more then met the eye seemingly meant nothing and the good feeling I'd felt when I discovered the note written four days before his death waned.

There were just a few more letters and news articles to go through, including several more letters addressed to Clarissa in what we discovered

Bruce Weiss

was a life long correspondence. I truly wished he'd put a last name on Clarissa.

'Dear Clarissa,

I'm not sure if you are fully aware of what's going on in Nicaragua so let me explain a rather complicated situation I've taken a very strong and personal interest in.

A man by the name of Somoza made himself president for life some years ago and he and his entire family once ran roughshod over the Nicaraguan people with total indifference to life or property. As in other Central American nations with their American backed dictators, the United States created policies favoring those leaders who bowed to America. If the dictator in power threatened American interests, they would face serious repercussions. In Nicaragua we began providing arms and soldiers in covert operations to keep Somoza in power because he was loyal to us. In time though he was overthrown in a popular revolution sadly splintering the nation politically. Civil wars broke out and you know, I'm no stranger to civil wars.

'Thanks to a team of young and very brave reporters I am currently working in Nicaragua and was able to obtain definitive proof of illegal doings by our government. What we are doing is prolonging the suffering the people of Nicaragua are experiencing. As many as a half a million have died in this travesty.

I believe I have enough documented evidence to prove the US government is illegally arming a group called the Contras. The funding for this does not come directly from Washington so I find myself on a convoluted trail hoping to expose wrong doing, possibly involving the president.

I'll keep you informed and in the meantime if you don't hear from me for a while, know that I am okay. Emil'

Little could Emil have known when he wrote that letter that it would lead to the doorstep of the White House months later.

Chapter 28

"It's all in the clicks my walking stick makes," Sucre said proudly. "It's exactly two hundred and five clicks to the Deli and the same number back. I hardly ever get lost."

We'd snuck out the back door several times avoiding the press and even with the sounds of rats moving about the alley it felt good to be free. Most of the streets on Beacon Hill were one way making it much easier for Sucre to negotiate.

"I've got all my regular destinations down to a certain number of clicks" she said happily," including the pathways I frequent at Harvard. Being in a familiar place often makes me forget I'm actually blind sometimes."

I said I was most impressed.

"I manage rather well and you know I truly relish my freedom."

Getting away from the reporters without getting caught delighted me, Sucre referring to them as tenacious pit bulls. I had a different view because I was once like them, always hungry for a good story. We enjoyed getting away from my place but when we decided to return I did something I immediately regretted. Without forethought, I placed my hand on her arm to guide her along. In a heartbeat I realized my mistake. Her recoil startled me.

No words were exchanged until Sucre stopped walking. A moment passed and to my great surprise instead of saying something she forcefully shoved me backward so roughly I tumbled onto the sidewalk, an aggressive side of her I'd never seen. I was bewildered, attributing the shove to her great disdain for my unwanted gesture. Her strength greatly surprised me as I lay on the sidewalk catching my breath. A heartbeat later I heard the unmistakable sound of a fast moving car heading seemingly directly

Bruce Weiss

toward us. From the sound I realized it was going the wrong way on a one way street, fearing we might be road kill.

The car passed by so close that I felt the engine's heat and looking far up the street I saw the car had already disappeared over a hill, tires screeching, black diesel fumes filling the air. I got up pulling Sucre to her feet, feeling her body trembling as I held her, her pants torn on both knees and blood oozing.

I was in a state of shock until I realized Sucre's reaction was not retaliation for attempting to guide her, but a move to prevent us from being run down. Had someone purposely tried to injure or kill us, or was it a case of extreme reckless driving?

"The car was an older Mercedes" Sucre announced.

I knew all too well she could not have seen the car so I asked how she knew.

"Because over the years I've learned the sounds each car's engine makes and you know, each one is different depending upon the size of the car and the size of the engine. I can tell when a Porsche drives by or an old VW and even a new Ford or an old Honda. If you listened to the traffic as carefully as I do, you too would inevitably learn those sounds. The car was definitely a Mercedes Diesel, probably ten years old because of the guttural sound to the engine. Can you still smell the diesel exhaust?"

In truth I could no longer. Sucre had most likely saved our lives knowing if I'd been alone, I would have been maimed or even killed.

Sucre's dark glasses had fallen off and for the first time I saw her beautiful face without them. She had truly remarkably eyes and I was unable to look away. The damage from the bomb blast hadn't marred her appearance so obviously the real damage was inside.

I looked us over concluding there was little damage, save Sucre's scraped knees and my nerves. When we started to walk again Sucre hobbled a bit. A fit of anger welled up, upset the sighted one had not seen the car.

"When I first heard the car" she said slowly catching her breath, "I knew it was a one street well and the sound was not what I usually hear. I've walked that street hundreds of times and I've always listened for things that appear out of place. I guess my brain became wired differently after I lost my sight because my senses told me a car was approaching at a high rate of speed, driving the wrong way. I didn't mean to push you so hard but there was no time to explain"

The sentiment made me smile.

Living near Beacon Hill I knew Mercedes, Range Rovers and BMWs were common sights. I was also aware of the expensive cars parked at the State House. It if was a local I thought it had to have been someone under the influence of drugs or alcohol. I was flooded with thoughts including the awful proposition someone had purposely tried to frighten us, or worse. When we reached the top of Beacon Hill I turned back, the sun light reflecting off the gold dome of the State House. Was someone working there our culprit? I felt Sucre trembling, or was it me?

Cleaning and bandaging Sucre's knees revealed little harm had been done but I couldn't say the same for my nerves. Someone might have been sending us a message or, was it simply reckless driving? One last application of iodine and Sucre was good to go, bringing up memories of fighting with my mother whenever the iodine vial came out. I knew it stung but Sucre never let on.

CHAPTER 29

There was another phone message from Attorney Sanford Roberts and with some hesitation I played the message back.

'The District Attorney graciously informed me he was dealing with an overload of cases and Emil's case had been put on indefinite hold for the time.'

I wasn't uncertain if that was good news or bad. Sanford suggested I arrange another meeting time to go over possible options should I be questioned by the detectives again. When I finished listening I anticipated a fairly benign meeting until I realized I'd had a death grip on the phone. We decided not to do any work the rest of the day, even too tired and upset to have our usual Pisco sours.

When I sat down the next morning in Sanford's tiny office something told me there was no time for idle chat. He looked all business, his tie usually loose around his neck taut.

"Lets start this meeting where we stand right now. The only solid piece of evidence the police have against you is the credit card charge with your name and account number. Handwriting experts compared your signature with other receipts of yours and they do see a slight difference. Three experts looked at the signatures and one said they were the same. The other two said no. The tape made of the transaction cannot be resurrected.

"I understand the detectives have not identified other suspects but I was told they're still keeping all options open. As to other possible people of interest, neither the detectives or DA Long cared to divulge that information so we're in is what I would call a holding pattern. I don't anticipate charges being filed in the near future so for now so put this in the back of your mind."

Emil's List

I was relieved to hear those words but something was troubling me. I had to say what was on my mind.

"Please don't take offense at what I'm going to say, but would I be better served finding another attorney dealing exclusively in murder cases? I don't mean to sound ungrateful or unappreciative because you've been here for me for several weeks now and you've certainly kept me well informed and positive. I need some assurance this is not over your head."

Sanford smiled and to my surprise laughed. I was free to choose any attorney I wanted he offered, and if I decided to choose someone else, there would be no hard feelings.

"How tall are you he asked?"

The questions caught me off guard.

"Six feet give or take a half inch," I answered.

"I drove north to the vet's office in New Hampshire two days ago and measured the height of the counter. It was five feet two inches from the floor to the counter surface. The man on the tape who bought the poison appears to be four or five inches taller. I passed that observation along to the detectives who will look into it. What I'm trying to say is that I'm working diligently in your best interest Charlie, but if you still want someone else, that's your prerogative. At some point the police will want to talk with you again and you should have an attorney who understands this case."

I apologized for being doubtful saying I'd be honored to have him represent me.

"Anything else" he asked?

In truth there was. I asked for a bottle of water, using those few precious seconds to find the right words because they hadn't gone over well in our last meeting.

"I want to bring up something that could have a bearing on the case, something you might call an old reporter's instinct kicking in. I won't sugar coat what I'm about to say so here it goes. Have you ever heard your boss talking about Raymond Baldwin?"

Sanford looked dazed by the question, shaking his head saying the only thing he new about Baldwin was what he'd read in the papers.

"Why do you ask," said with a look suggesting I'd better get right to the point.

Bruce Weiss

"It's a rather long story and I don't want to take up any more of your time, but would you listen. I gave you the shorter version? It's worth hearing."

There was no response unsettling me even more, figuring he'd stop me when he'd heard enough.

"I think Raymond Baldwin might have some bearing on Emil Breck's death and I'll tell you why."

"Go on," he said, a quizzical look on his face.

"Mr. Baldwin and I had a run in five years ago, actually it was really more like a head on collision. I once worked for a Boston paper specializing in investigative reporting and as I told you, I wrote a series of articles exposing treachery and deceit in Baldwin's office. My revelations eventually led to the announcement he was resigning the governorship, claiming total innocence. He stated he couldn't engage in a long possible legal battle and still hold the reins of the state government. I wrote truthful, well documented stories and I'd be happy to fax them over to your office if you'd like.

"A few weeks after the articles appeared in the press and just after things quieted down he retaliated, going to great lengths to get me fired and then eventually blackballed from my profession. In a matter of weeks my reporter's career was over, something I'd never anticipated.

"It took a long time for me to recover from that blow realizing I simply couldn't beat him. Baldwin played dirty and I refused to lower myself. My articles stood for themselves.

"There's something else I want to add. About thirty years ago Raymond Baldwin also played a major role in the life of Emil Breck. Baldwin was the chair of HUAC in the early fifties and he crucified Emil in a series of Senate hearings during the witch hunt for Communists in America. My point in telling you this is Baldwin might have decided to get rid of two old enemies at the same time before announcing his candidacy. Emil Breck was murdered and the evidence points directly at me, someone Baldwin would prefer out of the way once his campaigning commenced. It's speculation but the possibility exists Baldwin's up to bad things again."

I related what I'd discovered about the HUAC war of words between Emil and Baldwin, and how ugly it was portrayed on a national stage.

"There's more" I said." I knew Sanford was hooked on my story when he loosened his tie.

"Baldwin is merciless and a very vengeful individual yet I don't have a shred of proof that he was behind Emil Breck's murder or that he set me up to take the fall. I have an old reporter's sixth sense however there might be something to all this. I am in possession of Emil's personal papers and I've got a feeling someone doesn't want me to discover what Emil was working on. Why? I'm not entirely sure but a couple of unexpected new discoveries makes me believe there's more too it. I haven't finished going through all of Emil's papers yet but I have reason to believe he was working on something about Raymond Baldwin."

I eventually brought up the break-in at Sucre's place and the incident with the out of control car.

"Listen Sanford, someone obviously wanted me to take the fall for the poisoning so the questions is, why choose me? Why not just purchase strychnine with cash and leave no trail that might be followed? I believe it involves me because someone was afraid I'd discover something dangerous in Emil's writings I'd inherited. By the way, I'm talking about thousands of papers so our work has been a bit like looking for the needle in the haystack. I'm not being irrational or paranoid and although I have no specific proof, I can't help feel something terribly wrong is going on. I'll admit again I don't have a shred of proof Baldwin is conspiring against me, but this is the kind of thing he did when he was governor."

Attorney Sanford looked more troubled than satisfied with my story.

"Tell me a little more about HUAC and what actually took place between Mr. Breck and Mr. Baldwin. Those old articles you said you have, I'd like to read them."

What I thought might take five minutes to explain about Emil, my reporter's work, the HUAC hearings and my run in with Baldwin had me talking non stop for thirty minutes, all the while Sanford taking notes.

"This is all quite interesting but to use your own words, there's not a single shred of proof or evidence proving Raymond Baldwin was behind Emil Breck's death or your troubles. There's an awful lot of speculation here so I'll tell you what I'm going to do. Send me any papers about your and Mr. Breck's run-ins with Mr. Baldwin and I'll see if there's anything solid to pursue. Right now however, I'd like to keep this strictly between ourselves. No one else needs to know about our discussion."

There was one more thing eating at me I admitted, asking Sanford for just five more minutes. He nodded, note pad in hand.

"I'd like to talk about your boss Steven Gould and if you and don't mind me asking, would you know why or how he got involved in Baldwin's campaign? I know I've asked you this before but it's taken on more importance."

"Ouch, that hurts," he groaned.

"You believe there's something wrong if someone endorses a politician you don't like? Attorney Gould's politics should not be of any interest to either you or me. Are you implying one of the most distinguished barristers in the country is doing something decadent or wrong?"

It's more then that I replied.

"Attorney Gould knows I own Emil's papers and it's possible he knows there's something in them with the power to derail a political campaign he obviously supports. I think it's entirely possible Emil could have been killed because he was on the verge of going public with some shocking revelation about Baldwin. There are a lot of twists of fate but when my old reporter instincts kick in I'm rarely wrong."

Chapter 30

The days following my meeting were unusually quiet. Sucre and I went about our business reading and organizing the last of Emil's personal papers. I'd hoped we'd find another gold nugget but it was not to be. We spent one entire day again reading over his handwritten reporter's notes.

There were always new surprises and discoveries in each day's work, privileged to learn about the man who stood at the forefront of many life changing events in twentieth century America. It gave me more confidence that we'd have a great story to tell when the biography was eventually published. The only time spent away from the work was our special hour with one of Emil's novels. Emil read Dr. Zhivago to Sucre a year ago but she asked to hear the words and the story again. When we finished a couple of chapters we dove into a newly discovered cache of letters addressed to Clarissa. The letters had been written recently.

'Dear Clarissa,

The arthritis in both hands is beginning to effect my ability to write legibly. I hate to write letters on the typewriter but I know that is what I must do if I want to keep going. I feel like a musician who can no longer play his instrument but I do have some good news.

'I told you I'd narrowed my list down to three or four writers who might help me create the memoir I'm starting work on. With a great feeling of relief I think I've finally found the right person and if he accepts my offer we could begin the work in the very near future. I laugh at myself from time to time, wondering who would want to read long drawn out

Bruce Weiss

ancient history stories about me. I've also decided I will not have the work published until after I'm gone.

'Do you remember the name Charlie Darwin? I've mentioned his name from time to time, a hard name to forget because of the great biologist he's related to. The man was an excellent reporter, retired like me and if he says yes he and I will go over the ground rules and commence. Our first months together will be organizing thousands of old news reports, letters, court records and personal notes to see what we'll use and what we won't. It's a very long term project so I'll need a firm commitment from him.

'Many of my own papers I've not seen in decades, including the very first articles I ever got published. I know it will take a lot of time to go through my correspondence, probably starting with my experiences in Spain. I want to use your letters, some of the best first hand accounts of my life and if that's a problem, please let me know. I doubt many people would be interested in my young years in Romania but there's also a good chance I'll start there.

'The project is extremely ambitious, a very bittersweet experience for me. I just re-read one of the old Congressional transcripts from my appearance before HUAC and it made me quite emotional. I also found the application I made out in 1938 requesting a visa to visit the Soviet Union. How all this time passed so quickly I can never explain.

'I anticipate the actual writing of the memoir will take the better part of a year full time, possibly two or more. Charlie Darwin has a sharp mind and he's a bit familiar with my work because at times we worked together. The work will be laborious and certainly tedious with one of my biggest concerns figuring how to decipher my chicken scrawl. Many of the notes and articles were written in fox holes in the darkness of night. It's going to be breathtaking reliving such important events in my life, but I also suspect it will be heartrending when I realize the fright and horror I covered continues to happen over and over again. We'll do some of our work at the Harvard Library and as a bonus, I might get to see a few old friends who might still be around.

'I think about you often even though we have not seen each other in nearly 30 years, fondly remembering our days in the little stone house on the coast of Spain. We did such a wonderful job reporting the civil war, didn't we?

Emil's List

'Regrets at this point in my life? Only that I'm sorry we didn't take the time to see each other over the years. When I finish the memoir, for the first time since I was in my late teens I'll be free. I hope to have many more years because when this is finished I'd like to devote the rest of my life fighting censorship wherever it rears it's ugly head, anywhere in the world. Emil'

CHAPTER 31

Sucre kept her ears glued to the local news station on the hour, gathering important information to help her negotiate each day, particularly the local weather. News about Baldwin's campaign however continued to be the lead story.

I was getting edgier since Baldwin reappeared but tried not to make it too obvious when we worked. Sucre announced she'd be traveling to Springfield alone by bus to hear a speech delivered by Baldwin. I wanted to say no but I knew how dearly she cherished her independence.

She said not to worry because Baldwin was addressing the Veterans of Foreign Wars indoors so the crowd would definitely be on his side. I knew she didn't have to go because I'd be able to read about the speech in the paper the next day, but I knew it was important for her.

Sucre sweetened the deal reminding me there were things only she might hear, words or expressions and even comments by others that would not be found in the newspaper accounts. I hoped I wouldn't spend the entire day worrying about her.

When she left I managed to keep busy and the day flew by. I felt like I was seeing a rock star walk onto a stage when she got home a little after six. I was very proud of her but I'd learned she didn't like to be told that.

"Baldwin sounded even angrier" she claimed, "possibly because he was addressing veterans in language bordering on what I would call street talk. Like the earlier speeches I attended, he spent time launching attacks against liberalism, telling the veterans who'd won America's wars they deserved more recognition and help. His strongest and most vile rhetoric described our current military being in mortal danger because of policies created by leftist politicians who left our guard down.

Emil's List

"He said he was leading a nonviolent revolution committed to dealing with and solving America's problems our politicians have ignored. Promising a return to the past glory days, he denounced America's second rate military and its loss of face around the world. By the sounds of the whooping and hollering it was easy to discern the veterans were eating up his words. Let me see what else.

"Baldwin said he was one hundred percent committed to protecting the rights put into the second amendment, the eleventh Commandment he said. He pounded his first, insisting the right to bear arms made us all safer.

"He told the veterans he would end welfare calling it a failed system and stating emphatically it would be replaced with something the veterans could identify with; workfare. He promised to end immigration both legal and illegal until every single American had a good paying job, and that got the veterans to their feet. He also claimed it was time to wage a war against unions, claiming they had no further purpose in a free market economy. His attacks against his Republican and Democratic rivals bordered on slander I thought, insisting only an independent could do what was best for all the people. Charlie, The language was gritty and filled with rated X tirades."

The polls dutifully acknowledged his meteoric rise and the news on the hour proclaimed Baldwin was gaining ground every day. With three weeks to go before the election sadly there was still plenty of time to spread his word, what I called venom.

Baldwin was attracting larger audiences making the work with Emil's papers more urgent in case we could find a way to stop him. We were working late into the night, promising each other just another ten minutes and we'd knock off for the day, which never happened.

A ten minute snooze on the sofa usually refreshed me until one fateful evening in a deep sleep I was awakened by Sucre's screaming. For a confused moment I had no sense of time or place.

"I smell smoke" she shouted fretfully, grabbing my full attention. She'd once told me the idea of being trapped in a fire was her worse recurring nightmare, confessing it was because of the explosion in her apartment in Peru.

I ran around the apartment smelling nothing except our evening's dinner. Sucre insisted something was burning, having no idea where it

Bruce Weiss

might be. I'd never doubted her heighten senses but this time I hoped she was wrong.

"Let's go out into the hall and then tell me if you can smell smoke" she cried.

As soon as I opened the door a crack she put my arm in a vice lock, yelling we needed to get out of the building immediately. I still smelled nothing but a few moments later wisps of smoke drifted down the hallway toward us.

We both began yelling and pounding on doors to rouse the other residents. For a moment I thought about running back into my place to grab as many of Emil's papers as I could carry, but I didn't dare leave Sucre.

When we got to the front door of the apartment building the smoke was heavier. Someone shouted the fire department had been called and someone else shouted was anyone missing. The night air was frigid.

We heard the approaching sirens but none of us saw any sign of flames. I gave Sucre a play by play, explaining what the firemen were doing. The smoke was very obvious but the fire personnel reported they could not see actual flames. A half hour later the Chief summoned us together, declaring the danger was over but it would be at least another hour until all the smoke dissipated. My neighbor asked where the fire was.

"We found a large bag of trash smoldering on the back elevator so I'm afraid it's going to be out of order for a while. We searched the entire building and found nothing else so we definitely found the culprit. The fire marshal will be arriving shortly and he'll figure out if it was spontaneous combustion, a cigarette not completely crushed out or even possibly arson. My guess is someone dumped an ashtray into their garbage bag and for whatever reason left it behind in the elevator. Be patient because I've been informed the Red Cross will also arrive shortly to assist you."

Two hours later we were allowed inside; cold, tired and frazzled. Sucre and I had the same thought although we said nothing about it outside. Was it another attempt to warn us or even harm us, this time putting other folks in danger? What better way to get rid of Emil's papers then to have then incinerated I mused.

Sucre made a large pot of hot chocolate while I wondered what would have become of the papers or us if Sucre's sense of smell hadn't detected the smoke. One of the fire fighters said if they'd arrived only five minutes

Emil's List

later flames would have broken out and the old building would have gone up quickly.

Sensing we'd dodged another bullet whether it was intentional or not, I had Sucre to thank once again, making me believe the speeding car incident was probably intentional. Whether both incidents were serious attempts to harm us or to frighten us or just happenstance, it truly didn't matter because sadly, there was nothing we could do to prevent another incident.

Neither of us slept much that night, keeping out ears open and listening for unusual sounds. An hour later we were both still wide awake and began chatting.

"Emil lived a very distinctive life" Sucre remarked, "but I'll bet he made an awful lot of enemies during his lifetime."

I replied all reporters made enemies but Emil was certainly the king.

"His writings and political beliefs angered an awful lot of people" I replied, "some who certainly had vengeance in their hearts and minds. He never shied from controversy though saying if he'd taken every threat to heart, he might as well have gone off and lived on a deserted island. It came with the territory he said often and I agreed. How many people would purposely face an angry mob of white rioters armed with baseball bats in a bus terminal in Mississippi? Given all that Emil faced, I said he'd always taken the high road and the only hatred in his heart was directed at censors."

I wondered if Sucre had fallen asleep because there was no response. In the quiet I thought about the way Emil died, a man who most likely believed he'd die from a bullet in a civil war and not from poison

"He was my hero," Sucre whispered, "as were the nuns who I suddenly miss terribly. From what you've read to me in Emil's papers, he was certainly the most heroic and fearless person I've ever known. I wish he was here so I could tell him how much I admired his work."

I whispered that Sucre she was right up there in the bravery department herself, and that I was in awe of her inner strengths.

"Emil definitely put his life on the line many times and not all reporters were willing to do that" I added, "He never backed down when it would have been all too easy to run from danger. He stood for civil rights and human decency yet despite all that, he did not have a death wish. I've met a

Bruce Weiss

few presidents in my work as a reporter, even revolutionaries including Che and Fidel some years ago. To spend a few moments with Emil however, you truly understood you were in the presence of a very special man. You know, I was planning to spend months, perhaps years documenting an extraordinary life. There were certain things he said that I shall always remember, such as it only took one person to bring about good or great changes in the world. He rubbed a lot of good and bad people the wrong way but it never stopped his work."

The night sky began to brighten so I suggested we put all our thoughts aside and grab a few hours of sleep.

In the morning I let Sucre sleep in a bit longer but I wanted to get an early start on the papers. Re-reading an old letter to Clarissa made me sad when he said he'd hoped to be around a great many more years. I put the letter aside unable to finish, my mind feeling like a whirling cyclone.

The phone rang a few moments later waking Sucre. It was Sanford asking for still another meeting, once again not letting on what it was about. I said I wanted Sucre to come along this time because I didn't want to leave her alone but he replied, not this time.

Over morning cups of very strong Peruvian coffee I told Sucre we'd probably finish all the organizational work in a few days or so and then we should take a full day off and maybe think about our future.

Sucre looked very pensive, saying she had been thinking about her future, wanting to return to work full time at Harvard translating some of Emil's novels into Braille. She also said it might be the right time in her life to begin taking a few education courses. I was pleased she'd begun to see another life beyond the mountains of papers we'd been slaving over. I knew what I'd be doing the next year or more.

Three days later we read the last of the articles in the very last carton. Four months of work on Emil's papers created amazing highs and terrible lows, feeling as if the work passed by in the blink of an eye. I said we ought to celebrate that night, going out to an expensive restaurant we really couldn't afford.

I thought about all the sleepless nights, the days and days of pouring over documents and articles, exhausting work yet never failing to touch us deeply because everything was so poignantly. Even on that glorious day, Raymond Baldwin was never far from my thoughts. He'd taken up residence in my head and I simply couldn't evict him no matter how hard I tried.

I thought about all the Boston, Washington and New York newspapers I'd bought in order to keep up on the latest news about Baldwin. Sucre like clockwork monitored her twenty-four hour news radio stations. Baldwin's campaign theme, A New Day for America caught on all across the nation and was seen on tens of thousands of hats and t-shirts.

At campaign appearances too far away for Sucre to attend, we listened to the evening news, his audiences constantly growing. He always sounded mean spirited but sadly that that seemed to be a great hit with the voters.

"Welfare is a leftist plot we all pay for," he railed at every whistle stop.

Lecturing about America's failed social fabric, he insisted it was torn and broken and our nation was in danger of breaking down into civil violence. Promising to bring more law and order into America threw his audiences into a loud frenzies. His speeches began using buzz words like city dwellers, junkies, school dropouts, urban guerrillas, street thugs and meth suppliers. The crowds egged him on.

I thought about the way he appealed to the people he claimed had been shut out of the American dream for too long, a theme his audiences loved. He ranted about America's allies who didn't cleanup the messes they'd created, forcing us to rescue them time after time. The military he'd declared defiantly with hands on hips in a Mussolini pose, had it's hands tied by incompetent civilian leaders. Worse, creeping socialism was tearing the heart out of the nation.

I was sorry I was no longer writing newspaper columns because he needed to be called out again and again for his reckless rhetoric. I'd called him out once five years earlier and wished I could do it again.

After I'd read the daily papers I took a pencil and note pad and begin sketching an outline for a biography. Emil wanted his memoir to begin with Spain but I couldn't leave out his life in Fascist Romania because it had so much effect on his life as a writer.

Sucre and I'd spent many long hours working together, many days without a word spoken between us, knowing what the other was doing or thinking. I always looked forward to Sucre's Pisco sours.

"Charlie I'd like to as you a question that has nothing to do with the work or Emil, something I'm curious about. Do you know what Braille

Bruce Weiss

actually is or how it's read? I'm only asking because I plan to go back to work full time on Braille translations at Harvard and I wanted you to know a bit about how I go about my work.

We'd never discussed Braille so I answered what I knew.

"I believe its a system of raised dots on papers enabling people without sight to use their finger to read by moving it across the ridges. I know it's not a language but actually a system of markings. Is that the gist?"

"That's the nuts and bolts Charlie but did you know it had a very different purpose once?"

I told her I couldn't imagine what the original purpose might have been.

"What we know today as Braille was first used by the French army in the 1800's because it enabled soldiers to read messages at night. Nobody else figured out that a series of dots meaning words could be useful. I learned Braille from the nuns in Peru and I'm not bragging but I'm rather good at it. Of course once I mastered it in Spanish I had to learn all over again in English. Braille is the process of converting printed text to raised characters and that's what I do at Harvard."

"Is there something else about Braille making you bring the subject up or were you just curious?"

"Charlie, remember what Emil often said about his books?"

I wasn't quite sure what Sucre was getting at but I saw great animation in her expression. I also knew instinctively what she might say next,

"Emil said there was more to the books then met the eye, remember?"

I nodded, correcting myself saying yes aloud.

"He read nearly fifty of the books in his prized collection to me as well as the personal notes he'd written about each book. We've gone through those books countless times, page by page yet we found nothing unusual or out of place. How many times did we question whether Emil placed hidden clues or special coded words in those notes to keep them from prying eyes?"

I had a gut feeling Sucre discovered something but I didn't want to be disappointed again. We'd exhausted ourselves searching, finding nothing conclusive.

"When Emil used the expression about more than meeting the eye I never asked what he meant. Deep inside however I had a nagging feeling he was not talking about the books, but rather about his personal notes,

Emil's List

the interesting and informative facts he'd tucked into each volume. Charlie don't say anything until I'm finished because I think I might just have accidentally discovered something that was there all the time."

My hopes were up not by what Sucre said, but by the look on her face, like a child who'd just seen an angel.

"Go on," I begged.

"You've read all the notes found inside the books aloud to me and we did learn quite a bit about the stories and the authors. We held Emil's precious books in our hand hundreds of times, sometimes just for the joy of having them close. Charlie I've held those books in my hands many times but strangely, I never held Emil's written notes from the books in my hands. You read them all to me and I agreed that nothing seemed or sounded out of place.

"A few moments ago while you were reading I picked up the stack of notes to put them into a folder because we'd finished the organizational work. When I did something quite remarkable happened just by chance. Charlie, I believe I've discovered by accident what more to the eye meant. I'm having a hard time putting this into words so bear with me because my heart and mind are racing."

I couldn't handle another disappointment but I would not allow myself to think negative thoughts.

"Emil was trying to give me a clue to his work and when he realized I just didn't react of get it, he'd simply say that expression more often. I think you've used the expression fasten your seatbelt to me once or twice. Now it's my turn.

"Each of Emil's notes contains Braille characters embedded so lightly that only a blind person knowing Braille might detect it. I'm not bragging but I know Braille and I believe I've discovered what appears to be names and numbers in Braille. Honestly, if I hadn't picked up those notes just now and held them in my hands for the first time, we might never have known. Anyone handling these papers such as you or the person who broke into my place would not have known something was written in Braille, barely perceptible to the touch.

"Are you saying Emil knew how to read and write Braille?"

"I doubt he knew how but somebody at Harvard might have done this

Bruce Weiss

for him. There are actually several Braille presses in the basement of the library and he was well known at Harvard."

"So let me understand this. He put names and numbers into Braille, knowing only you could read them?"

"That's what I believe right now and if I can take this one step further, it follows what you've always thought. Emil was working on something very big and putting his investigative work into Braille was his way of making sure if the papers fell into the wrong person's hands, no one would discover his secret. I think Emil used Braille so no one except me would ever know what he was working on."

I was as dumbfounded as I'd ever been. If Sucre's words proved true we'd stumbled onto something huge.

"Charlie you've done all the reading but now it's my turn to read to you, something in my wildest dreams I thought I'd ever say. I know we've gone over those notes very carefully searching for clues and we've always come up empty, but no longer. Charlie, in my wildest dreams I could never have guessed there were tiny raised ridges embedded into Emil's notes, no doubt meant for me.

"I can't wait another moment so read me what you've discovered.

"The Braille on this note contains the name Hugh Kohn and after his name the words, former assistant director CIA."

Damn I thought.

"I used to know that name but I'm certain he'd retired from public service many years ago, never to be heard from again. I think Reagan appointed him I but I can't be certain."

"Charlie do you have any idea why Emil wrote this man's name down?

"Absolutely no idea," I replied. "I've heard of him because of his government service but I can't guess why Emil took the time and effort to write his name in Braille. What's on the other notes?"

I watched her finger move ever so gently across another page. With a look of amazement on her face I knew she'd found another name.

"The name Major General Kurt Priestly is in Braille on this one, followed by the words former ambassador to South Korea. Does this name mean anything?"

That one most certainly does I replied.

"The general was in the news several years ago because he'd been put on trial for treason. Priestly was recalled from his post as ambassador and a week later was terminated by the State Department. A Congressional committee uncovered evidence he'd been passing top secret information about our spying missions on North Korea to South Korean officials. As things turned out the South Koreans he'd trusted were actually agents of the North. He too disappeared after the hearings and was never heard from again. He's got to be involved in something big though or Emil wouldn't have put his name on the notes. That gives us two names but two doesn't make a conspiracy.

"The name in Braille on the next page is Alan Bateman, former Judge of the Alabama Supreme Court. Do you know anything about him?"

Who could forget Bateman, I muttered under my breath.

"He was a district court judge in Alabama trying to create his own system of justice based on the Bible. Probably six or eight years ago he did something gaining many supporters over a very contentious issue. He was ordered to remove certain items from his courtroom that he'd personally placed there, all considered contentious. I believe one item was a large crucifix, the second a painting of Jesus Christ and the third, a large granite plaque containing the Ten Commandments. Judge Bateman refused to remove any of them from his courtroom and as a result was censored, in violation of the separation of church and state. I think he eventually removed the crucifix and the painting but he refused to remove the Ten Commandments. His position was supported by thousands who held candlelight vigils outside the courthouse, claiming the Commandments cast a divine presence over court proceedings. I don't know if he's still a judge or if he returned to the law, but there must be a good reason Emil had his name written in Braille."

Sucre picked up the next note but before she read another name, I interrupted saying I'd just remembered something about Kurt Priestly

"North Korea exploded their first atomic bomb only months after the ambassador was recalled. Hardly a coincidence and most people agreed."

Sucre struck gold but unless we could figure out what those names represented and why Emil chose to put them into Braille, we were still in the dark. Were those people up to something evil? Were they in anyway connected to Raymond Baldwin? Were they the people who'd threatened Emil, doing him harm because of his writings? The three names were

Bruce Weiss

no longer newsworthy or seemingly relevant but like Baldwin, they'd disappearing from public life for years.

Emil had gone through extraordinary measures encoding the names in Braille and I wondered why go to that extreme? The only reasonable explanation at the moment was Emil created a method to ensure if his notes ever fell into the wrong hands, they wouldn't mean anything. How many more names might we find?

"Sucre, did Emil ever ask you about Braille?"

She shook her head no, saying not really.

"Was it possible after befriending you he took the time to learn the system of Braille?"

"I don't know the answer to that and besides, I don't know when he would have found the time. He did spend a lot of time in the Harvard library so I guess it's possible he used that time."

"I'd speculated several times before but now I was a bit more certain Emil was killed because someone found out he was working on something quite mind blowing.

CHAPTER 32

Sucre found more names in Braille discovered in Emil's personal notes, each containing the name of an individual I'd once known when I was a reporter. There were also many others I'd had never heard of but one thing was certain. It was becoming increasingly obvious the individuals identified so far once held important positions. Some had troubled careers while the others seemingly disappeared leading private lives. I wasn't certain but I began to believe Emil might have uncovered something quite disturbing.

Over the next few hours Sucre read names and positions or titles found on the notes Emil had written. Even with Sucre's extraordinary find, I couldn't fathom why Emil put those names into Braille.

It was well past our usual quitting time but there was no stopping us. I knew we were onto something big although where it was all going, that still remained a large question mark.

Harold England; Former Chairman and CEO, New York Stock Exchange

Admiral Philip Crowley, former Chairman Joint Chiefs of Staff

Honorable Lamar Brown, Mayor Washington, DC

Sidney Albertson, Chairman New York City Bridge, Tunnel and Airport Authority

John Devers, former Vice President of the United States

Bruce Weiss

General James A. Maxwell, United States Commander NORAD

General Oscar Truman, Commander SAC Northern Sector

General James Davidson, Southern Military Command

Attorney Armstrong Anderson, White House Consul

Commander Baron Revlon, Maryland National Guard

Colonel Montgomery Hastings, National Guard Pennsylvania

Emily Drysdale, owner Los Angeles Free Press

Captain Elrod Perkins, Coast Guard Commandant

Leonard Pearl, CEO Pearl Repeating Firearms Corporation

Former Senator Barney Langer, Chairman TVA

Raymond Baldwin, former Representative, former Governor

Burgess O'Hara, Weapons supervisor Fort Dix

Several names stood out because of their notoriety during my reporter's days while others meant absolutely nothing. One name in the notes however stuck out like the proverbial sore thumb besides Baldwin's. What in God's name was a former Vice President of the United States doing on that list? What have we discovered I muttered to myself until a curious thought struck. Would Gould's name eventually appear?

Near three in the morning we had one hundred and forty-eight names gleaned from the notes once tucked into Emil's books, each in

Emil's List

Braille. Many of the individuals once held very important positions in the military, the law, the press, industry and law enforcement, but were they all connected?

Devers and Baldwin were the only ones appearing in the national news recently, the others seemingly long forgotten. Devers however had been named Baldwin's campaign manager only days earlier.

It was near dawn and the lack of sleep finally caught up with us but we plugged on until every last note was read by Sucre. We desperately needed a few hours of sleep to clear our heads but it was impossible to stop.

I eventually stretched out on the couch and looked over the list of names and positions I'd written down. Two names stood out quite clearly; Devers and Baldwin and then it hit me. Why didn't we find Steven Gould's name? Keeping me awake was the thought, why did Emil think it important to write their names in Braille and what did he know about those people?

Sucre continued to listen to the hourly news and the seven in the morning lead story suddenly had us wide awake.

'Governor Baldwin is to announce today that Hugh Kohn, one time assistant director of the CIA has been chosen as a special adviser to the Baldwin campaign.'

Damn I said a little too loudly, making us miss the rest of the news and causing Sucre to jump. "We're now got another name in the news connected to Baldwin and maybe we're getting just a little closer to figuring out what Emil might have had in mind. We can clearly connect Devers and Kohn to the Baldwin campaign."

I had that old reporters gut feeling many more names on the list would somehow turn up in the news in the weeks ahead. If they did, would they be connected to Baldwin's campaign?

When the morning sunlight filled the room we had breakfast. Sucre's radio was always tuned to the news station making it certain we wouldn't miss anything related to Baldwin's campaign. I owned a television but had not turned it on in years, and would not do so with Sucre here.

"Did you just hear that Charlie" Sucre cried out? "Let me turn the sound up."

'Former Governor and presidential candidate Raymond Baldwin is set to announce shortly that Kurt Priestly will become his foreign policy

Bruce Weiss

advisor. Mr. Priestly was once the American ambassador to South Korea and before that, ambassador to Japan.'

Crazily the names on our list were popping up like spring daffodils. Did Emil have the foresight knowing certain individuals would one day join Baldwin's election team? Did he even know well before the candidates announcement Baldwin was planning a major comeback?

When the news report ended I said we should look over the list again.

"Of those names you discovered Sucre, I wonder if one of them had something to do with Emil's death? Had one of them deliberately set me up to take the rap?

I had that old reporter's instinct all the individuals Emil listed might eventually be connected to Raymond Baldwin, but the big question was, for what purpose? If Sucre and I were able to connect more names to Baldwin's campaign, I was willing to bet we'd discover something diabolic going on. If we discovered a secret plot, where would we go with it?

Former Governor Baldwin was gaining more supporters every day, his polling numbers rising in what the nation's newspapers called a meteoric rise. I'd never doubted Baldwin was exceedingly formidable but I began to sense there had to be something illicit in his candidacy few people other than his inner circle knew about. Sadly, we had more what ifs and why's then answers.

The election was two and a half weeks away, hopefully enough time for us to discover why Emil made a secret list of names, some directly linked to Raymond Baldwin. I wondered if there was some type of conspiracy being played out that could actually lead to a Baldwin presidency. Were there people of interest on Baldwin's team capable of using any means possible to turn the election in his favor?

Election day was on the horizon and I found myself overcome with an urgency to find out what the individuals on Emil's list were up to lately. My heart was pounding like a bass drum, making me feel more alive than I'd been in years.

CHAPTER 33

Candidate Raymond Baldwin was surprisingly shaking up the entire electoral process as a third party candidate, something once thought impossible. Reporters continued to ask the same question each day; can candidate Baldwin be stopped? Few outside Massachusetts had ever heard his name until his campaign began, and now the rest of the country was getting quite an education.

The latest poll showed him in front of the Democratic candidate but still well behind the Republican. Galveston the Republican and Arnold the Democrat refused to include Baldwin in their debates but the strategy came back to bite them in the ass, the empty chair on the stage on everyone's mind. Everywhere Baldwin spoke thousands cheered his message, his name seemingly on everyone's lips. I suggested we look at Emil's list of names again.

Cedric Smollett, Conservative radio host twelve hundred radio stations

Reggie Griffin, one time director of the Federal Aviation Agency

Connie Flanders, former head of the Internal Revenue Service

I knew very little about most of the names but a few I'd remembered. It was one thing to identify the individuals, another to find a connection

Bruce Weiss

to Baldwin if one even existed. We were moving forward but in what direction I fretted?

Gregory Stewart, CIA Latin America

Douglas Jacobs, former CIA chief Africa

Len Peterkin, Chief Scientist Los Alamos National Laboratory.

Ernestine Withers, Secretary of the Treasury

Father Monte Moore, Televangelist

The more I looked over the list, the more I had the uneasy feeling evil was lurking just around the corner. Lack of sleep, the need for urgency and the election getting closer unnerved me. Street noise outside my apartment felt like bad omens. Something as ordinary as a car door slamming on the street below or even the elevator stopping on my floor made me anxious. Could someone on that list be coming after us?

I continued to read several national newspapers each day but found no other names on Emil's list. Sucre remained glued to the news stations on her radio, hopefully finding a news story connecting someone on the list to Baldwin's campaign. Staring at the names until I'd nearly memorized them, it felt as if they were all in my apartment looking over my shoulder.

"Father Theodore" Sucre said excitedly. "I just heard his name mentioned during the hourly news update. He's to be Raymond Baldwin's spiritual advisor."

I'd also heard that name before but had not heard it in many years. If I was right he was the defrocked priest making national news five years ago for his terribly racist rants on his radio show. It eventually all came back to me.

"Sucre, Father Theodore was a disciple of Father Coughlin, taking a page out Coughlin's reproachful and disparaging rants against Jews, Blacks and immigrants. I can't quite imagine why Baldwin would appoint him religious advisor."

I put a check mark next to Father Theodore's name on my list. Just

Emil's List

below was the name General Corny Maxwell, the name suddenly jogging a memory. I told Sucre what I knew.

"The General once made the cover of Time Magazine because of his highly publicized fight with the president of the United States. The unpleasant state of affairs was front page news and if I remembered my facts correctly, the General became the first field officer fired by a president since General Douglass McArthur. He did not go away quietly though. His very first speech after his removal was delivered at the Veterans of Foreign Wars convention in Philadelphia, a speech filled with dire warnings and devastating scenarios for America. I once wrote a piece warning about his threatening rhetoric, especially when he told the veterans there was not one good reason to manufacture nuclear weapons if they weren't going to be used."

The newswoman on the radio confirmed General Maxwell had just been appointed Baldwin's military advisor.

A bigger picture was slowly emerging frightfully, the names attached to Baldwin were dangerous individuals with checkered pasts. Where had they been the last number of years I wondered? I thought if we could learn more in the coming hours and if we got very lucky, we'd find more names linked to Baldwin's campaign. Sadly, there was nothing we could take to the authorities so for the time being, it was just Sucre and me.

"Troubled personalities suddenly in the unique position of bringing their treachery to Raymond Baldwin." Sucre remarked. I smiled because she saw the bigger picture.

Might one of the names on the list be on to us, knowing we had possession of Emil's papers? Would we meet Emil's fate? I thought about Sanford Roberts, wondering if I could trust him with our suspicions and ask for his help.

"Baldwin's now the lead story on every broadcast" Sucre lamented, "and there's just been trouble reported on the campaign trail. Violence broke out at Baldwin's campaign stop in Omaha. Protestors were allegedly beaten, egged on by the candidate's command to his audience to take no prisoners."

Given his recent rhetoric I'd kind of expected that to happen. Many hate groups had taken up his cause, vowing to defend their candidate against the protestors. The language was heated, words turning his audience against the press and the result many broken cameras and a few heads. We were certainly looking at a group of individuals on Emil's list extremely capable of bringing havoc and confusion to the campaign and election I rued.

"I'm certain Baldwin is running the show" I said. "I'm thinking during the five years when he'd disappeared he wasn't sitting home doing nothing. I believe he was putting together a complicated and malevolent plot to steal the presidency."

Many on Emil's list had abused the power of their position or in some cases, were still exploiting their positions. Over the years many were condemned for their actions or words, some fired while others quietly moved into other positions.

Looking at Sucre I suddenly realized how tired she looked, concerned because we'd been putting in such long hours. I asked if she were okay even though I knew how she'd respond.

"I'm really fine" she said "but these days I'm having trouble getting back into my usual sleep routines."

That was my fault because I'd asked her to burn the midnight oil when knocking off would have been smarter.

"Why don't we go over the list of names just one more time and then put it aside and forget about it until another name pops up in the news. We can certainly both use a time out" I lamented.

My mind was still running at warp speed and nothing could seemingly slow or shut it down. I was deeply troubled by the number of military people on the list, some retired and others most likely still on active duty. Had Emil discovered a possible military plot to conceivably overthrow our government if Baldwin wasn't elected? Was Emil killed because some one, possibly directed by Baldwin feared Emil might be on to something exposing a nasty plot?

Put all the people on Emil's list together in one large room I thought to myself, and imagine what could possibly transpire? Military coups in many nations around the globe were often successful I knew too well. If just the military people were put in one room, there would probably be enough expertise and knowledge to create great chaos in America. We weren't anywhere near figuring out what the potential plot might be but I truly believed Emil had bits and pieces but most likely not all the answers.

Emil's List

Tragically it could easily take months to make sense of everything but by then it would certainly be too late. I considered going to the authorities but with only conjecture I was certain I'd be considered daft, either laughed at or ignored. No crimes had been alleged or committed plus I was still a suspect in a complicated murder. Was Emil close to exposing a plot or conspiracy against America and was that why he let me go, to make certain no harm came to me? It undoubtedly seemed all too plausible.

Sucre was always reading my thoughts, as if she could hear my thinking. "I think Attorney Gould could be the key to much of this because of his curious promoting of Baldwin's candidacy."

Sucre was right.

"I think I need to have a long talk with Sanford Roberts sooner rather than later, laying everything we've discovered on the line. Maybe Gould knew what Emil was working on, possibly discussed when the two met to change the will. If we can get some answers from Roberts we might be a step closer to figuring out this mystery. Then again, if Gould is working for Baldwin, maybe Roberts is working for Gould. It's all so crazy."

Sucre heard the uneasiness in my voice. Why wasn't Gould on Emil's list I queried?

"Sucre, given Baldwin's rhetoric, Gould must have realized he was pure evil."

My mind was a roaring forest fire badly needing a few hours of uninterrupted sleep. I'd forgotten I'd once lived a reporter's hectic life, seldom taking breaks. Lack of sleep in the old days seemed to fine tune my senses but no longer.

Sucre suggested we go over all the names one more time since neither of us was going to get any sleep, in particular the individuals associated with the military.

I didn't think I had the strength to go over the list one more time but Sucre insisted. I suspected we'd only find many more unanswered questions, pushing me toward a breaking point.

A few minutes into what was to be our last effort a name jumped out and then interestingly another.

"Sucre, I'd forgotten I once met Colonel Joseph Sebastian some years ago when he was chief of air operations at McGuire Air Force Base in New Jersey. I'd been working on a story about our military preparedness and he

Bruce Weiss

was the point man to talk to. I also now remember General Abe Somers I met when he was the commanding officer of Otis Air Force Base out on the Cape. I rented a home on the Cape one summer and he lived three houses away. He seemed like an intelligent person so why was his and Sebastian's names on Emil's list?"

Suddenly names I couldn't place before came roaring to life. Despite the incredible tiredness the idea of making progress refreshed me.

"I'd once met Abe Fellows when he retired from the military through a mutual friend, becoming an excellent source when I needed reliable information about certain military operations. Years later I'd heard he'd started up a think tank, focusing on how to use nuclear weapons in a limited war. I wonder if there was a way to get in touch with him but then again, what would I say except I'd discovered his name on Emil's list?

The tiredness was wearing off quickly and I felt alert and ready to concentrate. Several names that at first meant nothing began to flash like neon lights.

"Sucre, Avery Clark made a lot of waves during his tenure as head of the Federal Aviation Agency. I sat in on a few of his press conferences, a man always on the verge of losing his job. Clark oversaw all flight operations in North America when hijacking and bomb scares were rather routine. I remember one particular news conference when he discussed a collision between a passenger plane and a military transport over Staten Island. I thought he was very astute that day but he was actually fired shortly after when evidence surfaced he'd covered up the facts of the incident to protect the military. How could a person with knowledge about flight paths over America be valuable to Baldwin?"

Philip Snyder's name strangely rang a tiny bell, his name in the nightly news from time to time during the Reagan administration. He was the nation's book keeper I seemed to recall. I was certain he'd lost his position when it was discovered he was funneling illegal money to the Contras but I wasn't certain.

Why hadn't I made these connections before? Was I sleep working?

William Justice was once the director of flight operations at NASA I recalled, the point man directing the moon launches and landings. Jim Johnson I wondered. He'd become more noteworthy after he left NASA starting up an independent rocket development program in New Mexico.

Emil's List

It felt if I was tossing the dice and everything was stating to come up sevens. It was one thing to identify them but another figuring out what those men might have in common or why Emil created the list with their names. Each individual was extremely knowledgeable in unique fields, directing critical operations requiring great skill. Avery Clark I said a bit too loudly, causing Sucre to jump.

"I believe he found himself in very serious trouble when without informing anyone, he tested White House security by ordering an air control rookie to allow a passenger plane into restricted air space over Washington. The plane came very close to being shot down."

I wondered when Emil first started the list, suspecting he'd always kept close tabs on certain people he suspected of doing bad deeds. When and why were the names put into Braille? Why hadn't he said anything about the names or the Braille to Sucre or me? We had to assume he'd probably not discovered what those people might be up to, or had he?

We looked at the individuals as foot soldiers for Raymond Baldwin, a potent army that could deviously help Baldwin win the election, or worse. Steven Gould's association with Baldwin continued to drive me absolutely crazy so I thought about Sanford Roberts again, wondering if he could help us or harm us. As hard as I tried to quiet my overactive mind it was useless.

CHAPTER 34

Early the next morning the ringing of the phone nearly gave me a heart attack, wakening me from such a deep sleep I wasn't aware I was on the sofa perched near my front door. It was Sanford who I'd curiously dreamed about during the night. Sanford's first words baffled me while I struggled to clear the sleep from my head.

"Look Mr. Darwin, Charlie, I need to meet with you this morning to go over something materializing overnight. You can breathe a bit easier though because it's got nothing to do with the Breck case. I don't want to go into this on the phone so can you meet with me this morning?"

The words were terse, spoken with hesitation especially after saying he did not want to discuss anything over the phone. Hell of a way to start the morning I said to Sucre who began to stir.

What Sanford said next seemed most unusual and curious.

"I prefer not to meet in my office and I'll explain the why when I see you. Do you know Boston Bagels on Mass Ave?"

I replied I did. End of conversation. Was someone tapping my phone or possibly his at the law firm I wondered? Was there a reason I couldn't come into the Gould Building?

Sucre asked what was happening so I told her I'd found the conversation rather confusing. During the many long days Sucre and I'd worked together she seemingly always knew when something was troubling me. I repeated Sanford's words saying I had absolutely no idea why he needed to meet in a bagel shop. Sucre asked if she should come along but not knowing what was happening I said not this time.

"While I'm out you should get some rest because we've been pushing ourselves awfully hard lately. If you don't feel like sitting around you might

Emil's List

even want to check in with your boss to do a little work. Make sure if you go out though you leave a note. I should be gone for no more then an hour or so and if it's a warm afternoon, why don't we take a long walk down to the swan boats in the Commons."

I could not guess why Sanford wanted to see me outside his office, wondering if I should have insisted on hearing the reason. Not meet in his office? Was it merely a social call? Was Gould up to something?

I tried to put Emil's list out of my thoughts while I walked to Mass Ave but as hard as I tried, I found myself reciting the names aloud as if Sucre were by my side. Each one alone seemed rather innocuous but an uneasiness kicked in when I wondered what they might do as a team working for Baldwin. Would they use their knowledge and insights to make Baldwin a better national candidate, or would they create something scandalous? Was I watching too many science fiction movies at the local theater I wondered?

Arriving at the shop a bit early I took Sucre's recorder out and turned it on. She'd recorded Baldwin's latest speech off the radio and I hadn't had time to listen. Putting my ear buds in over my first cup off coffee, I listened to Baldwin's speech to the annual NRA convention.

'There are a number of amendments in our time tested Constitution under fire from what I'll politely call the leftists. Those people feel they have the absolute right to take away your guns and don't think for a moment they don't already have a plan. Let's be honest with each other. No one has the right to take my or your guns away today, tomorrow or ever. I promise to defend our gun rights until someone takes my guns from my cold dead hands. That is all I have to say about the second amendment for now but I wanted you to know where I stand.'

The ovation and chanting lasted nearly six minutes while I looked about the shop for any sign of Sanford.

"America's borders are so porous anyone can enter this country illegally. Six and seven years olds regularly walk across a shallow river into our country to plunder and create mayhem. A nation that doesn't or can't protect it's borders is simply not a nation. Ask the people of Poland how often their borders were crossed, each time bringing death and destruction to no end. Are we going to prevent another Poland from happening here? I promise you if elected we will not.

'We've lost all our moral courage because previous administrations have blindly allowed the courts to tell us how we ought to live. Judges have exceeded their powers and I will rein them in to protect your God given individual rights.'

I paused the tape to look again for Sanford, but still no sight of him.

'When I'm elected one of the very first things I will do is put an end to the abomination of abortion. How can the most civilized nation on this planet sanction the killing of the innocent unborn. Even third world nations don't allow that to happen.' This time the cheering was a bit quieter.

'I'll bring this nation back to a time when Christian values meant something, which includes bringing God back into the classrooms. Look at the chaos in America's schools today. God needs to have a presence in our schools and by the way, in our courtrooms and even in our board rooms.

'I'll stop the insidious creeping socialist programs strangling our nation. America has become a welfare state, supporting undesirables with your hard earned money. When the government tells us how to live, it needs to be told to back off in no uncertain terms.

'I'll sign an executive order on day one that the Ten Commandments must be placed in every school room in America. You know what's really wrong with children today? God and religion mean nothing to them. The Commandments have a place in our lives now more then ever and I'll order prayer brought back into the schools and hospitals and sporting events and anywhere good people gather.

'The poor, the ones liberals refer to as the underclass have to learn to live without government handouts. Enough is enough and mark my words, their free ride is over. Social and economic inequalities are natural and inevitable, something purposely overlooked by phony economists who get big bucks for their two cents. The government is not the answer to life's troubles and it should never be. I will stand for a strong social order with more law and order, certainly not less or the status quo. Do the crime and you'll do the time. We need to bring the death penalty back in every state and use it liberally.

'A civilized society needs state-imposed safeguards but it cannot be allowed to smother laissez-faire capitalism. Free markets and free trade should be our economic mantra, not government subsidies and handouts.

Emil's List

Get the government off the backs of all Americans rich or poor and watch us grow.

'I'm a strong believer in a formidable military force worldwide as well as strengthening our home forces. We need to stop knee-jerk reactions to every problem in the world and think more carefully before we act. We are not the cops of the world but let me make this perfectly clear. I'll make damn sure we have plans in place for any eventuality and I won't be bluffing. We'll go wherever evil rears it's ugly head but more importantly, we'll be prepared and those who dare challenge us will pay a heavy cost.

'I will scrap any treaty we currently have that limits what weapons we can build, use or deploy. We will never let our guard down under my watch, never.

'I stand before you at this NRA gathering of loyal Americans to say I will support laws allowing all Americans to carry concealed weapons of their choice. No person, family or work place needs to be unprotected or at the mercy of the bad guys. Every home, church, school and government facility should be well armed, guaranteeing our safety and security. The police, bless them, are overworked and under armed but I'll change that.

'Excessive taxes must be cut and we'll do that by slashing government spending. No more money to liberal programs encouraging promiscuity, especially Planned Parenthood.

'I have a great deal of respect for the Christian Right and I want to say I support you one hundred percent. Your message of bringing God back into our lives will be heard. Keep up the good fight and know my door will always be open to you. If we had mandatory morning prayers in our schools every day there would be far less delinquency and absenteeism. One more thing my brothers in arms. Marriage is between a man and a woman and don't you ever forget that.'

When the cheering began I looked up again for Sanford, worried we'd gotten our signals crossed because there was still no sign of him.

'When science disagrees with the Bible, I'll stand on the side of the Good Book. We need to reemphasize family values and not allow homosexuals to work with our children.

'The federal government has destroyed public education and healthcare with senseless and needless restrictions. We'll turn the clock back to the 1950's when both education and health were affordable and first class. Why

Bruce Weiss

are the systems failing today? Because Uncle Sam has put his nose where it does not belong.'

I stopped the recording just as Sanford walked into the eatery, clearing my head from the heart-wrenching rhetoric I'd just heard. I felt like screaming. How and why was the public buying into Baldwin's rhetoric?

Sanford placed the morning paper down in front of me, the headline stating Baldwin pulled well past his Democratic opponent in the polls and trailed the Republican candidate by only six percentage points.

Chapter 35

Sanford sat down but not before casing the place with a look on his face suggesting trouble. His first words were the need to speak very quietly because one never knew who was listening. I expected some very bad news.

We ordered bagels and coffee, Sanford saying nothing until our order arrived five minutes later. Pushing his plate aside he leaned forward closer to me.

"I have a problem I need to talk to you about because it does effect you."

Once more Sanford glanced about the room, making me wary and nervous, the way I felt waiting the results of a doctor's exam.

"This morning I was fired from the legal firm, something totally unexpected and it's still nearly impossible to comprehend. The reason we're meeting here is because I no longer have an office in the Gould Building. I'm still a lawyer with all the rights and privileges although I don't work for the Gould firm anymore."

I didn't know Attorney Sanford Roberts very well but I didn't mistake his anguish, feeling terribly sorry and even a bit responsible for his plight. Had I caused his firing by insinuating his boss Steven Gould was likely involved in something adverse? I could only manage to utter the word why. There was no immediate response.

"I can still practice law but here's the problem Charlie. I can longer represent you because your case belongs to the firm, not to me."

Sanford looked weary and despite my self indulging worry, I assumed I'd eventually be facing a possible indictment without a lawyer.

"Sanford, you've helped me and kept me abreast of the situation and I want you to know at first I resented being shuffled off to a newbie but I'm

Bruce Weiss

rather thankful for the time you gave me. I'm very grateful for your help so if there's anything I can do for you, please ask."

I got him fired was my only thought because I maligned his boss. I wondered if this man could be trusted with Sucre's discovery now.

"Here's the situation Charlie. Mr. Gould has an outstanding reputation in the legal world and he does more charitable work for the city than anyone. He's probably got his name on more plaques around the city than any Patriot who'd ever fought and died for liberty and freedom in Boston. I highly respect him and I should add he was a great mentor. He handed me your case not to get rid of you, but because he said he had great confidence in me. There were many more skilled lawyers in the firm but he decided to take a chance on a rookie and for that I was very grateful."

He could have told me about this problem over the phone I thought, so there had to be more to the story. I couldn't be Gould's client again and I assumed Sanford wasn't mine any longer. The thought of Sucre being alone made me to want to get up an run out of the shop.

"There's another reason I wanted to see you so give me another moment while I order a second coffee."

An inner voice screamed I too was in trouble and despite my concerns for Sucre, I needed to hear Sanford out to find out where I stood.

"Mr. Gould claimed I was fired because my superiors reported my work was not up to Gould standards. I won't go into their observations but what was written or said about me couldn't have been true. Mr. Gould didn't give me a chance to repudiate the evaluations but he did offer a deal. I would have to sign a waiver stating I would not discuss any legal business carried out by the firm during my tenure there. In return I was to pick up what Mr. Gould called a sizable check in accounting to keep me tied over while looking for another position.

"I had no choice but to sign and if I took you or any other client away from the firm, I'd be facing disbarment. I signed the paper and left without another word. A block down the street from the Gould Building I realized I hadn't picked up my check so I had to return and that's why I was late. I'll survive but I can't help you with your case anymore. Saying that, I'd still be very happy if you keep me on your speed dial in case you need legal advice."

Poor Sanford. Poor me I mused.

Emil's List

"You said there was another reason for wanting to see me. Can I ask what that is because I need to get home?"

"While I was in Mr. Gould's office he got a phone call he took in his side office. I assumed the papers on his desk were my evaluation forms so I walked around his desk to read them. To my great surprise it wasn't my evaluation but a note addressed to Governor Baldwin. You might be right about those two working together,"

My chest tightened hearing those words. The poor man had just been fired possibly because I'd asked about his boss and the word got out. Feeling as if I were sitting on a powder keg, I expected the news to get even worse.

"Sanford before you go on I think I need to tell you what Sucre and I are currently working on although I'm not entirely sure you want to hear this with your new troubles. I might be putting you in jeopardy telling you this, but I'm hoping I can trust you. Emil Breck was most likely gathering information about Raymond Baldwin and a team of troublemakers who'd signed on to help him get him elected one way or another. Sucre and I believe someone on the team he's assembled discovered what Emil was working on and silenced him to help Baldwin. Further, I'm not sure Emil finished his investigation but he left some pretty interesting work behind. Sanford, I need to find out why Gould is working with Raymond Baldwin. You must have overheard things at the office."

I was feeling worse and worse for Sanford. Why did Gould hand a murder case over to an inexperienced lawyer in the first place unless he wanted me charged with the crime, eliminating two people who'd been thorns in Baldwin's side. Which side was Robert's on was my new problem. Because of Sanford's inexperience he most likely would have lost my case if it went to trial. Was Baldwin behind Emil's murder, implicating me to successfully silent two nemesis who could stop him?

"Sanford, I'm awfully confused.

"I'm telling this because you deserved to know I'm no longer your lawyer. As to your question about what I might have heard, I'm really sorry but I rarely discussed anything other than the cases I was assigned."

A long silence ensued until Sanford finished his coffee. After looking about the place once again, he leaned in close.

"The second reason for this meeting is that I've suddenly found myself

Bruce Weiss

with some free time on my hands, thinking I might offer some free legal advice and in turn see if you could use my help on what you're dealing with. I don't know much but I do know you're working quite hard on something important."

The thought of Sanford working with us didn't sit well because it was still within the realm of possibility he and Gould were tied to Baldwin. Had I said too much already, lured into a trap by his sad tale? Before I answered yes or no I wanted him to understand a few things,

"Sanford before I say yes or no I'd like to know if Raymond Baldwin was or is still a client of Steven Gould."

Sanford shrugged his shoulders, saying he had a few trusted friends at the firm and asking the right questions might get an answer. I said finding out was one of the conditions for working with us.

"I'll also have to talk to Ms. Grande about you joining us in our investigation. You find out about Gould and I'll have a talk with Sucre and get her input. There is one thing for now though. I would still like you to remain my lawyer so is that possible without compromising your agreement with the Gould firm? Dumb question I quickly realized.

I rued the idea I'd been away from Sucre far too long and needed to go, but I expected that we'd talk again, possibly later in the day if he found the information about Gould.

When I got up to leave I wondered if any of my words would come back to haunt me. Was it possible Sanford was part of a shameful scheme to find out what we might have found in Emil's papers? I knew I should have said forget about me and I'd get another lawyer but strange feeling made me turn around to walk back to the table.

"Sanford, there's a back entrance to my place off Nutmeg Alley. Use that entrance to get inside my building and come on up to the sixth floor, apartment 614 late afternoon. There are reporters camped out in front and they might become suspicious seeing a lawyer come to my place so be careful. That should give you enough time to get any information about Gould's alliance with Baldwin and time for me to talk to Sucre about you working with us. If it works out, you need to know you're going to get yourself involved in something that could lead to great dangers.

"Thank you Charlie and remember, I'm still a practicing attorney and until that changes, I'll have your back."

On the walk back to my place it felt as if I were walking a narrow plank over an alligator infested swamp. Should I have discouraged Sanford from coming to work with us, a potential catastrophe in the making? I could barely handle the turmoil in my life so why would I look for more problems? Sucre and I were a team and we'd worked well together so why change that? Was I inviting the fox into the hen house? Would he prove to be a boon to our work?

I was pleasantly surprised seeing my super sitting on an old worn cushioned chair near the apartment building front door. The chair had obviously seen better days because when he jumped up to greet me feathers flew everywhere.

"I saw you go out the back way Mr. Charlie so I wanted your girl friend to be safe when she was alone. Sitting here I could keep my eye on who's coming or going."

I could have kissed him.

"Mr. Charlie, it's a good thing I was here because three well dressed men came into the building about thirty minutes ago. It was a big deal because you don't see well dressed people walking in here. When they saw me they stopped talking and walked out, getting into a very fancy car and driving quickly away. Maybe it was nothing but I thought you'd want to know."

"You wouldn't know what kind of car it was, would you?"

"One I could not afford. I think it was one of those Mercedes with blackened windows."

"Gas or diesel." I asked.

"Funny question Mr. Charlie but I'm certain it was diesel because of the smell."

I vowed not to let Sucre out of my sight again, my thoughts returning to Sanford nearly convinced it would be good to have an extra set of eyes watching our backs. On the other hand, who's back might he be watching?

When I opened my apartment door Sucre ran toward me, throwing her arms around my neck. I asked how she knew it was me and if there was a special reason for the hug.

She laughed saying she'd missed me. There was much to explain before Sanford arrived.

CHAPTER 36

Sanford took the back stairs to my place near five in the afternoon and when the door opened I saw he was cradling a large bouquet of flowers.

"For me, I asked?"

"Actually you once told me your friend liked to have fresh flowers around so I picked these up when I got off the T at Park Street."

I officially introduced Sanford to Sucre, saying she'd agreed to let Sanford work on the papers because we were stuck and the work was too much for two people. After the introduction I make certain Sanford understood that Sucre and I were equal partners totally up front and honest with each other. For a brief moment I wondered if I should tell Roberts about the men in suits who'd entered the apartment building but I thought not. Why add fuel to the fire when their appearance might have had no bearing on us at all.

We talked a little about the upcoming election sipping Sucre's Peruvian coffee, talking about Baldwin's chances to succeed. I asked Sanford to explain the strange circumstances surrounding his dismissal from the law firm to Sucre which he did.

After his confession Sanford said he'd also brought a gift for me. Raymond Baldwin was indeed a client of the law firm. I'd actually totally forgotten I'd asked Sanford to look into that.

Sanford added it might not have anything to do with his appearance on the stage. Somewhat more comfortable with the newbie, Sucre and I began to describe the work we'd done with Emil's papers, avoiding any mention of the list of names uncovered by Sucre, at least for the moment.

Nearly two hours later the only thing not discussed was Sucre's remarkable discovery. I'd used the two hour visit to sum Sanford up and

Emil's List

my old reporters instinct said I might trust Sanford, knowing too well there would be no going back. I let on that Sucre discovered something that could be dynamite.

Sucre and I took turns describing the treasured personal notes penned by Emil which on the surface contained remarkable information about books and their authors. When we finally got to the point where we'd reveal what was found, it was one of those moments in my life when I was going on pure gut instinct. I prayed it would not came back to bite us in the ass.

"Sucre discovered something a sighted person would never have found in Emil's notes."

I hesitated remembering never trust a lawyer.

"Sanford, Sucre discovered more than one hundred and fifty names in Braille written on Emil's notes, only something she might detect. At this point we can't say why Emil went through the trouble of finding these people and it must have taken some time. Without fully understanding what those names represent, we've managed to come to the conclusion most if not all the names are working on Mr. Baldwin's campaign. We both believe Braille was used to hide or disguise what he was working on from prying eyes. Baldwin is a rotten egg and from what we've been able to glean from the list of names, many individuals Emil identified have very dangerous and troubling backgrounds, just like Baldwin.

"The bottom line at this moment is the real possibility this team could be behind a treasonous plot to turn America's election into chaos, ensuring Raymond Baldwin wins the presidency legally or not."

I hesitated, then added that there were possible dangers lurking around every corner, especially if we asked the right questions to the wrong people. There have been a few incidents making us suspect someone doesn't want us to find evidence of a possible plot against America I emphasized.

"I want you to understand working with Sucre and I could put you in harms way so we wouldn't blame you for walking away. Of course if you do, we would expect you not tell anyone about our work."

Sanford had said few words, thanking us for sharing our work and deep concerns with him. At last he said he'd do what he could to assist us.

"We're probably dealing with some rather ruthless people so I do have a question for my lawyer. Sanford, do you think we should call the police and tell them about our work and our suspicions?"

"Honestly, I'm not sure what the police could do because no crime has been committed and no one has been harmed. I understand you believe you have names of people who might be involved in some type of conspiracy but you don't have any hard evidence suggesting those people are up to doing evil. As your attorney I suggest you keep this under the covers for now and don't go to the authorities until you have a tinge of proof those people are planning to commit criminal acts. I do have a question for you though. Do you have any definitive proof those so called incidents involving you and Sucre were more than accidents?"

"No and in truth we can't even say if it was someone on Emil's list behind the intimidation. Sanford, you know where the backdoor takes you so feel free to get up now or any time and leave. You certainly don't need more trouble in your life right now but if you'd like to be a part of our team, you're most welcome to stay,"

Sanford replied the only reason he'd walk away was if he felt he was getting in our way. That was good enough for us, thus it was time to get Sanford up to speed.

"First I want to go over the list of names Emil identified and ask if you if you've ever seen these people in the Gould firm or if you've ever heard their names mentioned."

Sanford nodded.

"There are approximately one hundred and fifty individuals listed so this could take some time. We know the election is on the near horizon so you'll understand there is much urgency in our efforts. Sucre and I will fill you in on what we know about these individuals and equally important, their work histories. Please keep this in the forefront of your mind. It's entirely possibly one or more of these people were involved in Emil's murder. Saying that is not easy because if it's true, we're looking at a list of murder suspects."

Sucre explained the positions the individuals held made them capable of creating great mayhem or worse around the election; most likely orchestrated by Raymond Baldwin. It's conjecture Sucre insisted as I'd reiterated, but a possible a goal might be the disruption of the election turning it in Baldwin's favor.

Emil's List

"Every day another individual on Emil's list is announced in the press as a new member of Baldwin's election team. I wish we knew how or why Emil got these names but if you knew his work, you'd know as an investigative reporter he was always capable of pulling a rabbit out of a hat."

Sucre handed the notes to Sanford asking if he could feel the tiny ridges of Braille. For several minutes Sanford rubbed his fingers across the pages. I watched Sanford's face as he moved his finger, finally nodding, saying aloud for Sucre's benefit he barely felt the ridges. I handed him a copy of the names and titles I'd written out. Sanford took several long minutes perusing the list, finally asking the million dollar question.

"Okay, assuming it's a group formed to disrupt the election, where can real proof be found?"

Sucre and I laughed because we knew Sanford just arrived at the place where we were stuck.

"So far we've identified twenty-five people with a direct connection to Raymond Baldwin's presidential campaign. That actually took very little investigating because all we had to do was read the news or listen to his speeches. The names keep popping up like corks."

"What about the others you haven't connected yet," Sanford asked? "Are you planning to find ties that bring them into Baldwin's circle?"

"We'd love to," Sucre answered "and with some luck it's possible. Right now however we both feel twenty-five individuals is very persuasive. We don't know what they might do for Baldwin but if you look at the important positions they once held, they could become a very formidable force.

Sanford said he needed a few more moments to go over the list of names more slowly

"There are an awful lot of people with military backgrounds. I assume that you're both aware of that," Sanford announced.

We said yes.

"What do you make of the others who are or were in essential and compelling industries and businesses Sanford queried?"

We collectively shrugged our shoulders.

"If I were Raymond Baldwin," Sanford replied, "I'd probably want these people with me because their expertise could be used to help his election chances. Sadly, it's a team that could also do evil things. What exactly made you think there's an actual plot afoot?"

Bruce Weiss

"Because Emil Breck was killed and there can be no reason other than he's discovered something toxic" Sucre replied angrily. "He was the absolute best discovering hidden secretive plots and conspiracies and that's why he was silenced."

"These truly are all high profiled individuals," Sanford remarked, "but you still need some hard fast evidence that you don't have. I know that sounds harsh but it's the way the justice system operates.

"The man who ran the Federal Aviation Agency," Sucre noted, "had the authority to ground every airplane in the country, possibly the military too. We don't have any proof he could create chaos but if you put all the people we've identified as cronies of Raymond Baldwin in one room, you'd certainly have a very contentious and dangerous force. If you examined Emil's illustrious life and career I think you'll find all the confirmation you'll need. Emil could smell out a rat."

"Stanford, the individual who oversaw America's electrical grid would have the ability to wreak disorder by literally pulling the plug" I interjected, "plunging most of the nation into darkness. Why would he conceivably do that? Right now we can't do more than speculate but he and the others have troubling pasts. Their goal might be to disrupt election especially if things aren't going well for Baldwin. Emil spent most of his life investigating and searching for answers and as we discovered going through his work, that often got him very unwanted attention.

"Sanford at our meeting this morning I asked you if your boss Steven Gould ever discussed why he was working for a man who'd abused power so badly he was forced to resign in disgrace. It's not a long stretch to believe Emil was killed because he was getting dangerously close to uncovering a plot most likely hatched by Raymond Baldwin. We can't answer the question how he was he able to discover a plot but Emil was a magician. It's also very possible he discussed what he'd found with Attorney Gould when he went to rewrite his will, conceivably alerting Baldwin. Sadly there's not enough time to look into each person on the list so I think our best option is to focus on the person who didn't make Emil's list. Would you care to guess who we've decided to zero in on?"

Without hesitating Sanford said probably Mr. Gould. The response told me we were on the same page and with little time to lose, I asked

Sanford to use any connections he might have to find out how and why Gould was involved in Baldwin's candidacy.

"Raymond Baldwin is immoral and dangerous and he's got the ability to hide his trail deceptive work very carefully. When I called him out five years ago causing him to resign, I thought I'd never hear his name again but now it appears he's had five long years to scheme and plot. It's only an old reporter's supposition but truthfully, I'm rarely wrong and I believe in Emil Breck. Baldwin is devious, ruthless and would probably do anything to become all powerful once again. Throw disgraced ex-Vice President Devers into the mix and it doubles the trouble. We truly believe that Emil uncovered a corrupt plot and if we can connect the dots, it might lead to Emil's killer and what the ultimate goal of Baldwin is."

The tension broke when my stomach growled like a lion making Sucre say she'd prepare some traditional Peruvian snacks for us. As always when she worked in the kitchen, she turned up her radio to keep abreast of the hourly state and national news. As if one cue Baldwin was the lead national story.

'The election is ten days away and according to the latest polls, the race is simply too close to call.'

"We've got a few pieces of a very perplexing puzzle but we're not even close to putting all the pieces together to see the big picture" I complained. "I too keep thinking about the large number of present and former military people on the list because the unfortunate truth is military people wage war. There are also several high powered media people who once had or still have the ability to sway an entire nation with a single word or headline. There are also several scientists on the list and even though their research theoretically improves our lives, they are also capable of manipulating such things as the environment right down to the air we breath. Some of the industrialists on Emil's list ran key weapons factories including two who oversaw the design and construction of the ultimate weapon."

"99 out of the148 names are military personnel" Sucre remarked over the sound of the blender.

"A who's who of warriors" I added. "If Baldwin was looking for the most formidable people to help him win the White House, he's certainly found them. Those individuals could certainly create mass chaos in America just before or on the day of the election if it appears their candidate might lose.

Bruce Weiss

It's possible he'd even groomed them for a possible coup during his years in seclusion,"

"Fourteen names on the list are current or former politicians, including former Vice-President Skip Devers" Sucre acknowledged. "People in politics know how governments work so they'd be extremely valuable to a candidates new to the national scene."

"There are eighteen individuals who work in the media" I offered, "including newspaper reporters, conservative television hosts and publishers of the right wing press. Any one of them could push fake news on the public creating false news stories before election day.

"Seventeen are CEO's in industries involved in some form of weaponry," Sucre said. "Four are still CEO's of important industries and utility companies, including the former head of the Federal Communications Commission. Each one of them could pack a powerful punch causing big trouble. As Charlie often said put them all in the same room and they could easily create pandemonium in America to ensure Baldwin gains the White House."

We'd just be wasting valuable time going over all our fears and assumptions, woefully admitting there was always the possibility those men and women on Emil's list might be good Americans doing what was best for America. The problem was, they were associated with Baldwin and he was definitely not an honorable man.

The hour was late. We needed answers so before we said goodnight, reluctantly I said we should go over the list one more time before everything turned into science fiction. Sanford announced it had been one hell of a day begging off, saying he needed to go home to start putting his new life in order. The words one a hell of a day was a great understatement.

When Sanford left there was much I wanted to say to Sucre alone that had no bearing on the names.

"Do you think Emil let me go because he inherently knew his life was in danger and possibly mine, and he didn't want to see me harmed?"

"Sadly there's no way to know Charlie but I believe that could be true, sparing you what he thought might be coming his way."

Sucre suggested she and Sanford work on the list of names while I turned my attention solely to Raymond Baldwin and Steven Gould. She added with election day getting closer, she still wanted to attend as many

Emil's List

of Baldwin's speeches as possible. The presidential election was less than ten days away and I wondered if we were running out of time. The late evening news report before we hit the sack claimed Baldwin's campaign chest was overflowing with cash while his rivals were pulling some ads due to lack of money.

Lying on my sofa near the front door it felt as if Baldwin was lurking in the dark in my place. I couldn't get him out of my mind. He was using the same angry buzz words and pointing the same accusatory fingers at anyone who disagreed with him, spouting empty promises for a better life for all. He was all bluster and to no surprise, he never brought up his past transgressions.

Harsh hateful words were sadly appealing to an audience falling under his spell. Relentless verbal attacks incited the crowds, bolstering his polling numbers after every speech. If Baldwin actually gained the White House the nation and the world would become a very contentious place I believed. He was as cold blooded as a rattle snake. I had no idea when the voices in my head would silence and for the first time since I was a child, I said my old childhood prayer and finally drifted off.

The morning news headline portended a troubling day, Sucre dutifully reporting the latest presidential poll was out and Baldwin was points ahead of the Democratic candidate and only two points behind the Republican. He just might be able to pull it off I rued.

Waiting for Sanford to arrive Sucre I killed time going over Emil's list again, although I didn't need a paper in front of me as I'd memorized the names. One obvious theme haunted me. Was there a conspiracy or a plot against America in the works? If Baldwin did not win the election, was his team of advisors prepared to step in and stage a coup? Before the election or after? The day of the election? I was grasping at straws yet every cell in my body was screaming Baldwin was preparing to sabotage our democracy. Emil battled Fascism all his life, often maintaining it could happen anywhere in any nation, even in America. I thought about how he'd once used the term 'hijacking' describing how a well thought out plot could undermine America.

I was at one of the lowest points of my life and if the worst happened, I hoped that Sucre would be as far away as possible, possibly back in her native Peru.

CHAPTER 37

Sucre had become a veritable fountain of information what she affectionately called Baldwin-ology. When I asked her what she was up to she said she was making travel plans to get to a few more Baldwin speaking engagements. The rallies were attracting hard fast admirers and the curious, some there to create trouble I feared.

Baldwin continued to defy the pundits who once said he had no chance to make it to the finish line. His ongoing attacks on what he called the leftist press got people's attention, declaring after being elected those papers would eventually be ignored and become irrelevant and disappear. He'd easily destroyed my career and was certainly capable of destroying others. His rivals for the office called him mad which only attracted more Baldwin supporters. I knew he was as formidable as a pit bull and he used that evil toughness to solidify his power and greed.

We had not heard from Sanford until a call near noon saying he'd be by in an hour. Rather than stare endlessly at the list I put the paperwork down and asked Sucre to tell me more about what she remembered about her Peruvian childhood, something she always enjoyed talking about.

This time though there was more sadness to her tale and I was very sorry I'd asked. If I'd known our work would become riddled with dangers I actually would not have asked the poor young woman to come along on the ride. She struggled to recall parts of her life when she suddenly turned very quiet. I thought it might occupy her thoughts if I related stories about my college life. I exaggerated much and when she began to laugh at some of my travails, she seemed to come back to life.

Our conversation eventually wound it's way back to Raymond Baldwin as always, the invisible person lurking around my apartment. Sucre had done a formidable task scrutinizing the language used by the ex-governor, gaining some very keen insights into his personality hearing what others did not, listening to his speeches two to three times to make sure she hadn't missed anything. He'd talked to quite a few veterans organizations often swearing like a drunken sailor, yet to religious groups he was always the God fearing Christian gentleman.

Waiting for Sanford I rued the election day was one day closer and the buzz surrounding the candidates seemed to focus on upstart Raymond Baldwin.

Sucre said he sounded more fanatical and warning bad things for America is he were not elected. When Baldwin attacked political correctness, he told adoring crowds that was the main reasons we were failing as a nation. Political correctness he insisted caused our leaders to ignore America's real problems. 'They're selling America down the proverbial river but Baldwin people are not buying it' he roared.

When Sanford finally arrived I told him we were still stuck in neutral but there was something important that he could do for us. I told him I wanted him to find Matt Roth's children. I related the details about Emil's appearance at the HUAC hearings and how I wanted very badly to ask either son a personal favor. I'm on it was his reply. I asked Sucre to work with Sanford because she could tell him more about the Congressional transcripts and the correspondence between Emil and Roth. Sanford said they were off to the Boston Library to do some research.

Near seven that evening the dynamic duo returned and I was not disappointed. Sanford found a copy of Roth's obituary in the Baltimore Sun, his hometown paper. He'd died of congestive heart failure which I had not known. His two sons followed in his dad's footsteps becoming journalists, each specializing in investigative reporting Where they lived and worked however was unknown.

"But there's more" Sucre chimed in.

"After searching newspapers in the library to try and find any articles written by either son, we actually struck gold. I was ready to give up but Sanford refused, discovering an article written by Ethan Roth nearly ten years ago for the San Francisco Examiner. Nothing very special but it told us at least one brother might possibly still live in the San Francisco Bay area."

Bruce Weiss

I asked Sucre to call the Examiner and ask if Ethan Roth still worked there. To our chagrin a junior editor who'd taken Sucre's call said he hadn't worked there for years. Any idea where he currently worked, Sucre asked? Sanford and I moved closer to Sucre to listen to the response.

"I don't know Ethan's whereabouts but if you're interested, his brother Damon Roth currently works as a political reporter for the San Francisco Free Press."

It was nearing eight at night but with a three hour time difference I prayed we might find Damon still at work. I dialed the Free Press a woman answering, asking what the call was about and could she help. I said I was a retired journalist who'd recently discovered a trove of articles written by his father, Matt. There was no response until we heard a man's voice saying what can I do for you? I took a deep breath.

"I've inherited scores of old news articles, transcripts of Mr. Roth's first hand accounts of the HUAC hearings taking place in the early 1950's."

I asked if I might speak with him and to my relief, he said I was. Damon said he was very impressed because most people had forgotten about his father and his stellar work. I mentioned among the articles we'd found were several op-ed pieces his father wrote descrying the terrible injustices many people suffered due to the committee's work.

"I honestly don't know much about my dad's Washington DC days but several years ago I tried to get copies of the transcripts from those hearings. I was told they were lost or possibly buried somewhere on a dusty back shelf in some storage facility. You say you have transcripts and articles my dad wrote?"

I said much of his father's reporting during the contentious hearings were written about one man by the name of Emil Breck, explaining Mr. Breck's testimony was well documented by his dad and was pure dynamite.

"Your father had a front row seat during what became known as an inquest rather than a hearing. I also have a small collection of personal letters exchanged between Max and Emil Breck.

"Could you possibly send them along to me?"

"It would be an honor and my pleasure. I should add your dad did a yeoman's job, making few friends in Washington exposing a committee ignoring most rules of civility and law."

I knew I'd gotten his attention so asked what he knew about Raymond

Emil's List

Baldwin, the man who led the hearings and now a candidate for the presidency.

"Campaigns and politics are not my field," he responded, "so only what I read in the papers. Sorry."

I talked about Baldwin's role in the HUAC hearings and how the committee turned into a modern day Salem witch hunt, running roughshod over many innocent lives. Baldwin has not changed for the good over the years I emphasized. "In my opinion he's still dangerous, cunning and deceitful."

"Tell me a little about Emil Breck because I'm not familiar with his work or his name."

"For nearly a half century he was the preeminent journalist in America, possibly the entire world. Sadly, he met an untimely death as someone poisoned him to silence his writings.

I gave a brief account of the time five years earlier when Raymond Baldwin and I'd crossed paths. "I'd exposed a great deal of graft and corruption in his governorship and I wrote pointed articles describing his evil ways. That eventually lead to his resignation and my being black balled from the industry."

I didn't want to take up anymore of his time but I wanted to ask the great favor, my real reason for the call.

"With the days to the election dwindling I need your help. I work with a young woman who is not a journalist but I'd like to get her accredited press credentials. If she can get them it might allow us to widen our investigation into a potential catastrophic election issue. Press credentials would allow my friend to get as close as possible to candidate Baldwin."

There was a very long heavy pause.

"Press credentials are sacred documents and very difficult to get" was the reply "I assume you're aware of that because of your own work. It's something not for sale and whoever earns one finds themselves with what I'd call a magic key, opening many doors and allowing access to very important people."

I said my own press credentials were long lapsed but they allowed me to get into places the public could not. Waiting for an answer was painful realizing it was totally unethical to ask for them The silence on the phone seemed unending. I knew anyone applying for credentials had to go

Bruce Weiss

through a full background check with lengthy interviews and questions. Anyone getting close to a politician had to be carefully vetted. The wait seemed interminable. I was asking a lot but hoping Damon might bend or even break the rules as a favor to someone who could tell him more about his famous father. I knew it wasn't illegal but it was certainly immoral. I had to break the silence.

"Would you be able to somehow get reporter's credentials from your newspaper? We're involved in an investigation of Baldwin's campaign and we're turning up some very dangerous possibilities. I can't ask my old newspaper friends because I've been away from the business far to long."

I heard a pencil tapping and though it best to say I understood if he said no because it would put him in an awkward position if it were traced back to him.

"Don't ask me why I'm going to do this Mr. Darwin but the thought of seeing the work done by my father I once thought impossible intrigues me. Look for a package in the mail in a few days and make sure it can't be traced back to me."

I thanked him profusely, promising to send along copies of all the HUAC articles written by his dad as well as the testimony given during Emil Breck's appearance. I then told him exactly what I needed.

When I hung up a feeling of guilt washed over me, knowing I'd done something inherently wrong. I was ruthless in my day but not that way.

Two days later via special delivery Sucre's press credentials arrived, making her the east coast political reporter for the San Francisco Free Press. It was the admission ticket to a very exclusive club allowing her special access to Baldwin. The only problem I foresaw was the reality we had little money for travel and Baldwin was hop scotching here there and everywhere.

A few hours later I gave Sucre a crash course on the finer points of journalism and in particular, how and when to ask the right question. I envisioned her asking Baldwin if he would describe his problems as governor. In all my days as a reported I could not recall a blind journalist ever covering a national story so she'd definitely stand out.

"Reporting can often be a very nasty business with much backstabbing and deception."

After saying that I started to fret, hoping her rivals would treat her

Emil's List

fairly. I explained what she might expect from the other reporters, some good and some rather crude.

"Be prepared to be pushed aside but when that happens, you anchor yourself and if need be push back. The competition for a story often borders on boorish and childish rude behavior so try not let it get to you. You're really there for a different reason and keeping that in mind, you want to get inside Baldwin's head. Anything you discoverer might tell us what he's really up to."

Sucre said she looked forward to getting close to candidate Baldwin. She looked rather pleased, unable to see the worry lines on my face. I couldn't emphasize enough her personal safety came absolutely first and to avoid situations that could possibly lead to harm.

A moment later I added one final thought. I knew she could do great work but I didn't want her to go alone. I'd ask Sanford to accompany her making me worry less. I hoped he might say yes.

Looking at the morning paper Baldwin's tentative campaign stops were noted. He'd be swinging through New York and Pennsylvania during the week, two places not terribly far away. Now all I had to do was convince Sanford to accompany Sucre, and Sucre to allow the company. I thought I'd seen something in Sanford's eyes and demeanor when he was near Sucre, suggesting he might want to spend time with her.

With no arm twisting Sanford agreed to tag along but I knew that was the easy part. When Sanford went home to pack I asked Sucre if she'd like to spend a few hours listening to the Diary of Anne Frank.

Chapter 38

Sucre dutifully had her photo taken and laminated for her badge, her shoulder bag packed with notepads, pens and pencils and her trusty recorder. On the evening news it was reported Baldwin would be making two unscheduled campaign stops in Providence and then Nashua, New Hampshire, both only an hour away. I was intrigued by the report ex-Vice President Devers would be doing the introductions at both stops.

A special delivery package arrived in the mail after my second phone call to Damon and the overnight delivery brought us a second set of reporter's credentials made out to Sanford Roberts. The badge identified him as a photographer for the San Francisco Free Press.

Sanford was a great addition because I believed he'd be very protective of Sucre, pulling him aside however explaining Sucre's need for independence. I also said if he had any job interviews scheduled that was his first priority. All that was left to do was tell Sucre she would not be traveling alone.

I got the response I'd expected. Sucre scowled, shaking her head furiously no. With an anger I'd rarely seen she told me in no uncertain terms that she worked alone and that was the way it was going to be. It took a half hour of consoling, repeating over and over that Sanford would respect her individuality. When I finally got an okay my blood pressure dropped.

Early the next morning the couple took the commuter train from Boston to Providence. I nearly decided to go along at the last moment but the old adage three's a crowd convinced me not to. Being alone also meant I could begin to outline the biography I hoped to start after the election.

In the back of my closet was an old black and white RCA television I hadn't seen in years. Providence was only forty miles away and with the set's aluminum rabbit ears, I hoped to get one of the Providence stations. Remarkably the set still worked and channel 12 in Providence came in with just a little haze.

At noon on the hourly news update the local Providence newscaster announced the station would cut away from it's regularly scheduled programming for live coverage of candidate Raymond Baldwin's speech on the Capitol lawn. Minutes later I saw live coverage of the large crowd waiting for the candidate. Many carried signs proclaiming 'I'm a Baldwin liker.' A roving reporter in the sea of people estimated the crowd at ten thousand. For a brief moment the camera caught a sizable group of protestors with their signs. It was obvious the protestors were kept far from the stage.

As reported Devers did the introduction, calling Baldwin a God-fearing flag waving one hundred percent loyal American. I remembered why I disliked Devers so much.

"There are rumors that when Governor Baldwin nicks himself shaving, he bleeds red, white and blue."

The crowd roared it's approval, clapping and shouting for nearly three minutes. Waiting for the cheering to stop, the camera panning the press corps allowing me to get a quick glimpse of Sucre and Sanford standing just below the podium. I couldn't resist smiling not because they had ring side seats, but because they were holding hands. Sanford had my 35mm camera around his neck while Sucre cradled her trusty recorder. While Dever's droned on I cut up pieces cardboard making placards with the names of the individuals on Emil's list. I planned on taping them on my living room wall to get a bigger picture. Baldwin naturally was placed in the center.

After much work I tore them all down, a waste of my good time, wanting them down before Sucre returned. Due to the small TV screen I moved closer to the set, the first time I'd actually seen Baldwin since the day he'd announced his candidacy.

The speech lasted fifteen minutes, the crowd's cheering taking up at least five minutes. Baldwin used the word deplorable at least nine times describing his rivals, each time igniting the crowd.

When the speech ended Sucre called me for what I suspected was a recap of her experience. Sucre however had something else on her mind.

Bruce Weiss

"If it's not a problem, Sanford and I will take a late train home because we want to have dinner in one of Providence's famed Italian restaurants."

I wished she could have seen the big Cheshire cat grin on my face. I did little the rest of the day, fooling with my new found television.

Sucre walked in just past midnight giving me the same feeling I had when my own daughters came home after their first dates. We spoke a few minutes, mostly about the restaurant. The rest would wait until morning. It had been a rough couple of weeks and at that moment, I couldn't have been happier for Sucre.

Sanford arrived early the next morning with some great photos of the dignitaries surrounding Baldwin and fresh flowers. I got a play by play analysis of the speech and all they'd taken in, deciding not to tell them I'd seen and heard the speech on my television safely back in the closet.

"I thought he sounded very tired because he mispronounced several words and was seemingly easily distracted. Still, he said enough to send his followers home quite happy because I heard many positive comments when Sanford and I were leaving. As usual, Baldwin hammered away for more law and order. He even went so far as to say he'd put National Guard troops into the city streets to combat illegal drugs and gangs. As to the military, the subject he spends a great deal of time talking about, he said as president he'd increase defense spending three fold. That statement got the loudest cheers."

"Charlie, nearing the end of his speech he got very theatrical, Sanford added, "raising an old Civil War rifle high over his head. He claimed it once belonged to his grandfather and said it could only be taken from his cold dead hands. The crowd went ballistic while a large contingent of NRA members sang the Battle Hymn of the Republic. That was the way the circus ended."

I knew most of that so I was more interested in Sanford's photos to see if I could identify individuals who might be on Emil's list. When I got to one particular photo I shook my head.

"You're right" Sanford remarked. "That is Steven Gould sitting right behind Baldwin."

"Actually we were so close I could smell his aftershave" Sucre chimed in.

Sanford claimed Gould could not take his eyes off of he and Sucre.

"Let me tell you what I overheard" Sucre said. "At the end of the speech many people remained on the stage milling around for what Sanford said were photo ops. I could hear Baldwin speaking just barely above a whisper and I knew right away the words were directed toward us. These are his exact words. There are two despicable and treacherous individuals in the press area. Get someone to keep an eye on them every minute of the day."

Sucre and Sanford were both a bit surprised when I said I hadn't looked at Emil's list all day. I didn't dare say that I'd been debating telling Sucre writing the biography was going to be a one person job. There was little left to do and I didn't want to keep her away from her job any longer. I hadn't figured out the right words to say but I'd save that for after the election.

The couple invited me to go along for breakfast but I reluctantly said no. In truth I was starved but I was going to stick to my silly belief three was a crowd. Dutifully Sucre phoned an hour later, saying they'd be out longer than they'd planned because Sanford was going to take her on her first swan boat ride on the lake inside the Boston Common.

I was beginning to relish my time alone working on the biography outline, the work once again energizing me. Despite the progress I was making something was not quite right. I finally realized I missed not having Sucre with me. Baldwin was due to deliver a speech in Hartford and then New Haven the next day and although I was happy she was going, a bit of sadness crept in because I would probably not see her for a while.

The pair returned after six when we had light snacks and Peruvian wine Sucre purchased in Providence. In the quiet of the evening I realized how terrific those two looked together. I was practically invisible.

Early the next morning Sucre and Sanford set off on their journey to Hartford. Two minutes after they'd left Sucre walked back into the apartment, asking Sanford to wait outside because she wanted to talk to me for a moment. Giving me a big hug surprised me so I asked what that was for. Her unexpected reply touched me deeply.

"I've been waiting my entire adult life to say these words and this is the perfect time. Charlie, believe it or not I'm going on a blind date."

My mind couldn't concentrate on the outline so I decided to read Orwell's 1984 again, recalling it nearly frightened me to death when I'd first read it in college. Not quite done with the first chapter I fell into a very deep sleep for hours. The day was unproductive, convincing myself I badly needed a day off even with election day another day closer.

When the pair returned late the next evening Sucre was bubbling with excitement.

"Charlie, we can now officially connect several more of the names on Emil's list directly to Raymond Baldwin. Just before he began his speech Baldwin recognized several people in the audience and I recognized the names immediately from our list.

"The first was Retired Lieutenant General Rex Standish and the other military man Retired Three Star General Frank Wilson. A moment later he called Ernestine Wither's name, the first woman board member of the NRA. I assumed each stood to be identified because I heard Sanford furiously clicking photos but that's not all.

"Attorney Gould passed several slips of paper to Baldwin during the speech according to Sanford and immediately after, Baldwin asked several more people in the audience to stand and acknowledge themselves.

"The first was Colonel William Prescott, introduced as the commanding officer of the Massachusetts National Guard. A moment later he asked Colonel Francis Anderson to stand, identifying him as the commanding officer of the Connecticut Air National Guard. On my recorder you can hear Baldwin's words about how heartwarming it was to have so many distinguished military people taking time away from their critical jobs to support him. He seemed to go off script at that point, lecturing about the sad state of affairs for the military and veterans. The crowd loved those words."

I became acutely aware Sanford had not taken his eyes of Sucre, making me hope it was more than friendship.

With election day another day closer we had more names connected to Baldwin. I felt refreshed, ready to stay up day and night if necessary to pull all the pieces together. With the new names I suggested we get back to work on Emil' list.

Sanford showed me the morning paper with the latest poll numbers, analysts still agreeing the presidential race was too close to call. Many so called experts suggested the very real possibility none of the candidates would pick up the necessary 270 electoral votes to get elected. It was a presidential race like no other.

We were only a week away from election day and I believed Baldwin would do whatever was necessary to win in the coming days. I had one more day alone because the duo was off to Syracuse, the last stop on the east coast for the Baldwin campaign. It was Sucre's last chance to hear the candidate speak and possibly our last chance to add a few more names connected to Baldwin. We wouldn't have enough time to connect all the names but I was almost certain each was involved in Baldwin's world. It was also becoming obvious that if Baldwin was truly plotting something evil, he'd corralled many formidable individuals with the expertise to wreck havoc on America's election.

The empty nest syndrome kicked in the moment they left, not only missing Sucre but the Peruvian music I'd come to love. Sanford turned out to be a true Godsend, showing up at the right time and making me feel more secure about Sucre's safety when traveling far from home.

Syracuse turned out to be another bonanza enabling us to put more individuals on Emil's list squarely on Baldwin's team. As the day to the election grew closer I began to wonder if there might not be any plot at all. The other haunting thought was, could Sanford actually be working for Gould?

We were able to connect more names to Baldwin. Listening to Sucre's recording I heard Baldwin introduce Four Star General Arnold, a member of the Joint Chiefs of staff and the National Security Council to his audience. A reporter spoke loud enough to be heard on Sucre's tape whispering Arnold had once been called before a select Senate Committee investigating the illegal sales of arms to right wing groups in Central and South America. Baldwin sure knew how to pick his associates I mused.

I said I couldn't remember if Arnold was ever charged although the word on the streets was he wore Teflon clothing. Baldwin painted a very rosy picture of the man, asking him to come forward to receive a plague from the National Veterans Organization.

I was no longer counting the days to the election but hours. On the evening news that night we heard something quite unexpected. Baldwin for unknown reasons was suddenly losing support, trailing the other two candidates. Rumors circulated that the Republican candidate might withdraw from the race throwing his support to Baldwin. The nation was rife in rumors.

I told Sucre and Sanford I was very proud of them and because of their efforts we were able to identify more than thirty-five names connected to

Bruce Weiss

Baldwin, most in positions of power in America. The nagging question in the room however remained, what exactly could these people do for Baldwin?

Sucre and Sanford went out for a night on the town and even though I was seeing less and less of her, I loved the idea of she and Sanford together. I'd never heard her sound so happy but fortunately she was level headed enough not to let infatuation hinder our work.

CHAPTER 39

There were only four days left before the election and the campaigning continued without any new surprises from candidate Baldwin. The biggest news story was about the political pundits being unable to account for Baldwin's sudden fall from grace. News reports predicted all three candidates would stay to the end, acknowledging if no one got the majority of electoral votes, the election would go to the Democratic controlled House. Would Baldwin drop out due to his low numbers or stay the course?

Concentrating on the biography was nearly impossible, Emi's list of names never far from my thoughts. Not lost in all the work however was the fact that Emil had been murdered, most likely directed by Raymond Baldwin. If Emil had been able to live for several more weeks I was certain he'd have exposed a devious secret plot against America.

Without a shred of evidence though I still believed Emil uncovered something quite explosive suggesting great mayhem, possibly just before election day. Our little team could not guess when, where or how Baldwin's team might strike and there was still nothing we could take to the authorities. Our case was built on assumptions and coincidences but without concrete evidence, who would listen to us? What would happen if Baldwin actually won the election or worse, what would happen if he lost?

There was little left for Sanford and Sucre to do. I felt bad when Sucre told me Sanford's savings were running low. I tried to lend him a few dollars but he refused. With the election seventy-two hours away Sanford gracefully bowed out saying it was time to move on, hopefully catching on with another law firm. When he left, Sucre looked forlorn breaking my heart. I felt the full weight of the world on my shoulders again The work

Bruce Weiss

I'd begun with the biography was in shambles and there would be no more work until after the election.

The evening passed with a great heaviness in my place, interrupted by a phone call from Sanford with excited news for Sucre. He'd gotten two solid job interviews set up. Sadly if Gould did to him what Baldwin did to me, he wouldn't stand a chance.

In the morning Sucre and I admitted we hadn't gotten much sleep and just as Sucre started breakfast there was a loud knock on my door. Sucre ran to the door as if she knew who might be there. She'd smelled the fresh cut flowers. Their reunion was joyful and seeing them together again lifted the gloominess from the room. We ate breakfast together wishing Sanford good luck when he left for his first interview.

Sucre said she'd decided to go back to work at Harvard full time. She'd been away for quite a while and she had some plans cooked up to put Emil's collection into Braille. An hour later Sanford returned, a hang dog look on his face so I didn't have to ask. The bottom line rung true. Sanford said he'd been black balled, asking me to sit down because there was something he wanted to discuss. My immediate thought was here comes the words he'd been working with Gould. Bear with me he insisted.

"When I was let go by Attorney Gould it happened so fast and so shockingly I neglected to turn in my keys. I've been toying with a strange idea every time I hear a new connection between Steven Gould and Raymond Baldwin."

I had no idea where Sanford was going.

"I have the keys to the building so I'm wondering if we might put a plan together allowing me to get inside Mr. Gould's office."

I tried to interrupt Sanford but he wouldn't allow it.

"It's possible I might find Baldwin's real intentions. I know the Gould building inside and out, even how to get around late in the evenings when the place is dark. The cleaning staff leaves at midnight sharp and there's only on person on duty in the entire building, patrolling the lobby until the offices open in the morning. I'd have Mr. Gould's office to myself and who knows what I might find."

My response was an absolutely no. Before Sanford could raise the issue again I said Emil Breck was most likely killed because he talked to the wrong people, possibly even Gould when he made his last visit to rewrite

266

Emil's List

his will. Sanford I argued emphatically, if you break into a legal office and got caught you'd never practice law again and you'd certainly be arrested. It's an insane idea we need not discuss any further."

"Charlie it's impossible to get caught in the hours between midnight and seven in the morning. The time spent in Gould's office would be no more than an hour."

"And if you did manage to get caught don't you think all hell would break loose? Do your remember Watergate? One slipup and you'd be facing very serious criminal charges."

Sanford pressed his case, claiming nothing could or would go wrong. I asked about silent alarms and he replied only the downstairs front doors were alarmed to let the sentry on duty know someone wanted to come in.

"I know the back way into the building and the staircase near the rear door taking you up to the sixth floor landing. Nothing ventured, nothing gained."

I refused to let myself relent but I had to admit I was somewhat intrigued by the idea. If Sanford found incriminating evidence in the office it might be the hard proof we had not able to find. Was it worth the price of all that could go wrong? Didn't Sanford know he would certainly be disbarred for life? I was relieved Sucre was in her bedroom with her ear buds in and didn't hear the insidious plan. I was so absorbed with Sanford however I didn't realize Sucre was standing in the doorway listening to our conversation. The look on her face told me she was going to take Sanford's side.

"If Sanford says he can get in and out without being caught, I don't think there's much of a risk. We've put an awful lot of time and effort into this and we're coming down to zero hour. If Sanford can do it, I'm unequivocally telling you both right now I'm going with him. I might be a blind as the proverbial bat but there's nothing wrong with my ears. If I'm with Sanford and something stirs inside the building, I'd be the first to know. If Sanford goes, so do I."

We were both stunned, looks of incredulity on our faces while Sucre insisted it was a done deal with no debate. I knew Sucre well enough to know I couldn't dissuade her so my only hope was convincing Sanford it wasn't worth the risk. Not to my surprise, Sanford announced yes it was a done deal.

What would happen if Sanford was caught I wondered and what would happen to a Peruvian national with him?

Bruce Weiss

"These are the company keys" Sanford announced, "and one of them goes to the back door and the other to the rear freight elevator. I know for certain there are no internal alarms, just the single guard far from the back of the building where we'll be."

I'd hoped Sucre would be kept in the dark, hating myself for thinking those words. She tried to convince me all she would do would listen for any footfalls or voices. We'd be in an out like Patty Hearst in a bank heist she joked.

"I'll be okay because Sanford will be with me. Charlie, consider what we may gain. If we can find evidence of a plot involving the election, we could accomplish what Emil was unable to finish. Besides, Gould has attended every Baldwin rally and I happen to know he'll be in Cleveland tomorrow night, far from his office. If something terrible is going to happen before election day, it's possible it could be stopped."

I had to pinch myself because curiously I was beginning to find merit in Sanford's plan. We'd been up against some very formidable people but in the darkness of night something in Gould's office could possibly break everything wide open.

"Sanford, tell me exactly what Sucre would have to do."

Before there was an answer Sucre spoke up, saying she'd be out in the hallway listening for any sounds in case she had to alert Sanford.

"Sanford knows his way around the building so if someone is walking about the building or near the sixth floor, I'm certain he'd lead me to a safe place. I'd strictly be a look out or in truth, a listen out."

I pictured myself pacing my place as night time passed, fearing for their safety and well being. Did the lone guard carry a weapon? Would Sanford know that? My mind was on fire sensing it would be the right time to go against my threes a crowd philosophy and invite myself to go along, prudent to have an extra set of eyes and ears just in case. It would not be a walk in the park but if Sanford somehow found incriminating evidence, we'd have something to take to the federal authorities, putting the exclamation point on what Emil was working on. I truly had nothing to lose although a Peruvian national and a lawyer could be looking at some unpleasant business. I insisted that it was no go unless I went along. There were no objections.

CHAPTER 40

To get our minds off the caper I suggested we go over Emil's list one last time to see if we'd missed anything. If Sucre had not discovered the Braille I knew all to well we'd be terribly lost. My mind drifted at times going over each name, wondering if it would eventually help us uncover a possible hideous plot against America.

There was no more time left trying to associate more names with Baldwin I declared. We had roughly forty names connected to Baldwin and that was enough for me. Was it a conspiracy or paranoid speculation? If I only knew how and why Emil put the list together long before Baldwin declared his candidacy, we'd be on more solid ground.

With the hours flying by incredibly quickly there was nothing more we could do with the list and considered the logistics of the break-in. Just hearing the words break-in didn't sit well with me. Monitoring her ever present radio, Sucre announced the so called experts were predicting when all the votes were tallied, Baldwin would not influence the election. He'd lost too much support but for what reason, no one knew. That report did not make me feel better because even as a loser, Baldwin had a team capable of waging war against the nation.

With time dwindling we stayed in my place, talking nearly to dawn about anything and everything except Emil's list. There were only two and a half days left before the election and only sixteen hours until we invaded Gould's office.

Sucre and Sanford went out for breakfast but I said I wasn't hungry, too nervous to eat. Sucre informed me they'd not return to the apartment after they ate but instead take a bus to Rockport for the day, returning in plenty of time to arrive at the backdoor of the Gould Building just after midnight. I would meet up with them there. Sanford repeated nothing could go wrong so many times I nearly lost my temper. Alone when they left I took out the book Fahrenheit 451 to take my mind off what awaited. As I'd done with each of Emil's, now Sucre's books, I touched the author's signature. A few minutes into the reading I realized my mind wasn't into the book so I walked to my bookshelf looking over the thirty books Sucre insisted keeping at my place. With very tired eyes I was curiously drawn to one volume I'd somehow not seen before.

I'd stared at those magical books too many times to count but this time, I spied a volume on the shelf I'd somehow managed to overlook. A very thin book nearly invisible between Anne Frank's Diary and Marx's Das Kapital caught my eye. The binding was made of fine leather like the others but so thin, possibly no more than ten pages I'd somehow just not seen it. I removed it from the shelf examining it closer.

The title on the binding was in Spanish, causing to me wonder if Emil might have purchased the book during his years in Spain. I looked for the author's name on the cover page and was quite surprised to find the author was Emil Breck. The first page was an introduction in English, followed by Spanish. Had Emil written a short story?

I leafed through the pages scanning what Emil wrote but to my chagrin, all the pages were blank. Was it going to be a diary that he'd not gotten too? About to put the book back on the shelf it felt as if lightening bolt suddenly struck me. Could Sucre's discovery of Braille in Emil's personal notes be connected to the blank pages?

I ran my index finger cautiously across the pages and although not one hundred percent certain, I thought I'd detected tiny ridges. If it was Braille the book was definitely meant for Sucre because she would be the only one able to read Emil's words.

What could Emil have had in mind I wondered? Sucre was away with Sanford and I couldn't reach her so there was nothing I could do until I saw her after the undertaking at Gould's office. The words had to have been meant for Sucre so did it have anything to do with Emil's List or was it simply prose written to a blind woman?

I paced the room, talking to myself trying to guess what I might have found. Leafing through the pages again I was certain that I could feel tiny ridges just barely perceptible. Anyone looking at the book would have assumed it was simply a blank book as I had. Sadly, until I caught up with Sucre there was nothing I could do, adding a bit more frustration to my life. The discovery and the scheduled break-in portended one hell of a day, my mind telling me life was a mess.

Baldwin spent five years in self imposed exile but I'd lately come to believe those years were spent planning a comeback. With hours to go before our meeting in the alley behind the Gould Building, I was suddenly overcome with great tiredness, but worried if I fell asleep, I'd probably miss the rendezvous. Despite my best efforts to stay awake I dozed off, shaken again by a loud knock at my door. It was Mrs. Delvechio, a kindly elderly neighbor who'd grown concerned by the sounds of screams inside my place. I'd been dreaming someone was trying to poison me. I thanked her for her concern and said I was alright, knowing I truly wasn't. To my vexation there was a phone message I'd obviously slept through.

'Sanford and I are in Rockport and I was just calling to make sure we're set on the meeting time. For your peace of mind Charlie, I don't want you to worry. It's Brewery Lane, the back entrance to the Gould Building and as I've said many times, I'm a big girl. Remember we meet between 12:15 and 12:30 in the alley way. Hope you're enjoying the peace and quiet.'

I'd missed her phone call so the new found book would definitely have to be put aside until after our late night, early morning business. Afraid to close my eyes again, I walked back to the book shelf to look once again at the book I'd found. Cradling it in my hands it felt curiously alive. For a moment I wished I'd gone with them but then if I had, the book would have gone unseen.

Looking out my window the sky was clear with the promise of a moonless night. Should I have put my heavy foot down and said no, that it wasn't worth the risk invading a legal office? As the minutes passed fortunately only positive thoughts surfaced, hoping everything would work out.

By 11:30 the city lights were going out, getting closer to the time I needed to leave my place. I held Emil's surprise book in my hands again, seemingly rubbing the binding as if it were a magic lamp. As the midnight hour approached a sense of calmness soothed my nerves, resigned to the notion there was no turning back. The city turned a bit more dangerous after midnight but when I finally took my first cautious steps away from my place, the sight of many couples walking arm in arm gave me a warm feeling.

CHAPTER 41

I repeated the mantra over and over again, the idea was fool proof although a tiny voice in my head kept whispering it was not. I envisioned Sanford unlocking the back door with his key and immediately running into trouble. In our favor however was the reality time was not critical and there was no need to hurry. I'd insist no matter what Sanford was doing, Sucre remain in the hallway with me. Nothing could go wrong I repeated over and over in my mind.

Walking blindly down the unlit alley, as dark a place as I'd ever been I heard the sounds of Boston rats scurrying all about. It was so dark I feared I'd end up at the wrong doorway. When it seemed as if it couldn't get any darker I thought about Sucre and how well she managed a dark life.

Hearing footsteps in the darkness I prayed the sounds were Sucre and Sanford. Sucre heard my breathing, whispering we would all be okay.

Entering the building was both quick and easy but with no interior lights, I wondered why we hadn't thought about bringing flashlights. Sucre reached for my hand while we meandered through the darkened halls to the back staircase. This time there would be no magical look into the old Revolutionary war cemetery, nearly out of breath when we reached the sixth floor landing.

"I'm going into the office. You and Sucre wait here" Sanford whispered. "You'll hear the opening and closing of drawers but let me know stat if you hear anything else."

In Sanford we trust I whispered. Sucre had my hand in a death grip saying nothing. We heard the sound of a key go into a lock and a door opening. So far so good I thought. Even some distance from the inner office I could see the green glow of the computers. I pulled Sucre into the outer office and just as I did, the door to Gould's office opened and in that instant, a blinding flash of light exploded blinding me. My first thought was some kind of powerful alarm light went on in the inner office when the door was opened. It actually felt as if a bomb had gone off, seeing Sanford's shadow near the door when my eyes focused. I briefly wondered if that was the kind of flash Sucre saw when the bomb went off in her Peruvian home.

I couldn't guess how much time elapsed as more areas of the inner office came into view. When I was fully able to see clearly a sickening feeling hit me so hard I thought I might fall to the floor. I reached for Sucre's hand, staring in shock at the sight of Steven Gould sitting behind his oversized desk, too overwhelmed to tell Sucre what I was seeing. In a heart beat I knew that we were all going to jail or worse. No one said a word as I felt the life slowly being sucked out of me, much like a deflating balloon. I knew Sucre had no way knowing what had just happened and I had no idea how I might explain. Looking about I realized Sanford was no longer in sight, guessing he'd probably run off. The silence ended when I heard a familiar voice. It was Steven Gould.

"I think you and the young lady need to come into my office and sit down. Charlie, you look like you've just seen a ghost."

After more minutes of silence we heard the words, we have important things to discuss.

I didn't understand why Gould wasn't calling the police, whispering to Sucre the jig was up. What happened to Sanford I wondered? I felt Sucre shaking but couldn't be certain if it was her or me. Sanford somewhere in the distance declared everything would be alright. When I turned around I saw him with his arms crossed, nestled on a sofa against the far wall. Oh God I groaned.

"It's time we have a very serious discussion" Gould announced. "But first, I want you both to know you are not in trouble. I've actually been expecting you thanks to Mr. Roberts."

Here comes the axe down on our necks a knew.

Sanford Roberts is not quite who you think he is but after he explains, I'm certain you'll understand."

Dear God I thought, believing what we were about to hear Sanford like Gould was working for Baldwin. I'd invited the fox into the hen house

Bruce Weiss

and it was now time to pay. Had he joined us in our work to discover what Emil was working on?

My thoughts turned to Sucre who hadn't said a word and who must have been as terribly confused as I was. To my incredulity, Sanford got up from the sofa and walking to Sucre he put his arm around her shoulder. The crazy hits kept on coming. Was he going to harm her?

"Sucre, I sincerely apologize for deceiving you" he said, "but after Mr. Gould and I explain everything you'll understand. I want you to know that despite what you might be feeling right now, I've fallen hopelessly in love with you. I think you know that. Give Mr. Gould a chance and he'll explain everything. Before he begins however, I hope you'll find it in your heart to forgive me for not telling you certain things."{

"What the hell is going on" I shouted angrily."

"Charlie and Sucre" Gould announced, "when this all unfolds you'll both understand what's happening. First, I am an attorney and I manage the Gould legal firm. Mr. Roberts however is not a lawyer but an FBI agent working under cover out of my building. His mission was to discover what Mr. Raymond Baldwin was really up to, based on some evidence the FBI gathered. Folks, we're dealing with potential catastrophe. Just as Mr. Baldwin declared his candidacy, the FBI received information a possible plot was afoot meant to derail our election. All that was known at that time was that Raymond Baldwin was likely the ring leader. When Charlie inherited Mr. Breck's the papers the FBI felt it put him into harms way. Emil Breck being the first victim. Roberts and other undercover FBI agents were actually watching your backs from the day you inherited the papers. After my meeting with Mr. Breck rewriting his will, I contacted the Boston FBI office with the information he'd uncovered some potentially dangerous information about a Machiavellian plot traced to Raymond Baldwin. The agency painstakingly poured over every single document in Mr. Breck's papers before Charlie inherited them, sadly finding nothing. The agency hoped that Mr. Darwin might uncover Emil's investigative work. With no answers and the election getting closer, Mr. Roberts found a way to work with you."

I wasn't sure what Sucre was thinking but her sobbing was quite obvious, taking many deep breaths before speaking her first words.

"Sanford, was everything between us just a lie?"

Emil's List

"Sucre darling, I took absolutely no pleasure deceiving you but I had to get into your and Charlie's lives in order to stop a mad man on a dangerous mission. The FBI was well aware Charlie might find answers in Emil Breck's valuable papers. The agency couldn't confront Baldwin because there was nothing solid so it all came down to this; could Charlie decipher a mystery. You were both in danger and my becoming part of your lives was to ensure you both remained safe. Despite thousands of hours agency work, our last best hope was Charlie. We'd been following Mr. Baldwin for some time hoping to find a smoking gun but it was not to be."

"When Mr. Breck came to my office to pen a new will" Mr. Gould interjected, "he let on to me that he was investigating a possible plot that would create great disorder during our election process."

I was too stunned to say anything, overwhelmed by all I was hearing.

"Time is running out," Sanford added. "Even though you were able to find the names of the individuals allegedly associated with Mr. Baldwin, we still couldn't unlocked the great mystery of when and where a possible coordinated attack against America might take place. We also concluded that Mr. Breck was unfortunately silenced because of his work. To that extent, we asked the Boston Police Department not to arrest Charlie.

"Sadly, the agency is still in the dark," Sanford lamented "and we're still not exactly certain what we're dealing with. Thanks to Sucre however we were able to put a watch on the people on Emil's list. Your assumptions about those people were right on the mark. That group is very capable of engaging in acts that potentially could do great harm to this nation. America has certainly taken it's licks in past contested elections but this was on another level. Even though the polls now clearly show that Baldwin is not a threat to win the presidency, we believe he still has the capability to destroy the entire electoral process, which might have been his real focus. We've never faced anything like this before."

I was still stunned although simmering with great anger at the thought we'd been used I didn't know whether to thank them for protecting us, or damning them for not telling us what was happening.

"Would anyone like a drink," Gould announced. Neither Sucre or I responded.

"I knew Emil Breck for more than thirty years," Gould said barely above a whisper. "He was one of the finest gentleman I'd ever known. I

Bruce Weiss

learned much about his life over the years, possibly more than anyone until Charlie here inherited his personal papers and began working with him. Charlie, the day you inherited Emil's papers was the day you popped up on the FBI's radar screen. Many years ago believe it or not, I was actually Emil's co-counsel when he was called to testify before the House Un-American Committee. We go back a long way and interestingly, I was also acquainted with Max Roth.

"Emil and I touched base over the years not as lawyer-client, but as friends. On our last visit together he let on he was close to exposing something so lethal and toxic it could devastate America's election. Emil affirmed he hadn't put all the pieces of the puzzle together but was getting very close. He couldn't or wouldn't elaborate but he hoped to eventually discover what Raymond Baldwin was up to and then inform the FBI.

"He told me he was working to uncover irrefutable proof an unthinkable plot against America was in the works, believing something harrowing could occur either on the eve of the election or on election day. As to how and where, he said he wasn't there yet.

"How did I get involved? Sanford Roberts came to my office asking for my assistance because I was also Raymond Baldwin's long time attorney. Regretfully, because of attorney client privilege I was not able to be much help.

"We tried to protect Mr. Breck but regretfully his killer found a way to silence him and then place the blame on Charlie. If you hadn't inherited Emil's papers in truth, you'd never have been involved. Regretfully we're only hours away from election day and we still haven't figured out what Baldwin might be up to. I do know the agents are working round the clock to find answers. I'm very sorry we couldn't keep you in the loop but I hope you both now understand we needed you to discover the plot."

The words crazily made sense but I was still as angry as I'd ever been. I wanted to scream fuck you or go to Hell but I held back because of Sucre. I glared at Sanford because of what he'd put her through.

I was surprised when Sucre reached out and took Sanford's hand.

"You could have trusted me because you know I'd have kept your secret. I'm terribly upset you wouldn't tell me who you really were. Why couldn't you have just been honest and up front?"

"Sucre honey, I couldn't reveal who I worked for because one wrong word might have led to great harm for you and Charlie and Mr. Gould here. My first priority was keeping all of you both safe and sound. Strangely, after I got to know you I allowed my feelings to affect my work, something very dangerous for an agent. I want you to know I fell head over heels for you and everything I ever said about us came straight from my heart."

A tear rolled down Sucre's cheek, something she once said could not happen. Maybe the tear ducts were not totally damaged, a surprise to us both. She was soon sobbing but before I could reach out and hug her, Sanford put his arms around her, the growing silence in the room deafening. For several moments no one spoke until Gould cleared his throat rather loudly, saying time was critical. As if I'd just awoken from a dream I suddenly remembered the small book I'd discovered on my book shelf.

"Thanks to Sucre" Sanford whispered, "We were able to put hundreds of agents on the case in nearly every state in the union. From the latest polling numbers curiously, Baldwin doesn't have a chance in hell of winning the election but we believe that makes him even more dangerous. Unfortunately we really don't know what he' s capable of doing."

Sanford reiterated that elections in many foreign nations were subject to chaos and we were certainly not immune, the results catastrophic. I knew in my heart my discovery of Emil's book of blank pages was possibly the last chance to derail a plot. I shouted everyone needed to shut up and listen to what I had to say.

"Hours ago I found a book on my shelf that just might provide answers to what Baldwin could have planned. It took me a while to figure out what the book truly was eventually understanding the words were meant for Sucre. The blank pages hold a message in Braille only Sucre can read. This could be the key to unlocking a mystery so I suggest we leave here immediately and go to my place so Sucre can determine if it's the real deal."

A moment later Sanford gave marching orders.

"Sucre rides with me and Mr. Gould and Charlie will take Mr. Gould's car. We have to move quickly because there's no time to waste."

CHAPTER 42

Driving like a madman on a moonless night we got lucky. The streets were empty, suspecting we were all wondering the same thing. Had everything come down to a single volume mysteriously put into Braille.

I thought about the difficult life Sucre lived. certainly more than one person should have to handle. She'd seen her parents killed and she'd suffered horrible injuries. Still, she managed not only to survive but to endure, one step always forward. In truth I'd never met a braver person in my life and the fact she'd never surrendered made me admire her even more. If she'd chosen to give up, who could have blamed her.

The two cars pulled up to my building at the same time and without a moment to lose, the four of us ran up the six flights of stairs to my apartment. The book was exactly where I'd left it and removing it from the shelf, I handed it to Sucre, so incredibly proud of her I could barely hold back my own tears. Before she opened the book Steven Gould said something putting us a bit more at ease.

"Put on the lights so the poor girl can see what she's reading."

We all broke into nervous laughter, even Sucre. When the laughter died silence took precedence. Sucre's first words were be patient because she was a slow reader. The look on her face when she touched the pages reminded me of the look I'd seen when she so lovingly talked about her Peru.

"I believe Emil but these words into Braille for me so I'll read it word for word.

'All my life I've relentlessly fought censorship and Fascism, using the written word to expose it's darkness and evil ways. In my life I've seen Fascism up close, particularly the early years in my native Romania. In the years since my childhood I've traveled thousands of miles over mountains, across deserts and through small villages and large cities. When Fascism reared its head, I wrote how it's wicked ways destroyed hopes and dreams.

'America has not been immune to Fascism. I once had a front row seat in the United States Capitol Building in Washington DC before the dangerous HUAC committee, chaired by then Representative Raymond Baldwin. Fascism begins like a tiny pebble tossed into the sea. At first it's just a ripple but later, huge waves are created and they destroy. I've heard the screams and protests from innocent women, children and poor peasants, especially in the villages of Spain. One never forgets the pain and suffering. I heard those same cries in Panama, El Salvador and Nicaragua, especially in the rural villages. Facism must be stopped cold in this country.

I have enclosed the names of individuals in Braille to protect my work. My conclusion? I believe these men are involved in a heinous plot to destroy our democratic ways. The individuals could have used their expertise for the good of the nation and the world, but sadly that was not their intent. Each of the following individuals are to have a role in a new unwelcome government, created by Raymond Baldwin.

Cedris Smollet…. the Minister of Food and Agriculture

Len Peterkin….Minister of Labor

Paige Griffin…..Minister of Postal Affairs

Gregory Steel…..Minister of Transportation

Kurt Priestly…..Minister of Public Enlightenment and Propaganda

Leonard Pearl…. Minister of Aviation

Lamar Brown…..Minister of Science and Education

Father Monte Moore…..Minister of Church Affairs

Hugh Kohn….Minister of Armaments and Weaponry

Philip Crowley…..Minister of Annexed and Occupied Territories

Harold England…..Minister of Oil, Gas and Coal Industries

Sidney Albertson…..Minister of the Army

Anthony Hastings…..Minister of the Navy

John Devers……Minister of Justice

James Maxwell…..Minister of Transportation

'Those individuals will attempt to strike a knife into the heart of America the morning of our national election. Their goal? To seize control of our government in a coup. The cadre is well schooled and trained, thanks to the efforts of Raymond Baldwin. The following are their targets, chosen to create havoc before out time tested process of a free and fair election.

'Power generating stations, high-voltage transmission lines, dams, underground armories containing nuclear weapons, transportation facilities, airports and military bases.

'I have evidence the plotters stole three small nuclear weapons from a facility in Kentucky, not to kill but to create Electro-Magnetic Pulses creating large geo-magnetic storms, disabling our communication systems. The ensuing blackouts on the east and west coasts will create panic. A plot is also in place to shut down all air traffic, including the military, grounding all aircraft.

'Radio and television stations will be seized and forced to broadcast pre-taped speeches announcing a new revolution in America. Government agencies will be hit quickly and hard, destroying vast computer systems in the Pentagon and the While House. All those targets and more cannot be protected so it is important the individuals that I've identified by stopped before they can act.

'Raymond Baldwin spent the last five years of his life organizing a depraved plot and with a great deal of investigative work and luck, I was able to discover their plans. Mr. Baldwin covered his tracks quite well but fortunately he made several revealing mistakes. Part of the plot is to access multiple media outlets stating that ex-Vice President Devers will initially take control of a new government. In a secret memo obtained by one of my valuable lifetime sources, the message is to be broadcast to the entire nation exactly one hour before the election polls open on the east coast. This is the message.

'America's democratic political systems have paralyzed our great nation and as a result, many fear that our way of life has become obsolete and unresponsive. Our political parties are unable to work together or manage our affairs. Our nation is floundering and the future of our nation is at stake right now. Like all of you, we fear that our leaders can no longer keep us safe. We've been fooled too often by grandiose responses and promises, but few are fulfilled. Millions of Americans are not blind to the malaise, treachery and the failed promises. Too many of you have seen and felt the decline of our prestige and have given up hope. Why in America, the land of the free does less than fifty percent of the population vote? The answer is they know nothing will ever change.

'The very existence of our nation is in question. We live in an era when laws and more importantly, order means nothing. We have become used to the words we have unsolvable problems, choosing to ignore them. The wretchedness and misery of the American people is a terrible thing and we no longer have the foresight to make a better life. Our middle class doesn't exist anymore and no society without a working middle class has ever survived. We are moving at warp speed toward total destruction.

'The warning signs have been there for a long time but our current political parties have turned a blind eye. Left wingers continue to make insidious attacks against our liberty and left unchecked, they will destroy all we've fought for. We sit on the edge of chaos, a sad negative spirit choking the life out of this once great nation.

'The traditional American family no longer exists. Families were once the great foundation of morality and faith, but no longer. Justice and honor are things of the past.

'The future of this nations is at a breaking point so we must move quickly to get America off life support. What we are experiencing today has destroyed great civilizations in the past. History books have recorded the rise and fall of great empires and a failed nation has no hope for the future. We need to all come together to allow us to reach our God given potential. We have to renew our basic tenets in order to continue the dreams of our founding fathers.

Bruce Weiss

'The task of rebuilding America is a challenge and we are up to the task. There is anarchy in our streets and misguided judges in our courtrooms have failed us. Teachers in our public schools have also failed us. We have lost national discipline and it needs to be restored including making our churches the strong foundation to rebuild on.

'We've lost our national discipline and I promise we will work hard to restore it. Institutions including the church are the strongholds of this society and sadly, we have taken God out of our lives.

'Better days for you and America will be here soon. One of our first duties is to attack unemployment and create a livable wage. Our emphasis will be to return to the way we used to do business. We will create real economic freedom for all loyal Americans.

'I promise we will succeed in our mission to end the chaotic state of affairs our current and past leaders have created. Orderly life is our mantra, doing all to end bipartisan politics. We will bring to an end to the chaotic state of affairs our past and current leaders have created. The lackeys have had their day yet they continue to disappoint us. God will guide us and strengthen our purpose.'

We sat in stone silence, stunned for minutes until Sanford announced he had to leave because he had some serious work to do. What might happen in the next hours none of us could guess but one thing was terribly obvious. In less than twelve hours it was entirely possible our election could be hijacked, replaced with anarchy.

Attorney Gould said he needed to return to his office to remain there until the crisis passed, leaving Sucre and I alone. We huddled by the radio to hear Baldwin's taped address, or hopefully the words the FBI nipped a plot in the bud. The only clue something was happening was the ongoing message the President of the United States would address the nation before the polling stations opened.

One hour before the early polls were to open, the president went on the air. Americans listened on portable radios while lining up to cast their ballots.

'My fellow Americans, a very good morning to all of you. I need to speak to you at this early hour on America's very special day. Two hours ago I ordered a series of raids to be conducted by numerous federal agencies and the justice department, seeking out known individuals who planned to sabotage our election process. I won't go into specifics at this time other than to say, a plot aimed at disrupting this election has been thwarted. Therefore, I encourage every American to get out and vote. Several hundred individuals have been taken into custody and will be facing various charges, including sedition. The people who were determined to deny you the right to vote for the candidate of your choice are no longer a threat. The exact number of conspirators is still unknown, but authorities all across America have assured me there is no threat to the election process.

'Attorney General Arthur Palmer has ordered the arrests of several high profile individuals who were preparing to disrupt the long held American tradition of free elections. Due diligence on the Attorney General's part has made the difference between chaos and the time worn practice of the American people speaking out through the ballot box.

'The raids have enabled us to gather much evidence and it will be used to prosecute to the fullest extent of the law. Those who would deny you the right to vote will pay dearly. This President, who is not a candidate knows that we change our government by free elections, not by devious plots. I am very pleased to announce there is no threat to our nation and our election will go on as scheduled. I will now read a memo I received from Attorney General Palmer a few moments ago."

'Two hours before the polls in America were set to open, hundreds of FBI and treasury agents in conjunction with local authorities executed a series of raids deemed successful. Agents cast a wide net over a cadre of plotters who's goal was to sabotage our elections. Caches of arms were seized and more than three hundred individuals involved were captured, most without violence.

'The raids took place in more than two hundred cities and towns in thirty-one states. In several locations, weapons capable of doing great harm were seized. In the process no agents were harmed. I will be holding a news conference in the coming hours detailing the conspirators plans and our response. I urge all Americans to get out and vote as a way to show your support for our nation. There are many people to thank for stopping this plot but I would be remiss if I didn't mention one remarkable woman who asked to remain anonymous. A young woman broke the code enabling authorities to identify the individuals involved in the plot.'

The media continued to air assurances from the White House,

declaring it was safe to go to the polls both as a civic duty and to send a message to those who would change our government by force.

Near noon eastern standard time the While House released a statement that the ringleaders of the plot were all in custody. Candidate Raymond Baldwin and former vice president Devers had been arrested and charged with conspiracy and treason, a charge that could lead to the death penalty. A spokes person for the President told the voting public that Raymond Baldwin, the chief conspirator would have his name remain on the ballot. He and others had not had their day in court and therefore were still eligible to seek office. More information about the situation would be forthcoming.

Sucre received phone calls from Sanford nearly every hour, not with news about the raids or their aftermath, but to declare his affection for her. Sucre looked happy again and seemingly at peace. Flowers from Sanford arrived on the hour until we had no more room for them.

We took great solace in the fact that we'd done Emil well, turning our thoughts to the real hero of the day. We decided we should go to his grave, leaving all the well deserved flowers. The FBI was crediting us but it was Emil who deserved all the credit.

The news station that sustained Sucre over the months reported the polls were seeing extraordinarily long lines and everything was going off without a hitch. By late afternoon eastern standard time, the national news reported more people had gone to the polls than ever before. Voters interviewed claimed they were not necessarily voting for a candidate, but for America. Instead of change by revolution, all was peaceful. It was also reported that hundreds of thousands of voters leaving their polling places went to the church of their choice and gave thanks.

Sadly, few people would never know that Emil Breck gave his life to save the union. If it wasn't for his work, a dastardly and violent attempt to overthrow the government might have succeeded. I could not stop thinking about Emil's biography, needing to let people know that Emil was responsible for saving the nation during one of her darkest hours.

Days and then weeks after the election arrests were still being made but the leaders of the insurrection were no longer a threat. Raymond Baldwin was given access to an attorney and held in isolation at a secret military facility. Regretfully, he'd still received twenty one million votes

Emil's List

in the general election, not enough however to send the election to the House of Representatives. Ex vice president Devers was taken to a military base in Texas and put under twenty-four hour observation because of a suicide attempt. Thirty others had been charged with the crime of treason and held in detentions centers scattered across the country. Newspapers printed names and charges, keeping Americans abreast of the ongoing investigation.

When President Elect Mark Gordon took the oath of office in January, he reaffirmed that only in America did power pass without violence or trickery. In his speech he never mentioned the plot, urging all Americans to become more active in the affairs of their nation.

Sucre and I slept well for the first time in weeks but before we drifted off one night, she'd say it was the right time to go back to Peru to see old friends, including the nuns. Sanford who'd been on the job without sleep for nearly three days called often, professing his love for Sucre. A day later Sucre returned to her own apartment, tired but at peace. In light of Baldwin's arrest, the police announced we were no long suspects in Emil's murder.

Chapter 43

Sucre began packing for her journey back to Peru, asking me to take possession of Emil's book collection because she'd never be able to read them. I refused her offer because all that we'd been through, I knew Emil wanted her to own his prized possession.

In the days and weeks after the election Sanford was seldom home, working on FBI business digging through thousands of papers recovered in the raids. I continued insisting Sucre and I we were a team and there was much work to be done on the biography celebrating Emil's life. Days later she surprisingly declared the work was a one person endeavor, what I'd always believed. There was no argument. It was obvious she'd fallen in love with Sanford, preferring to spend almost all her free time with him when he returned to the Boston FBI office.

Sanford was recognized for his extraordinary work insisting Sucre stand by his side. I was happy for her. We'd been through an awful lot together and nothing could change that. My only sad thought was she'd be in Peru for at least a month and I would miss her terribly. Still, the thought of her going home made me feel good, knowing she'd find redemption and peace. She asked not to receive any credit for our work and although I said okay, I would always consider her my equal partner.

I managed to convince Sucre to partake in a few award ceremonies held in her honor. She'd received a thoughtful letter from Attorney General Arthur Palmer, including an invitation to Washington to receive on one of the nations highest civilian medals. With much prompting she accepted the offer.

When Sanford concluded his work we had a farewell dinner and after Sanford announced he'd been granted a month's leave and would accompany Sucre to Peru, Sucre tried to convince me to come along but I answered as always, three was a crowd. I said I'd found a great publisher who'd given me a very generous advance, meaning I'd have to start work on the biography immediately.

Our parting was bittersweet, especially when Sucre said she and Sanford were going to climb Misti Mountain together. I'd always thought I'd be the one accompanying her.

I was extremely grateful Sanford entered Sucre's life. They were the team now. Sucre promised to call the moment they descended the mountain, reporting how the climb had gone. When I last saw them they were walking hand in hand toward the gate for their flight.

I found myself very teary on the drive back to my place from the airport, wondering what it would feel like to take an entire day off and do nothing. I was so emotional the toll booth collector saw me sobbing, asking if I was alright.

I knew in my heart the dynamic duo would always be a part of my life yet it was with relief starting work on the biography I had a clear mind. The writing was going well, the goal producing a rough draft for my publisher in less than a year.

Nine days after Sucre left I received a call telling me it was a most difficult climb but the good news was they'd both summated Misti Mountain together. It was one of the most wonderful experiences of her life she proclaimed, sobbing saying those words.

I asked if she'd seen the nuns and between sobs she said yes. She also said she and Sanford visited the newly built post office on the site where she used to live, where her life was changed forever. She said Sanford bought flowers and they left them on the steps in honor of her family, admitting she'd actually felt tears on her cheeks and it felt so good.

There was some bad news however.

"Sanford is in the hospital in the city as a result of a nasty tumble on our way down. He broke his left hip and right wrist during the fall. Despite a lot of initial pain he feels rather well though and is on his way to a good recovery. Charlie, because of that we can't home right away."

Six days later Sucre called again, saying they'd decided to remain in the city, leasing an apartment for at least six months so Sanford could recover fully. I asked what they would do during that time.

"Sanford is enrolled in a Spanish language school and getting therapy for his bones. Although he walks with a slight limp, he's able to get around although sometimes with great difficulty,

I was so damn proud of them both, missing Sucre terribly.

Months passed with occasional phone calls from Peru. My good news was that I was well into an introductory draft of the biography and the writing was going well. Another few months passed and I'd become so involved and even obsessed with my writing I'd often forgot to eat or rest. I was on a high I wished would never end.

One day something extraordinarily happened. I heard an unexpected knock at my door, something rarely happening lately. When I opened the door I was taken aback seeing Sanford standing there. We talked all through the night about old and new times and what the future held for he and Sucre. Near eight in the morning there was another knock at the door and to my surprise, it was Sucre, a baby cradled in her arms. It took a few moments for me to fall in love with that beautiful child, a girl given the name Emilia. I was informed I was to be here Godfather. After hours of fawning over the baby I had something wonderful to tell them. After countless revisions my biography of Emil had finally gone to press. Exhausted I still found myself suddenly charged up I said.

"I got a few author's copies and one was done in Braille."

By late morning we were too tired to stay awake, agreeing to meet for dinner at a Peruvian restaurant. Sanford and I joked about possibly having to eat guinea pig. Even though we'd just spent time with each other later, the parting was filled with tears.

At dinner Sanford announced he'd be starting a new job with the FBI in Washington with no more field work. There was more good news. Sucre would soon be starting her first teaching job at a school for the sight impaired in Arlington. We promised to see each other often, especially since I was Emilia's godfather. I wished the time together could have lasted forever but it was time to get on with our lives.

Epilogue

The biography titled Emil's List was published receiving great reviews and as a bonus, a terrific write-up in the Sunday New York Times book review. Everyone was talking about Emil Breck which elated me to no end. Inundated with phone calls, I was asked to appear on talks shows and to speak at various author's functions. It was a thrill for a while but because I'd become so used to being alone, I began dreading traveling the book circuit.

Emil was a shining star, his lifetime work extolled. Reviewers said again and again the journalist led a magical life.

Every so often there was something in the news about Raymond Baldwin, remaining as defiant as ever, vowing to take his case to the public one day. During a Sixty Minutes interview he encouraged new revolutionary groups to organize, many people calling him the new Messiah. One of Sanford's new tasks was to investigate the sudden explosion of hate groups.

Eventually the biography fell out of the best seller list and the calls about speaking stopped. I unexpectedly fell into a deep depression immediately after with thoughts if my work was done, why wait. I knew I was drifting aimlessly, unsure what to do with my time.

I tried to write a novel but it went nowhere. For days at a time I couldn't go out or even answer the phone. Everything began to frighten me, especially sirens on my street. I was certain they were coming to get me.

For weeks I avoided leaving my place carefully hiding my misery. It took some time to realize I could fool most people, but not Sanford. He encouraged me to get some professional help, knowing I was struggling.

One warm summer day Sanford showed up at my door asking me to accompany him on a visit to an old friend in Boston. His friend turned out to be an FBI psychologist working with agents who'd experienced traumatic situations on the job. Reluctantly I agreed to sit down with Dr. Claudia and to my surprise, I began to feel better. New ideas about writing began to stimulate me, forgetting journalism for the time to concentrate on writing a novel in my head. HUAC stood out in my mind and a fictional account of it's dirty dealings could be a good read I sensed.

I thought about Emil every single day vowing to continue his work fighting Fascism and censorship. I began writing letters to the editors when I heard about wrongs instead of ignoring them. One of the highlights of my recovery was an invitation to the White House honoring retiring Attorney General Arthur Palmer. I met the president who said he'd loved my book, asking me to sign his edition.

Life was good again. Sucre and I talked on the phone nearly every day, the latest news she and Sanford would once again be traveling to Arequipa in a few weeks to see the nuns. She insisted I come along this time. When I hesitated she said Sanford wanted to climb and descend Misti Mountain again fulfilling a promised he'd made to himself. A few days later Sanford called saying he wanted to do the up and down without incident, suggesting I get in shape and climb with him.

Arriving in Arequipa I toured Sucre's beloved city, including a stop at the main post office and later her family's cemetery plot. Days later Sucre drove us to the base of Misti Mountain, wishing us luck and above all to be safe. The hike was exhilarating and certainly the most difficult physical activity I'd ever undertaken. To my surprise, I realized it was my birthday when Sanford and I summated.

With a second child on the way I saw less and less of Sucre, Sanford and Emilia. My first novel was a hit, a fictional story about a rogue senator plotting a coup. Thanks to Emil who was never far from my thoughts and Sanford and Sucre and especially Doctor Claudia, I learned much about perseverance and the courage and strength to move on. Love your life they urged. Life was good and when I felt low, all I had to do was think about Sucre's courage and my problems disappeared.

Finis

CPSIA information can be obtained
at www.ICGtesting.com
Printed in the USA
LVHW111929311018
595437LV00004B/34/P